Praise for the novels of Tarryn Fisher

"You'll have whiplash until the very end. *The Wives* will leave the most sure-footed reader uneasy until the last word is read."
—**Colleen Hoover, #1** *New York Times* **bestselling author**

"Fisher smoothly inserts moments of self-doubt, longing, paranoia, and triumph into her unsettling narrative.... Suspense fans will be rewarded."
—*Publishers Weekly* **on** *The Wives*

"Fisher is a slick writer who keeps a tight rein on her lightning-fast plot, and the lengths that her feisty narrator goes to in order to reclaim her life make for salaciously satisfying reading.... Fisher is a writer to watch."
—*Kirkus Reviews* **on** *The Wives*

"Fans of Gillian Flynn's *Gone Girl* will revel in *The Wives*.... Fisher's story, like the score of a film, builds to an emotional and psychological crescendo that will keep readers on their toes until its final page."
—*USA TODAY*

"*The Wives* author delivers another un-put-downable psychological thriller."
—*E!* **on** *The Wrong Family*

"Fisher's latest thriller is electric, like riding a roller coaster in the dark. Hairpin turns plummet to heart-stopping depths. You won't devour this book. It will devour you."
—**Author Tess Callahan on** *The Wrong Family*

"A wholly original story of two women with dark pasts on a crash course with one another. This smart, claustrophobic thriller will keep you up reading...and just plain keep you up at night."
—**Andrea Dunlop, author of** *We Came Here to Forget*, **on** *The Wrong Family*

"Utterly absorbing."
—*PopSugar* **on** *The Wrong Family*

"Nothing is as it seems in this twisty new thriller."
—*Bustle* **on** *The Wrong Family*

Also available from Tarryn Fisher
and Graydon House

The Wives
The Wrong Family

For more about Tarryn Fisher, please visit www.tarrynfisher.com.

TARRYN FISHER

AN
HONEST
LIE

GRAYDON
HOUSE

GRAYDON
HOUSE®

Recycling programs
for this product may
not exist in your area.

ISBN-13: 978-1-525-81157-9

An Honest Lie

Graydon House
22 Adelaide St. West, 41st Floor
Toronto, Ontario M5H 4E3, Canada
www.GraydonHouseBooks.com
www.BookClubbish.com

Printed in U.S.A.

For Jolene

AN HONEST LIE

AT THE END OF THE *highway sat an old town, not completely dead, but on its last breath. There was no reason to go there unless you were lost or, in her case, trying to be found. She stared past the candy-colored lights, the reds and blues and lilacs, to the empty desert beyond…to Friendship. That's where it began fifteen years ago and what had begun there would never really end.* Two birds with one stone, *she thought.* Two vultures.

Her phone lit up, drawing her eyes away from the window.

Braithe: I'm going to kill her. You better come if you want to save her.

1

Now

It towered on high, a black house throned on a mountain and surrounded by lush foliage. The constant flow of water from the sky nourished the succulent shades of green on Tiger Mountain. Her house was at the highest point, a cake topper. She liked to think of the mountain as hers, but the road that led to the bottom of the mountain passed by many houses. She knew only a handful of their occupants. She felt less determined than she had five minutes ago. She could go home, say she wasn't feeling well or give another flimsy excuse, but duty kept her left foot jumping between gas and brake as she navigated the curves.

Duty to whom? She met her own eyes in the rearview mirror, and then quickly looked away before turning left down a driveway. Rainy felt her tits lift and slap back against her rib cage as her old truck cleared a pothole; she'd forgotten to put on a bra. *Trashy*, she thought. Braking sharply in front of the shed, she threw the truck into Park and hopped out. The house was a Cape Cod, painted white with black trim and set back from the road on a cozy lot bordered by mountain hemlock. So stark was the comparison to her own ultramodern home that Rainy always paused to admire the warm charm of the Mattson house. Each of the houses on Tiger Mountain was marvelously different; that's what both she and Grant loved the most about living there.

As she stepped away from the car, her boots crunched against the gravel in the driveway, and she kept her head down against the rain as she climbed the three stairs that led to the door. She could hear them inside, their voices filling up the house with a cacophony of sound. Rainy hated this part: walking into a room and having all eyes on her. They would check her clothes, noting the lack of effort, see that she was braless, wonder—she was sure—what Grant saw in her. She rang the bell and bent to unlace her boots. By the time Braithe Mattson opened her front door, Rainy had kicked them off and was standing in her socks. One, she noticed, was of the floral variety, and the other plain white. It was too late to do anything about it.

"I told you to stop ringing the bell and just come inside," Braithe said.

She didn't have time to respond. Braithe pulled her through the door, and Rainy had to rework her face as her host corralled her toward the kitchen where the women usually hung out.

"Working today?" Braithe glanced over her shoulder, eyeing Rainy's black jeans and T-shirt. But Rainy didn't sense any judgment, just curiosity. Braithe was—for lack of a more interesting word—kind. She nodded, and Braithe's face lit with happiness. She was a rarity: a friend who understood that, for an artist, a productive day of work was hard to come by. Rainy felt a surge of affection for her. She'd only known Braithe for the year she'd lived there, but they'd fallen into an easy, noncommittal friendship that included an occasional dinner downtown and texts about nothing in particular. That dip you made on Friday night was amazing. Did you watch the Justin Bieber documentary? The boys want to go bowling Friday night, you down?

Following Braithe past the formal areas of the home, she braced herself, keeping her eyes on the back of her friend's head, dreading the routine of the next five minutes. There was nothing more painful to Rainy than the way women greeted each other: the high-pitched squeals of joy, the touching and hugging, the exaggerated expressions that accompanied the small talk. The high, singsong voices saying, "How are *youuuuuuuu*?" Bonus points if they delivered a compliment about hair or outfit. In her circles in New York, her artist friends never touched; they kissed the air beside her cheek and asked how she was in the same sentence they inquired about her bag. They didn't wait for the answer—that was the best part to Rainy—but here, they wanted her answer. Here, they asked and expected to receive.

Braithe Mattson's kitchen was stark white, aside from the large black butcher-block island that sat at its center. A cluster of women were seated around it, seeming to glow under Braithe's mood lighting. These were the faithful, the loyal, her ladies-in-waiting. The room smelled of her signature scent, a Tom Ford candle—Rainy had once Googled the price of it—called Lost Cherry. It was cozy, even if it was a little overly curated. Rainy did not see herself as one of them; she was the newest, still in the first year of her feel-out phase. She came to their weekly happy hours, and since some of their partners and husbands were friends, there were crossover dinners and summer barbecues, the group discussion centering on sports, their respective jobs and family gossip. All in all, they were nice… and they were Grant's friends. She'd come because Grant was important to her, and he had asked her to.

Rainy made a split-second decision: she sneezed violently into her elbow, and by the time she opened her eyes, a unanimous "Bless you" echoed from the women across the room. Suddenly, everyone was laughing, including Rainy, who was able to avoid the hugging and touching part as she sniffled past them. No one wanted to get sick or touch the snotty girl.

The Tiger Mountain group was composed of mostly childless, married women in their thirties and forties who connected via a Facebook page, but the Baby Tigers—as Tara called them—were a handful of newlyweds in their midtwenties. They brought a fun, energetic vibe to the group; it felt like hanging out with your little sister and her friends. They were cute, but there was a disconnect that happened whenever the thirty- and fortysomethings spoke about things the twenties hadn't reached yet. The two that came to happy hour with the most consistency were Ursa and Mackenzie, best friends who seemed to enjoy the company of the slightly older women. The other twenties had broken off into their own group that Ursa and Mac still hung out with occasionally. Rainy felt bad calling them the Baby Tigers; Tara had only come up with that nickname because she was threatened by their youth.

Braithe came back and pushed a glass of white wine into Rainy's hand. Her lips were lined in gold, as were her eyes. She surveyed the room.

"Sit over there by Viola, will you—she's miserable because she can't drink." She said it loud enough for Viola to hear.

Braithe winked at Viola, who in turn made a face at her. Rainy made her way over to where Viola was sitting and slid obediently into her seat. She would have chosen to sit next to

Viola, anyway. The clock on Braithe's range read 7:47; she'd stay until nine-ish, and then say she had to get home to let Shep out. These were dog people; they would understand. That meant an hour and fifteen minutes for happy hour and she could call it. She grinned at Viola, who returned her look with raised eyebrows. Her pursed lips were a perfect matte burgundy.

"Don't think I don't know what you're thinking. I am thinking the same damn thing." Viola leaned back in her seat, cradling her belly and looking miserable. Rainy eyed the gaggle. They were talking about a new restaurant and were distracted for the moment.

"Well, why do we keep coming to these things?"

"Good question. Pass me that water, would you?"

Rainy leaned forward, reaching for the glass, and Viola took it from her gratefully. She drained it, eyeing Rainy over the rim.

"Indigestion," she said before Rainy could ask. "Samantha made some shit, and now I can't tell if I'm in labor or if hot sauce is leaking into my chest cavity from her rice." She pounded her chest with a small fist and grimaced. Samantha was Viola's partner. Rainy had only met her once at one of these things; she was one part goth and the rest awkward computer nerd. Since Rainy was equally as awkward, she'd hit it off with Samantha, who shared her dry sense of humor.

"Why did you put hot sauce on your rice?"

Viola looked at her sideways, eyeing her with disapproval. "Why do you not?"

Rainy laughed. "Touché."

Braithe seated herself on the last empty bar stool, her glass of white wine in front of her. To her left was Tara Hessler, her right-hand woman and main lady-in-waiting. Tara was a little flushed tonight, her creamy skin rosy with anticipation. She was, in Rainy's opinion, a social scavenger, but a smooth one. She needed to be the prettiest girl in the room, but that was Braithe, so she settled for a close second. Tara adorned Braithe like an unnecessary tiara. Rainy avoided having close friendships for that reason: the last thing she wanted was costume-jewelry friendship. She didn't have time for that. Codependency sucked up large chunks of time.

Rainy, being the newest to the group, was always pelted with questions when she showed up to happy hour. It was like they were trying to fast-track her into their group with these little Q and As.

"The new-girl novelty will wear off soon and they'll stop hounding you." It was a promise Viola made to her a year ago when Rainy moved to Washington. They wanted to know who she hung out with in New York—*a handful of close artist friends from college.* Who she dated before Grant—*two art students and a gallery owner, nothing serious.* Where were her parents? *Dead.* Did she miss the city? *Yes and no. She liked the solitude and vast openness of Washington.* And finally, the most painful question of them all—was she going to marry Grant? Viola had called them out after that, told them to stop being nosy.

Rainy did not want to play house for the next ten years— she did want to marry Grant—but she also had no intention of talking to them about it. He was the only man she'd ever felt this way about, unless she decided to hold these little happy hours against him.

"Get to know some people, this is your new home," he'd said.

"What people?" she'd argued stubbornly. "You are my people."

"Friends," he'd said. "Friends are good, friends are healthy."

Ursa, in a pink silk top and jeans, was lip-synching along with Braithe's playlist, forcing Mac to be her audience. She got right up in Mac's face as she sang, "You make me, make me, make me want to cry!" Mac giggled and shoved her away; undeterred, Ursa began grinding against Tara on her other side. She paused her dancing to point a finger at Rainy and wink.

Viola laughed from beside her. "She is on tonight."

Rainy had never really seen Ursa *not* be on. She was energetic: matte skin, leggy, shaggy hair. She worked in marketing and was smart as a whip. Rainy liked the way she could make anything sound fun—even a bikini wax. Mackenzie was her best friend: sweet, less sure of herself, a kindergarten teacher by trade. Rainy thought they were both in their late twenties, but she wasn't sure; Botox made it impossible to guess a woman's age. When Grant set her up with the group—the wives of some of his friends—he'd called them "fun" and "easygoing." She'd wondered if he'd remembered she was uptight and not fun at all, but loving someone meant talking yourself into things on occasion. And besides, Viola was one of the realest people Rainy had ever met. The group was worth it solely for her friendship. And then there was Braithe: the glamorous, put-together adult friend. Her job was to make everyone feel like they had a place at the table—her table.

Rainy sipped her drink, content for the moment. She looked around at their faces, her gaze finally resting on Tara. To her consternation, Tara was looking at her, as well. Rainy crossed her legs, suddenly nervous. Maybe it was the way Tara had repeated her name the first time Braithe introduced them, dropping her chin and raising her brows. "Rainy like our damn weather...?" Everyone had laughed, including Rainy, but she'd had the distinct impression that Tara didn't like her. And over the last year that feeling had grown, fanned to life by Tara's lack of eye contact and her occasional snarky remarks. When they were in a group, it was easy to overlook that she usually hadn't said a word to Rainy all night. With Tara being

the life of every party, she seemed inclusive, drawing everyone into her stories and jokes. Rainy had never minded the
slights; these were, of course, Grant's friends, and she didn't
take offense, since she didn't want to be there, anyway. But
here was Tara, smiling at her warmly, no hint of dislike on
her face. Her full lips were curled nicely, the mole above her
lip punctuating her smile. The result was *French model holds a
secret she's about to spill.*

Rainy put her drink down and leveled her shoulders, the
tag from her T-shirt scratching her neck. She could feel the
energy building in the room, and it was making her nervous.

They all were staring at her now, smiles picking up the corners of their mouths. Rainy suddenly felt a knot form in her
throat; she was going to choke on her own panic.

"Um…what? You guys are weirding me out."

"Look at my face, Rainy…look at my face." Ursa wiggled
her eyebrows and made kissy faces until Rainy cracked up.

"Rainy…" Tara scooted forward in her seat, drawing
Rainy's attention back to her. Tara was seated directly across
from her, on the side of the island nearest the kitchen door. In
one hand she loosely held her vodka tonic, and the other was
sliding something across the counter to Rainy. Tara tried to
control the cogs of every situation and Rainy did not want to
become one of those cogs. For that reason, she was hesitant
to look down at what Tara was passing to her.

She'd lived in Washington for a mere four months when
her thirty-fifth birthday snuck up. She hadn't been thinking
about it. She'd been preoccupied with settling into her new
home, finding a comfortable groove with Grant. The things
on her mind back then: wondering if Grant secretly hated her
cooking and stressing about whether she needed to go to bed
when he did. When he told her he wanted to plan a dinner
to celebrate, she'd been surprised.

She'd been content to spend the night at home with Grant. She secretly hated her birthday, anyway; since her mother died, it had been a reminder of who she didn't have. But at the time, it seemed important to Grant to plan something for her, so she'd let him.

"What type of food? Vietnamese, Korean—I know this great Mexican place in Tacoma." He was excited as he opened his laptop and said, "It's Seattle, I can find you almost anything you want—or at least something similar."

The New Yorker in Rainy highly doubted that, but she kissed him to get a taste of his excitement and said, "Seafood sounds great." Grant had booked a place on the water that he swore up and down served the best crab legs in the state. He'd sent a group text to his friends and their wives with the date and time. Everyone texted back, excited, and then Tara's text had come.

Hey, don't mean to be a vibe killer, but that's the weekend of the annual chili cook-off.

The texts came in fast little pelts: everyone suggesting that they combine the two.

Rainy had been embarrassed that her birthday plans were disrupting something they all wanted to do. We'll have a cake for her at the party! someone had texted. But she was already mortified by then, trying to make some big weekend about herself when they barely knew her.

"I've never celebrated my birthdays. I don't want to be the center of attention," she'd argued when he said it was no big deal to reschedule the dinner.

"This is your first year here with me. Let me do this."

Grant was so set on the issue—so pleased with himself— that she couldn't bear to burst his bubble. She'd relented, but with a sinking feeling. She didn't want his friends to think she was the one pushing the issue, demanding to celebrate even though they barely knew her. It had been a rule among her New York friends to ignore each other's partners until they were too embedded in the circle not to. A cruel but caution-ary way to not get "too attached." As she half hid and healed, the coldness had suited her, but these were Grant's people. She was thirsty for his approval—and the last thing she needed was to be the topic of their gossip.

She agreed to a six o'clock dinner on Friday night with four other couples: Braithe and Stephen, Tara and Matt, Viola and Samantha, and Gary and Linney—a couple Grant knew from high school that he affectionately referred to as Old Faithful. Ten minutes before they were supposed to leave, Tara had texted links to the group with several reviews she'd found online about the restaurant.

Five cases of food poisoning in the last four months, she'd said. Didn't know if you wanted to chance it...

No one had. And by that time, it was too late to get a res-ervation for ten people anywhere else. The dinner had been canceled, and Rainy was left with the distinct impression Tara had wanted it that way. Rainy had never figured out why Tara disliked her, and she'd learned to not care. There were plenty of people who liked her well enough.

Now, she glanced around and saw five sets of eyes pinned on her. The sudden surge of attention from everyone at one time was making Rainy dizzy.

"Take my hands, Lorraine Ives." Tara's nails were painted a pearly white. She flipped them over and held two small palms toward her, so soft and unblemished Rainy was fixated. Had the woman ever so much as fried bacon in her life? Tara cleared her throat and Rainy offered her hands apologetically.

"Sorry, artist acknowledging beautiful hands."

Tara flushed, pleased with the compliment. Viola kicked Rainy under the table and Rainy shot her an apologetic look. *What? She has beautiful hands.*

Before she could make sense of why everyone was watching her and what was happening, Tara launched into her sell.

"So! We know you're new to the group, and we don't always like the new people," she said, winking. The others murmured their agreement, and Rainy wondered who the last new member had been. Maybe one of Grant's other girlfriends? Tara continued. "But we're all totally obsessed with you—that's why—and you can absolutely say no, buuut we won't let you." They all laughed at the joke she didn't get and Rainy held her breath as she waited for the punchline. Were they going to suggest matching tattoos? Were they swingers, asking her into their circle? The possibilities were endless as Rainy sat sweating beneath their eyes. She could feel her eyebrows dancing comically in confusion.

"Picture sun, heat—" she said the word *heat* with reverence "—and drinks by the pool! We're inviting you on our girls' trip…to Vegas!"

At first, Rainy's relief was immense; a girls' trip was kind, inclusive. And then she processed the word: *Vegas*. She glanced over at Viola and wondered if they would have invited her instead if Viola wasn't in her last trimester, and then corrected herself for thinking that way. It was a nice gesture, one she never intended to accept. But she couldn't tell them why.

They were waiting for her to say something, but she was having trouble forming words.

"You guys," Viola said from beside her, "give her a minute to swallow what you eager beavers are saying." She felt a much gentler kick under the table: Viola saying, *You okay?*

Tara loosened her hold on Rainy's fingers, which was a good thing because Rainy's hands were starting to sweat, and she doubted her sweat was organic enough for anyone in the room.

"Okay, let me explain." Tara pushed her hair behind her ears and scooted forward on her stool. She had pale blond hair that on the average day was scooped back into a ponytail, but tonight she wore it parted and past her shoulders. "Every year we go on our annual girls' trip. We've done all sorts of things," she said, waving a hand in the air. "Camping near the hot springs, we've driven up to Canada for the week and stayed in a lodge…"

"What about the year we rented those tree houses?"

Rainy glanced over as Braithe set down a baked brie, surrounded by a cluster of fruit, in front of them. The room seemed to hinge on Rainy's answer, but it was one thing eating cheese with these women a few minutes from her own home, another entirely to go away with them. Shit, why had she drunk the wine so fast? She couldn't think of a good lie fast enough.

"Vegas is not my thing. Trust me, I'm not fun, not even a little bit. Look, you sat me next to the pregnant woman—you all know it's true in your hearts." That brought a cry of outrage from Viola, and a few laughs from the others.

"That is not true, Rainy! We love hanging with you!" This came from Mackenzie, who was always positive, always inclusive. She was married to Bryan Biggs, a software engineer; the group fondly called them BigMac.

Rainy reached for the cheese, slamming back a mouthful to buy herself time. They wouldn't understand this, her hesitation. They had just emerged from a bitter winter, and everyone was jumping at the chance to travel again. She should want to go. Any normal person would want to go.

"Well, we certainly aren't going to force you to come," Braithe said a little hesitantly. Her face was conflicted but

Rainy couldn't tell why. She was a fairweather member of the group and they'd always been okay with that.

"But I for one am going. And you know what else? I'm not going to feel bad about all the money I'm going to lose at the slot machines…and I plan on losing a lot of it, more than last time." She pointed around the table, daring anyone to contest, and Rainy breathed a sigh of relief. She owed Braithe one. The banter continued, and the air of planning descended on the group. Rainy was content to listen to them talk about it, laughing when Tara and Ursa got into an argument about setting drink limits, so no one would be chaperoning anyone else.

"Last time we were there I had to drag you back to the room as you vomited into my bag," Tara complained.

"Well, leave me where I am next time and mind your business," Ursa shot back. "Besides, I am not sitting at a slot machine pressing buttons the first time I get a vacation in two years. Send me to a club and let me dance!"

She spotted the time on Braithe's range right as they were discussing hotels and stood up a little too abruptly; her chair screeched painfully against the floor.

"Rainy, no! Stay longer!" Tara said. Her teeth were stained purple, like she'd been feasting on the wine instead of drinking it.

"I have to go let Shep out." The planned excuse tumbled easily out of her mouth. She wanted to give herself a congratulatory pat on the back.

Tara had a poodle named Stacey that she treated better than most parents treated their kids. She nodded right away like she understood.

"Promise us you'll at least think about it, okay?" Tara was smiling, the blond daggers of hair contrasting with the sweetness of her tone.

Rainy knew this tactic, and she wasn't going to allow herself to be guilted or strong-armed into something she didn't want to do.

"Think about what?" She said it casually, but she supposed if you listened closely, there was a nip to her voice. Tara's smile became fixed. Rainy could see her thoughts ticking behind her eyes.

"Think about coming, silly." She leaned in and Rainy had the urge to pull away. "I know it would mean a lot to Braithe if you did."

She stared into Tara's eyes and saw something she didn't like; what was that? Desperation? She blinked back her thoughts, casting a glance at Braithe, who was chatting with Ursa and Mac. The only one paying attention to them was Viola, who was pretending to text, but Rainy knew the look on her face—she was listening. Rainy highly doubted Braithe's happiness was hinging on her going to Vegas, especially since she'd be surrounded by her groupies. If Tara wasn't getting it, she'd help her.

"I already said no, but hey, hit me up if you guys decide to do the tree houses again. I'll see you guys next week." She tucked her hair behind her ears, avoiding Tara's eyes and winking at Viola, who gave her a thumbs-up.

She was moving toward the door; a few more steps and her hand would close over—

"Rainy." It was Braithe, walking toward her, an apologetic look on her face. Her shoes made pitter-patters on the hardwood as Rainy turned to face her.

"She comes on strong, but she means well." Braithe's mouth was pulled into a tight little bud; she only made that face when she was worried. Little tendrils of hair had come loose around her face. She looked like a painting.

"How did I know you were going to say that?"

Braithe sighed and opened the door. "Have you considered

that we actually like you?" Rainy hadn't; she'd been too busy trying to like them. It felt more like they were tolerating her, but she smiled at Braithe and nodded.

"I'm behind on work. I can't really take the time off right now. Maybe next time. You guys will have to let me know how it all goes."

Braithe laughed, reaching out to squeeze Rainy's shoulder. "That sounded rehearsed."

Rainy grinned, guilty. "I'll see you, Braithe."

She'd already bounded down the stairs when Braithe called after her again. "We're at Viola's tomorrow, remember? Throwing her a little sprinkle before the baby comes. You signed up to bring sparkling apple juice and the couscous."

"I remember," Rainy called over her shoulder. She hadn't, and was glad Braithe couldn't see the lie on her face. The mist soaked into her clothes as she walked. She could feel Braithe watching her from the doorway, wanting to say one last thing before sending her off. She'd only known the tiny, articulate former ballet dancer for a year, but she was the unofficial group mother. And there it was: "Don't be a stranger this week. Come down for coffee."

Without turning around, Rainy lifted a hand to acknowledge that she had heard, and walked quickly to her truck.

2

Now

When Rainy pulled past the end-of-road sign and up their long, looping driveway, the lights on the basketball court were on and flickering gingerly under the mist. Grant was shooting hoops; he had his shirt off, and she could see the top of his boxers above the line of his shorts. The floor of her stomach dropped out whenever she looked at him; sometimes she had to look away very quickly so he wouldn't see how much he affected her. It wasn't a bad problem to have, she supposed.

He stopped playing when he saw her and jogged over, the ball tucked under his arm. Rainy's fingers hooked through the fence until they touched Grant's chest, and she looked into his sincere brown eyes. The corners crinkled when he smiled at her, and for a moment, she was so captivated by him she forgot everything else.

"You look like you need to be kissed." He pressed himself right against her, bending the fence outward and tangling his fingers with hers.

"Oh, yeah?"

He kissed her through a chain-link diamond, and she relished the salt and sweat of him.

"There's a bottle of wine waiting for you inside, Miss Ives."

"Great." She looked over her shoulder at the house, the sharp angles of it black against an even blacker sky. "I better go let him out."

Grant leaned in for one more kiss. "I'll be in in a minute. Dinner is in the oven."

Had she been hungry a short while ago? She remembered the cheese, and her stomach rolled.

"I'll wash up, too. See you."

At the center of the round driveway was a very large western hemlock, its roots beginning to split the asphalt in places. Rainy knew where to step so she wouldn't trip. Grant threatened to have it cut down, lest the roots reach the house, but Rainy loved the tree, and she wouldn't have minded if the roots popped up in her living room.

Grant had made a fire before he'd gone outside. Rainy could smell it as soon as she walked in the door, along with whatever he was making for dinner. To her left was a staircase, curving up toward the master bedroom; to her right was another that led to Grant's office and the rooftop deck. Instead of taking either, she walked down three steps into the dropped living room where, during the daytime, the windows looked out over the mountain. It was for this view, this house, this solitude, that she'd agreed to leave her apartment in New York; Grant had offered to move there to be with her, but when she'd seen this place... She'd called it Goth House the first time she'd seen it.

Putting a log on the fire, she called for Shep and heard him scrambling up from wherever he'd been sleeping, nails clicking on the wood floors. Bending down, she greeted the old mutt by pressing her forehead to his.

"Need outside?" she asked. He whined. She'd adopted Shep from the Humane Society a day before he was to be euthanized. He was already old when he came home with her five years ago, and now he reminded her of a grouchy old man who hated his naps interrupted. At the far end of the living room were three stairs that led up to the kitchen, and she followed Shep through it and to the back door, where he pawed at the floor impatiently. After she let him out, she stood with her back pressed to the door, massaging her temples. She needed to process what had just happened. Had they been able to see how shaken she was? She'd tried to keep her cool and get out of there as quickly as possible, but Tara had sensed something. *Get your shit together, Rainy.*

As she glanced around the kitchen, her eyes swept across the gray cabinets and clean quartz countertops until they landed on the nook where Grant had set the table and put out candles. The nook was surrounded by the same grand windows that were in the living room, and Rainy glanced at them uneasily before going to the control panel and hitting a button that made the shades roll down automatically. Better. She grabbed a box of matches from the drawer and lit the candles before sliding into her chair to wait for Grant.

It had taken her years, but she'd trained herself to live solely in the present, because the past and future were in competition for what frightened her more. But how fragile was her current reality if just the mention of a place—*that* place—could still make her feel like this? And what did she feel exactly? Unnerved. Unsettled. Unsafe. In New York, none of her friends ever spoke about Vegas; it was garish and vain, not up to their standards. Here in this rainy, cold state, it was paradise. People popped over there for sun and a nice stay in a hotel all the time. She told herself she was a drama queen, tried to brush off the feelings of doom that were making a playground of her mind, but in the end something bad *had* happened there. She was only human.

The pipes groaned upstairs as Grant turned off the shower; she opened the wine and carried it over to the table, splashing it into the glasses. The kitchen smelled of pepper and oregano.

The kitchen smelled of *him*.

No, it doesn't, Rainy reminded herself. *It smells fine. They're just spices.*

"So, what happened?" She jumped when he walked in, wearing pajama pants. Damp hair rested on the neck of his T-shirt as he bent to pull something out of the oven with her flamingo-patterned mitts.

"How do you know something happened?"

When he put the casserole dish on the table, he made a face that made her both angry and want to kiss him at the same time.

"You get a look on your face," he said. "A panicked look in your eyes."

She laughed without looking away. "A panicked look, huh?"

This time, he raised a lone eyebrow as he sat down, like, *You gonna tell me or what?*

"They invited me to Vegas. Their girls' trip." She picked up her fork and realized there was nothing on her plate.

"Oh?" He reached over to slide a piece of lasagna onto her plate.

Rainy didn't answer. Instead, she took a sip of her wine and stared at her partner over the rim. Grant was one of the most chill men she'd ever met. It was why they worked. He thought she was reclusive because of her art. He'd spent a lot of time convincing her to hang out with his group at first.

"So, will you go?"

"To Vegas?" Rainy swallowed. "No, I hate that place."

He looked crestfallen and she felt awful. Grant was a good man. It was her fault he didn't understand.

Again, she lied easily, by omission, though it wasn't without a price; the guilt settled in her throat and she tried to swallow it down. Grant was watching her carefully.

"What is it? What are you not saying?" he asked, frowning.

She was startled at how perceptive he was, and that she liked how he saw through her.

"It's just one of those places that holds bad memories for me," she said, looking away. "And besides, do I look like the type of girl who enjoys a Vegas good time?" This time, the joke fell flat to her more discerning audience, and Rainy turned to her meal, head bowed.

"Could be fun. You're all about the human experience." He was prodding her, and she'd have to give him something. "I could take care of all the details for you," he said hopefully.

She chewed enthusiastically for several minutes to stall. How to explain that there were certain human experiences she had no desire to revisit? Grant didn't know certain things and that wasn't on him; she just wasn't ready to let him see those parts.

"Wait a minute," she said. "Did Stephen say something to you about this?" Stephen was Grant's best friend and also Braithe's husband. They'd gone to school together, and it was Grant who'd gotten Stephen the job with his company.

He glanced up at her and she could see the guilt in his eyes. She waited to see what he would say, her nerves spiking. Her foot began a vigorous side-to-side shake under the table.

"Stephen did mention that they were going to invite you on their trip. To be honest, I thought you'd want to go. And," he continued, "my work trip is coming up. I'd feel better if you weren't alone up here the entire time."

"I won't be alone," she said, glancing at Shep, who was asleep in the corner. It sounded nice actually: a few days of uninterrupted work would allow her to catch up on things.

"Rainy, I'm serious. If you get a random snowstorm while I'm gone, you're going to be trapped up here without power. The soonest I can get the generator installed is late spring."

"We can manage," she said, sounding more confident than she felt. "If the power goes out, I can build a fire, and we have plenty of supplies, don't you think?"

Grant made a face, and she knew what he was thinking: city girl. And that had been true of the last decade. But Rainy hadn't always lived in the city: quite the opposite.

And anyway, what was she supposed to say? *I've survived worse than a snowstorm? I'm terrified of people, not nature?*

"All I'm saying is, if you have the chance to get out of here before bad weather hits, take it."

"And what about Shep?"

"Are you kidding? He loves going to Mr. Bean's house." Mr. Bean was their closest neighbor, and his name was actually Mr. Beade; Grant had come up with the nickname, saying he looked like the TV character. She couldn't tell him that it was Nevada she was afraid of, not snowstorms, and that she'd rather starve here than go there.

"I'll think about it," she lied.

After they ate, Grant cleaned up while she went down to her studio. It was an industrial space with heated concrete flooring and the same floor-to-ceiling windows that the upper levels boasted. There were doors to two adjacent rooms: one that she used for her office, and the other held a full-size bed that she crashed in when she worked late nights. The area was large, and there was also a garage-door entrance, which allowed her to get her larger pieces in and out easily. She was working on a sculpture for a private commission, a beehive using wire as its base. She stepped over the mess she'd made earlier in the day and walked briskly to the little windowed room that held her desk and computer. There wasn't much privacy in there, and at any moment Grant could walk into her studio and see her through the glass, but he hardly ever came down, saying he wanted to give her space. She sat down at her desk and only then did she allow herself to feel what she'd been holding in. It was as if balloons of anxiety floated in her belly, bloated and ready to burst at any moment. She bent over her desk until her cheek rested on the cool surface and waited for the feelings to pass, breathing deeply as tears ran in a steady stream down her cheeks. She felt frozen, unable to navigate through the maze of emotion that had taken over.

"It's over," she said, her voice husky and thick with tears. "You're gone from that place and that time."

Rainy hid in her studio that night, plugging her earphones into her ears and turning up her music until it was time for bed. Then, in an exhausted zombie shuffle, she walked the three flights of stairs to their bedroom and fell into a dreamless sleep until morning.

She woke alone with the rain sprinkling the window. Rolling over, she was sad to see Grant had left for work, his side of the bed rumpled. Grant was an architect in the city, and had a love of sculptures in particular. He'd visited her show in New York while he was at a conference and bought a piece called *Our Father* in which she'd used industrial metal wires to construct a man's face. The face, Grant claimed, looked just like his dead grandfather's. He'd paid thirteen thousand dollars for the four-foot sculpture, while confessing to Rainy he'd seen her work in an architectural magazine, and then he'd asked her out on a date.

She'd been flattered, of course, and she'd gone back to his hotel room that night and proven that flattery will get you anywhere with an artist. Over the next year, he'd made several trips back to see her, and eventually their meetups developed feelings.

Deep feelings. She still didn't quite know why she'd done it. Her entire life was in New York, her friends and business acquaintances; and yet, when he'd offered her the chance at a wet mountain life, she'd taken it.

She'd moved out of her studio apartment in Soho nine months later and made the trek to Washington state with Shep in tow and fear trailing behind her. No matter where she went, no matter who she was with—

One day, Taured would come for her.

3

Then

What she remembered about that first day was sitting in the back seat of their old Monte Carlo, her bare legs sliding along the leather because of how much she was sweating. The air-conditioning had never worked in the Tin Crap, as her mama called it, and it smelled like maple syrup for some reason. The radio was the only thing that provided some comfort of home, playing songs they could sing along with, like the Cranberries and Destiny's Child. They'd driven from California, sleeping in the car at rest stations and Walmart parking lots, eating peanut butter sandwiches when they got hungry. Summer still felt sick about the way they'd left: in the middle of the night so that the landlord wouldn't see them. No good-byes, no nothing. And they could only take what could fit in the Tin Crap—which was practically nothing. She'd had to leave her books behind and the telescope her dad bought her for her birthday. Now, they were headed to Nevada, where her mama had a friend who could help.

"What type of help do we need exactly?"

Her mother blew air out of her nose; glancing to the right, she honked at a car and sped around it. "We need everything, Summer! A place to live. I need a job, support, God…not in that order." Her mother's braid hung between her shoulder blades, thick and shiny, as she leaned forward to change the radio station. She bypassed a couple songs Summer liked, only to stop on a station that was playing the blues. Summer rolled her eyes, falling back against the seat. The change in music seemed to make her mother happy; she rolled the window down all the way and sang out at the desert. Her nails were painted a deep red, chipped at the tips. Normally, she never let her nails look like that, but things had been weird lately. Her mother was always tired, always working, always crying. Not in that order.

"Who is your friend?"

This time her mother met her eyes in the rearview mirror. She turned down the radio and pulled a piece of hair out of her mouth before answering.

"We were friends when we were kids. I haven't seen him in a long time, but we kept in touch. Kind of, anyway…and when your dad died, he reached out to see if there was anything he could do."

"Like what? Bring him back from the dead?"

There were a couple minutes of prickly silence as her mother stared her down in the rearview mirror. Summer, who was sitting in the back seat as protest for this whole ridiculous trip, looked out the window.

"Hey! Promise me you aren't going to run your mouth like that when we get there. The last thing I need is—"

"I'm not trying, Mama!" And it was true: the first thing

that came to her mind always seemed to shoot out of her mouth like shrapnel.

"You sound like your father." Her mother's voice was wounded, but Summer felt stung, too. *You sound like your father* were mean words from Lorraine, who'd spent the whole of Summer's life complaining about the man. She didn't want to talk about her dad, anyway. When she thought about him her chest hurt with how empty it was. The word *dead*, which had held little meaning to her before, could now trigger a frenzy of bad electricity in her chest.

She knew enough about how people worked to formulate her next question. "What does he need from us?"

"Nothing." Her mother rested an arm across the bench seat, steering with her left hand. There had been nothing but flat red dirt for hours. "Some people just care, they want to help."

Where were these people when her dad needed help? But she didn't say that—couldn't say it—or she'd get in trouble.

Lorraine caught her daughter's eye via the rearview mirror again, two brown orbs of intensity.

"There will be plenty of kids your age. And we're all going to live together, contribute together and be a community."

"Dad hated socialism."

"It's like this experiment, really," she explained, obviously pretending she hadn't heard Summer. "Taured was this…this… gangly teenager with adult ideas. It was hard to take him seriously until he started speaking, then everyone would shut up and listen. Anyway, he had this idea when we were just kids and it's neat being able to be a part of helping him build it."

"If you've been friends with him for so long, why have I never heard of him?"

Lorraine tensed, her arm sliding off the back of the seat where it had been resting.

"Your father didn't like me having friends, least of all male ones."

Her mother had never said anything like that to her before. Summer straightened in the back seat, her body tightening with this secret.

"Why not?"

"He was jealous."

She pictured her dad's big smile and bigger sideburns and something flipped uncomfortably in her chest. In her memory, his face took on a strange look—the light in his eyes snuffed out and burned like coals. Now that it had been said out loud, she could see it: her dad's crazy moods. He had yelled at her mom a lot. She always put her Walkman on when they were fighting, but sometimes she heard snippets of what he was yelling. When she looked up, her mom was studying her in the rearview mirror.

"He was different with you than he was with me," she said simply.

They hadn't known a lot of people in California, just her dad's family, and they were kind of strange, but it was still the only place she'd ever lived. Her mama had left her family behind when she'd met Summer's dad and gotten pregnant. As much as Summer scanned her memory, she couldn't recall a time her mom had friends over or went out to lunch with someone. Anger bounced up into her chest and she didn't know what to do with it: anger at her dad, anger at her mom— she was even mad at herself.

"You hate talking about Dad." Her voice was hurt, accusatory. Again, it had just sprung into her head and she'd said it.

"I don't," her mother said, and then she sighed deeply. "Look, Dad owed a lot of people money. That's why we had to leave. Awful people…no, scary people," she corrected herself. "We couldn't stay there."

"Why couldn't you keep babysitting and pay them back?" Summer asked.

"Hon..." Her mother's voice was strained. "I could babysit for the rest of my life and still not be able to pay those guys."

"Okay." It was the best peace offering she could make.

"It's you and me now, kiddo."

"And, like, all the people we're going to live with."

Her mother's laugh filled up the whole car and Summer felt happy again. Sometimes the things she said made her mother upset, and other times she'd laugh harder than Summer had ever heard. She tried not to say the wrong things, but it was hard to know what exactly it was that made adults upset—they were like seesaws.

An hour later, a row of small, stucco homes appeared on their right: they looked like toenails painted pink and green and yellow.

"Is that it?" Summer asked, scanning the desert for more homes and seeing only scrub bushes.

"The town is called Friendship, isn't that cute?" Lorraine said, ignoring her. She pointed to the sign as they sped by and Summer caught a glimpse of the name with the words *Established 1913* beneath it.

"Why is there a town way out here?"

"It was a mining town, part of the boom at the turn of the century, I'm guessing. When the minerals run out, the people do, too."

They passed a row of buildings and she craned her neck around to see what they were: a diner, a place called Red's and a two-pump gas station next to what looked like a motel... then more nothing. That was it. She slouched back in her seat, disappointed. When her mama had told her they were going to Nevada, she'd been excited about the bright, flashing lights of Las Vegas. But Vegas was at least an hour from

where they were going. Friendship was just a boring town in
the middle of the desert.

"There's some kind of famous cactus back there. People
drive from all over to see it!" Lorraine was using her overly
cheerful voice, something she did when she was nervous.

Summer hated when adults tried to make boring things
sound fun; who did they think they were fooling, anyway?

"Cool." She traced the stitching on the back of the seat,
not bothering to look.

Her mother, who usually called her out when she was rude,
was leaning all the way forward in her seat, oblivious as she
studied the road ahead of her.

"It should be coming up…"

Summer rolled her eyes but scanned the desert for it, anyway.

"Does it *look* like a prison?" She'd seen them on the Life-
time movies her mother watched: gray places with bars over
the windows and people dressed in orange.

"Don't think of it like a prison," her mother said. "He's
renovated the inside with the money his adoptive mother left
him." She was checking her reflection in the rearview mirror.
"It's more like living in an apartment building. They have a
vegetable garden, an apricot orchard and goats and chickens.
There's a cafeteria where everyone has their meals together."

"He": her mother's friend—the help-promiser. "Are the
goats and chickens in prison, or to be eaten by the prisoners?"
She'd meant for it to be funny, but by the look on Mama's face,
she'd said the wrong thing again—the thing her dad would
have said. Summer could taste the dust from outside coating
her mouth.

"Sorry," she said quickly, not wanting to ruin the mood.
"Can I have a sip of that water?"

The plastic water bottle crackled when Summer took it

from her mother's hand. She was lifting the bottle to her lips when an odd shape rose out of the desert, on her right.

"Look, is that it?" She pointed out the window at the pale building that rose out of the dirt like a squat sandcastle. A single road led down to the building. To reach it, they would have to pass through a gate. The gate was an ugly, solid, metal thing; Summer resented that she couldn't see through it, but now someone was stepping out of the little shack to their left and she switched her attention to the thickset woman wearing a guard's uniform.

Her mama said a bad word, tapping her fingers on the steering wheel like she did when she was nervous. "Summer, sit back," she said.

The woman was around her mom's age, and she had crunchy-looking blond hair that zigzagged out from her head like electrified noodles.

Noodles took a step toward the car, scanning the road behind them like she was waiting for an ambush or something.

"Name?" This one word, spoken through her teeth, with no smile to accompany it.

"Lorraine," her mama said to the woman. She said it in the nice voice she reserved for Summer's teachers. The woman didn't react to the name or her mama's friendly tone. She didn't check a list or smile; she stared straight at Mama—stuck her jaw out at her, even. And then, in a less friendly voice, she heard her mama add, "Taured is expecting us."

Bending at the waist, like she hadn't heard, Noodles scanned the interior of the car for…what? Summer scanned along with her, looking for a problem. There was none. They both seemed to come to this conclusion at the same time. "Pop the trunk." The woman's voice was deep and impatient.

It came as an order, not a request. Summer felt rather than saw her mama tense. Sometimes she thought she could hear her mother when no one else could, feel her feelings, and she couldn't really explain that to anyone, because it was weird. The trunk unlatched and she heard things being moved around. A few seconds later, the woman reemerged next to the driver's-side window. She nodded to Summer in the back seat and stepped into the shed, picking up a walkie-talkie. She turned her back to them when she made the call, and Summer watched her walk back into the little shed, nod and press a button to open the gate. The two solid metal doors opened to reveal a long stretch of road.

Mama let go of the brake and the car bounced through the gate. Summer spun her head around, gripping the back of the seat with both her hands to stare out of the back window at Noodles. She was watching them.

"What a nutjob," she said, turning back to face the front.

"Don't say things like that. You have no idea what you're talking about."

"Daddy would have thought she was."

"Enough!" Lorraine's voice was angry, and her eyes were worse; Summer looked away, at the sandcastle, instead. The closer they got, the less interesting it looked. She wanted to go home.

"Remember what I told you," Mama said.

"You've told me a lot of things." She could feel her mother's eyes in the rearview mirror, but she refused to meet them. Instead, she focused her gaze outside the window and on the bumping of the car as it rolled over the battered road. The closer they got, the more disappointing the scene: dirt, more dirt and then a dusty parking lot holding eight crappy cars.

"How many people live here?"

Her mama hesitated. "About a hundred," she said as they neared the building. "Taured bought this place right around the time I got pregnant with you."

"Why?"

"Why what?"

"Why did he buy a prison?"

"Oh." She said it in a way that made Summer think she didn't want to talk about it. "It fit his dream, I guess." Lorraine turned into a parking spot next to the other cars. "When we were kids, he lived in a foster home up the street from my house. He was the only other kid on our street that was my age, so we kind of just had to play together. Anyway, this is what he'd talk about even way back then."

"Living in a women's prison?"

Her mother shot her a look that said she better shut up or else. "Creating a family of like-minded people."

Summer opened her mouth, her next words forming on her lips, when a door opened on the side of the building. She saw his boots first—gray—and then long legs followed. Gangly, her fifth-grade teacher, Mrs. Eli, would have said. He was tall and lean like the cowboys in movies. He wore jeans, a black T-shirt and a smile spread so wide you couldn't help but smile, too.

"Oh my God, he still wears that damn outfit." Her mother said it more to herself than to Summer, her fingers running underneath her eyes and then through her hair. She watched, interested, as her mother clapped her hands in delight and then jumped out of the car, sprinting toward him.

There was a commotion outside as Summer scrambled to look out the back window.

"Look at all this, Taured!" her mama said, holding him at arm's length and gazing up into his face. "You did it!" He looked so pleased at her words that he hugged her again, lifting her feet off the ground.

Mama walked slowly back to the car with him, never taking her eyes off his face as they spoke. It was like she was thirsty for him.

Summer checked that her braid was neat, then pulled it over her shoulder. Then he was there at her door, opening it and bending down to smile at her. His face was mostly covered by a thick, black beard, but the skin around his nose and eyes was tan, like he spent all his time outside. There was a freckle on one earlobe, almost making it look like his ear was pierced. He held out his hand to assist her out of the car and she felt very *la-di-da*.

"Summa, Summa, Summatime..." he said when she was standing in front of him. It was so hot, hotter even than California. He smelled nice and he held out his arms for a hug. She hugged him because she'd seen her mother do it and because she missed her dad.

"You're going to love it here," he said, looking Summer in the eye. "We're a family."

"Why do you have to live way out here with your family?" She kept her voice light and innocent so her mother wouldn't chide her for it later.

"Because the rest of the world gets in your head and tries to teach you its way of thinking. Bad men sold your dad the stuff that killed him, that's how messed up the world is."

"Drugs," she provided.

"Yes. You're a smart kid, just like your mom." He tugged her braid and she smiled at him, and then her mother smiled at her. Normally, her mother would never let anyone call her a kid, but here was Taured breaking the rules, her mom grinning like she enjoyed it.

"Let's go check out your new digs," he said, putting one arm around her shoulders and another around her mother's. And then the man in the snakeskin boots led them into the Flatlands Women's Correctional Facility, the place where her mother would be murdered.

4

Now

Lorraine had been her mama's name; she'd taken it when she'd left—or rather, when she'd escaped that place—shortening it to Rainy. She'd taken her hair, as well, but that had not been by choice. The Ives women had hair so deeply black it reached toward blue. It grew straight and thick like a horsetail and she hated it, but because it reminded her of her mother, she couldn't bring herself to cut it. Grant was always touching it, running his fingers through the strands until her eyes rolled with pleasure. It was heavy, and the most she could do to get it out of her face was wear it in a braid, which hung between her shoulder blades like a sword.

For breakfast, Rainy made fried eggs and toast. She lounged at the table in her robe, drinking her coffee and passing bits of crust to Shep, when Grant called.

"What's on the schedule for you today?"

"Oh, you know, thought I'd fire up the gun and blow some metal."

"I love it when you talk welding to me, baby."

"You home tonight at the normal time?" She carried her plate to the sink, cradling the phone between her ear and shoulder. She heard his hesitation and knew what was coming.

"Happy hour with the office."

She didn't mind, but he acted like he was doing something wrong whenever he went somewhere without her. Rainy knew he felt like that because she'd moved here for him, leaving her own social life behind. But the truth was that she was glad to leave it; none of those relationships had meant what Grant meant to her. She listened to him as she watched the yolk of her egg spread like paint across her plate.

"I figured since you had Viola's baby shower tonight..."

Shit. Rainy almost dropped the plate. She'd forgotten, even after Braithe's reminder last night. She put everything in the sink and turned on the faucet, letting the water scramble the stains.

"You forgot about it, didn't you?" Grant's voice was teasing, but the reality was there; she was forgetful, too lost in her art to keep in touch with the real world.

"Yeah, I did. I better run to the store. So much for working today, huh?" She could hear the disappointment in her own voice. She was uncomfortably behind schedule on the hive—three weeks behind, if she were honest with herself.

"Baby, this is how it's going to go down, are you listening?"

"Uh-huh." If there was a phone cord to wind, Rainy would have wound it around her finger. She was familiar with this particular timber of his voice.

"You're going to wear that black dress I like—"

"It's a baby shower," she reminded him.

"You're an artist, so you get to wear black. When you get there, you're going to talk to Viola and Samantha—they'll look for you, too, because they like you more than any of the others—"

"That's not true," Rainy cut in again.

"Hush, this is my story."

She stifled a laugh while Grant kept talking. "You'll wander over to the drinks table and make yourself a double without anyone noticing, then, bravely, you'll manage small talk with Tara, who will ask where I am even though she knows, then she'll make a comment about your dress and how she's not brave enough to break the rules of fashion to wear black to a baby shower."

Rainy lost it at this point, the laughter escaping her throat in ripples. That was exactly what Tara would do.

"Braithe will, of course, rescue you. She'll see what I see with the dress, and she'll grab your arm and make you go with her to the drinks table."

She knew all this was true. Grant couldn't have written a better script.

"After a few shots with the Baby Tigers, you'll be ready for the big rocking chair presentation—"

Rainy groaned at this part. Shots with them wasn't what she was groaning about, though; it was the rocking chair she'd made for Viola. Rainy loved making art; she just didn't love being around for people's reaction to it. The oohs and aahs, the questions that came about the process, she hated all of it. She didn't want to talk about what she made.

"Anxiety," a therapist had once told her, "comes in all shapes and sizes."

"You'll grin and bear it, and it won't be as bad as you

thought because Viola will be so, so happy. You made her a chair with your bare hands, like a beast."

They were both laughing now, Grant unable to continue. When they caught their breath, Rainy was the first to speak.

"I love you, and I love that you can do that."

"S'why you keep me around, baby."

She got dressed, dreading her afternoon. The promise of a quiet workday forgotten, she resolved herself to another night of vapid social fanfare. There would be even more of them there tonight. Her only consolation was how much she liked Viola. Supporting her on her special night was easy; making small talk with twenty-plus women was not.

But instead of going to the store, she changed into a pair of coveralls and headed straight to her studio. Then, shivering, she turned on the gas fireplace, standing close to the blue-orange flames. She rubbed her thumb along the ridges of her necklace, stroking the same spot absently. There was something bothering her, something just out of reach.

For the next few hours, she got lost in her work. When it was time to get ready for the party, she hastily threw together the ingredients for her mother's couscous salad recipe and went to get dressed. Hopefully, no one would notice that she hadn't brought the sparkling apple juice. She stared into her closet. Her options ranged from black to gray. Instead of the black, she chose a gray dress so fair it was almost heather, and dug out an earthy cardigan to throw over top. *A for effort*, she told herself, shrugging. The dress was expensive, but it looked snobby instead of stylish.

Slipping her feet into orange Birkenstocks, she walked back and forth in front of the mirror, sizing herself up. She sent a text to Grant, telling him whoever got home last had to drag the garbage cans to the curb, and she ran for the truck.

Viola and Samantha lived in a ranch house halfway down Tiger Mountain. It took her ten minutes to pull up and another two to gain the courage to enter. Their three-bedroom house was ablaze with orange and cream balloons, dancing in the corners and around the fireplace where a gold-lettered sign was stretched from one side to the other: Baby Makes 3! Rainy swallowed a memory: *balloons. Not orange and cream, but blue and yellow.* Her head began to swim.

"The sign is dumb, right? Baby makes three what?" Viola said, taking the bowl from Rainy and making a face. "I told them it was stupid, and they looked at me like I was being too emotional."

"You probably were." Rainy didn't have to check Viola's face like she had to do with other people; Viola always got her jokes.

"Anyway, you look great," Viola said, eyeing her dress. "You look like a dove in an exotic bird shop."

Rainy didn't have time to ask Vi what that meant because Samantha was walking toward them. Samantha—who Viola called Tata—was wearing dark-rimmed glasses and a black T-shirt on top of severely ripped jeans. The only thing missing tonight was the beanie, and she guessed Viola had something to do with that. Samantha was the stereotypical Pacific Northwest hipster with a hint of goth, and she wore it well.

"How come Tata gets to wear jeans?" Rainy widened her eyes, letting her mouth fall open in jealousy.

"Because Tata didn't sign up for the Tiger Mountain Desperate Housewives' Club." Samantha smiled widely at Rainy, lifting her hand for a high five. As soon as Rainy's hand met hers, she turned toward Viola. "They want you in the kitchen. It's about the cake."

"For what? They can't do anything themselves?" Both of Viola's hands were pressed against her belly as she spoke.

Rainy watched them bicker playfully for a minute, and then Samantha steered Viola toward the kitchen. A sharp burst of laughter issued from the next room, and then Tara's tinkling voice calling over the noise: "Ladies, let's get this party started!" All of a sudden, everyone was pushing into Viola and Samantha's dining room, where the cake and presents were set up. There were at least thirty people there, half of whom she didn't know. They'd called this a "sprinkle," which was supposed to be smaller than a typical baby shower, but there was nothing small about this gathering. A woman who looked like a younger, emo version of Samantha breezed past from the living room to join them. *Must be her sister,* Rainy thought, lingering near the front door. She hesitated; she wanted to get the chair out of the back of her truck, but she knew that if she didn't go in and make her presence known, they would hold up the whole thing till she was back.

When Rainy walked into the room, she skirted the group so that she was standing at the back of the small crowd. Rainy spotted Tara at the center of the group, wearing a silk jumpsuit and holding a glass of champagne. Her signature ponytail was held back with a gold scrunchie. Rainy did not envy Tara's gift of holding court. Without Braithe present, all the women were enraptured with her second-in-command. Tara's eyes were busy scanning faces, checking attendance. Her eyes briefly rested on Rainy before she began announcing the night's festivities.

A few minutes after the first game ended, Rainy slipped out the kitchen door and headed for her truck. The night air was sharp and fresh, and it swept through her lungs, revitalizing her. She planned on grabbing the rocking chair and leaving it on the front porch with the card she'd taped underneath a white bow. Rainy had been secretly working on the chair for two months, after hearing Viola say she "couldn't find anything but basic bitch rocking chairs." Rainy had constructed the chair out of metal and wood, combining Samantha's mid-century modern taste with Viola's industrial.

"Hey! Hey, Rainy." She turned to see Tara tiptoeing toward her over the gravel, trying to keep her heels from sinking.

"You're not leaving, are you?"

It was dark outside. Rainy could just make out Tara's expression as she passed the kitchen window and trotted toward her. She looked...strained.

"Um...no. I just have to run back out to the truck to get Viola's gift." Her fingers drifted to her neckline, where they pinched at the links of the gold chain that rested there.

"Oh." Tara stopped where she was, looking embarrassed. "You're coming back in, right?"

A slow drizzle was falling on Rainy's head and shoulders. She nodded, confused by Tara's sudden interest in her comings and goings.

"Is there...do you need me for something?" Someone cheered inside the house, followed by a round of laughter. Tara glanced over her shoulder toward the kitchen door, and then looked uncertainly back at Rainy.

"No," she said finally. And then: "I'll see you inside."

Rainy didn't watch her walk back into the house; she turned, eyes wide, and jogged to the truck. *What the—?*

She'd wrapped the chair in old sheets, and she pulled them off before carrying her gift to the front porch and setting it down where they could find it later. She checked her phone, hoping Grant had texted. Nothing. Then, steeling herself, Rainy walked through the door.

Halfway through the baby shower, Viola pulled her into the pantry and handed her a fresh glass of wine. "I've got the tea," she said, and dipped her head around the corner to make sure no one was in earshot, her braids sliding across her bare shoulder. Then she did a little dance without lifting her feet off the ground, shuffling left, then right.

"What is it?" Rainy laughed, taking a sip of her wine. Their pantry was neatly organized and labeled—even the pasta was in matching glass jars with labels that read Bucatini, Angel, Bowtie. "Wow, okay..." Rainy said, looking around. "I definitely feel like a failure."

Viola waved an annoyed hand in her face. "Pay attention!"

Rainy faced her in the cramped space, barely able to lift her wineglass to her mouth. "Go," she said.

Viola didn't need further nudging.

"So, I accidentally picked up Tara's phone earlier instead of my own—you know how we both have that same phone case."

Rainy nodded.

"Dude, Braithe is not sick. Her text said, 'Thanks for covering for me, I owe you.'"

"It might not mean anything," Rainy said. But the pantry, no longer charming with its labels, suddenly felt smaller. Her breath caught and she felt *hot*. Viola was blocking the door with her body, her belly between them; Rainy's back was now to the pasta, and she wanted out.

"This party was her idea. She has no reason to not want to be here." And that was true; Braithe was consistent, and she adored Viola.

"Okay, but I'm not finished. The next text from Braithe said, 'I'll tell you everything tonight. Come over after the party.'"

That was harder to explain. Rainy bit her lip, trying to

think of something so that she could get out of the pantry; it felt like the walls were squeezing tighter by the second.

"What are you thinking?" she asked Viola.

"Honestly, I have no idea. She told me she was sick when I texted her—'I can barely stand up' are the words she used to describe her situation. Do you think she's mad at me?"

"Can Braithe be mad at anyone?"

Viola took a minute to consider that one. Then she shook her head. "No, she's not like that."

"Maybe she's mad at me," Rainy suggested. "Or one of the others. Or maybe she really is sick, and she needs Tara to come keep her company later." With her non-wine-holding hand, she reached past Viola and turned the door handle. The door swung open and cool, fresh air reached her lungs. "Either way, this is your baby shower, and you shouldn't be worrying about this."

"You're right." Viola backed out of the pantry.

Rainy thought about how Tara had chased her outside earlier when she went to her truck for the rocking chair. That had been weird. "You'll text me if you hear anything, yes?"

"Yeah," Viola said. "You want to sneak out the kitchen door now, before anyone knows you're gone?"

"Don't you need me here?" Her voice was laughably flat.

Viola winced, holding a hand to her belly, and shook her head. "Go, before they come in here. And drive slowly past the Mattson place and see what you can see."

"Oh my God, I love you so much." Rainy's relief gave way to affection and she gave her friend an awkward, over-the-belly hug before heading for the door.

"Your present is on the front porch."

"It better be good," she heard Viola say as the door closed behind her.

5

———

Then

Tanned faces stared at her from all around the room. No one was pale here, Summer noted. Even in California there were pale people, but not here. She liked that; it meant they were outside a lot. Everyone was wearing the same white T-shirt. She felt silly in her brightly colored, mismatched clothes... and then she felt embarrassed. She didn't have much to choose from: a couple T-shirts with flowers and pants with stripes, everything faded. Taured had them stand side by side next to a table ringed with blue and yellow balloons as he spoke into a microphone, introducing them. The room squealed with glee and everyone clapped their hands for Summer and Lorraine, their newest family members. She felt so important in that moment she didn't see the gift being handed to her, a basket overflowing with things. Her mother was handed another, and she politely thanked the room for them both. Summer was counting the kids in the room, all looking at her with equal parts jealousy and curiosity.

"We're celebrating someone else tonight," one mother said to a crying five- or six-year-old.

"What about cake?" the kid screamed. "I want my cake!"

There was, indeed, a cake set out on a table—white with pink roses. Summer was allowed to cut the first slice like it was her birthday. She cut a giant square where all the frosted roses were clustered and was told that that was her slice. The kid from earlier screamed again and his mom carried him out by the armpits as he kicked and wailed. *Little brat!* Summer thought. The adults were all drinking beer—the one her dad called "bitch beer." Even her mama had one in her hand. She wasn't smiling like Summer thought she'd be, but at least she was talking to people. The mother came back in with the bratty kid. She was holding his hand and his face was red.

"Come here," Taured said. The little boy went to him. Summer stopped chewing as she waited to see what would happen. The kid didn't seem afraid of Taured. In fact, he hugged his leg and stared up into his face.

"Enoch Aaron, let's welcome our guest and not be selfish."

"Yes, Papa." The boy seemed chastised, dipping his head.

Summer's eyes shot back to Taured's face. He was a dad? Her mom hadn't mentioned that part. She looked around for the boy's mother, wanting to remember which of the women it was, but everyone looked the same: smiling, smiling, smiling.

At some point, an older woman with bushy gray hair wandered over to where Summer was finishing her cake and handed her a card. The woman was moon-faced and rosy, like a storybook character.

"I'm Appy," she said, folding her hands at her waist. "That's 'Appy' with an *A*—not 'Happy'—a common mistake. Though I am very happy." She grinned. "Everyone signed it—even the babies," she said, pointing to the card. "We are all so happy you've come to live with us. You can't even imagine how excited we've been to meet you."

It all felt so overwhelming and good, like syrup on pancakes. And then there was a feast, the food unusually colorful compared to what she was used to: pistachio salad, gelatin molds with the fruit floating inside like bugs in amber and a popcorn machine they said they only used on special occasions. They grilled hamburgers and hot dogs and chicken legs outside by the playground, and a tall girl with blond pigtails came to take her hand and offered to show her the animals.

That night, Summer sat in a bath with a blue bath bomb—her favorite color—and watched in fascination as the foam built and then fizzled away to nothing. The bath was in the guesthouse, where they were staying until the paint fumes left their smaller room. Taured had told them that the guesthouse had been used for visitors to the prison, and occasionally the warden when he spent the night, so it was special. Despite her comments in the car, Summer didn't think it was creepy at all to be in a prison; it was an adventure. Her dad always talked about taking her to Alcatraz, but then he'd died. To her, it was the perfect setting: corridors and secret rooms, an animal farm with tiny piglets and chicks, and, very best of all, a large family. For the first months at the compound, Summer was radiant.

"Look at her, Lorraine!" Taured would point to her on the playground, smiling at her in pure delight. "She's so happy." Summer shone brighter and brighter to meet their comments, while her mother watched her, guarded. She smiled less and less, Summer noticed, and she wasn't very friendly to the other women when they tried to include her in things.

They had moved into their new space exactly four days later. Two twin beds sat on either side of the small room, with a wardrobe between them. Up near the ceiling were two shoebox-size windows; Summer would have to stand on her tiptoes on the bed to see out of them. It was kind of dark, even with the lights on. The room had a metal sink for water, but Taured explained that refrigerators weren't allowed in the rooms. "We want everyone to eat together and not have an excuse to hide away," he said, winking at Summer.

"Who wants to eat alone?" She spun around the room, arms stretched wide. There wasn't really space, and her mama told her to stop.

"Exactly," Taured said. "But adults get weird sometimes and want to hide instead of fixing the problem." He looked at her mother then. It was a strange look that she didn't understand. Her mother had loosened her braid and was shaking out her hair, something she only did when she wanted to hide her face.

"Right. No hiding," Summer announced, drawing his attention back to her.

"So…what do you think, Summertime?"

She grinned at the nickname. The room was small and weird, but she felt happy.

"It's good. I like it."

She turned to her mother as soon as Taured left, hands on hips. Just as she expected, Lorraine was sour-faced and pensive. She hated when her mother got like this: her lips folded, the seam between them a bright white. Too much in her own head, her dad used to say.

"You hate it," she said accusingly. "You made me come here and now you hate it!" Summer wanted a fight; sometimes it was the only way to draw the truth out of her mother.

"I never said that." Lorraine was digging around in her purse, murmuring something to herself that Summer couldn't hear.

"I want to stay." She almost stomped her foot but thought better of it.

Her mother's head snapped up.

"Why, because they gave you cake and a basket of T-shirts?" Lorraine slapped her forehead once, twice, and then she got up and strode across the small room. She opened the door, looked out and closed it again.

"Well, you're going to get your wish for a little while yet, Summer." Her voice wasn't nice. Summer didn't like it.

"What's that supposed to mean?"

Lorraine dropped her voice. "Look, we don't have another option right now, so we have to stay...but not for long, okay? Just to get on our feet." She was talking to herself now, pacing the small space between the beds. Summer sat down cross-legged on her own bed to listen and to get out of her way.

"Why don't you like it?"

Her mama stopped abruptly and looked at Summer like she had a thousand things to say. Summer braced herself for a lecture, but instead she got only a handful of words.

"This place isn't right. He's different than I remember. I don't trust anyone here and you aren't to, either, do you hear me?"

Summer nodded, her eyebrows lifting on their own. "But they paid all of your credit cards. I thought you said—"

"We're going to be foreigners in their land—do you know what that means?"

"Um, no," Summer said.

"We live here, we eat their food, we heal up and wait, but we are not to think like them. Their ways are not our ways."

Summer smiled. She only cared about the food, anyway.

"How long can we stay?"

"I don't know yet. I'm trying to decide if I should call your grandparents."

"You hate them. You said living with them was a nightmare," Summer reminded her. It wasn't fair! Her mother couldn't just drag her around the country, could she? She had to go to school and have stability. Her mother used to yell that at her dad when they fought. "Summer needs stability!" And she was about to bring that up when her mother said something that made her shut her trap.

"Some nightmares are worse than others."

6

Now

She didn't want to lie to him when she was already omitting most of her truths, so when Grant brought up the girls' trip again while they were having dinner in Seattle, she took a large sip of her water and buckled down for a squall.

"Stephen mentioned that you were considering going on the trip with the girls. Still thinking about it, according to the Tiger wives." His voice had a hopeful tone.

Her hand stilled halfway to her mouth. She set her fork down instead of taking the bite and sighed.

"No, actually, I specifically told them I wasn't."

Grant looked—not crestfallen, but worse than that. Disappointed.

"Why is it so important to you where I spend my weekend? You're going to be ten thousand miles away."

She'd just tossed back an oyster and was licking brine from her lips.

"Look, I'm not going to be available for most of the time I'm there. As soon as we land, we're going straight to the Tokyo office, and I'll be in meetings all day. It would give me peace of mind knowing you were...not alone." She heard him choose that word carefully and it bothered her. *Suspend your feminism for a moment and hear him*, she told herself. Picking up her fork, she speared salad and filled her mouth until she was unable to talk.

"The weather forecast says it's going to snow, and I don't like you up here by yourself. If you lose power, you're not going to be able to work, anyway, and you won't even be able to see four inches in front of your face."

She knew this was true.

She glanced at him, annoyed, still chewing. It was nice to be cared about; it wasn't so nice to be controlled.

"Then why did you ask me to move here? This is my home now, and I have to get used to all the weather and quirks that come with it."

She thought she was doing an excellent job of defending her position, and besides, she liked her chances by herself more than she liked her chances in a group of women she'd only known for a year.

"Grant, I—"

"I already bought the ticket." It came out in a rush and flopped between them like a dead fish. Grant was sweating, a nervous tell; Rainy studied his face, half amazed and half horrified as she tried to form words.

"What?" She caught the edge of hysteria in her own voice and cleared her throat.

"I'm sorry, Rainy, I really am." He stared at the ceiling, a look of pain on his face.

"Spit it out," Rainy sighed.

"They talked to me about the trip before they asked you. Two weeks before. I was so thrilled that when they sent me the links I booked your ticket right away, not even thinking to ask you." He looked really uncomfortable now, and Rainy remembered how enthusiastic he'd been the night she came home and told him.

"I never considered that you wouldn't want to go, I'm sorry."

Why would they talk to Grant about it before they spoke to her? And why would he not even consider that she might not want to go? Did he not know her at all? She felt betrayed and, beyond that, annoyed. Were they checking with him for permission, or to be considerate? Either way, she didn't like it.

"I'm an idiot. I just thought it would be good for you, but it's really not on me to decide what's good for you. You left everything for me in New York and, in a way, I'm trying to force you to put down roots by making friends."

She was almost as touched by his honesty as she was upset by the weight of what he was saying. She might not have told him everything about her past, but she had explained to him who she was and what she needed.

"Grant, I'm not super into having relationships outside of my partner. It's hard for me to trust people, and you know that."

"I do, but I've known some of these people since high school. I trust them, and I want you to trust them, too."

Rainy licked her lips. "Okay, I get that, but it can't be on your terms, it has to be on mine."

Grant, who had been looking more than sorry for the last five minutes, said, "I surrender. I was wrong. I've never felt like this about anyone before. I want to make you permanent in my life."

You could just ask me to marry you, she thought. Something she would never say out loud, for fear it would make her sound desperate. *That's some misogynist shit right there.*

Grant was obliviously happy; now that he knew he was forgiven, the relief was pooling off him. Rainy gave in because she didn't want to fight anymore, and because it wasn't Grant's fault that he didn't understand certain parts of her. He tried, but he was mostly fumbling in the dark, figuring her out by trial and error. *You could just tell him.* And then what? He'd see her differently if she told him about her mother and Taured.

And if she went on the trip to Vegas, would it satisfy his version of who she was supposed to be? She could tell him why she didn't want to go to Vegas particularly, or she could just go to Vegas.

"I'll go," Rainy said.

Grant blinked at her like he hadn't heard right. That made Rainy smile.

"Am I allowed to be excited?" he asked seriously. Rainy rolled her eyes, then nodded.

On the day of their flight, Rainy accidentally slept in. At ten past twelve, she tossed her carry-on into the truck's passenger seat and raced to drop Shep off at Mr. Bean's before setting off for the airport. They'd tried to get her to drive with them—the Tiger Mountain carpool—but she'd insisted that there wasn't enough room for them all to sit comfortably in Ursa's Jeep and that she'd meet them at the gate.

When she finally did make it to their gate, the plane was already boarding. The women were lingering around the gate, talking to the flight attendant, when she arrived, flustered and rosy-cheeked from her brisk walk over. Braithe embraced her in relief, while Ursa and Mac fussed over her. Tara, she noticed, glanced at her watch before reminding the girls they needed to board. High on the near-miss, they clambered down the walkway to the plane, recounting their morning to Rainy in code words and raised eyebrows. Mackenzie had had a pregnancy scare, but she'd taken a test in the airport bathroom, and no, she wasn't, but what a morning. Their seats were all separate, and Rainy had to check her carry-on at the last minute due to lack of overhead space. But when they finally did take off, she felt oddly relaxed and ready.

For what? she asked herself as she closed her eyes and settled back into her seat. She slid a Xanax between her lips for good measure and tucked her AirPods into her ears. Before she knew it, they were landing, their plane bouncing happily along the runway like a puppy. They hauled their carry-ons to baggage claim, where the rest of them grabbed their oversize suitcases off the rack. Rainy looked down at her own tiny bag and temporarily panicked that she hadn't brought enough, then consoled herself with the fact that the shopping in Vegas came as easily as the slots. A memory edged its way into her mind: she'd been a kid at the time, barely a teenager, and her mother had pulled her through this very airport, jogging, she was in such a hurry. And then she'd heard her mama ask for two tickets to Albuquerque, New Mexico, and her panic had gone into overdrive. Her grandparents? That was her mother's big plan? But then her mother had vanished, leaving her alone in the airport.

Braithe snapped her fingers near Rainy's face. "Hey! You okay? What are you doing?" She'd rolled her two bags, one big and one small, over to where Rainy was waiting, and her eyes were wide. "You, like, had this look on your face. I thought you were going to scream or cry."

Rainy smiled at her weakly.

Braithe was wearing a white silk top and white pants, and somehow, even after the flight, she managed to look fresh.

"Yeah. I'm fine. I was just—it was nothing. Are they ready to go?" She spotted Ursa, motioning for them near the doors that led outside.

"Looks like there's a cab ready," Braithe said. They ran for it, and then they were outside, Nevada's warm breath reacquainting itself with Rainy's skin. She brushed off the familiarity, allowing their excited voices to fill her head instead. Mac was telling them where she had made reservations for dinner. How many outfit changes would they need? Mac was asking. She'd had two cocktails on the plane and was slurring her words.

"Hey, guys." They all stopped talking and turned to look at her at the same time. Rainy pointed to the sky, her nose scrunched up.

"Oh, no, no, no!" Tara had her nose pressed to the window behind Rainy. "Did anyone check the weather? Was this supposed to happen?"

A flash of lightning punctuated Tara's words, and everyone made their own sound of distress.

"Sudden storm, turned this way," the driver said. *Jersey*, Rainy thought. *He's from Jersey.* "Hope it don't ruin your plans."

Ruin their plans. *Taured had ruined her mother's plans that day at the airport.* She reached up to touch her forehead, where an ache had already rooted itself behind her eyes. Her head hadn't felt right since...

When?

And why in God's name was she having these memories now?

The memory felt so real, with the confusion and fear. And then there was what had happened after. There was one thing that scared her right down to the center of her gut and it was a man who was governed only by his own sense of right and wrong.

7

Then

"**W**hat is Kids' Camp? Why can't I go to it and still sleep here with you?"

"That's just not the way they do things." They, meaning Tauredians, as Summer had dubbed them after the first week. If Taured wasn't going to name them, Summer felt entitled to. Her mother had scolded her for using the name, so now Summer used it solely in her head.

"But it's the way *we* do things," Summer argued. "You said I would never have to sleep away from you—you promised me after Dad died." The Kids' Camp argument had been gaining speed for a week, becoming a bristling point between them. At the last group meeting, held in what had been the old prison chapel, Taured had informed everyone that the children would no longer live in the main building with their parents during the week, but would be assigned to sleep and be educated in the children's building. Before anyone could ask, he cited the reasons: "Your children are too dependent on you, and they need to be taught to be dependent on God. They can't hear His voice if they're hearing yours."

There were murmurs of agreement, but there were also whispers of concern. The loudest being Summer, who immediately turned to her mother and said, "What?"

"Now, I know what you're thinking," Taured had said. "We will still share all of our mealtimes and free times together," he explained to the confused faces. "Kids' Camp is an exciting time for your children's education and your growth as individuals. Each parent and child team will have time together and time apart." He looked directly at Lorraine when he said this.

He'd taken a long time to drag his eyes away from her before saying, "As some of you have expressed, now that our numbers are growing, we need a more scheduled way of life. We're going to try this and see if it works. If not, we'll adapt to what's best for the group." That had seemed to soothe the room.

They'd been here through the summer, their life merging with this place: its people, its chores and its quirks. For the most part, it had felt like a vacation to thirteen-year-old Summer, who delighted in her farm chores and enjoyed the overall community bustle of mealtimes and evenings. But as she'd listened to Taured's words, she'd known things were about to change, and she had a sick feeling. Her mother had the uncanny ability to look her in the eyes and calm her down, and she was doing it now, slow and steady, from her own bed, where she sat propped against the wall, her legs hanging over the side of the bed.

"I'll be mere yards away. I hardly think that constitutes sleeping away from me."

"It's a different building."

Mama's words made sense, but Summer didn't care. Adults lied all the time: they told you things were fine when they weren't, and they acted like they themselves were fine when they weren't.

"Look, this is the way they do school here. We said we'd stay and try this out. You and I both agreed, remember?" Mama's eyes were large as she spoke, and Summer knew what she was thinking because she'd said it a hundred times: if this didn't work out, they'd have to go live with her parents. Summer's grandparents sounded pretty awful. They'd made her mother earn her dinner when she was little by how many prayers she said in a day. And she had to go to church five days a week, no matter what. They didn't believe in music, or television, or card games, or even holidays, because those things were evil distractions.

"Grandpa and Grandma would let us sleep in the same room." She said this with finality, and she knew it would hurt her mother. Suggesting she'd rather be at the place her mother hated the most was her lowest blow yet.

"You don't know what you're talking about."

"I do," she said back. "You said your parents made you do things you didn't want to do and that made you hate them. And now you're making me do things I don't want to do."

Her mother stood up, like she'd had enough, but instead of shrinking back, Summer stepped forward, her anger reaching a new peak. "You're a liar like Daddy!" she shouted.

Whatever her mother planned to do was drained out of her in that second. Her face went slack and soft and then she began to cry. Summer felt low. That's how her dad described his worst moments. But instead of saying sorry like she wanted to, she turned her back on her mother and went to her own bed, where she lay facing the wall. Shame was her blanket as she lay perfectly still, hardly breathing, listening to her mother cry. Sometime after that, her mother left the room. It felt like something had changed between them in those few seconds. Summer couldn't stand it. After an hour of sulking, she swung her feet off the bed and went to find her.

The cafeteria was empty at this time of day, a gray room with gray tables and gray chairs. The air always smelled like canned corn and wet cement. But the lady who ran the kitchens, Alfreda, left the coffee out, and sometimes her mother would stop there to fill her mug.

She found Taured instead.

The strong smell of oregano lingered in the air from a previous meal—lasagna. He wasn't sitting at his usual spot, and at first, Summer didn't recognize him. He was wearing a T-shirt and jean shorts and he had a baseball cap turned backward over his dark hair. Summer felt strange seeing him like this. He looked like a normal person, someone you'd see walking down the street in California. She stood frozen in the doorway, wondering what she should do, when Taured looked up. He smiled when he saw her, and the ruptured feeling in her gut mellowed out.

Summer widened her lips in a smile to match his, and he gestured her forward.

"You looking for your mom?"

"Yes," she said, taking a hesitant step forward. "Have you—?"

"Yeah, she was just in here. Come and sit down, Summertime."

She looked around to see if anyone else was around; Taured was hardly ever alone, and Summer thought about saying no, but it was hard to say no to an adult she barely knew. She was supposed to be polite, so she walked slowly to the table closest to the kitchen door and sat opposite him. A bowl of apricots sat next to his elbow, and as he watched her, he split one open and flicked out the pit, eating that half first. He pushed the bowl toward her and Summer chose the brightest, orangest one. Imitating his movement, she split it open and stared at the brown pit inside. It was the shape of an eye, and when she popped it out, it was rough to the touch. Summer ate the apricot, pushing the pit into the pocket of her shorts. The fruit was soft and sweet, like a marshmallow. It was cool that they grew them here; she'd seen kids her age hanging out in the orchard from a distance.

"Did you have an argument?" he asked. He split another apricot and again pushed the bowl toward Summer.

"Yes," she said. She swung her legs beneath the table, feeling guilty all over again. What if he asked them to leave and they'd have to go live with her grandparents?

"I had a little brother, he was barely younger than me—eighteen months—so we were like twins," Taured said. "One of my first memories is of us—me and Chris—fighting like our lives depended on it: biting, hair pulling, kicking. That's all we did, fight. It drove my mother crazy." He stopped to laugh at something Summer couldn't grasp, his entire face glowing with the memory. She wished she had memories that made her face glow like that.

"Until it was time for me to go to preschool." Taured paused to stare at the ceiling, one corner of his mouth lifting, and Summer got the feeling he was somewhere else. "I remember being at preschool and missing him so badly all I wanted was to go home, and then when I did get home, we were happy to be together."

"No more fighting?" Summer asked.

"We were best friends after that. As it turned out, we needed space to be our own individual people."

"But you were just little kids." Summer rolled one of the apricot pits between her palms under the table.

"Little kids are people, too!" he insisted with mock outrage.

Summer laughed at his expression and shrugged. She hated this part, when you were supposed to say something back that made the adults feel good about what they said.

"Cool."

Taured stretched, lifting his arms high above his head and closing his eyes. When he was looking at her again, he said: "I tell you what, Summertime, you and your mama need some time apart." He stood suddenly and Summer looked up at him with a frown. Did he know about the fight? She sniffed the air, seeing if she could smell Lorraine's perfume, but the air still smelled like leftovers.

"Come on, I want to show you something." He walked for the door, clearly expecting Summer to follow him, so she did. Summer's face went red at the thought of Taured knowing what she'd said to her mother. If he knew she was capable of saying such awful things, maybe he *would* ask them to leave.

She followed him out of the cafeteria, where he took a left and walked toward the doors that led outside. When they stepped into the white-bright of outside, she shielded her eyes with her forearm, curling it around her face. Taured handed her his sunglasses and she tried to play it cool as she slipped them on. Summer knew he was heading in the direction of the school, and despite her reservations, she was curious about it. She trotted on his heels, feeling important. When they arrived at the entrance to the children's building—as her mother called it—he turned back to look at her, winking. Her stomach clenched. A twist of his wrist opened the door, and then a blast of smells—paint and crayons—reached her nose. They were comforting smells. Summer reached for his hand and they stepped inside together. She propped the sunglasses on her head like her mom did.

He showed her the dorms, with white bunk beds lining the blue, green and yellow walls, each one with a shared desk and wardrobe. There were colorful shag rugs, and in the center of the room was a swing, hanging from the ceiling.

"Sara's dad put that in," he said when he saw her looking. Summer tried to play it off, but she was impressed. They moved on to what he called the canteen, where a rec area was set up with tables and chairs. In the far corner, and made to look like a tiki hut, was the Snack Shack, where they could trade good behavior tokens for cans of pop, chips and chocolate bars. Taured pointed to the projector, mounted on one of the walls.

"Movie nights," he said.

"Awesome." Summer couldn't help herself; she was into it.

From the rec room, they passed through another set of double doors until they were standing in a room larger than the last. Instead of sitting in the center of the room, the desks were pushed against three of the walls. In front of each chair and stuck to the wall was each student's name and daily schedule.

"Everyone works at their own pace here. There isn't a teacher for every subject like in public school—we let the books teach you and you decide how much you want to learn. We had someone graduate high school at sixteen last year."

Summer's head darted up from the desk she'd been eyeing. It belonged to a boy named Jonah. She'd seen him around. He stared at her a lot with unblinking blue eyes, but he never spoke to her or pulled her into games like the other kids did.

Jonah had a jar full of colorful pens and pencils sitting on his desk, and a drawing he'd made himself of a hummingbird flying above a lion's head. Summer liked it. She liked the sunny schoolroom, and the tropical Snack Shack, and the three colored walls in the dormitory. She liked the swing the most. She wondered how they took turns on it.

"This building was just used for storage before. It's amazing what a little paint can do."

"It's a lot nicer over here than it is there." Summer jerked her head toward the main building.

"Kids are the future, and we believe in investing in our future." Summer couldn't think to do anything but nod. No one had ever said anything like that to her before.

"So, Summertime, what do you think? You want to try out Kids' Camp or what?"

"Oh, yeah," she said.

It didn't feel quite right, but she did it, anyway, the promise of a ceiling swing and snacks bought from a tiki hut fresh in her mind. Also, there was the promise of friends, and she wanted those more than anything. She'd seen everyone as they left Kids' Camp and walked back to the main building. They were outside for some sort of field day, leaping and climbing through an obstacle course. They were on teams, judging by their red and blue shirts, and for a moment, Summer stopped to watch them, letting Taured get ahead.

They were having a pizza party that very night in Kids' Camp, he'd told her, and after ice-cream sandwiches, they were going to watch a movie about Moses. It felt rushed, the way she was instructed to pack up her things and join them that night, but when she'd protested, Taured told her that they had planned to surprise her with a cake to welcome her and to not show up would be rude. Because she wanted to please her mother and to make friends, Summer agreed. As Taured watched from the door, she said goodbye to her mother. It felt silly, sure, because she was only going to be sleeping a few hundred feet away, but at the same time, it hurt so much she could barely breathe.

"It's going to be okay," Lorraine said, wrapping Summer up in her arms. Burying her face for a moment in her mother's neck, she allowed her hair to be stroked and she breathed in that *mama* smell of comfort and soaped skin. Her mother was breathing hard as she touched Summer's hair, like she was sighing with each breath.

"Lorraine." Her mother's hand froze at the sound of his voice, but then the stroking started again.

"I'm really proud of how brave you're being," she said into Summer's hair. "Daddy would be proud, too." She said that part softly, so Taured wouldn't hear. Taured made it clear that anything her dad had said was influenced by the poison he had been taking; both Lorraine and Summer had taken to only talking about him privately, which was fine with Summer. She liked Taured, but the truth was, he hadn't known her dad.

He was watching from the door and she was too embarrassed to let him see her cry, so Summer bit the inside of her cheeks and tried to think of something else as she let go of her lifeline and stepped away.

"I'll see you at breakfast," she said, lining her voice with a cheerfulness she didn't feel. Lorraine nodded, tears edging her eyes.

"Take care of her?" Her eyebrows were drawn when she looked at Taured, who bopped his head at her request.

"You'll see her in the morning, and you can confirm she was well fed and well taken care of, mama bear."

The smile didn't reach her mother's eyes when she nodded, and then she turned away, facing her bed.

Taured led Summer to Kids' Camp the same way he had earlier, but instead of coming inside with her, he stopped at the door. He knocked twice, and a woman Summer recognized as Marcy opened the door. Her smile was wide and her eyes were excited.

"Summer!" she said. "Everyone is waiting for you!" That sentence shot twin firecrackers of excitement and fear into her belly. She glanced back at Taured, who nodded at her. He was happy with her. Marcy reached for her hand and Summer allowed herself to be led inside.

Marcy took her to the dorms. At the back of the room was an empty bunk pushed against the wall. It was closest to the bathrooms, which would mean foot traffic and flushing toilets; she understood why it was the last one chosen. Marcy told her she could choose either top or bottom, since no one else had claimed it. A couple kids had trickled into the dorms after the movie and were pushing each other around and laughing. Summer stared at the bed, uncertain. She usually conferred with her mother about these things, but Taured had been insistent that she do this on her own. Lifting her chin, she said, too loudly, "I'll take the bottom."

As soon as she'd said it, a very tall girl climbed the ladder to the top bunk closest to Summer's and settled back against her pillows.

"Wrong choice," she said as she picked up a book and began to read.

It was Sara. Her dad had built the swing in the rec room.

"I'll take the top, then," Summer said to Marcy, who winked at her. Later that night, after everyone had taken their showers and gotten into bed, Summer whispered across to Sara, "Why was it the wrong choice?"

Someone shushed her from across the room. "Lights out," apparently, was taken seriously.

"Cockroaches, mice and spiders," Sara said. And that was enough. Summer felt a wave of affection for the girl who had saved her from every grossness on the planet. Not four hours later, a girl named Lydia woke everyone up in the middle of the night, screaming, when she felt tickling on her cheek and reached up to find a cockroach. She was shushed by one of the adults who slept in the dorms with them at night and told not to be so weak-minded. Summer didn't think Lydia weak-minded at all; she would have screamed louder and probably not stopped, even when told to. She made sure to smile at Lydia the next day as they made their way to the cafeteria for breakfast. The girl looked embarrassed to be noticed at all, but she raised a small hand in greeting before scurrying away to find her parents. Summer caught up to Sara near the buffet of scrambled eggs, fried ham and tomato. With her plate under her arm, she stood in line behind the girl, keeping an eye out for her mom, who should have been here by now. After a moment of contemplation, she elbowed Sara gently in the ribs to get her attention.

"Hey, thanks for warning me about the bugs."

Sara shrugged like it was no problem and reached for the tongs in the tomato tray. The room was really starting to buzz now as people arrived for breakfast from the main building. *Still no Mama*, Summer thought. She redirected her gaze to her potential new friend. Sara had the palest skin. Summer could see her veins threading through her arms as she moved down the food line and dropped a scoop of eggs onto her plate. She offered the spoon to Summer. It was a small gesture, but a nice one. Summer took the spoon, smiling, and Sara smiled back.

"This is a really great breakfast," Summer said, taking two spoonfuls of egg.

"Yeah," Sara said. "It's not always like this." There was something in her voice that made Summer look up.

"What do you mean?"

Sara, clearly realizing she'd said something wrong, turned a shade of red like the tray of tomatoes as she plucked a piece of ham out of the serving tray and dropped it on her plate. Summer didn't want to blow it. She had a few seconds to salvage the situation, so she said, "Hey, want to eat together?"

Sara froze, her plate between her hands, and then, decidedly, she nodded.

"We sit there," she said, pointing with the serving spoon toward the far wall. Summer could see Sara's mother and father sitting together with their coffee. They were watching.

"Okay," Summer said. "Can my mom come?"

Sara shrugged, and Summer went off to find her mother, feeling happy.

She didn't find her, however, and after five minutes of circling the cafeteria with her plate, Sara came to collect her and lead her back to the table where her parents were still drinking their coffee. Sara's mother and father seemed glad to have her and asked her questions about where she'd lived before and what her dad had been like. Summer answered as politely as she could while she kept her eye on the door. Her mother had said she'd meet her for breakfast so that Summer could tell her about her first night at Kids' Camp.

"Summer..." It was Sara's mother, Ama. "She probably got caught up. She was meant to start her new job today."

"Oh," Summer said stupidly. She hadn't known. She knew that everyone here had to work, on the compound or off, that they had to contribute. She remembered asking her mother what she was going to contribute. Had she answered? Summer couldn't remember.

"Where does she work?" she asked Sara's mother. Her voice was meek and confused, and the woman, sensing her distress, put an arm around Summer's shoulders and squeezed gently. It was a mom thing to do, and Summer began to cry.

"Well, look there, sweetie, I see her now."

Summer's head snapped up, and lo and behold, her mother stood in the doorway of the cafeteria, eyes searching for her daughter. Summer didn't say goodbye to Sara's family; she launched herself from her seat and across the room, dodging bodies and plates until she was face-to-face with her person.

"Sorry I'm late," Mama said. She didn't hug Summer like she normally would have, just stood with her arms at her sides.

"I was worried," Summer shot back accusingly.

"I have a job," her mother said simply. "I'm really tired. Come with me while I get some coffee."

She followed after her, tripping once on her heels. When they found a spot at the end of an overcrowded table, her mother slouched over her mug and looked at Summer with droopy eyes.

"Did you have a nice time?" she asked. Summer launched into the stories without being pushed, ending it with eating breakfast with Sara's family.

"Her dad is the doctor?" her mother asked.

Summer nodded.

"What was he like?"

"I don't know. Sara's mom talked more than he did. They just asked me stuff."

"Like what stuff?"

Her mother was sitting up straighter now, more alert.

"I don't remember," she lied. "I have to go to class now." She started to stand up, but her mother grabbed her hand.

"I'm sorry," she said, and she looked it. "I'm just tired." Seeming to force a smile, her mama squeezed her hand once more before letting go.

"Okay, kid. I'll see you tonight for dinner."

Summer raised a hand and ran after Sara, who was waiting near the door for her: the school bell had rung.

8

Then

It was February of 1999; Kids' Camp was double the size it had been the previous year. Summer turned fourteen quietly that month. Her mother was away, and if anyone knew it was Summer's birthday, they didn't say. Most days consisted of a steady stream of chores, schoolwork, journaling and leadership training, and by the time she climbed into her bunk at night, she couldn't say what day of the week it was. They woke early—four a.m. early—to run two miles before their day started. Fitness and discipline were important, Taured told them. To learn bodily discipline, they would watch what they ate, report on their exercise and calorie intake each day and sleep exactly six hours each night. If they didn't meet their assigned weight goal each week, they lost an hour of sleep. And if they weren't sleeping, they had to be working.

In March, Monica Lewinsky was interviewed by Barbara

Walters about her affair with the president. Taured wheeled
the big TV into the cafeteria so everyone could watch. Plates
of cookies were passed around, the chocolate warm in their
mouths as Miss Lewinsky explained why she hadn't dry-
cleaned her dress. It felt like they'd barely dusted the cookie
crumbs off their laps when the TV appeared again in April,
with bowls of rice pudding: this time, Eric Harris and Dylan
Klebold had murdered twelve students and one teacher in the
Columbine massacre. Summer couldn't eat the pudding; sprin-
kled with cinnamon, it looked like freckled skin. She watched
as hundreds of students ran for their lives across the grass, arms
behind their heads lest they be mistaken for a shooter, and
wondered what she'd do in that situation. The building Harris
and Klebold had terrorized looked similar to the compound,
filled with windowless hallways and limited exits.

In May, a tornado ripped through Moore, Oklahoma, and
for forty-five minutes, its winds fluctuated around 301 mph,
devastating everything in its thirty-eight-mile path; it killed
thirty-six people and injured five hundred more. Taured ushered them into the cafeteria for this, too, and they ate a dinner of sweet potato, watching survivors being pulled from the
rubble. Why were these things happening? Both in nature
and to the nature of people? America, Taured told them, had
become godless, and as a result, the country as a whole was
under a spiritual attack. They'd had a hard year money-wise,
eating their crops instead of selling them. Even so, Taured sent
missionaries out that summer, her mother one of them, and
they came back with a widower named Jon Wycliffe and his
teenage daughter, Feena. After that, they ate okay again, and
they got a couple new TVs for the main building.

The first time Summer saw Feena she was in the cafeteria,
standing near the soda fountain, her hands clasped politely at
the waistband of her jeans. She was elfin and pretty-faced, with

spiral-curled red hair and creamy yogurt skin that the Nevada sky would eat up. Below her neck, she was all woman. None of the other girls had rounded breasts or hips that curved like an S, and because of that, every single one of them was looking at her. She was standing with her father and Taured, and despite that she was the news of the evening, her eyes were watching their exuberant leader, and only him.

Taured wasn't like the other adults; Summer and Sara agreed on this. He spoke to them with the same respect he used with their parents. There was no difference between young and old, male or female; if anything, he was nicer to women than he was to men. She noticed that they all looked at him in the same hungry way—not just the older girls, but all of them: the men, the women and the children. But who was Taured looking at?

At the moment, he was looking at Feena, and the feelings Summer experienced could only be explained by one very basic word: *envy*. Her eyes dragged between them as they spoke: Feena polite and nervous, Taured interested. Jon was smiling between them, a content chaperon. The smell of frying onions reached her nose, and remembering that she was here to meet her mother, she dragged her eyes away from the group and began to look for her.

After Summer moved to Kids' Camp her mother had worked different jobs around the compound for months before Taured began sending her on the four-to-eight-week trips. The missionaries stayed in motels, her mother told her, some really gross, but recently Taured had bought an RV, and they were going to use that instead. When she asked Lorraine if she liked going on the mission trips, she said yes, and then pressed her lips together so tight they'd turned white. They saw each other less and less, it seemed, but Summer was so busy she hardly had time to recognize it. She spotted Lorraine at a table, her tray already in front of her, and made her way over, still thinking of the way Taured was looking at Feena.

"Aren't you going to eat?" Lorraine asked when Summer sat down without a tray. Summer studied her mother's face for a moment, trying to understand what had changed, and then saw the tiny gold studs in her ears.

"You got your ears pierced?" Her tone was accusatory, she realized, but the women here were restricted from tattoos and piercings, especially a woman such as her mother, who was sent on mission trips.

Her mother shrugged, leaning her chin on her fist, and looked down at her soup and bread indifferently.

"Here," she said, pushing the plate toward Summer. "Have mine."

"I'm fasting," Summer said quickly. She hid her hands under the table as to not be tempted by the food. She was trying not to look at it. When had she eaten last? *It doesn't matter*, she thought. *The longer you go, the more blessed you'll be.* Taured had said so himself.

"Why are you fasting? Did he make you fast?"

Summer drew back like she'd been slapped; she hated when her mother got like this.

"Why did you get your ears pierced?" she tried. If they were going to be asking questions, she had a few of her own.

Lorraine, who seemed to realize the trade of information her daughter was asking for, leaned back in her seat with a sigh. They were in the back corner of the room near the AC vents. No one liked to sit there because of the noise, but Summer suddenly realized her mother might have chosen the table for a reason. The area was often used for dry storage, the table stacked with overflow boxes of instant mashed potatoes and macaroni when the storage room was full. Today, it was empty.

"I guess I thought, why not? I've always wanted to." Her

mother tilted her head to the side, making her little earrings flash attractively. Summer felt disgust as thick as vomit fill her esophagus.

"But it's against the rules."

"Not mine."

The soup sat between them, no longer steaming, as Summer considered what to say next. She wanted to know when she'd had it done, and who had gone with her, and what she'd been thinking at the time. Instead, she settled on a more direct question: "Has Taured seen?"

That drew a reaction. Her mother's expression seemed to curdle, her eyes growing dull and her lips shriveling up like dried fruit.

"Why are you acting like this?" Summer lowered her voice, though she didn't need to; the air conditioner was groaning loudly. "When you brought me here, you told me that these people...these people were here to help us. Now you're acting...ungrateful. Like you don't want to be here."

Something passed over her mother's face—she couldn't tell what. Then, all of a sudden, the look disappeared from her face and she leaned back in her seat, crossing her arms.

"Ungrateful." She said the word as if she were tasting it. "Taured should be grateful to me. Can't you see the new meat I bring him?"

Her mother was purposefully staring over Summer's shoulder. She turned around in her seat to see Taured, now sitting at a table with Feena and Jon.

"'New meat'? That's terrible. What's wrong with you?" Summer was appalled. She shook her head, a sneer pulling the corners of her mouth. For months, her mother had been changing, looking different with each appearance she made at the compound. She journaled her thoughts about it to Taured and then sent them to him through the computer like a prayer.

He never responded, but she knew he was reading. Now, she wished she'd asked him for advice on how to handle a situation like this. She sat up ramrod straight and practiced her leadership abilities. She doubted it would work on her mother, but it was worth a try.

"The work that you do is important. You gather lost souls and bring them to help."

Her mother laughed. The sight of her with her eyes closed, white teeth exposed, was beautiful. The sound that her laughter made was not. Feeling cynical and raw, Summer flinched away from it. No one looked, thankfully. Everyone was too busy being nosy about the new people.

"I don't bring them to help, Summer," she said. "I bring them to hell. He's brainwashed you—they're all brainwashed."

"Mama—"

"Yeah, I am your mother, Summer, I am. And I made a grave mistake bringing you here. I need you to listen to me, and listen carefully, okay?" Lorraine reached for her daughter, but Summer's hands were under the table in her lap. She would have yanked her hands away, anyway, if her mama had dared touch her.

"No," Summer said very softly. "No, I don't want to. You're embarrassing me. You're acting crazy. And if you say things like this again, I'm going to tell Taured."

The look on Lorraine's face made Summer's stomach ache. She'd only ever seen her mother make that face once before: on the day her dad died. She stood up from the table suddenly, not caring if she drew the attention of everyone in the cafeteria. She wanted to get away. Turning, she heard her mother hiss her name, then call it loudly as she charged past the soup bar, and then the soda fountain. She would have to walk past the table where Taured was eating dinner with Feena if she wanted to go back to Kids' Camp. Taured paused in his con-

versation with Feena and Jon to look at her, and instead of
walking past them, she veered left out the double doors that
led into the main side of the compound. She needed to think.
Her heart was hammering around so hard it hurt.

What had happened to her mother out there? If Taured
found out what Lorraine was really thinking, would he ask
them to leave? The thought sent panic, pure as pain, through
her insides. Then she felt angry. Her mother couldn't do that,
ruin their lives here like she had with their last apartment,
forcing them to leave their home in the middle of the night.
Summer had left her things behind, things her dad had given
her, written to her. People in the compound were headed to
dinner, and she seemed to be the only fish pushing upstream.
People said her name, but Summer acted like she didn't hear
them. She was almost to the chapel now, and the chapel led
to the doors out front. Light-headed, she reached the corri-
dor where the chapel stood, its doors propped open for anyone who needed a safe space to pray and think.

Summer stepped inside and smelled new paint and fresh car-
pet. Taured had had the whole thing redone last month. She'd
been in there a couple times since, but never alone. The newly
installed pews were modern and made the space look less
threatening than before, when it was covered in dark wood.
Through the chapel and to the back, where the Bibles were
kept on a wheelie rack, was an alcove used for storage, and
through that was a door that had been kept locked while the
compound was a prison. Guards had used the hallway, which
circled the perimeter of the building like a vein. There were
access points to this vein through the chapel, the infirmary
and Taured's office. Sara had shown her where each one was.
She'd been at the compound since the beginning—her family
was the first to leave their former lives and join Taured here—
and she told people that with pride. Summer knew where the

key was stashed. To the left of the door was a framed picture of a Bible verse: plucking it from its hook, she turned it over, and wedged behind the frame backing and the frame itself was a key. She needed the key to get back in, so she pocketed it and slipped through into the dark hallway.

It smelled funny back there, like wet concrete and something sweetly rancid. The light bulbs hadn't been replaced in years and the only light came in from the tiny rectangular windows near the ceiling. Summer walked a ways until she reached another door marked with an exit sign. This lock took the same key. It slid in and she shoved the door open, letting the fresh air pool in her lungs. There was a narrow sidewalk, and beyond that, the ground dropped off at a sharp, odd angle, a mini–Grand Canyon. On the other side of the mini-canyon was a fence and, beyond that, the desert. Summer followed the sidewalk around the building to the old prison entrance. From there she could see the guard shack perched on top of the hill. Not wanting to be seen—Marta, whom she'd called Noodles on that first afternoon, still manned the booth most days—she walked toward the carport where Taured had greeted them on their first day here.

Her mother's words—"new meat"—were still echoing in her head. What had she meant by that? It had sounded so ugly. And if her mother was opposed to bringing back new members, why was she going on those mission trips, anyway? But Summer already knew the answer to that: the mission trips had been chosen for her mother. People were assigned to jobs based on their strengths, and it was their duty to serve the community with those strengths. Summer served here, leading the younger girls by example. *And what type of example are you setting now?* she thought, keeping her eyes trained on the guard shack. The carport looked different than the last time she was there: there were three SUVs this time, a shiny new

RV—an Airbus—with a lightning bolt painted on the side and parked horizontally, taking up six spots, and a black convertible BMW that looked brand-spanking-new, as her daddy used to say. She walked alongside the RV, and when she got to the driver's-side door, she tried the handle. It was open.

Climbing into the driver's seat, Summer closed the door gently behind her and looked around. Everything smelled new. She leaned around the front seat to see into the back. The gut of the RV had a living room preceded by a small kitchen. To the rear of that were two closed doors that must be the bedroom and bathroom. There was no indication it had been lived in. Reaching across the passenger seat, she opened the glove box. When she was little her dad had kept Tootsie Rolls in the glove box. She pressed the button that sprang the little door open and found a pile of notebooks stacked inside. Rainy's forehead creased together as she reached inside to retrieve one. Opening it, she saw with surprise that it wasn't a notebook at all, and she was staring at a photo of her mother, but the name beside it didn't match. Staci Cartright, it said. Born August 3. That was not her mother's name or birthday, and yet the passport she was holding said it was. Shaking her head, Summer reached for another. They were all photos of her mother, matched with strange names. She put them all back as she'd found them and moved this time to the stack of driver's licenses, bound by a rubber band. Summer found her mother's real driver's license. She squinted at the address: Forsythia Drive. It was the old one, the apartment they'd left in the middle of the night. According to the front of the card, it was expired. Among the other cards, she found another face that actually matched the name: it was Feena's father, Jon Wycliffe, his thinning hair limp across his forehead, his eyes two dead brown puddles. They were from a place called

Rolla, Missouri. She stared at his photo long and hard, wondering if Feena got her looks from her mother.

She put everything back as she'd found it except her mother's expired driver's license and Jon Wycliffe's—which she slid into her back pocket. The last place she looked was in the large armrest between the driver and passenger seats. Popping it open, Summer stared inside: it was messy, unlike everything else in the RV: a polaroid camera, a pack of Doublemint gum, a handheld voice recorder and two pairs of rolled-up white socks. She heard a door slam and instinctively ducked her head, thumping the armrest closed and sliding down in the driver's seat so that her body was half under the steering wheel and her legs jutted awkwardly toward the pedals. Footsteps and voices. Summer made a mewling sound in the back of her throat. If she were to be caught… She tallied up her crimes, knowing the harshest punishment would come from the stolen items in her pockets. They'd be angry she'd used the key and snuck out, even more that she'd gone through the RV without permission, but Taured hated stealing—said it was the most dishonorable of all the sins.

The driver's-side door was still open and unlatched; she pushed on it roughly with her shoulder. It would leave a bruise, but it opened enough for Summer to wriggle out from under the wheel and drop to the asphalt. She hit the small of her back on the step as she went down, landing on her haunches. The pain was sharp and she gasped from it, clapping a hand over her mouth. They were on the other side of the RV now, and any minute one of them would walk around the front of the vehicle and see her, crouched and panting. She pushed the door closed silently with her palms, but there wasn't enough force to latch it. Two men: Taured and someone else. Real fear flowed through her now, making her tremble, as if she were cold. But she wasn't cold, it was a hundred and four degrees outside. The only option was under, so she dropped to her belly and rolled. Summer came to a stop faceup, the underbelly of the RV staring back at her. Her heart was hammering and she'd swallowed a good amount of dirt, but she lay as still as she could, afraid the slightest movement would alert them to her presence.

"The money is under the seat, passports and IDs in the glove box." The voice belonged to Sammy, one of the men who went on the mission trips with her mother. Sammy did most of the driving, her mother had once told her. His boots stopped on the passenger side, so close Summer could see the yellow stitching on their soles. She blew out her cheeks, holding her breath, her hand still over her mouth, and followed the other set of shoes to the driver's-side door. Nice boots: gray snakeskin.

"The photos?" Taured's voice this time.

"In your car," Sammy said. "Front seat."

The driver's-side door didn't open as suddenly. Taured was hesitating. Summer breathed through the hand cupped over her mouth. It was the door. He never missed anything that was half-finished, half-closed or half-assed.

"You didn't close the door."

"What—yeah, I did. I always— You're right. I probably didn't. It won't happen again, boss."

Summer couldn't hear what Sammy said after that, because both doors to the RV were now fully closed and the engine had started, with her still underneath.

9

—

Now

Ursa was taking her bags from the Lyft driver, her eyes hidden behind the largest sunglasses Rainy had ever seen. Her shoulders were hunched forward, and the rain pounded her back as she sprinted for the lobby. A woman jogged past them in a dress so short Rainy could see her underwear. She was barefoot and clutched her Louboutins against her breasts as she screamed, "Javi! Let me have my bird!"

Only when they were in the hotel's lobby, the air-conditioning chilling the raindrops on their skin, could Rainy relax. By force of habit, she reached up to make sure her necklace was still there, flat against her skin. Her fingers caressed the metal as she watched Ursa dust raindrops from her clothes.

"Do not play with me, rain! I am a pro." Mackenzie, whose blond hair was plastered to her face, shot Ursa a woeful look and escaped to the bathroom, presumably to dry herself with paper towel. They had come to escape a snowstorm and had found a rainstorm instead. As an artist, Rainy appreciated the comedy of the situation, though she'd never say so; the rest of them looked ready to cry. Didn't most of what happened in Vegas happen indoors, anyway? They could still gamble and see shows while the desert got her watering.

"Will you watch the bags? I'm getting a drink," Ursa said. Rainy followed her eyes to the hotel bar and nodded. "Want anything?"

Rainy shook her head and watched Ursa's leggy stride as she made her way to the bar. Braithe and Tara stood in front of the check-in counter, their shoulders pressed so closely together they looked like conjoined twins. Not for the first time, Rainy noted that two of them seemed to have nothing in common but time—a grandfathered-in friendship. She thought of Sara then, wondered what had happened to her; it was fleeting and uncomfortable, and she pressed it to the far back of her mind. Sara didn't belong in this world with these people, and Rainy had practiced hard at separating that life from this one.

A check-in attendant became available, and they shuffled forward together. Rainy might not have grandfathered-in relationships, but if Viola were here, she'd be standing with Rainy, making sarcastic comments about the whole situation. As Rainy stood in the center of their little luggage brigade, she slipped her phone from her back pocket and texted her friend. If partners existed in this strange Tiger Mountain square dance, Viola was hers.

The hotel is gold.

Stop bragging, came the quick reply. One corner of Rainy's mouth lifted at Viola's snarky humor.

Anything yet? Rainy asked.

The only thing arriving today is four inches of snow. This baby is stubborn. How are things there?

There's a really bad rainstorm. Girls are freaking out.

Rain is better than snow, Viola texted back, and Rainy scrunched up her nose in disagreement. Sitting by the fire while the world outside was still and white sounded nice.

Is Tara still acting weird?

Rainy glanced over at the check-in desk, where a receptionist was handing Tara their room keys. She was gesturing wildly, probably making jokes about how she was going to get lost every time she left the room. She sent one last text to Viola.

It's like she's mad at me about something.

She slid her phone into her back pocket and smiled at Tara and Braithe as they made their way over. Tara didn't make eye contact with her as she passed Rainy her room key. Rainy looked around their little group to see if anyone else had noticed, and then felt foolish. Braithe caught her staring at Tara and gave her a weird *what's going on?* look.

Rainy shrugged, embarrassed at being caught. She was being crazy; of course she was. Making things up in her head. She got like this with relationships sometimes, trying to find things wrong that weren't there. How many therapists had confirmed she had trust issues? Not that she needed to be told that, but it stung a little every time she had to hear it. The truths you didn't want to hear, right? She could accept that she avoided most relationships because of what she'd experienced. What she could not accept was when a well-meaning therapist tried to tie that distrust to her mother, painting her as weak and unable to protect her daughter. Rainy did not have trust issues because of what her mother had done; she had issues because of what was done to her mother. If they started in on her mother, she'd look for a new therapist. That's how it went.

"Up, up and away!" Braithe called. With the grace of the former dancer she was, she wove through the crowded lobby toward the elevators. They followed behind her single file, like little ducklings, Tara in second place, Rainy at the rear. When they crowded into an elevator, Mac had a sneezing fit that lasted four floors and made the other six people in the elevator scootch to the far side. By the time they reached their floor, they were giggling uncontrollably. Mac's face was shiny with embarrassment as she whacked her friends playfully on the arms.

"Ya'll don't understand. I get nervous around this many grown-ups and then I hiccup and sneeze!"

That sent them into a fresh round of laughter with Mac admitting that she hiccuped through parent/teacher nights.

Their suite had four bedrooms, a communal living room and a kitchen. They oohed and aahed over the view while Rainy shrank back from it. She didn't want to see the desert. Beyond the colored pinnacles of a castle and the pyramid-shaped tourist traps were several fucked-up years of her childhood. From the plane, everything had looked like a sandbox, sectioned off into smaller sandboxes with houses dropped in the middle of them. Grant thought that it was Las Vegas that she hated, but it wasn't the Shangri-La-ness of the city that got to her; she'd only driven by it as a girl. All the snakes were in the desert, and from their room, she could see clear across it.

"Holy mother of all slots this view is amazing!" Ursa said. "But only three of the rooms have a view."

"I'll take the viewless room," Rainy said quickly. When they all looked at her, she shrugged. "I'm afraid of heights and won't be looking, anyway." She hoped they wouldn't call her on that; after all, she lived on a mountaintop like the rest of them. But no one said anything—they were probably relieved that she had volunteered to take the crappiest room.

Ursa and Mac paired up in the largest room and Rainy, Tara and Braithe each got their own. Rainy dropped her bag on the bed and had a quick look around. The room was simple, in sharp contrast to the garish strip outside: creamy whites and dull gold accents. As Ursa had indicated, her view was obstructed by the Eiffel Tower, which suited her just fine; she was going to keep the drapes closed, anyway. At the moment, the rain angled harshly toward the window, slapping the glass rhythmically like she was in a car wash. *When nature imitates life!* Rainy thought. She had the urge to pull up the corners of the linen and hide herself under the covers like the antisocial person she was.

When she wandered back into the living room, Ursa was standing with her nose pressed against the window, whining mournfully. "It's pouring!" She had a habit of stating the obvious, but in a gloriously funny way. Once, when they'd sat down to a meal of dry chicken and burned rice in the dining room of the blue rambler she'd bought with her fiancé, she'd announced, "The chicken tastes like shit but I'll be offended if you don't eat it." It was funny and true, and they'd all cleaned their plates, smiling through the burned pieces of rice like supportive friends. Rainy had been even newer to the group back then, and she'd been charmed by the beautiful gazelle with no filter. This time, however, Ursa sounded genuinely deflated. Her weekend plans had been derailed, and she was a hundred percent not okay with that.

"So what?" Tara shrugged.

So what? Rainy mimicked to herself. Then, *Stop. Be nice.* She massaged her temples as a headache tightened behind her eyes.

"The restaurant I booked is an outdoor venue." Mac was staring at her phone, her thumbnail between her teeth. On the drive from the airport, they had discussed two things: the rain and their hunger.

"Just call them and see if they have a table inside," Braithe suggested.

Mac's face was red. "Yeah, okay. I'll call." She disappeared into her room with her phone, shutting the door behind her. Everyone busied themselves, either heading to the bathroom or checking their phones while they waited; when Mac walked out of the bedroom ten minutes later, she didn't look happy. "So, due to the lightning storm, the restaurant we were going to has closed their patio and they don't have any tables inside."

"Baaa!" Ursa threw up her hands in defeat.

"Relax, I got us in somewhere else—"

They all cheered, but Mac was holding up her hands to quiet them. "But only at ten o'clock...so I ordered pizza."

Rainy smiled at Mac's handling of the situation: bad news delivered by semigood news with a snack as consolation. It seemed to work; everyone accepted the news with optimism, and an hour later they were drinking and scarfing down barbecue chicken pizza like they hadn't eaten in a week. Ursa put on the hotel robe and was digging around in the minibar while the others propped themselves in armchairs, slices drooping in their hands. To Rainy, it looked like a scene out of a magazine: *Tiger Mountain Takes Vegas.* The city was the backdrop, spread beneath the windows like a neon quilt. Tara had not looked at her once since they arrived, and it irked the hell out of Rainy, who still remembered the urgency with which Tara had invited her all those weeks back.

"This is just my luck. First getaway in a year and we're stuck in a monsoon." Ursa uncorked a minibottle of vodka and sipped miserably from it as she stared at her magenta toenails. Rainy sat in the only armchair with its back to the large expanse of windows. She was trying not to look anxious.

"We should play a game," Braithe suggested. "Until this clears up."

"Like what kind?" Mac asked.

"Leave it to the kindergarten teacher to vet the game!" Tara sang. "Might as well play something good, since this isn't going anywhere."

"We could do dares!" Ursa chose a bag of M&M's from the minibar and studied the wrapper.

"Stop counting calories!" Braithe threw a pillow at the younger woman, who started, then smiled.

"I'm too old for dares," Braithe said. "Maybe something more…inspiring."

Tara chortled from where she sat on the sofa. "Who wants to play an inspiring game? This isn't a women's conference. I thought we were here to have fun." To emphasize her point, she raised her arms above her head and shook her hair around like a dancer in an eighties music video. In her year of knowing them, Rainy had never witnessed Tara mock or question anything that Braithe did. Braithe was staring at Tara, equally as disturbed. She looked around to see if Mac or Ursa had noticed, but they were alert and interested in the game idea, not the sharp tones in which it was presented.

"That's right," Ursa agreed. "Why don't we each ask a question that everyone in the room has to answer. That way, you can customize your game-playing experience and ask inspiring or nosy questions."

"Ooh, I like that," Mac agreed.

From across the room, Tara rolled her eyes and mouthed, "Of course she does." At some point, Tara had changed from her jeans into cotton shorts and a tank top. She strolled over to the chair next to Rainy, considered it and moved to a chair on the other side of the room instead.

Rainy felt uncomfortable with the game right away. Being forced to answer personal questions directed at her by Tara, Ursa and Mac? No, thanks. But the rest of them were reluctantly crowding around the suite's living room, finding chairs. Braithe was ripping the hotel's notepad into thin strips of paper.

"Here," she said, handing them around. "Write your question on this paper and try to disguise your handwriting!"

They all took a slip and one of the pens Braithe passed out and stared at her expectantly.

"Do we all have to answer the question, or is it one person per question?" Mac wanted to know. Ursa yawned and Mac said, "No, you have to stay awake. Dinner is at ten." Rainy scratched her foot with her other foot and tried to pretend she wasn't terrified of what they'd ask her. *Let it be one question per person*, she pleaded mentally.

Tara settled it. "One each or it'll take forever." They'd each draw a question and, unless it was their own, they'd have to answer.

"They can't just be any questions. You have to ask really prying questions," Tara emphasized. But they all knew each other—had known each other for years. They'd only be prying into Rainy's life with their drilling nosiness. *You only have to answer one*, she reminded herself, tapping her foot with the pen.

She scribbled down her question, hoping the others would

be just as straightforward, and tossed her slip into the ice bucket Mac had put on the table for that purpose. Maybe she shouldn't have drunk her wine so fast; she was feeling weird. She wished Grant would call her so she'd have an excuse to leave the room. It would be a great time for Viola to go into labor, she thought miserably.

"Okay, okay," Mac called. "Here it is...first question." She held the slip of paper up, reading it carefully to herself before her face underwent several expressions, one of them embarrassment.

"Spit it out, Mackenzie," Ursa said, and then added: "I hope it's mine!" She rubbed her hands together theatrically.

Mac cleared her throat. "What was your first sexual experience? Describe in great detail."

Braithe cackled.

"Yessssss!" Ursa sat upright.

Mac looked around at them nervously and then reached for her wineglass.

"My youth group was on this camping trip," she said. "So the guys were in one area and the girls in another and we had a chaperone in each camp. One day, the girls arranged to meet the guys at the lake after our youth leaders fell asleep. They were going to skinny-dip, but I didn't want to do it, because I was, like, terrified we'd get caught, so I stayed behind in the tent." Her face got really pale, and Rainy felt sick. This wasn't going to be good. She wanted to reach out and tell Mac that she didn't owe anything to these women, and she didn't have to say another word if she didn't want to.

"Anyway, there was this guy I kind of liked but he never really spoke to me, even when I tried to talk to him. The others hadn't been gone for more than ten minutes when he crawls into the tent where I'm lying in my freaking purple sleeping bag...and he starts to kiss me."

"Wait, he didn't ask? He just starts to...kiss you?" The delighted look had left Ursa's face, and she was staring at Mac in horror. Mac nodded.

"But then he starts feeling me up, too, and I'm still so shocked by the kissing that I'm letting it all happen."

"Whoa, whoa!" Braithe said, cutting her off. "How old were you?"

The room had taken on a new feel. Everyone had stopped drinking and eating and fidgeting and they were all focused on Mac. She looked exceptionally small and fragile as she sat on her knees on the hotel floor, wearing her Britney Spears T-shirt. She probably hadn't looked that much different when she was a teenager. Rainy blinked hard, trying to clear her vision.

"Fifteen," she said. They all flinched. It was an age where people stopped thinking of you as a child, even though you still were one. Grown men made sexual remarks to fifteen-year-old girls all the time. Rainy knew that on an all-too-personal level. She shivered as she stared at Mac, not wanting the story to go where it seemed to be headed.

"We—he had sex with me. It all happened really fast and I genuinely feel so stupid for not saying anything, or screaming, or anything like that. I just laid there, honest to God, and waited for it to be over. I never told anyone." She folded her lips in after the last sentence and stared fixedly at the blank TV screen.

"Mac, holy shit," Ursa said. "Does Bryan know?"

Mac shook her head. Bryan Biggs was a really nice guy, there was no other way to describe him. He reminded Rainy of what she was supposed to be: kind, patient and outgoing.

"Omigod," Mac said in one breath. "I can't believe I just told you all of that." She covered her face with her hands, and Ursa went to sit by her. Mac started to cry.

"No, Mac, please don't. We're your friends." Braithe reached across the table between them and placed her hand over Mac's protectively while Ursa nodded. Rainy felt torn between comforting her and staying the observer. She noticed that Tara was watching everyone's reactions carefully from where she still sat perched in her chair.

"What happened to that guy?" Rainy asked.

"Who the fuck cares," Ursa said, rubbing little circles on Mac's back. "I hope he died a thousand deaths."

"Nothing. He never really spoke to me after that."

Tara said, "What?"

At the same time, Braithe said, "Hell, no!"

Mac shrugged. "He never spoke to me before then. He just kept coming to youth group and I pretended not to know him and then finally we moved and…"

"This is messed up," Tara said.

"Someone take a turn and change the subject fast," Mac laughed through her tears. She shoved the ice bucket toward Tara, who wordlessly stuck her hand in and pulled out a slip.

She didn't bother to read it first like Mac had, wanting to digest the question before she shared it. Tara cleared her throat. "Why haven't you had any kids?"

Tara's smooth white throat spasmed as she laughed. Her face was tilted all the way up to the ceiling like she was conversing with God. "Who asked this?" she said between tears. The tension in the room deflated under her cackling and Rainy started to laugh along with the others. The question, though very valid, could have been posed to any of them; they were all childless. As the author of the question, Mac raised a hand, which for some reason made Tara laugh harder.

"Okay…okay…sorry," she said, spreading a palm over her chest. "I don't know why that tickled me so much. Matt and I tried for about four years, then we talked about adoption, but we never actually made a move toward those first steps. That's really it. I don't think we wanted it enough. And we're pretty happy just the two of us. You're going to be a great mom, though," she said, pointing a finger at Mac, "when you're ready. You and Viola are the graduating class." No one said anything for another minute and Rainy considered that they were all wondering about everyone else's reasons.

"What about you, Braithe?" Mac asked. So that's who her question had really been directed to. Rainy was more interested in her answer than she'd like to admit. Stephen and Braithe had a box at the Seattle ballet, they vacationed to places like Greece and Italy and had a wine cellar in their house with bottles that cost anywhere from three hundred dollars to three thousand. Rainy had assumed they were too busy to have children; she'd never considered that maybe they couldn't have them.

"I used to want children," Braithe said. "I always thought I'd have three: a boy and twin girls. I wanted to name the girls Juniper and Orla, isn't that funny?"

"Those are pretty names," Mac said. "What about the little boy?"

"He'd have his dad's name."

Everyone fell silent, imagining a little Stephen with tight curls and dimples and waiting for Braithe to tell them why it never happened. But Braithe didn't explain. She reached for the ice bucket. Her hand emerged and she curled her knee up to her chest and wrapped her arm around it to read the slip. She absently fingered the ends of her hair, her mouth moving as she read. *Three to go*, Rainy thought. Would she have to lie? If Ursa asked the first question, and Mac the second. That left her own, Tara's and Braithe's questions unanswered. She'd already decided that she wanted to be the last one to go. That way, she could make her answer short and sweet and end this game.

"Are you going to read it or not, Braithe?" Rainy wasn't the only one watching her. To her right, Tara was smirking at Braithe. "Let's hear it." Tara nudged Braithe's shoulder with her toe. "I'm getting bored with this, fast."

"Well, I'm down to be done." Braithe crumpled the slip in her fist and made to toss it away.

"No way, everyone has a turn. I'll read it for you." She wrestled the paper from Braithe's grasp with a triumphant smile and, with the slip in her possession, Tara began to read silently, ignoring Braithe's protests. When she saw the question, Tara exclaimed, "Yass, girl."

"Ohhh, why doesn't she want to answer her BFF's question?" Ursa was sitting on a chair behind Mac. She'd retrieved her curling wand and was sectioning off the brunette's hair.

"Because she's being rude," Braithe said, giving Tara a look. But instead of continuing to fight with Tara, she let her read it.

"Who was your first true love? Describe them."

Rainy sat up a little straighter; that wasn't Tara's question, it was hers, but for some reason, Braithe had thought her best friend had written it. *Why?*

"He was, like, so handsome," Braithe said to the room.

"Stephen is still handsome!" Ursa called from behind a piece of Mac's hair.

"Just real easy to be around, you know?"

And now it seemed to Rainy that Braithe was talking to herself more than any of them.

"We were just around each other and it was this energy, like putting spit to pop rocks."

"Oh, ew," Tara laughed. "Can you not wax poetic about bodily fluids?"

"So you...popped?" Mac asked, clearly unsure of herself.

Her eyes were still red from crying, but thanks to Ursa, she was starting to look like...Ursa. Waves framed her face, easing some roundness into her square jaw; with a little bronzer and wet lips, she'd be set for the twinsie life.

"We popped *and* we meshed, and he was this perfect combination of Chandler from *Friends* and that guy from *The Notebook*. Like, superfunny and snarky and comfortable with his obsession with me. We were obsessed with each other—"

"What's *The Notebook*?" Mac asked. But no one answered her; they were waiting for Braithe to keep talking. *Now that she's going she's* really going, Rainy thought. But this was her favorite topic, even if she was hesitant to admit it: love.

"And he'd do this thing where he'd rub little circles on my palm to tell me he wanted me, and like, wherever we were he'd do that and we'd just go running out like—"

"Two horny kids?" Rainy finished for her.

"Yeah," she said, and her mouth curled up in a secret pleasure as she traced over her memories in front of them.

"Um, so are you not talking about Stephen?" Mac's face was genuinely confused.

"Have you ever loved anyone other than Bryan? Hush," Tara said, but not unkindly; Mac was like everyone's little sister.

"I'm more of a Christian Grey fan myself," Ursa said. "I need you to spank me, not read me stories in a nursing home."

"Your turn," Braithe said as she pushed the ice bucket toward Ursa, who was finished with Mac's hair.

Ursa reached in, her hand, with its candy-colored nails, drawing out the second-to-last question. Rainy watched her eyes scan the paper and widen considerably. When she read it out loud for the rest of them, she was trying not to laugh.

"Have you ever...squirted?"

It sounded like a series of murders were taking place all at the same time. Rainy joined the choir of screams and screeches and then laughed behind her hand as Ursa recounted her the story of the first time she'd done it (freshman year of college with a premed major).

"And he explained the whole thing in medical terms. I legit thought I was dying of an STI. No one had ever told me about it—"

Rainy stopped listening, remembering that her turn was next. *So had that been Tara's question or Braithe's?* she thought, doing the math. There wasn't long to think on it because they were done asking Ursa their prying questions and ready to sink their teeth into Rainy.

They didn't even bother to pass her the ice bucket. Braithe dug the last piece of paper out and passed it to Rainy without looking at her. She was still engaged in the conversation, pointing a finger at Ursa as she said, "It is not right that a man had to explain that to you!"

It was stupid, but Rainy's palms began to sweat.

Unfolding the slip, she mumbled out the words as soon as she saw them and felt herself immediately go cold. Her voice abruptly cut off and Mac asked her to repeat the question. Rainy read it again, slowly this time.

"Have you ever been married before?"

"Um…weird," Ursa said. "We all know each other's dating history."

"Not so weird," Tara piped up. "We don't know very much about Rainy, since she's our newest."

On cue, they all looked at Rainy, who was still reeling and desperately wanting there to be an earthquake at that very moment to end this game and suck them all into the ground.

"I—"

Had they done this on purpose, included that question for her? But how could they know what had almost happened to her? And how could they know that she would draw that question?

Her heart was pounding, and a familiar panic was rising in her throat. If she gave anything away, they'd know the truth before Grant did.

"No." The word rolled from her tongue, firm and hard like a boiled sweet. It was easier than she expected it to be, though her heart was hammering around in her chest. Rainy, who had spent many years learning to be silent, chose that approach now. Sitting squarely and blinking lazily, she stared at them as they stared at her. When no more words were said, the room took on a weird energy. The white living room with its white furniture blurred in and out of focus. Rainy wanted to stand up and leave. She was almost relieved when Tara spoke, but her relief curdled as soon as the words were out of Tara's mouth.

"When do you and Grant think you'll tie the knot?"

The knot that formed in Rainy's belly was not the same as the knot Tara meant.

Momentarily tongue-tied, she stumbled over her words before saying, "We're not sure we will. I...er...I'm not so much a fan of the whole thing...?" The end of her sentence seemed to drop off in a question. *Stupid, stupid Rainy.*

Tara raised her eyebrows before glancing around the table to gauge everyone else's response to this bit of news. To Rainy, she looked hungry as she searched their faces. Ursa and Mac, satisfied with her answer and already bored, looked indifferent. Marriage wasn't a thing anymore; if people didn't choose it, it was no big deal. They'd moved on, game over. Braithe and Tara were the only ones still looking at her, and Braithe's eyebrows were drawn in what Rainy could only assume was concern.

"Does Grant want to get married?"

Tara was really pushing it with these questions. Rainy felt herself nearing anger as she licked her lips and lied again.

"No. We're on the same page."

Braithe gave her an odd look, like she knew Rainy was lying, and she probably did—she'd known Grant since they were teenagers. He'd no doubt expressed his desire to get married at least a couple times over the twenty years of their friendship. Her next words surprised Rainy, however. "Not everyone wants to get married, Tara," Braithe said tightly. Tara shrugged, but there was a small grin on her lips that Rainy didn't miss. Had they spoken about this together, the possibility of Rainy and Grant getting married? She supposed they had. After all, they'd known Grant longer than she had, and it was only normal to speculate about your friends' love lives.

"Game over." Braithe stood up, stretching. "We need to get ready."

Getting ready, for Rainy, involved a three-minute shower, putting on an uncomplicated outfit and mascara.

"We're gonna be a while, Rainy," Braithe said, looking embarrassed. She had no makeup on yet, and she was wearing one of the hotel gowns. A hair dryer roared to life in one of the rooms, and Ursa began wandering around in a towel, looking for her curling iron. It was female chaos.

She should have taken a longer shower, washed her hair, put on a more complicated outfit...but the trouble was, Rainy didn't know how to take a long time to do things; she rushed through everything, which made her feel like she was failing at being a woman. These women were part of a ritual that she didn't understand: bonding through talk and preparation. *It's just not how you grew up*, she thought, and then flinched. Sara always seeped into her memory when she was in a group of women, even when she tried to keep her out. The normalcy of these women, talking and laughing together, made her long for something she hadn't allowed herself since then... since Sara.

"The shops and bars downstairs are great if you want to get started without us." Braithe's voice pulled her out of her feelings, dropping her into less complicated ones. They were trying to get rid of her. Did she care?

"I'll go walk around for a bit," she offered, standing up. If they wanted to talk about her, let them. They needed to dissect her answers to the game, right? Well, she needed space.

"I'll text you when we're heading down," Braithe called to her.

Grabbing her bag, Rainy chewed the inside of her cheek as she made her way to the door. The sounds she left behind were familiar, the sounds female friends made when they were together. Happy sounds. And more importantly, *their* sounds; she was not included.

When she saw how crowded the lobby was, she decided to wait downstairs in the hotel bar instead of fighting her way through the bodies that clogged the hallways. Soon, she was sipping a beer and watching the TV as an excited meteorologist updated them on the storm. She hadn't liked the vibe in the group since they'd arrived at the hotel, but that was probably just her. God, if she had to be here, she wished it were with Grant. She stared at her phone, willing him to text, but knowing it wouldn't happen for another few hours. She'd marry him if she could. It was that simple. But these women didn't get to weigh in on that.

Things are weird, she texted Viola.

Stop it. Try to have fun.

She nodded, as if Viola could see her. She put her phone away and drained her beer.

"You need another?"

She jumped, then relaxed when she saw it was just the bartender. He was middle-aged with a receding hairline that was charming on his angular face.

"Another beer?" He pointed to her empty glass. He had a New England accent and he looked like a talker.

"Nah, switch me to your cocktail of the night, if that's okay."

He nodded. "I made this one up myself. It's on the sweeter side if that's okay...?" He was mimicking her, but in a friendly way.

She gave him a thumbs-up and he came back two minutes later with brown sludge in a martini glass.

"Coffee-flavored," she said, taking a sip. "It's good."

"You know where I get that? Rhode Island, baby. It's coffee syrup. Grew up on that stuff. I call that a New England Russian. I tried this out on another guy who came in here, and he loved it. Makes sense—he was from New England, too."

"Coffee syrup?" She said it out loud, though she hadn't meant to. *She'd heard that before...*

He showed her the bottle and Rainy had a sudden, dizzying sense of déjà vu.

"I drank white Russians in college," she said. "It's my kind of drink." He looked pleased enough that he wandered away to offer his New England Russian to some fresh new faces on the other side of the bar.

"You waiting on someone?" he asked, coming back around fifteen minutes later.

"Four female someones," she answered.

He nodded. "Bachelorette party?"

Rainy played along. "Sure."

He scooped up her empty glass. "Another?"

She shook her head. "I'll close out." His concoction was curdling in her belly as she signed the receipt.

"Hey, I know you girls like to party hard when you come here, and I like you. So, listen up—whatever you do, do not buy drugs from Barry. He works at the Bellum, but he comes around to all the hotels within a few blocks." He was pouring someone else's beer but looking at her. "Last week, that little bastard sold roofies to four girls here. He told them it was cocaine, and they all ended up in the ER. I served them before they left—just like you. I told them to stay away from Barry, too, but do you think they listened?"

Rainy gave him a look that was part fear for what was happening in her stomach, and part interest. He glommed on to the interest part.

"He's a New Englander, too. You'll know that slimebag because he wears a fanny pack. But don't worry about it. You're a nice girl."

The nice girl felt better when she got up from the bar stool to walk around some more. She'd just bought herself a water at a little grocery in the lobby when Braithe texted her to say they were coming down.

"I can do this," she said to no one. "Maybe not well, but I can do it." She sped up when she saw them step off the elevator. She was definitely underdressed. Why hadn't they told her?

Get over yourself, Rainy. Tucking her hair behind her ears, she presented her best smile to the night ahead.

10

—

Then

Summer had not been crushed when the RV rolled forward, its brakes hissing. She'd lain flat on her stomach, cheek pressed to the road so hard she could feel the heat of the asphalt digging into her skin, and she'd been praying like hell. And then she'd felt the breeze on her back, lifting her shirt, and she realized she wasn't pavement paste, after all.

Taured had driven the monstrous thing straight over her body. When she dared look up, it was turning at the maintenance shed. And that's when she understood he meant to turn the RV around: cut a U-ey, as her dad would have put it. In a few seconds, he'd back the behemoth up and turn the wheel left. He'd see her lying in the middle of the parking lot, covering her head like the sky was falling. The other cars in the lot were parked neatly alongside the building, and she ran in a half crouch for those, diving between the BMW and the

Chevy just as the thing came rolling back around. Sammy had said something about the envelope being in Taured's car—the very car her right hand was resting against. Summer scuffled backward, opening the car door as the Airbus neared. She probably had about sixty seconds before one of them spotted her. She reached her arm inside to feel the passenger-side seat and her fingers caught the edge of an envelope. It was heavier than she expected; she pulled it toward the opening in the door and adjusted it to slide out sideways. A door slammed. Sammy had jumped out of the passenger side of the RV and was asking Taured what he thought of it. Summer tented the envelope and reached inside.

"Everything's good," Taured said. "I drove the Airbus home from the dealership. Jon signed the papers, no problem. If you get pulled over, show them the paperwork, everything's clean."

The envelope rattled. Her fingers grasped something hard and square. She pulled out a floppy disk—one of several in the envelope—holding it up to her face.

"Sure, boss."

She had just enough time to slide the envelope back onto the front seat. She was about to close the door when she saw another envelope, this one spilling its contents—what looked like Polaroid photographs. She could only manage to take one. It was a much easier grab, but it almost cost her. Sammy's steps were heading toward her. There was no time to hide. Summer stuffed the disk in the waistband of her jeans and crawled under the Chevy. She was breathing so loud she was sure Sammy was going to hear her, but lucky for her, the guy never stopped talking.

"Marvin over at Nirvana asked if we had a couple of wait-resses we could send over, said the girls you sent to the motel and post office are working out real good."

"Send the sisters," Taured said. "Tell them to listen and learn and be good little employees."

"On it."

The sisters were Rhodi and Dawn, two of Taured's earlier converts who'd moved into the compound with him eight years before. Her mother called them loyalists, in a not-nice way. They looked like twins but got pissed if you said so. Dawn had a tattoo on the back of her hand, a mandala, as she called it—that's the only way Summer knew how to tell them apart. Not that she needed to; she didn't like them or the way they watched her mother with little smiles on their wiry lips. They smoked their cigarettes and leered and listened like desert snakes.

The BMW's door opened and closed. Summer watched Sammy's boots stir up dust as he walked the two envelopes over to Taured.

"This it?" Taured asked.

"Yup."

"Good, go gas her up. I'm sending you out again."

"But we just got back." Sammy's voice was incredulous.

Taured kept talking like he hadn't heard the upset in Sammy's voice. He was rattling off the next set of plans. Summer was lying in a pile of her own sweat, realizing that her mother would be gone again by morning. They always left in the night and were gone by the time everyone was up for breakfast. If she wanted to talk to her, it was going to have to be tonight.

"You're going to Florida."

"Man, we have to go so soon? You said there'd be a break after Minnesota, and we went on to do two more cities—"

"Lorraine is causing problems."

There was a thick silence as Sammy reevaluated his position. Summer, who had never seen the underside of any car before today, much less two, was praying, her lips moving without sound. In her mind, she saw her mother's pierced ears—was he referring to that or something else?

"I told you about that when we was in Saint Louis," Sammy said. "I can't control her on these trips. She's getting the other women riled up, telling them they don't need to do things—"

He was shifty; Summer could see the little traitor's feet stirring up dirt as he sold her mother out. She let the air rush out of her nose as she ground her teeth, all praying done.

"You threatened her kid, man, she's agitated."

She grew stiff waiting for what Taured would say next. Her? Taured had threatened to do something to her? Summer was on edge now for several reasons: Sammy was talking to Taured with open disrespect, the type that usually received a punishment. If they fought and Sammy fell to the ground, he'd see her. But instead of an explosion, Taured's next words were measured.

"Replace Shanna and Desiree with Frank and Chord on this trip. Remind her about Summer if she acts up again. The sins of the parents will be visited upon their children."

Summer felt real fear then. It was cold and it tingled as it crawled up the backs of her legs and settled in her gut. She wanted to roll on her side and curl in a ball right there under the Chevy's hot belly. Instead, she looked at the photo clutched between her sweaty fingers.

"All right," Sammy said slowly. "But she ain't gonna like going with Frank. She'll have something to say about that."

Summer didn't know what she was seeing, not at first. The photo was taken at an odd angle, low, like the camera had been resting on a counter.

"Don't tell her. Load up an hour earlier and be ready to go. If that cunt gives you a problem, call me on the walkie."

She peered closer, the sweat dripping down her sides and

onto the asphalt. What she was seeing wasn't right, but she didn't fully understand why.

Sammy offered no further argument. There was the sound of breathing and the crunch of gravel as the men parted behind the BMW. Summer tore her eyes away from the photo and listened for their feet. She was biting her bottom lip so hard she was sure it would leave a mark. Even when she closed her eyes, she could still see the photo. She waited until she heard the hissing of the Airbus engine and heard Taured open and close the side door of the building. They had both been gone for a few minutes before she scooted out from her hiding place, tucking the photo into the waistband of her jeans. She was filthy, and more than that, she was afraid.

Lorraine is causing problems. The sins of the parents will be visited upon their children.

She wanted to speak to her mother again. If she didn't find her now, she'd be gone for weeks, maybe months. They had never gone on a mission trip without Shanna and Desiree; what would her mother think of that? Frank had been there long before Lorraine and Summer arrived on that dusty day. He was one of Taured's first recruits, and her mother had hated him on sight. She could remember the way her mother tensed whenever Frank walked into a room. She would not be happy he was going. *Taured did that on purpose*, Summer thought as she made her way back to the side of the building. He was angry with her mother.

It wasn't until she was back in the dorms at Kids' Camp, riffling through her clean clothes for a new T-shirt and jeans, that she remembered the items she'd taken. They suddenly felt hot against her skin. Looking around, Summer saw that there were only a couple girls milling about. Everyone else was in the orchard at this time of day. Slipping into a stall in the girls' bathroom, she pulled the floppy disk and photo out of the waist of her pants, then reached behind to slide the driver's licenses from her back pocket. She had to hide them for now. God, if anyone found them in her things… She could sneak to the computer lab later and have a look at what was on the disk, but she had to find her mother before lights out. Changing into clean clothes, she put all four items inside of her sports bra and went to find her mother.

Lorraine was not in her room. While Summer was there, she reached into her shirt, pulling the four stolen items from her bra. Looking around the room, she searched for a place to hide them. The wardrobe? Too obvious. Under the mattress? What if her mother found them while changing the sheets? She spotted a crocheted pillow her mother had brought from their apartment in California. Lorraine had told her daughter that it once belonged to her grandmother, and Lorraine had used it to hide Summer's dad's love letters from her parents by pressing the letters into the stuffing. Summer had found the hole in the seam many times as a child, sticking her fingers inside in search of a forgotten love letter. Now, she widened the opening with her finger and pressed everything inside. Instead of love, she was putting sin into the pillow; it felt wrong. She set it back on the bed and backed out of the room, making sure everything looked okay.

Her mother was not in the cafeteria nor any of the other common areas in the main compound. Summer walked with her head down and avoided making eye contact. If someone asked her why she wasn't in the orchard with the other kids, she'd say that she was on an errand. No one would question that because everyone knew Summer was one of Taured's favorites. Hours ago, that thought had comforted her, but now it made her feel strange. She turned right, away from her mother's room and toward an area everyone called Music Street because of the three musicians who lived there.

Summer headed over to the room Desiree shared with Shanna and found the women sitting cross-legged on a rag rug playing Scrabble.

"You seen my mama?" Summer asked. She leaned against the doorframe as Desiree laid R-E-S-P-E-C-T on the board.

She saw the women exchange a quick glance before Shanna took her turn.

"Not since dinner when she ran out after you."

Summer felt heat crawl up her neck. So she'd made more of a scene than she'd intended, but she couldn't change that now.

"When are you guys leaving again?" She pulled on a corner of her hair, studying for split ends, and tried to look casual.

Again, they exchanged the sort of look that made Summer uncomfortable.

"Why don't you go join the other kids in the orchard, Summer. You've caused enough trouble for one day."

"What's that supposed to mean?" There was no more grinning, no more playing with her split ends; she was staring at them now with her hands fisted at her sides.

"Close the door on the way out, will you?" Shanna wasn't looking at her; she was frowning at her Scrabble board. Both women had always been warm to her, so the whole situation made Summer feel uneasy. The first bell rang for bedtime. Everyone would be heading to their rooms now, so if Summer wanted to make it back to Kids' Camp in time for second bell, she would have to leave now. Instead of turning to the hallway that would lead her to the dorms, she cut a left and went back to her mother's room. She'd wait there all night if she had to.

Summer woke. She'd fallen asleep on her mother's bed, her arm trailing the rug. Disoriented, she sat up. She thought she'd heard a scream. Glancing at the digital wall clock, she saw that it was 3:36 in the morning. Had she been dreaming? The room was the same it had been before she fell asleep, with the bedside lamp on and the door closed. She listened for some other sound to confirm she hadn't been dreaming, but nothing came. It was hot, she realized, really freaking hot. Scooting off the edge of the bed, she slipped into her shoes; if the Airbus hadn't left yet, she could catch her mother there. And then what? *You're going to get her alone somehow and tell her what you heard.*

Summer stalled halfway to the door as a realization slipped like ice into her head: Taured. What would he do if he knew she'd been hiding under the Chevy, listening to his conversation? Had they noticed she wasn't in her own bed, or had Sara covered for her? She reached for the door, determined to find her mother one way or another, and found it locked.

Locked? She tried again, yanking at the handle. Had there been a key? She tried to remember the first day, if Taured had given her mother a key, but there was no such memory. No, no one in the compound had a key to their room; she'd been watching people open and close their doors for years without keys. And besides, the door was locked from the outside. *Mama installed a lock after you moved to Kids' Camp*, she told herself. That was it. And she probably left for her trip and locked up without coming inside. She pounded until her fists were numb.

Wherever her mother was, she didn't know this was happening. Summer screamed until it felt like she'd swallowed broken glass. Her mother kept bottled water under the bed, so she crawled forward on her hands and knees, pulled out a bottle and, unscrewing the cap, gulped down the whole thing. The room was hot, too, like the air-conditioning wasn't working. But someone would find her. They had to.

★ ★ ★

No one came for Summer until hours later. By that time, she was cried out, hungry and defeated. Sara's mother, Ama, heard her pounding and had gone to get Taured, who came back with the master key.

"My God, Summer," he said, looking at her in amazement. "How long have you been in here?" He looked rested, fresh, like he'd just gotten out of the shower.

Summer stood by the bed in socks, shorts and a T-shirt and asked in a half daze, "Where is my mother?"

"She's gone, left on mission trip to Florida. Didn't she tell you?"

"No," Summer said numbly.

"She's known about it for a while, Summer. I'm so sorry."

That was it: that was the lie. He lied with clear, bright eyes and an easy smile. It wasn't his true self; she'd heard his true self speak to Sammy. Summer, who was tired and hungry, began to tremble. Just yesterday, she'd trusted this man with her whole entire heart, and now she could barely look at him. The things she'd taken from the envelope were just feet away. If he found those...if he knew what she'd seen...

"She never came back to the room. I waited here for her."

"She must have come back because she locked the door," Taured said.

"It's never been locked before," Summer argued. "It was like someone locked me in here on purpose."

"Why would someone do that?" He was frowning now, his eyes alight with curiosity. "No one wants to hurt you here, Summertime, you know that."

She looked at his face: it looked honest...kind. When he smiled, creases appeared at the corners of his eyes. He smelled like soap and cloves—good things. He played with the little kids, tossing them into the air and tickling them until they

squealed. He sang on some nights, while he played the gui-
tar, and his voice froze everyone to complete stillness until
the last verse.

The sins of the parents will be visited on the children.

"She always tells me when she's leaving and she always says
goodbye, so I was confused," Summer said.

Taured seemed to look right into her when he said, "Did
y'all have a fight? You certainly ran out of the cafeteria in a
hurry..."

So he had been paying attention to more than just Feena
and Jon. If she said yes, he'd ask her what the fight was about,
but if she denied it, he'd know she was lying. Either way, she
was royally screwed. She decided her best bet was distraction.

She kept her voice light so it didn't sound like she was chal-
lenging him. "I'm surprised you noticed. You seemed to be
very focused on what you were doing." She could keep her
expression scraped of anger, but her voice was another story
altogether. Everything she said sounded like a challenge and
she hadn't intended—

"And what was I doing, Summer?" There was a threat dan-
gling in his question.

Summer imagined herself standing on a tall ledge, balancing her weight so she didn't fall. Her mother was en route to
Florida, and she was stuck here for the next few months on
her own. She would make it hard for herself by picking a fight
with Taured. She'd seen what happened to the people who
did it. Her dad, her drug-loving con man of a father, used to
say, *"Tell an honest lie when you need to."*

"You were welcoming our new family members."

"That's right," he said, locking his eyes on to hers. "And
what were you doing?"

She shrugged, trying to flatten her tone, but her heart was

racing. "I left dinner early. I didn't eat because I'm fasting. I didn't want to be tempted, you know?"

He seemed to consider this for a moment, and then in a gentler tone, he said, "Was your mother upset that you were fasting?" His eyes were scanning back and forth across her face like he was trying to read her.

"I don't know," she lied. She tried to look bored.

"Come with me," Taured said, his eyebrows raising in concern. "I think we need to have Doc look you over."

Her head jerked away from the wall. "I'm fine," she said. She didn't like Sara's father; his eyes and hands lingered where they shouldn't.

"It wasn't a suggestion, Summer."

"Okay," she said. She would have said anything he wanted in that moment; she just wanted out of that room with its pressing walls and suffocating air. Feeling small and afraid, she ducked her head in shame to hide her tears.

"Can I call my mother?"

He didn't answer. She fell into step behind him. He was walking quickly, like he wanted to be done with her. Summer had never felt lonelier than in that moment, following a man who meant her harm—who meant her mother harm. When he was speaking to Sammy, he'd sounded like a different person. Summer had the urgent idea that maybe it wasn't Taured all along; maybe she'd just thought it was Taured and she'd been listening to someone else entirely. Her hope fizzled out when she remembered that Sammy had called him by name. Just yesterday morning she'd trusted him, probably more than she trusted her mother. How long had her mother known that her daughter was a traitor, ready to rat her out? She was as bad as Sammy. The shame Summer felt was consuming. She could barely look at Taured now. When had she made him her most important person? Her mother said they were to be foreigners in this land, but here she was, lapping up the hometown honey.

Mama, help me. Summer could try to summon her mother all she wanted, but she was not there.

Summer was alone.

Taured stopped walking and faced her. Summer looked around. She'd been so focused on her thoughts that she hadn't been paying attention to where they were going.

They were in the hallway, near his office, but he'd walked past it. Only two doors stood on this side of the hallway, which dead-ended at a brick wall. Taured opened the closest one. He stood with his hand on the knob, smiling at her.

"Go on in," he said. "I'm going to get Doc."

Fear drove her feet forward, through the doors and into—

Darkness.

She looked back at Taured and for a second he smiled. Then the door closed.

Summer was alone in the dark.

11

Then
A year later

"You swing like a rookie, Summertime."

Her name sounded wet in his mouth. She didn't like it when he called her that anymore.

Her hands gripped the bat, her breathing hitching in terror as she stood over home plate; she wouldn't look at him, but she could always feel his eyes as they probed. It was a sixth sense she wished she hadn't acquired on that terrible afternoon a year ago. Since the day she'd overheard his conversation with Sammy, everything had been...different. The change was noticeable to everyone; she'd gone from being attentive and eager to sullen and rebellious overnight.

"We don't have all day." He scratched his chin, eyes narrowed, focused on her.

She took the stance he'd taught her, and it pained her to do so—to obey him—even if it were something she cared little about, like softball. Softball was merely the newest way he'd found to torture them. Before that, Taured had become obsessed with the chemicals companies were putting in food: he made lists of bad foods and good foods, posting what they were and were not allowed to eat on the doors of the dining hall.

"Isn't that very Luther of him?" her mother had mumbled when she first saw them nailed to the door. As the weeks went by, Taured had added to the list, saying that anyone who ate what was on them would be sent to isolation, insisting they work together as a community to bring about change in their own bodies. The list grew and their meals shrank. For three months they ate one meal a day consisting of nothing but broths and the vegetables they grew at the compound. Taured called it detox fasting. The crux: people started passing out, falling down while they worked outside, malnourished and dehydrated from the laxatives he made them take. When productivity went down, the food came back, this time in the form of potatoes, which they also grew themselves. When he got something in his head, Taured's obsession would overtake the compound.

They were less hungry than a year ago, but as his focus shifted to softball, he was learning more creative ways to break their bodies.

He'd keep Kids' Camp on the field behind the compound from sunrise to long past dark, suspending schoolwork, with no exception for the heat. They sat beneath the unrelenting sun, waiting for their turn to be "conditioned." She heard the boys refer to their long days of softball as boot camp. They woke, they ate, they ran two miles in the desert, and after that Taured would have them work out in the obstacle course he'd created, having them do sit-ups and push-ups at various points until it was time to break into teams and play softball.

In the evenings, they'd have more games, during which the parents would gather to watch. Most everyone was pretty okay at it, but there were a couple kids who largely sucked. Summer was one of them, and she was on this week's rotation of humiliation.

"What's the matter with you? I've never seen a more useless woman." He was rough when he repositioned her, his eyes glassy. She recognized the look inside of them; his eyes got like that when he was in his bad moods. When he was in one of these moods he was dangerous; he'd put words in your mouth if he needed to punish you, create conflict where there was none. Her dread picked up speed when she looked over at third base and saw that a kid named Skye was pitching. Kids' Camp was divided into the boys' side and the girls' side, and the two sides didn't interact much as a rule. But what she did know about the man/boy who had eyelashes that looked like pale spider legs was that he was cruel. And worse than that: Taured liked him. Skye made eye contact with her, and she felt a plunging in her belly as his flaxen hair lifted in the slight breeze. There was a look of solid determination on his face. He wound the ball above his shoulder in little circles. Taured had told him what to do, she realized, and he wasn't going to take it easy on her. She licked the sweat from her upper lip and glanced to her left, where Taured had the men set up the makeshift bleachers with benches from the cafeteria.

She pictured her mother's pale face, her expression earnest and solemn like the statues of saints she'd seen in Taured's education slideshows about idol worship. But education was for Wednesday nights, she thought. Tonight, they were here for Taured's amusement: to play his favorite sport and be his favorite sport. She positioned herself over home plate, holding the bat like she'd been taught. She could hold the bat, but she couldn't hit anything with it, that was the problem. He'd put her up here week after week until she did. People were getting antsy, sensing the tension; they were out here sweating, and they wanted to be paid in drama. Summer braced herself for the imminent show in which she was to star. Taured looked cool as a cucumber. Happy. And why not? He wasn't the sport.

She glanced around at the faces watching them: the people she'd come to know over the last four years. Some of these people were doctors and nurses. Gary Hoeff sat in the front row of the bleachers, his arm around his wife Paula's shoulders—they'd been owners of a gymnastics academy in their former life. But then something had happened, and they'd come here. Next to them was a young family: a pretty mother and a baby on her knee, her husband a former marine, discharged—for what, Summer didn't know. None of these people thought this was strange: a grown man using his power to bully a girl. And if they did, they didn't let on. Everyone here seemed to enjoy it when someone was being humiliated, so long as it wasn't them.

Fuck you all, fuck you all, she thought, the sweat running like fingers between her breasts.

"Another week of the rookie show!" Taured declared with charismatic good humor. His hair had been freshly cut, and with his blindingly white teeth, he looked like a TV game show host. There was laughter from the makeshift bleachers; to Summer, it sounded relieved. They weren't going to care what happened next because it wasn't happening to them. This was going downhill fast. She shut her eyes. *You can do this*, she thought. *You know how.* She could sense the building aggression in his movements; he was fixated on her. It was her newest role in their fucked-up "family": torture pet. He'd liked her so much at the beginning. But things were so different now.

The sins of the parents. New meat. She couldn't stop thinking about that, and about how her mother's entire attitude had changed after a few weeks of being there. Maybe this wasn't about Summer at all. She saw Feena in her mind's eye, naked in the photo and lying spread-eagle on a gray bedspread; she saw it as if the photo were in front of her and not buried beneath Charlie Cactus a dozen miles away.

Glad her mother wasn't there, she clamped her jaw, resigned. It would be fine; she could do this. If her mother got involved, he would hurt her and then he would send her away again. The thought of being alone at the compound for months at a time was frightening. Lorraine was in the infirmary tending to two sick toddlers, though when she'd seen Summer earlier in the day, she'd grabbed her hand meaningfully and told her to be careful.

Softball was a dangerous sport when played with a maniac.

"You have to *want* to hit the ball, Summer!" He clapped his hands, once, twice, and looked at Skye, who was watching him like an attentive puppy.

Yes, yes, yes—she nodded, agreeable. Like she wanted to miss it and be humiliated in front of these people. She'd tell him anything he wanted to hear. She felt the strong urge to pee and clenched her thighs together, ashamed of her own fear.

He was in her face now, his own features alive with the same fervor he had when preaching one of his sermons.

"Watch it, Summertime. Don't take your eyes off the ball." And how pleasant did his voice sound to those who could hear him? Just a guy coaching the local softball team. Could they hear the threat beneath the words, or was it just her ears it was meant to sting? When she'd stopped complying, stopped journaling, stopped worshipping, he'd changed. She'd quickly become his favorite person to humiliate. *"I'm not trying to embarrass you, Summer, though sin is embarrassing, and you're filled with it."*

She gripped the bat harder, her palms sweating. If she missed the ball, she'd be deemed unteachable. Unteachable people were shamed publicly. Was that what he was after? She had to think fast. The adults watched with smiles on their faces; they were excited because Taured was excited. She could smell her own sweat and fear.

"Watch it...watch it." His voice a low hum like a mosquito. She tried to block him out and concentrate.

Don't tell me what to do! That's what she wanted to say, to scream, but she didn't have the guts. His presence was unnerving. It made her chest feel tight and uncomfortable. With her vision blurring, she couldn't focus on the ball even if she wanted to. Skye wound his arm and then the ball was hurtling her way. It seemed like a fist was coming to punch her in the face—Skye's or Taured's. She dropped the bat as she swung; it slipped out of her slimy fingers, landing with a plunk on the ground. The ball hit her on the shoulder, and she was too stunned to cry out. Her shoulder was hot, a dull sting that grew into fire. She stood there, cradling her hurt arm, tears stinging her eyes. A strange sound was coming from somewhere behind her and she swiveled, confused, the pain so intense a single line of tears was soaking into the neck of her T-shirt. Taured was laughing so hard he was bent over. It was a belly laugh, so filled with joy that anyone who heard it would suppose he'd heard the most fantastic joke. *You're the joke, Summertime*, she thought.

"You dropped it!" he shouted like a madman, spittle flying from his lips. He walked away like he couldn't stand to be near her, clapped three times, then suddenly turned around and came back faster than he'd left. He was angry now. She'd seen him like this before, with other people. Why hadn't it bothered her then? She'd thought they'd deserved it, just like most people probably thought that now about her.

"You know what to do, Summer, pick up the bat. You can't afford not to." He swung around to everyone else, spread his arms wide as if he were an Old Testament prophet. Perfect for *The Taured Show.* "None of us can afford to drop the bat when God hands it to us. You cannot let fear dictate what you do." He turned back to her, the smile still on his face, but something else in his eyes. When she just stood there, staring at him, he said it again: "Pick up the bat, Summer. Swing again."

Her fingertips tingled as she bent to obey him. Her face felt funny, like it was frozen despite the heat. She tried to arrange her expression into something besides horror, but everyone was staring at her and it felt like too much. Taured's eyes on her felt like too much. She covered her eyes with her palms, pressing. She didn't want to pick up the bat, she didn't want to do it again.

"Pick up the bat, Summer," he said. "Or else..."

Or else what? She'd have to eat broth for a month? Did she care what he punished her with? She thought of isolation then, and a small shiver crept up her spine; she did care. She was afraid—especially for her mother.

Maybe that was why she didn't pick up the bat—she couldn't, she was clutched in anxiety's grip, her heart racing so quickly it felt like it was going to rap right out of her chest— *ra ta ta ta.* Taured's hands circled her wrists, gently at first, and then his grip bit down harder and harder until she wanted to scream out for him to stop. Before she could open her mouth, he yanked her hands away from her face. She could smell his breath, the soap he'd used to wash himself that morning. His face was suddenly so peaceful, and she hesitated, thinking that maybe he wasn't mad at her, but then she looked into his eyes and the pupils almost felt like they were reaching for her. She tried to look over his shoulder to find her mother, though she knew Lorraine wasn't there. The silence alarmed her. Everyone was watching to see how this would play out.

"Pick up the bat," he said again, this time so close to her face his spittle landed on her cheek. She tried not to have a reaction, because that's what he fed on. Keeping her face stony, she bent to retrieve the bat from the ground. Her fingers scraped across the dirt, and then she was upright with the bat in her hands. The grains of sand steadied her grip, soaking up the damp on her palms. Taured stepped back and Summer took her position, her back as straight as the endless Nevada horizon. The strain of holding back her tears was stinging her nose.

Taured delivered one curt nod to Skye, who looked to Summer like he couldn't wait to do it again. The next time the ball hit her in the stomach. The third time, it broke her nose.

There was blood; Summer wasn't sure where it was all coming from, but when she touched her face, her hands came away dripping.

"Taured, she needs to see a doctor, a real doctor." Her mother's voice was pleading and urgent.

"Is our doctor not good enough for you, Lorraine? Is there a reason you're so eager to leave here?"

Summer was barely able to see through the pain. His voice was loud, agitated. They were inside the cafeteria; she recognized the lights on the ceiling. Someone had propped her in a chair and her mother was holding a towel to Summer's nose.

"M-kah," Summer said. "I'm okay" gone wrong. "M-kay." She didn't want her mother punished because of her. Grabbing the towel out of her mother's hand, she held it there herself, crying out when she nudged the wrong place and lightning-sharp pain careened through her head. She looked at Taured first. He was still in one of his cat-and-mouse moods; she could see it on his face.

If Lorraine argued with him, she'd be taken away from her injured daughter and punished in isolation. That's how it had been: to disagree was to be sent to solitude for a day or two, "to cool down," or so he called it. What he meant was: here's a few days without food, water or light to reconsider your stance. When her mother had come back from her last mission trip and had confronted Taured with what Summer told her, Lorraine was sent to solitude for four days, after which she wouldn't speak about what had happened to Summer or about her time in solitude. "There's nothing to say," she said when Summer asked. "We need to get out of here. And when the time is right, we will."

Summer had immediately understood that she and her mother couldn't talk about their plans to leave for fear of being overheard. She stared at him silently, the answer burning in her eyes but held wisely on the tip of her tongue.

Their old Tin Crap had been sold long ago, "for the financial benefit of the compound." So Lorraine, with no access to a car and being twenty miles from the nearest hospital, took her fifteen-year-old to the infirmary, where Sara's father had seen to her.

Summer would remember his words exactly, the hard-to-cover excitement on his face as the latex of his examination gloves slapped cheerfully against his skin.

"It's just a small break." He asked her to turn her head from side to side, which hurt to do. "I don't want to cause more harm by trying to reset it." He leaned back decidedly, though he'd barely examined her. Her fifteen-year-old horror seemed like vanity—she'd have to look like this, a crooked nose for the rest of her life.

Her mother lowered her eyes and said, "Tom, she's a child, like Sara. She cannot be punished because of my decisions."

Summer didn't understand what her mother was talking about. And by the time she would, her mother would be dead.

"Your decisions affect everyone, Lorraine." And then he

dropped two pills onto the metal counter and walked out, his back sending a clear message.

Her mother gathered her from the bed—scooping the pills into her palm, her petite frame so strong in the moment she had to be—and dragged Summer back to their room, locking the door behind them. She pressed her fingers to Summer's lips and said: "You know I trained a little as a nurse. I didn't make it through the program, but I know a little bit. Do you trust me?"

"Yes, Mama." She allowed her mother to push the pills between her lips, taking a sip of water to wash them down. At one time, her mother had wanted to be a pediatric nurse.

"Here, drink this." She handed her a bottle with a straw in it. But before she could lift it to her lips, her mother grabbed her wrist and said, "Summer, it's not water...go slowly. It will help with the pain."

Her mother set her nose and gave her three stitches where her nostril had split open. When she was done, Summer asked for a mirror. Her mother hesitated, but in the end, she brought it to her, her eyes earnest as she watched for her daughter's reaction. She stared at herself in her mother's handheld mirror and thought, *Oh, good, you're Frankenstein's monster.*

"You won't be able to open your eyes in the morning. They're going to swell shut. There will be bruising, too."

But Summer didn't care. All she wanted was sleep. She tried to close her eyes, but her mother hauled her into a sitting position, propping pillows around her until she felt like a stuffed animal.

"I can't let you sleep. You might have a concussion."

"Ever again?" Summer slurred.

Her mother laughed softly. "No, just for a little while. I need to make sure your eyes don't get weird and you don't throw up." Her mother's voice was light, but Summer knew that she was worried.

That night, as she sat propped in bed like a stuffed animal, high on painkillers and vodka, she listened to her mother talk about her father. She didn't often speak of him, especially how he used to be, and Summer loved those stories. Things had been good before they went bad. Fighting to stay awake, she bit the insides of her cheeks as she listened to the good parts. Her mother told her she had her father's nose and that his had been broken, too. "In a fight," she said with a sense of pride in her voice. She wondered if her mother had been there for the fight and wanted to ask. Instead, she lay very still and listened to the emotion beneath her mother's words. She'd heard love. In a way, her mother had given her her nose, a shape she now shared with her father. Why did he have to die? Why had they had to come here? Why couldn't her grandparents have loved them better? With the way things were, everyone suffered.

When she was finally allowed to sleep, she settled into her pillow as her mother sat on the edge of her bed and stroked her hair.

"Mama…?"

"Go to sleep, love."

"We have to get out of here."

The stroking stopped. "I know."

They tried to leave two weeks to the day after it happened. That was the beginning of the end.

12

—

Now

"I have a surgeon in LA who could fix your nose." Tara briefly made eye contact with Rainy in the mirror before she stood back to examine the feathered sleeves of her top. "He's the best."

"I can see that." Rainy lacked the will to smile, so she made large eyes instead—*I am so, so interested* eyes. She knew from living in New York for a decade that not every nose was equal and that some of them cost more than a new car.

"Well, it wasn't my nose I had done, just some other... work," Tara rushed. And then, as if the need to explain was pressing on her, she detailed the *work* done to her face as she vigorously washed her hands. "So, noses—easy-peasy. If it was a break, even a long time ago, he can reset the bone." She waited for Rainy to say something as she dried her hands.

"Some things are best kept broken." She didn't look at

Tara as she shook the water from her hands and stepped to the towel dispenser.

It wasn't the first time someone had mentioned the slight bend in her nose, but it was the first time they'd done it so rudely.

"I mean, you're beautiful either way, but if you ever want to fix it…" One last check in the mirror and Tara moved toward the door in a noiseless pink breeze. There was a rush of sound from the restaurant beyond and then Rainy and her nose were alone. She turned back to the mirror. The bathroom was a goth grotto with slick black walls and eerie lighting. She studied the nose that wasn't quite straight and blinked at herself. They'd taken an Uber to the restaurant and Rainy had offered to sit in the front seat with the driver while the rest of them climbed into the rear. By the time they'd arrived, she was behind on the conversation and they didn't try to include her as they made their way inside. The girls ordered drinks right away while Rainy stuck to water. She could blame Tara's rudeness on her drinking, but she'd felt that strange hostility since she boarded the plane. She was so deep in thought she jumped when the door opened and two women walked in. With one last, quick glance at her nose, she headed back to the table.

Worst idea ever, she thought now. *This trip, this gaudy, neon-crusted city—these women!*

When Rainy sat down at the table, she was just in time to see Braithe slip her American Express into the billfold and hand it back to the server. Ursa, Tara and Mac were bent over their phones. Had they all chipped in? Why couldn't they have waited the two extra minutes for her to get back? She was annoyed at not being included in whatever decision they'd made.

"You weren't here so I just took care of it," Braithe said, waving her off.

"Well, I'd like to pay my share." Everyone looked up at the same time and Rainy realized too late that her words had come out more aggressively than she'd intended. Her nose throbbed.

"It's not a big deal, I got it," Braithe said, emphasizing the last three words.

"But would it have hurt to have waited the two extra minutes for me to get back?" She knew she was overreacting, but in the moment, she didn't care.

"Honestly, Rainy, if I knew it was going to be such a big deal I would have gladly waited."

Guilt and shame rang like a bell in her chest. Rainy ducked her head, her eyes briefly visiting her lap. When she lifted her gaze and met Braithe's eyes, her friend looked on the verge of tears.

God, Rainy, maybe she was just trying to do something nice.

"I'm sorry," she said, and Braithe's expression relaxed a little. Tara, Ursa and Mac looked tense, waiting to see what Braithe would say next.

Braithe clapped her hands and everyone jumped. The moment was so comical they all started laughing.

"Let's go to Bubbles to get drinks." It was like little light bulbs lit all their faces.

Rainy turned to Braithe. "What's that?"

"A bar," she said, scooting out of her seat and standing up. "And don't worry, you're buying me my first drink."

Rainy would have preferred a shower and a movie in bed. Braithe must have sensed her hesitation, because she grabbed Rainy by the arm and whispered, "Please come," in her ear as the others walked ahead of them, their jewel-toned heels snapping like fingers on the marble floor.

"Okay, but just one drink and I'm going to head back."

"Fiiinnne," Braithe said. They walked like schoolgirls, their arms linked as they lagged behind the others. When they got to the bar, Braithe slid into the seat next to her and ordered an old-fashioned. "What are you having?" She turned to Rainy, her chandelier earrings dancing above her shoulders.

"I'll have the same," she said to the bartender.

She hated the drink, but for some reason all of Grant's friends drank them with enthusiasm. Looking around, Rainy noticed that most of the clientele were their age and remarkably beautiful.

"What is this place?" She darted her eyes around the space; it was themed, like the restaurant they'd just come from.

"It's a champagne lounge." Ah, now it made sense: the blush colors on the walls and the stools that resembled champagne bottles. *But why order an old-fashioned in a champagne lounge?*

"I really am sorry about earlier." Braithe's voice drew Rainy back from her thoughts. Her face was earnest, and Rainy believed her—not because of that, but because Braithe had always been honest with her. She glanced over at Tara, who was on the other side of Braithe, and saw her staring at them. Rainy looked away quickly, uncomfortable with the whole vibe.

"I was just having a moment," Rainy said. "Forget it, it was an overreaction on my part and I'm sorry."

Braithe smiled, tucking in the corners of her mouth and dimpling her cheeks. She'd styled her chestnut hair high on her head and was wearing a black choker. Rainy would have loved to sketch her. Their drinks arrived with lids. Even the champagne flutes had lids with little spouts to drink from. Rainy picked her rocks glass up in confusion at the same time as giant soapy bubbles began to shoot from the four corners of the room. Everyone began to scream at the same time, holding their hands up for the soapy, wet bubbles to kiss their skin. Rainy looked around, horrified, and then began to laugh as she noticed everyone holding drinks in outstretched arms as they danced around the bar, getting soapy; the sippy cups were brilliant.

Ursa and Mac hopped down from the bar to dance where people were passing clear plastic balls over their heads in a weirdly chill mosh pit while Rainy, Braithe and Tara stayed at the bar. Rainy wished Tara had gone with them; she was making everything exceptionally tense. Tara knew...something. Rainy could see it in the way Tara looked at her, the wary eyes, the way she sucked in her cheeks whenever Rainy said something, like she was holding back an eye roll. Tara drank her champagne facing the dance floor so she could watch Ursa and Mac, while Braithe angled her seat toward Rainy.

"Steve's not texting me back. Have you heard anything from Grant?"

Rainy shook her head. Her hair was heavy on her shoulders and she reached behind herself to gather it together and pull it over her shoulder.

"I think it's going to be like this for the next three weeks," she admitted, looking at Braithe's crestfallen face. It was weird: Braithe and Stephen had been together for ten years. Shouldn't she be comforting Rainy, who was new to these extended work trips? It was sweet how cute Braithe and Stephen were together. She always brought it up to Grant, who said they'd been like that from the beginning.

"You're right, I'm being silly. I always get anxious when they leave."

Rainy smiled at her. Maybe that's why Grant had been so insistent she come with; he'd known how lonely Braithe was when Stephen left and figured they could do the whole lean-on-each-other thing.

"We're in a club of two now, I guess," Braithe said, and Rainy saw Tara flinch. In that moment she wanted to hurt

Tara for how unnecessarily cruel she was being, for the games she was playing that Rainy didn't understand.

"Yes, we are," Rainy said with enthusiasm. She held up her glass and Braithe knocked her own against it.

"Let's dance," Braithe said, hopping down from her stool. She was looking at Rainy, avoiding Tara's eyes. She allowed herself to be led to the dance floor, swallowing the last gulps of her drink as she clutched Braithe's hand.

She began to wind her hips to the music, all thoughts gone from her head.

13

Then

They waited until everyone was in church to leave, putting most of what they wanted to take into two backpacks and walking up the long road to the guard shed. There they had to pass through the gate, where one of the sisters was on duty.

"Mama…?" Summer looked at Lorraine, her eyes wide. There was no way either one of the sisters would let them pass without alerting Taured. Lorraine's eyes were set, her jaw up and out like she meant business. Summer glanced over her shoulder every few minutes, expecting to see the compound's occupants pouring outside to stop them, but there was no movement, not even a breeze. Up ahead, she could see the black gates looming, the fence alongside them running endlessly to their left.

"Stop doing that," her mother snapped the next time she looked over her shoulder. "You're making me jittery."

"Sorry."

When they reached the gate, Lorraine walked to the box on the right-hand side of the road. She flipped up the grate to the keypad and typed something in. They both looked expectantly toward the gate; nothing happened. She touched her necklace as her face pinched in worry.

"I put it in wrong, that's all…" Lorraine tried again, and this time the gate groaned and swung open. Lorraine grabbed her daughter's hand and walked her across the threshold. Dawn was waiting for them on the other side.

"Where ya going?" Her voice was deceptively cheerful as she squinted at them. She wasn't wearing her knockoff Ray-Bans, which were a fixture on her face most days. Lorraine let go of Summer's hand and went right up to Dawn, her back to Summer.

"Lose your sunglasses? Why don't you go look for them and mind your business?"

Summer did a double take; had it been her mother who'd said that? But as Lorraine stepped backward, Summer saw that Dawn didn't look mad; she looked afraid actually. She nodded once, plucking the toothpick from the corner of her mouth and tossing it away before retreating to the guard shed. She was about to ask her mother what that was about when Lorraine's attention diverted left.

"There it is—hurry!"

A cab gently crested the horizon, the sun seeming to melt the air around it. Summer could feel the sweat on her back and running down her legs. She was too afraid to look back now. She imagined Dawn walked directly into the shed and calling down the wrath of the whole compound.

The cab seemed to take an extraordinarily long amount of time to get there, the air feeling hotter with each second. When it stopped next to them, due to her mother waving her arms, Lorraine shoved her daughter inside the car and slid in beside her. Summer scooted all the way across the seat, taking her mother's bag with her.

"The airport," she said. "If you could drive quickly, we'd appreciate it."

The cabbie seemed to understand their urgency and he turned the car around, the cab's tires squealing as he shot forward. Summer twisted around to look out the back window. The dust spun up behind them, like a curtain. She thought she saw Dawn come out of the shed, but then her mother pulled her down.

"Don't look back, Summer."

She sank into the seat, the smell of cigarette smoke rising to meet her. It was then, as her hand accidentally slipped inside her mother's bag, that she felt the hard metal. Pulling one side of the bag toward her, she looked inside to see a gun. It was small and cold to the touch. When she looked up, her mother's eyes were large in warning. She was not to react, she understood. Turning to look out the window, she pretended she hadn't seen anything at all, but it made sense now, the way Dawn had behaved. Her mother must have shown her the gun to scare her. But where had she gotten the gun? She must have snuck off to buy one while she was on a mission trip and hidden it, waiting for this day.

And the cab that had shown up at exactly the right time. That one seemed easier to explain; her mother must have secretly called for it from the compound somehow. Why hadn't she told Summer the plan?

"Where are we going?" she asked eventually. Her nose, still tender, was hard to breathe through. They were passing Red's, and the straggly little town, Friendship, that was built around a famous cactus.

"New Mexico, to Grandma and Grandpa." There was no

dread in her mother's voice when she spoke about her parents this time. It sounded nice to Summer, who wanted to be anywhere else.

She was looking earnestly out her mother's side window now at the row of pastel houses, one of which had broken toys in the yard.

"What is it?" Lorraine snapped.

"I buried something there," she told her mother, "by the cactus." She thought Lorraine would ask what, but she was the one looking behind them now, checking the road. Summer watched the depressing little patch of buildings pass by.

"Does it matter?"

She didn't know. She hadn't told her mother what she'd taken, just what she'd heard. Despite who she had stolen from, she still felt the shame of being a thief, and—even more so— the shame of what she'd seen in the photo.

Her mother began to speak then, quickly and very quietly. She had managed to sneak into Taured's office one night and call Summer's grandparents. They'd gone to the bank and put money in Lorraine's account so she could buy plane tickets. They were going to board a flight to Albuquerque, where they'd be picked up in her grandparents' minivan. Lorraine told her the rest of the details in a voice that didn't sound like hers at all.

"What did they say when you spoke to them?"

Lorraine looked at her hands, her bottom lip caught between her teeth.

"That I was in a cult. That they'd help me."

Summer frowned considering her mother's words. *A cult?* Could that be true? What was a cult, anyway—rules and religion?

"Aren't they in a cult, too?"

Her mother cracked a smile, her dimple flashing. "You'll have a hard time convincing them of that."

They drove in silence the rest of the way. Up front, the cabbie listened to R & B, turning it up when Biggie came on. He didn't speak except to ask what airline they were flying. When he dropped them at the curb, her mother paid him in twenties, thanking him profusely. Where had she gotten this cash? Summer felt like she didn't know anything anymore.

"Come on." Lorraine grabbed her by the wrist and walked her through the doors. Summer trotted alongside her mother until they reached a trash can at the far end of the passenger drop-off area.

"What are you doing, Mama?" She stumbled over her own feet as it dawned on her exactly what she was doing.

Her mother was looking down into her bag when she said: "Sometimes, the key to not being seen is being seen."

Then, with a flick of her wrist, her mother tossed the gun inside and dusted off her hands. Summer looked around to see if anyone had noticed. Her mother had done it fast enough—hadn't she?

All around them, the airport was being the airport, an endless hustle of bodies and luggage.

"Let's go." Lorraine grabbed her hand this time and led her through the doors, the air-conditioning as violent against her skin as the heat had been moments ago. They fell into step, walking toward the counter, Summer's heart pattering like a frightened animal. She was as tall as her mother now, her legs longer; she wished they could run instead of walk.

Would he come here? Follow them? The way her mother looked over her shoulder, scanning the faces of the people behind her, told her yes. The man at the ticket counter took his time, his fingers hitting the keys like fat sausages, and then, suddenly, Lorraine had two tickets in her hands. They didn't speak as they made their way forward, still arm in arm. Her mother's braid had come loose, and her hair cascaded around her shoulders. When her mother caught her looking toward the bathrooms, she said, "Go. I'll wait here."

Summer stood in line for the bathroom, biting her thumbnail. Her mother stood a few feet away, watching the board with the arrivals and departures. The line wasn't moving very quickly; in front of her, an old lady with glasses was complaining about the terrible facilities to her friend. A toilet flushed; the line moved forward. Summer stood just inside the bathroom doors now. A mother was in line behind her, trying to wrangle her toddler, who was bouncing from foot to foot, saying he was going to pee his pants. When a stall opened, she let the mother go ahead of her.

Summer washed her hands, thinking about her grandparents' house. Her mother said they had a porch swing facing the sunset. They hadn't spoken about any of the details yet, but she imagined she'd be allowed to go to a real school. Her mother would get a job, and Summer would see her every day. She felt the start of something sparking in her belly. Excitement? No…maybe hope. Things were about to get better.

Summer dried off her hands and left the bathroom, noticing that the line had doubled since she'd been in it. Her backpack was heavy, and she wanted to sit down and not think about anything. She wanted to sleep. When she walked over to the board where she'd left her mother, a new line of people stood staring up at the screen. She spun on her heels, checking the line of chairs against the wall, and then the bathroom line. Deciding her mother had probably gotten into line behind her and was now in a bathroom stall, Summer took a seat.

The bathroom emptied out three times over. She walked the area twice, scanning every face she passed. She checked the two coffee stands and the ticket counter, where the man with the sausage fingers had helped them. There was no sign of Lorraine. Summer tried to remember the gate number from the tickets. Maybe her mother had gone there. But even as she thought it, she knew it wasn't true; her mother would never leave her, especially not during a time like this. Going back to the board, she searched for the departures to Albuquerque and found that their flight had left ten minutes ago. Summer tried not to cry, but it was all too much. She did another lap of the airport, past the flashing, pinging slot machines, and past tourists in brightly colored shirts, wearing their vacation faces. She could smell coffee and the sweet aroma of baked goods mixed with a man's cologne.

Where was her mother? This felt like a nightmare within a nightmare, Summer thought, like a Stephen King book she had snuck back from Red's one time. This felt like when her dad had died and she didn't know what to do with her hands or face, because nothing made sense. She had no money, no way to make a phone call—and who would she call, anyway? She didn't even know her grandparents' phone number. She wandered outside, back to the trash can where her mother had deposited the gun. She stood there for a good few seconds before she noticed the man standing against his car, looking at her. He was casual, arms crossed over his chest, his glasses reflecting the activity of the drop-off. It was Taured.

She sat in the back seat of his car, the BMW she'd stolen the photos from. Her mother sat beside her, pale, her hair tangled and her lip swollen. When Taured pushed Summer into the back seat of the car, Lorraine had looked at her daughter with scared, wet eyes, but didn't say anything. Summer quietly folded herself into the seat, eyeing the police officer who was watching traffic a few yards away. Could she jump out and run to him? Would Taured drive away with her mother if she did? Would he be arrested? She looked at her mother, who was breathing nosily from the seat beside her. She was hurt. Then the car was moving, and it was too late to do anything. Summer reached across the leather seat to hold her mother's hand.

They grabbed her by the arms, fingers digging into her thin flesh as they pulled her from the back seat of the car. She didn't cry out in shock or pain but kept her posture rigid as she watched them do the same to her mother. They dragged her through the prison kitchens and toward the courtyard outside. The courtyard was an eight-by-ten concrete block, fenced in on three sides. It had a drain in the center and a waterspout low on the wall. It stood to the side of the prison and ran along a steep gully. Someone had told her that they slaughtered the livestock there.

She didn't resist when the sisters stripped her, leaving her naked aside from her panties. It was too hot to shiver, too bright to hide. The elders started to arrive, Taured's most faithful, most likely not to question him. She saw them through the diamonds in the fence: bodies surrounding the cage to witness her shaming. She couldn't look at their faces; if they wanted her to feel shame, she did. It was so great she touched her chin to the hard bone of her clavicle and let her hair hide what it could. Standing above the drain, Summer knew Taured would appear at any moment. She knew what was about to happen. She'd heard about this punishment, heard about the humiliation that some of the adults had to endure in their path to righteousness. She'd always felt separate, better than those people.

Now, she was displayed like a thing, not a person—Taured's thing. She couldn't see Kids' Camp, but she could hear the younger kids playing on the equipment, their squalling and their laughter making happy noises. She couldn't see her mother. She imagined they were keeping her in one of the solitary rooms. *Until it's her turn*, Summer thought, buckling under the nausea of this thought. She dropped to her knees, her bare skin digging into the grate as she heaved above it. She would rather do this a hundred times over than know her mother had to stand in front of these pigs. But nothing came: no vomit, only contempt. She stood up, hid behind her hair.

Her mother wasn't here to protect her and neither was her father, who had died and allowed this to happen. But she wasn't afraid, no. Taured had already pushed the fear out of her, and now there was nothing. She was a void; you couldn't frighten something that didn't exist.

Marshall Carruthers, one of Taured's goons, was attaching the hose to a spout, making sure to keep his eyes on her body. Taured stood in the doorway, filling it up. Marshall handed him the hose and stepped back.

The water stung her skin, especially her breasts, where it hit her hard as rocks. She struggled to stay upright, her body bending under the pressure. But she'd heard that was the important part: if you could stay upright during a cleansing, the punishment was less severe. The water sprayed in her eyes, her nose, her mouth—it felt like it was being driven up into her brain. She coughed, bending at the waist, and almost toppled when the spray hit her face. There was no more hair to hide beneath; it was plastered like fat leeches to her back and arms. She heard the school bell and thought about screaming.

Why didn't anyone think this was wrong?

And then it was over. She'd stayed on her feet, but as soon as the water stopped, her knees gave out. Marshall threw a blanket over her shoulders and Dawn pulled her to her feet as she trembled. Taured was gone. But if he was punishing her, he wasn't punishing her mother.

They took her to isolation.

★ ★ ★

When Taured spoke about the isolation rooms to Kids' Camp, he framed it as a wonderful, sacred time. She'd once asked what the rooms had been used for when it was a prison, and they'd told her they were the cells used for pregnant, incarcerated mothers. Inside, they'd been painted cream, the floors concrete. The only light came from a single bulb that was operated by a switch outside the cell. Once you were inside, you had no control over the light, and were only allowed brief periods of illumination through the day. This, he claimed, was a test of trust and a time to reflect on your bad and grow into your good.

"Will one of us ever have to go in there?" a kid named Ginger had asked. He was a couple years younger than Summer, and he'd moved to the compound from New England with his family the year before. He'd brought some weird habits with him, like some strange taste in junk food. He was always complaining about the contents of the Snack Shack. She'd noticed the older boys enjoyed picking on him, while most everyone else ignored him. The kid seemed to latch on to strange ideas and not stop talking about them.

"Are you scared, Ginger?" yelled someone from the back of the room. Summer knew the voice belonged to Skye.

"Of course he is—he's scared of everything," another voice called out.

Ginger, who had light strawberry blond hair (Sara said his mother had been ambitious with his name), turned around to give the speaker a dirty look. "What do you know, you big meatball?"

Summer liked his spunk, but he was probably going to pay for that later; Skye was a bully.

"I'm not afraid," Ginger said, turning back to address Taured. "I would go in there voluntarily. I would."

Summer and Sara had turned to each other at that point and rolled their eyes. They usually sat somewhere in the middle of the room.

Taured spoke directly to the boy. "If you focus on fear, you'll live a life of fear. Do you understand that?"

Ginger nodded enthusiastically. He was sitting in the front row of the chapel, in the seat directly in front of Taured. When they worked the orchard, he tried to outpick everyone by double and he was always trying to get Taured to notice him. The other boys would chant, *Ginger has a finger up Taured's ass!*

"He thinks Taured is his daddy," Sara would say, shaking her head. Summer had to agree, but wasn't that what Taured wanted them to think? Most of the kids here were missing one parent or the other, and the ones who had both were a little cocky about it—Sara included.

"So rather than worrying about being in the isolation rooms, worry about doing the right thing so you don't get there." Taured ruffled his hair and Ginger looked pleased.

"Think about it," he'd told them. "I'm an adult and I can tell you that I don't know how to trust. But you guys aren't jaded by the world. You know how to trust. And by giving me your trust, by allowing me to make healthy decisions for you—well, you guys are ahead of the game. Your parents don't even know how to do that. Will you guys trust me when the time comes?"

She didn't know how everyone else reacted, hadn't looked around to see, but when he asked them to trust him, she had. At least back then.

14

—

Now

Rainy forgot her earlier desire to go to bed. When she danced, it felt good. When Braithe chose her over Tara, it felt good. Maybe it was the alcohol working her limbs into a frenzy of dancing. She was almost acting like a normal person, and in that moment, as she lifted onto the balls of her feet to hit one of the clear orbs that was bouncing around, she couldn't remember who she'd been before now, or who she'd be tomorrow. Only now.

As they were leaving the bar, Braithe stopped midstep; it was sudden, and they all stopped with her.

"We should find somewhere to have our cards read." Her voice was breathy and excited.

The adrenaline that had pushed Rainy through most of the night drained at Braithe's words, and suddenly she felt gross,

AN HONEST LIE 149

and sweaty and tired. But more than that, she felt empty, and all she wanted to do was curl up in bed and talk to Grant.

"I'm in," Ursa said. "This one time, a psychic told me I'd meet a guy named Oscar while fishing and I did. I was in Miami and he was just right there."

"But you don't want to meet anyone now, right? Since you have Alex." Mac looked nervous.

"They don't just tell you things about love," Ursa shot back. She started listing the other topics on her fingers: "Careers, dead relatives, unfinished business—and this one time, my aunt went to a psychic to tell her why her cat, Sequins, always bolted from the downstairs bathroom like its tail was on fire."

"And?" Rainy couldn't help herself; she wasn't a believer, but she wanted to know about the cat.

"She said that my dead grandfather was haunting Sequins. And honestly, my grandfather hated cats, so it came as no surprise to any of us." Ursa shrugged. "My family is weird. We got rid of the cat, but not the ghost."

They laughed so hard they held their bellies, holding on to each other for balance as they maneuvered the sidewalk in their high heels. A slow rumble of thunder came from the sky and Braithe yelped, grabbing Tara's arm and staring at the sky suspiciously. It was all humorous and fun beneath the veil of alcohol.

Maybe this isn't so bad, Rainy thought. She walked alongside Ursa, who was recounting her time with Miami Oscar. Tara and Braithe were up ahead, leading the way, and Mac was somewhere in the middle, calling out directions as she read them off her phone.

They found a place online: readings for forty dollars apiece, group discounts available. There was no such thing as psychic ability, Rainy assured herself. This was like a show: they were going somewhere to be entertained, like any other place in

Vegas. They had to navigate their way across puddles, making a game of leaping dramatically, arms flying. Rainy felt silly. She hadn't even done these things when she was a kid. As they walked, Braithe told them she'd tried to get an appointment with a famous psychic her mother had seen here in Vegas, but there were no openings.

"Stephen always makes fun of me for wanting to go, but I swear to God that guy knows what he's talking about."

"She's obsessed," Tara announced to the rest of them. She was tiptoeing on a narrow strip of pavement to avoid a puddle. Braithe didn't seem bothered by Tara's comment; she looked happy, almost beaming.

"Ohhh," Ursa said. "Does he have dark hair and a scar on his cheek? I've seen him on TV."

Braithe nodded. "Yeah, that's him. My mom went to see him before she married my dad. There was this other guy before my dad and I guess she was unsure about which man to go with. So she went to see the psychic and he said stuff about her that no one knew. Freaked her out, but it gave her such clarity. She said he changed her life. I just think it's cool." She dipped her head, laughing, and Rainy marveled at how beautiful she was.

Rainy sidestepped a wad of gum. She was starting to feel the exhaustion; it was tag-teaming the alcohol, making mush of her thoughts. And then they were there, the shop a blur of neon and incense and pastel crystals that looked like candy. She ran her hands over the lip of the shelves, listening to the others talk to a man who introduced himself as Luc.

"Is that your real name?" she heard Mac ask. She didn't wait for Luc's answer; she ducked behind a display of shirts and pretended to look for a size. Places like this freaked her out: people claiming to hear from other beings, relaying messages. She was chilly, the night had dried uncomfortably on her skin and her buzz was a faint hum now. Had she really been dancing beneath a ceiling of bubbles only an hour ago? She eyed the door, wondering if she could slip out and send them a text saying she wasn't feeling well. Peeping around the display, she saw that Tara had taken a seat at Luc's little table and he was laying cards in front of her. The words came back to her.

Do not be deceived by liars and manipulators. Astronomy, psychics and mediums are signs of a nation perverted by the idea that they can control their futures. They are evil manipulators of truth.

She tugged her phone from her pocket, hoping to see a text from Grant. Nothing, but there was a text from Viola.

I've got heartburn. You up?

The Tigers are getting their cards read and I'm here, too, she wrote back.

Viola's text came back at record speed.

Say what? And don't try to act like you're not a Tiger, okay? I saw you in Tara's story and you looked like you were having the time of your life.

Rainy rolled her eyes, trying to squeeze the smile off her face.

That part was fun but now they're acting weird and I want to leave!!!

Whoa, whoa, you never use excited punctuation. How bad is it?

She bit her lip, thumbs paused. It wasn't that bad, was it?

Things had been weird, then great, then weird again. She decided to say exactly that to Viola.

Weird in what way? Viola asked.

They're asking a lot of prying shit. Braithe is floating around superhappy and Tara keeps looking at me like I'm wearing tampons for earrings.

She's just territorial, Viola sent back. Ignore her and don't answer any of their questions. They're always like this with Grant's girlfriends. Don't let them play you.

Play her. Grant's girlfriends.

In the beginning, when she'd first started going to their happy hours, they'd made suggestive comments about Grant's exes, but Rainy had never taken the bait, had never pried for information about who came before her. He was hers *now*. It didn't seem fair to ask questions about his past when she wouldn't answer any about her own. She heard her name being called and slipped her phone into her pocket, bracing herself. It was Ursa.

"Do you want to go next, or...?"

"I don't want to go at all," she said flatly. Ursa nodded once and went back to the group.

Maybe they'd only invited her to see where she stood with Grant. Was it possible that the entire year she spent going to their little gatherings they'd been fooling her, making her think they were her friends when—

"Hey, Ursa said you seemed upset." Braithe stepped around the corner and Rainy froze.

"I...just don't feel great."

Braithe's eyes crinkled in concern. "Yeah, we don't always drink that hard. Well, you can go next if you like, and then head out early."

Rainy's mouth was dry, and she felt the buildup of pressure in her chest. She knew what was coming and she didn't want to have a panic attack in front of them.

"I need the bathroom." She looked around desperately and spotted the sign. She tossed Braithe her best *I'm sorry* look and darted for the back of the store. From somewhere behind her, she heard Braithe tell the others that Rainy was sick.

Once locked in the bathroom she called Grant, her panic increasing from drizzle to downpour. This had been a mistake of epic proportions, coming here—especially *here*—with these women. She called his cell; it rang twice before going to voice mail. What could he be doing at this time of night? *Get a grip, Rainy. He's in a different time zone.* She slid her phone into her back pocket and covered her face with her hands.

If she'd told Grant about her past, then he wouldn't have pressured her to go on this stupid trip; she should have just been honest with him. She hated herself; she hated her inability to know what was best. Leaning against the wall, she listened to her own breathing as she calmed herself down. She knew they'd come to check on her if she didn't come out. She washed her hands, avoiding her own gaze in the mirror, formulating the words she needed to get the fuck out of there. The knock came before she'd dried her hands.

"You okay?"

It was Mac. Rainy opened the door, and before Mac could react, she grabbed her wrist and pulled her into the bathroom.

"I need you to get me out of here. I don't want to do this."

At first she thought Mac was going to ask why, but then her face transitioned from worried to confused to determined right in front of Rainy.

"Okay," she said. "But they're waiting for you, and you know how Tara is…"

Rainy nodded.

"Splash some water on your face. Make your makeup run more."

Rainy wasn't expecting the burst of laughter that came from her own mouth, but Mac being sneaky was a treat.

They left the bathroom together, arm in arm. Rainy dipped her head and tried to look even more miserable than she was.

"It's your turn!" Ursa spotted them first, her voice filling up the store with its bold, smooth tenor. Mac squeezed her arm, leading her forward.

"She doesn't feel well," she told them. "I'm taking her back to the hotel."

"Oh, no, Mac, you were looking forward to this!" Ursa said. "I'll go back with Rainy."

Rainy flinched. She didn't want to ruin either of their experiences because she was having a ridiculous emotional breakdown. Squaring her shoulders, she loosened herself from Mac's grip.

"Go. You should. I'm feeling better. I'll just sit right here and wait."

Mac's look said that she didn't believe her.

"I promise. Go."

She had to shove Mac toward the table a few times before she went, glancing back at Rainy like she wasn't sure. To make her feel better, Rainy sat in one of the armchairs facing the table and smiled at her. She ignored the looks Braithe and Tara were exchanging and focused solely on the table where Luc was laying out Mac's cards.

The reading didn't take more than ten minutes. When Mac stood up, she was beaming. They all turned to Rainy, and she shook her head.

"Come on!" Ursa urged, grabbing her arm and pulling her to the table. Rainy stopped short, yanking Ursa to a halt.

"I really don't want to."

Tara's head swiveled around to catch Rainy's eye. "Why not? It's just for fun."

Tick tick tick—Rainy felt the seconds prickle by with no solution. If she didn't have her cards read, she'd look like the same sourpuss who hadn't wanted to come in the first place. But if she just did it, they'd move on. Pressing her palms to her shorts to clear them of sweat, she walked cautiously over to the table where a dude of indeterminable age—wearing a fishing hat, of all things—sat beneath harsh lighting. There was nothing special or showy about him, which bothered her more than if he'd been in some ridiculous costume. Maybe he didn't need to play the part because he was *real*.

She almost laughed at herself as she gripped the back of the chair and pulled it out so she could sit. Mr. Fishing Hat Dude had a soul patch. He didn't smile at her when she sat down, tucking her ankles underneath the chair and sitting forward nervously. He laid the cards out without show, keeping his eyes down as he worked. She could feel the others watching from around the shop, and she tried not to think of Tara, who made her feel angry and embarrassed at the same time. What was he going to say to her? Had they brought her here to see how she would react? No, that was ridiculous—stupidly narcissistic. She pulled herself back to the sound of his voice. He read the cards, blinking slowly as he tapped each one, explaining what they were. What was his name again? She didn't remember.

"You don't like to be known. You hide." He splayed his hands as he spoke, and Rainy wanted to scream for him to stop. Did they know she was dying inside? She refused to turn around to read their expressions, afraid of what she would see.

"You got the Four of Cups. So, in the tarot the suit of Cups talks about love. You love someone." She nodded, for lack of anything better to do. Didn't everyone?

"And that someone loves you back, but Four of Cups is the

moment when your love temporarily pulls away from you. Make sense?"

"Not really..." Rainy said.

He turned over another card. "The High Priestess." He glanced at her. "This card is about killer instinct. Do you get that?"

"I get it, thanks, dude." Like, was this guy for real? Maybe it was part of his show. Settling back into her seat, she gave him a dramatic sigh. His lips twitched. *Almost made you smile,* she thought.

"You have those instincts, but they're clouded right now. You can't see things clearly." He flipped another card before Rainy could respond.

"The Emperor," he said. "Okay...that's a strange follow for the High Priestess. So the Emperor is about power and authority. So, another power could be seeking to usurp yours."

Rainy couldn't help it: she glanced at Braithe, who was looking back at her. She looked away quickly, her skin warm with embarrassment. This was stupid. Why had she drunk so much, anyway—her head was foggy.

He flipped another card; Mr. Psychic Energy was really into this now, his eyes getting more intense.

"So, this card is also about keeping secrets." He tapped it with his pointer finger. "If someone confides in you, keep that dirt on the down low. On the other hand, this card could also be a warning about bad vibes and someone else keeping secrets."

It was funny how something could be a joke one minute and then start to sound creepily familiar the next. Rainy lost her smirk at the end of his last sentence. She was over it.

"You know..." Rainy's chair screeched when she stood up. If the women hadn't been looking before, they were now. "I'm not feeling so great. I think I'm going to head back to the hotel." She put three twenties on the table in front of him, smiled and headed for the door.

"Rainy, wait!" She heard Mac call out to her, but she kept walking until she was out of the storefront and on the pavement outside. Mac clambered out after her in her colorful dress, hair damp from the weather.

She took a deep breath before she turned to talk to Mac.

"Just not my thing," she said, folding her lips all the way in and looking over Mac's shoulder.

"That's fine." Mac put an arm around her shoulders and walked with her, the two of them in sync. "It doesn't need to be your thing. Let's go back to the hotel and get in our pajamas." Rainy felt overwhelmingly grateful as Mac steered her toward the street, where a cab was idling.

"What about the others?" She glanced over her shoulder to see Tara, Braithe and Ursa still in the shop.

"I'm texting them. They can take their time. I wanted out of there, too."

Rainy nodded. The cab was on a break, so Mac called an Uber, which arrived in less than two minutes. She caught a glimpse of the shop and the three of them standing inside as they drove past. Braithe was sitting in the chair again. Rainy strained her neck to see, but then they were gone as the car made a turn.

The rest of the group was back in the room just past three, tossed on their beds in loose-limbed, sweaty heaps. Rainy heard someone throwing up sometime during the early hours. She covered her ears with the pillow and drifted back to sleep, her head wobbly like the yolk of an egg.

She woke up at eight a.m. to a missed-call notification. Swearing, she tried calling the number back, but was met with a weird dial tone. She was about to text Grant when a chime told her that she had a message. Lying on her back, Rainy pressed the phone to her ear, her heart beating furiously at the sound of Grant's voice. He sounded upbeat, but she could hear the exhaustion there, too. Stephen would tell him to rally, she thought, smiling, and he would. He was funny when he was tired, saying everything that came to his mind. She grabbed on to the sound of his voice, listening as he told her that they'd arrived safely and the day had gone amazingly well. She edged her way upright against the headboard and snaked her arm to the nightstand for the bottle of water. Where was her aspirin? Grant's message wound down with, "I'll try to call if I get a few minutes after lunch." She had no idea what time that meant. She held the phone against her ear long after the message ended, feeling stupidly needy. Love was exhausting. It felt like a sore muscle...or a healing wound.

15

Then

Isolation wasn't enough of a punishment for Taured: a bed, a blanket, food…those were all comforts of the flesh. To cultivate the change he wanted in a person, he needed them humiliated and afraid.

Bob and Marshall—trailed by Sara's mother, Ama—led her into the room with the blanket still wrapped around her shoulders. The room smelled of urine and bleach and looked as bleak and yellowed as an old toilet seat. In the center of the room was a metal stool bolted to the floor. She sat down because she knew she was supposed to. Bob got on his knees to strap her ankles to the chair, avoiding eye contact even as she tried to catch his eye.

"Bob. My mama?" she pleaded, but his only response was a grunt as he stood up, work done, prisoner shackled.

A minute later, they both left, leaving her with Ama. She

was a serious woman, a woman of conviction and discipline, as Taured so often praised her. Ama did not smile or meet Summer's eyes. All the warmth from their previous encounters, like when Summer had eaten breakfast with them in the cafeteria, was gone. Ama stripped her of the blanket, leaving her naked on the stool.

She wanted to beg for the blanket, but she kept her mouth shut, knowing it wouldn't do any good.

"Ama..." she said before the woman could leave. Her back was to the door, but she craned her neck all the way around to see the woman. Ama had stopped, but hadn't turned around.

"Has he been in to see my mother?"

How many seconds ticked by as she waited for Ama's response?

"No."

And then she heard the door click shut, the lock grate into place. No one could hear her screams of protest.

She drifted in and out of sleep the first twenty-four hours, exhausted and in pain. When they let her out, there would be a celebration to welcome the renewed version of herself back into the group. She held on to that, tried to think of the party, the bacon sandwiches that sat on red-and-white paper, the table piled with pink frosted cakes and cookies, the way everyone in the compound would clap and smile as she walked into the room as she'd once clapped for others.

She'd known nothing then. She couldn't believe she'd helped celebrate something so awful. After the feast, the women would take her to the communal bathroom, which would smell like eucalyptus and be filled with hot steam, and they'd let her shower for as long she liked. She'd be clean and have a full belly, and they'd put her in a white dress, brush her hair and then lead her to the chapel, humming in the creepy way they did sometimes, but it would be okay—because it was over.

She'd assisted at an "after" ceremony when she was thirteen: her mother's. But all she'd seen of it was the celebration; she had no idea what her mother had gone through, the hours she'd spent behind the doors where she herself now sat imprisoned. Why hadn't her mother told her? She'd let her daughter believe these things were good, let Taured tell her that they were. Summer screamed as loud as she could, straining against the ties that bound her; she screamed so loudly that her throat felt like it was on fire.

She guessed that twelve hours had passed before Rhodi came back to release her from the stool and give her a bowl of broth and a bottle of water. She tried to take it easy on the water, knowing she should save some for later. She wanted to know if her mother was receiving the same punishment or something worse; she knew in her gut the latter was true.

Why had she gone to the bathroom in the airport? Why hadn't they made more of an effort to hide after they left instead of going to the most obvious place of escape? She lifted the bowl to her mouth while Rhodi undid the ties on her ankles. Her muscles felt bunched up and useless. She considered her chances of darting past Rhodi and out the door, but how far would she actually get before they dragged her back? Taured had walked into the airport with a gun in the pocket of his tan jacket and jabbed it into her mother's side. That's all her mother had imparted to her in the back seat before they were separated at the compound. Summer rested the bowl in her lap, letting the warmth seep into her thighs.

"Rhodi...my mother?"

"She's in isolation, same as you." Her tone was matter-of-fact, her touch rough; she didn't look at Summer as she finished undoing the straps. Summer's eyes followed her to the door, where she grabbed a few things off her cart and brought them back into the cell, setting them on the floor.

"Is she okay?"

Rhodi clearly wanted to say something. She puckered her lips, leaning against the doorframe, and craned her neck to see if anyone was coming.

"She's taking the brunt of what y'all did. You know that, right?"

Summer stood up, the bowl of broth flipping off her lap. She stepped through the puddle to get to Rhodi, but she wasn't fast enough. Rhodi was out the door, metal slamming in Summer's face, blowing her hair back with its force. The steel had not touched her nose, yet it ached from the threat, anyway. Resting her forehead on the cold metal, she rolled her head from side to side. The sounds she made were sharp and high, a choked-off scream. She wept, folded over her own knees, face slimy with tears and saliva and snot. She dripped onto the floor as her wailing scraped over her throat again and again.

Rhodi had left her with another bottle of water, a dress and a blanket. Wrapping herself in the blanket and ignoring everything else, Summer sat facing the door, her back against the wall. Taured's voice was the only sound in her head now, and she whimpered, remembering the last thing he'd said to her outside of his car before he had the sisters take her mother away: "I'm going to have fun with her punishment, Summertime."

She's going to be okay because she's strong—stronger than Taured. She closed her eyes, leaning her head against the wall; the air smelled like pee and bleach and soup and it made her want to vomit. She didn't want one more smell in here with her, so she took deep gulping breaths until the feeling passed. She must have fallen asleep, because when she woke up, the lights were out again. Crawling on her hands and knees to the door, Summer pounded on it until the sides of her hands were tender and her voice was scratchy.

On the evening of the third day, they came for her: Ama, Sara, Dawn and Rhodi. She started crying as soon as she saw Sara. No one would look at her, including her friend, who glanced nervously at her own mother as they helped Summer dress.

"Sara?" she said under her breath, but either Sara had been warned not to talk to Summer or she was too afraid to, because her body grew stiff at the sound of her own name. This was not like the last time: there were no greetings of joy, no hugs or words of affirmation; they were brusque in their handling of her. As they ushered her into the hall and toward the cafeteria, she trembled beneath their hands, light-headed and weak.

Summer felt relief so sweet that her feet moved with new energy; they were taking her to her mother, they must be. Instead of feeling her fifteen years, though, she felt like a kid—a small one, needy. All she wanted was to be held by her mother, her hair stroked, her back rubbed, Lorraine's comforting words in her ear.

But the procession started out slow and got even slower. There was no joy, no celebration, just the shuffle of feet as they walked through the empty hallways. When Summer was led into the cafeteria where everyone was usually gathered and waiting for the feast, the normally heavily laden food trays were empty except for the two coffee urns they used at breakfast.

Summer had been sure something was wrong before, but now, glancing around at the furtive faces of Ama and Sara, at the identical smug expressions of the sisters, she was certain. And the most astonishing part: only Taured stood in the room, presumably waiting for her.

"Where's my mother?" she asked them one more time.

"She's in the chapel," Ama said simply, looking her in the eyes. Taured motioned for her to step forward. She glanced behind her at the procession of women sent to collect her from hell, and they nodded encouragingly. Her discomfort stalled her feet; from behind, she felt one of the women give her a little shove forward. *Was she more afraid or less afraid after being locked in that place?* Summer considered that as she moved slowly toward him. He looked like an actor in a movie, but not a handsome actor like she used to think. He looked… She couldn't find the word.

You're too tired and hungry to be scared, she thought. But she knew that wasn't true.

The word came to her as she came to stand sentinel in front of him: *Small*, she thought. *He looks small. Or did I get taller?*

Taured didn't say anything until she was right in front of him. He looked sick. His eyes, which were usually alert and dancing, now looked dry and red. She shifted her feet, fixing her gaze on his face. What she saw in the deadness of his stare made her so uneasy her bladder stung for release.

"Congratulations and blessings on you, Summer, for the tremendous feat you have accomplished. You have shunned your flesh, defied it and risen above in triumph."

She'd heard all this before. Her mouth was dry, and swallowing made it worse. She flinched halfway through his speech as a result, and his eyes focused sharply on her face, his words becoming more clipped. She didn't know what he was saying and she didn't care.

When he was finished, he nodded to the women behind Summer, who stepped forward at once to collect her. Their procession would now move to the chapel. She kept her eyes on him even as they steered her toward the doors, twisting her neck as far back as it would go, conveying her hate and her weakness all at once. He stared back unmoving, the cold of his eyes reaching for her, as well.

She could hear singing as they turned down the hallway where the chapel was, the hypnotic hum of voices. It wasn't so much singing as it was chanting, the men and the women holding hands, eyes closed, their mouths molding over the words *holy, holy, holy*.

Sara had left the procession at some point and had gone ahead to the chapel, because when they entered through rear doors, she saw the back of her friend's head in the last row. They'd snuck in here together many times, using the key they'd stolen. Now her back was to Summer, her shoulders pressed forward; Sara wouldn't look at her.

Look at me, look at me, Summer thought, focusing all her energy at Sara's head. It was like Sara could sense her there, because she twisted her body away from Summer, toward the wall. And then they were past Sara, and she focused her attention ahead.

It all happened in one ugly moment, the moment that would burn into her memory with a hot, shocking pain that throbbed through her already depleted body. The song, the flowers, the glossy box ahead. She didn't believe it right away, or maybe she thought it was someone else—one of the elderly. But there was the photo, the name. She still looked through the faces frantically with every step forward they took; when she slowed down, she felt Dawn's hands on her lower back, moving her forward.

"Walk," she said into Summer's ear. Before they reached the front row, the row where they meant for her to sit, she started screaming. The wails of "Mama" shrill above the singing. She looked back at the faces behind them. Maybe she was sick, too, maybe she had what Taured had, and she was hallucinating. But then they were at the front of the church, near the place where Taured addressed them, and she could see it all.

She was at her mother's funeral.

She didn't stop screaming until they removed her from the chapel, Bob and Marshall hauling her down the hall, her feet dragging. Her breaths were ragged gasps. A boy—Ginger— was in the hallway. He looked to be exiting the bathroom; when he saw them coming, he flattened himself against a wall until they had passed. It was like the last time, just with a few different players, except now, she didn't care what they did to her; in fact, she wanted them to kill her—she wanted to die.

They took her to her mother's room this time and locked the door. She curled up on her bed, on the quilt with the tiny, embroidered roses, and howled as loudly as her vocal cords would let her, the grief growing heavier by the second. Eventually, her voice gave out to a skinned, gravelly sound, and she was only able to sob. When she woke, she remembered, and the pain started again, fresh, a billowing wound that was all-encompassing. She lay in one spot, refusing food or drink until they sent Sara to comfort her. But she didn't want to see Sara, who had betrayed her. In the end, they left her alone with her grief.

On the third day, Taured came to see her. He was dressed in his nice clothes: black pants and a blue oxford rolled to the elbows. In his hands was a tray with what she assumed was breakfast. He set it down on the little table where Summer sometimes did her homework and turned toward her with a brilliant smile.

"Good morning, Summertime. I've come to keep you company."

Her stomach clenched.

"I've made you breakfast. Will you eat?"

He motioned to the table and Summer froze. She had eaten

very little, mostly drinking juice and eating pieces of bread rolled between her fingers into little balls. She'd pretended they were communion and she was eating her mother's body and drinking her blood in remembrance. On the table was a plate, piled high with steaming yellow eggs and thick pieces of bacon. Her mouth was wet and her stomach groaned miserably. But then, out of her rolling stomach came a memory: *another table covered in food…Taured leading her into his office…his smile as he closed the door.* The vision ended as soon as it came, skirting something significant she couldn't recall. When had that happened? Lifting her hands to her head, she cradled her own face. She was outside of herself, a coating on her own body like sweat.

She was hungry, but she did not want to eat. Eating would be disrespectful to her mother, who would never eat again. She swung her legs over the side of the bed, keeping her eyes low, and walked over to the table. She sat, smashing her toes into the rug and staring down at her hands.

"Eat," Taured commanded. Still, she hesitated. He picked up the fork and placed it in her hand. Summer gripped the metal and scooped egg into her mouth. She chewed, staring straight ahead. The egg dropped into her stomach with a plop, she could feel it—all the while Taured watched.

"I know you're in deep pain, Summer. We are all grieving Lorraine. She was a very important member of our community and we loved her very much."

The eggs threatened to come back up. She held the back of her hand to her mouth and breathed in the scent of her own skin, closing her eyes. She didn't want to listen to him talk about her mother. The fork clattered to the plate when she dropped it. Her hands moved to her eyes, palms open to cover them—a childish gesture, but what felt like the right one. A moment later, she heard the sound of a chair being moved. She dropped her hands to see him across from her. His knee brushed hers and she yanked it away, squeezing her thighs together.

"Your mother was not well these last months."

"She was fine. She was the same as always."

She saw a flash of annoyance in his eyes at being interrupted. "Parents shield their children from the ugly truths to preserve their innocence, Summer. You were not privy to all of the things your mother was moving through emotionally." That was true, though it hadn't been her fault, because Taured kept her mother away on his mission trips, and they barely had time to communicate when she was at the compound.

"And you were?"

"Well, yes, I'm her mentor and spiritual leader, and she confided in me when she was having a hard time."

Summer shook her head; she didn't believe a word he was saying. He went on speaking, anyway.

"She never got over your father. You know that. She lost her will to live." His voice was low, like he was telling her a secret, but it wasn't true—her mother had been fine. At the airport, she's seen the signs of her old mother again, and then...

"What did you do to her in there?"

Her balled fist hit the table, rattling the orange juice in its glass. She registered the look of surprise on his face, but this time there was no remnant of fear on hers; he had killed her mother, and she was angry. He didn't answer.

"I'm going to go to the police and tell them you killed her!" His face changed, grew angrier with each word she said, but she didn't stop. "You put her in that room and she died!"

The slap came like a whip, striking fast enough to bob her head and leaving a terrible sting.

She touched her cheek with her palm, trying to draw out the pain, staring at Taured not in shock but in anger.

"You can't call the police, Summer, you can't do anything. You belong here, to me. Especially now that your mother is dead. Where would you go? Do you know that her father molested her? That's why she didn't want to take you back. She knew that you were safe here."

"She would have told me—" But she knew her mother hadn't liked to talk about her parents. Had it been for the reason Taured said? *No.* It was another of Taured's lies.

"Then why was she taking me to them?" Her voice was a wail, her mouth open; she knew how she looked. Standing up from the table, she took a step back, her fingers gripping the flesh of her cheeks in a panic. She molded the skin there as she thought, and an image flashed in her mind: *eating food, spread out on a desk. Taured's office.* A desk? Was that real? She'd never eaten in Taured's office, she'd never laughed as he touched her hair. Then she was back in her mother's room, her shoulder blades pressing against the wardrobe.

But Taured didn't answer her question. Instead, he said, "She was taking drugs to deal with her grief. We tried to help her, but she wasn't thinking straight."

Drugs? No, never. She tried to say so, but her voice was as wobbly as her legs. Her dad took drugs, and her mother hated them. Her mama would *never.*

He opened the wardrobe, then pulled out one of its drawers, waiting for Summer to come over and look. Inside the drawer was a book she didn't recognize, one her mother would never read. It was self-help: *How to Live Well and Free.* She stared from the book to Taured, not comprehending.

"Open it," he said.

"Why?"

The flash of anger in his eyes made her reach forward and flip open the cover. But there were no pages—the book was hollow. Inside were several needles, a glass orb and four foil-wrapped packages the size of quarters.

"It's not hers." She looked him squarely in the eyes. "It's. Not. Hers."

He hit her again, this time hard enough to move her whole body. Before she had time to recover, he left. Summer crawled onto her mother's bed and wept. She would not believe that liar; she would not turn on her mother, not even to save herself. *"Stubborn like your dad,"* Lorraine used to say. *"Stubborn to a fault."*

She thought briefly of the memory before she fell asleep: the food, the feeling of being at the desk. Feelings she couldn't identify with words. Then...nothing.

That night, Marshall and Dawn came to collect her. She'd been asleep when they opened the door and now, as they led her through the familiar halls, she was in a half daze. In the kitchen, they led her to one of the freezers.

"In you go," Marshall said.

Taured was, of course, waiting for her, standing beside a table with his hands in his pockets. On the table was a lump covered by a light blue sheet. Before she could process the sight, Taured had pulled the sheet down. Beneath it was the bluish body of her mother, naked and still.

There was nowhere to go. She could see Marshall's head outside the small window in the freezer door. Taured lifted her mother's arm and held it up for her to see.

"These are track marks," he said of the pinprick scabs that freckled the skin on the inside of her arm. He dropped her arm roughly and it landed with a thud on the table. Summer heard her own breath wheeze from her throat like she was being strangled.

He walked to Lorraine's feet and stood in front of them

ceremoniously; then he pushed apart her big and second toes. Summer wanted to scratch his face off for touching her. She didn't want his hands on her or her mother, ever—ever.

There were marks between her toes, so tiny and hidden. While Taured spoke about her drug use, explaining how Lorraine had taken pains to hide it from everyone, Summer was thinking about how to kill him. How to make him lie dead on that table instead of her mama. The closest thing to her was a block of meat, so hard and frozen it was purple. While his head was still bent, her arm darted out to pluck it from the shelf. It was heavy but it felt good. Summer lifted it as Taured looked up. She threw it like Skye had thrown the baseball at her, a projectile of her anger. For a moment it sailed toward him, a strong line. Summer felt a pure pulse of adrenaline. And then the rock-hard meat hit the wall beside his head. He looked stunned, and then he smiled.

Marshall dragged her out as she screamed, "I'll kill you!" over and over.

16

—

Now

The elevator doors were already open, so she stepped in, joining a middle-aged man in swim trunks who looked overly pleased with himself for some reason. He was dripping on the floor, his fleshy shoulders already showing a painful sunburn. He smiled at her, and Rainy felt nausea creeping in. She wished she'd thought to bring some aspirin. When the elevator doors opened, she rushed out, holding the back of her hand to her mouth. *I will never drink again*, she told herself.

She could barely hear her own thoughts over the humming of people and machines. Sweat was swimming across her skin despite the air-conditioning. She'd written a long text to Grant before she got out of bed, detailing their night, but leaving out the parts that were uncomfortable to remember. She trotted through the lobby and saw Braithe just through the doors, walking quickly, her phone pressed to her ear like she was trying to escape the noise. Maybe she was talking to Stephen. Rainy tried Grant again as she kept walking toward signs for the pool. She had no idea where she was going, but she didn't want to be in the mess of noise and lights. When she stepped into the sunshine, she felt a thousand times better than she had ten minutes ago. Lying by the pool was exactly what she needed to decompress from last night. The concrete around the pool was still wet from the previous day's rain; hotel workers were sweeping up the dirt from a potted palm that had fallen over.

"Wow, some storm, huh," she said to Ursa as she tossed her bag on the lawn chair.

"Apparently, the wind blew some bottles over in their little bar, so they don't have vodka for my screwdriver. How cruel is the wind." One long leg was tented up and swaying from side to side as Ursa watched the bar over the top of her glasses. "They've gone to get more," she told Rainy.

The thought of more alcohol made her stomach turn over, but Rainy nodded, pulling her cover-up over her head and tossing it on the chair. She sat down with her sunscreen in her hand, eyeing the twentysomething carefully. Last night, Mac had been tight-lipped for most of the cab ride back to the hotel. She'd reached across the seat to squeeze Rainy's hand once, which made Rainy feel like she was apologizing for something. Ursa, on the other hand, didn't apologize for anything, and had the type of blunt honesty that was shocking at times. If Ursa was in the mood, she'd tell Rainy what she wanted to know.

"I saw Braithe as I was headed over. She was outside the lobby doors, talking on the phone. She looked upset."

Ursa's leg stopped swaying and Rainy could see her blinking rapidly behind her oversize sunglasses. When Ursa didn't say anything, Rainy swung her legs to the ground and stared her down.

"Is something going on, Ursa? Because I am getting really weird vibes from you guys." She must have sounded as desperate as she felt, because something broke in Ursa's face. Her lips pinched together, making a tight little rosebud, and she blew air out of her nose. She took off her glasses and set them on the small table between their chairs, where a bottle of Tylenol stood sentinel. Rainy wanted two of those little pills, but she didn't want to interrupt what was about to happen. When they were knee to knee, Ursa tilted her head, pushing her lips into a frown.

"You're right, things have gotten weird." She tied her hair in a ponytail, avoiding eye contact with Rainy. "They planned that whole thing last night, Tara and Braithe. I don't know why, but they wanted you to sit down with that psychic and they asked for our help getting you there. I feel really bad, I'm sorry."

Rainy was momentarily speechless; the confirmation that something weird was going on the night before felt like a victory. *You're not crazy.*

"Why?"

Ursa shrugged. "I think they're jealous, honestly. Not everything is what it seems with those two. All I know is that after this trip I am taking a Tiger Mountain break." She slung her legs back up on the chair and put her sunglasses on.

That was about as much as she was going to get from the woman, who was facing the sun with determination. *She feels bad for telling me.* Resuming her position on the deck chair, she turned her head casually toward Ursa.

"One more thing…"

Ursa didn't face her, but she nodded.

"Did you ever meet any of Grant's other girlfriends?"

This time she smiled. "I only met one of them. Tara had

a barbecue at her house one summer and Grant brought her with."

"What was she like?" She felt like the shittiest human in the world asking Ursa when she could have asked Grant, who would have gladly told her.

"Not like you." Ursa glanced at Rainy, looking wary, like she thought Rainy might be offended.

Rainy chewed her lip, wishing she'd get on with it. She didn't need to be coddled; she needed to know what was going on.

"Anyway, everyone was really drunk by the end of the night and Marchessa—that was her name—got into an argument with Braithe, and then all hell broke loose."

"What type of hell?" she asked. A server appeared with Ursa's drink. She set it down next to Ursa and looked expectantly at Rainy.

"Same, thanks," she said. *I guess I am drinking again*, she thought wryly.

"Put it on my tab." Ursa waved over her first sip. "So, anyway," she said as soon as the server was out of earshot, "I was pretty new back then and have never revisited this with them, but Braithe and Marchessa were in the kitchen and all of a sudden Tara comes hurtling out the back door, still holding a tray of hot dog buns, and runs up to Grant to tell him they're fighting." She paused to sip her drink and check her phone simultaneously. "Sorry, just have to answer this."

Rainy waited while Ursa texted. Her drink arrived and she was so thirsty she drank the whole thing before the server left. "Another," she said. "And two waters."

"Hair of the dog, get it, girl." Ursa tossed her phone on the towel at her feet and stretched languidly. "I still to this day do not know what started the fight, but I do know that Grant had to pull Marchessa off Braithe, and then Stephen came running and they were screaming cunty things at each other. After that weekend I heard Marchessa and Grant broke up, and then we didn't hear much from him until he started seeing you."

"Wow, okay," Rainy said. "That's a lot. Did she look like me?" She asked it before she lost the nerve. Ursa laughed her full, deep, brazen laugh, and it made Rainy laugh, too.

"Get right down to it. No, she did not look like you. She was blonde and bouncy and vegan. You're like dark and artsy and carnivorous. That's why it was such a surprise when you came along. I've heard them say that he normally dates blondes. You're his first emo girl."

"Ha!" Rainy couldn't help it. She could see Grant dating leggy blonde models and it made her sticky with insecurity. *Were they better? Did he like them better? Why did he change his mind and date a brunette?* She was glad her eyes were hidden by her glasses, or Ursa would have seen the turmoil behind them.

"You know what they say about girls like us—one bite and you never go back."

She was both moved and deeply confused at being grouped with someone like Ursa; she'd never considered herself in the same realm.

"Because I'm an artist," she said.

"Yeah, like, I think his other girls were type-A personalities, perfect and superfeminine like Braithe…oh my God, this is sounding so bad. Perfect as in Little Miss Perfects, if you know what I mean. They'd drink one glass of rosé and get wild, and think a fun night in was organizing the closet with their boo. And that's what she called him by the way—boo."

"Marchessa?"

"No, Braithe. That's why Marchessa got angry and said something to her. You know how they've all been friends since the beginning of time and all." She said the last part, Rainy noticed, with a note of bitterness. There was a club within a club when it came to these women; the original group had a secret language and traded private jokes as easily as siblings.

Rainy opened her mouth to say something, but at that moment Braithe swung through the doors, wearing a long black cover-up and dark sunglasses. Rainy kicked Ursa lightly on the foot to let her know they weren't alone. She had no idea if Ursa would recount their entire conversation for the others later, but at the moment, she needed to process what she'd just been told. Braithe barely looked at them as she dragged a lounge chair next to Ursa's and dropped into it.

"You feeling okay?" Braithe directed this at Ursa, who gave her the thumbs-up without turning her head. "I'm never drinking again," she announced before popping in her AirPods. During the four minutes it took for her to get settled, she hadn't so much as glanced at Rainy.

It felt like a slap in the face after the previous night. Hadn't they danced arm in arm hours ago? Had she imagined Braithe pleading with her to join them? Perhaps she'd misinterpreted something. Or maybe, after a morning of reflection, Braithe was pissed about the way Rainy had acted at the restaurant.

Her feelings were further validated when, five minutes later, Tara arrived and Braithe took her AirPods out to chat with her.

"Hey," Rainy said, leaning over to Ursa. "I'm gonna head out for a few hours. If anyone asks, just say I don't feel well." Ursa nodded, and Rainy gathered up her things. No one acknowledged the fact she was leaving or said goodbye. It stung worse than she wanted to admit. It took her what seemed like forever to make her way back to their suite, maneuvering around the slow-moving gambling crowd and then waiting for an elevator that wasn't packed so tightly you could smell your neighbor's shampoo.

When she finally made it to the suite, it was empty. She

must have just missed Mac on her way down. Rainy stood at the vast window in the suite's living room, staring down at the dusty city she'd long come to hate. Her mother's words the first day they arrived—*Everything is going to be okay now*—echoed uncomfortably in her memory. The most honest lie she'd ever been told. Nothing had ever been okay again. She'd learned to maneuver around the not-okay-ness until she met Grant. He made it all better than okay.

She replayed the voice mail he'd left earlier. When she put her phone away, the longing for her mother hit her so deeply she hugged her arms around herself and held her eyes closed against the threatening sting of tears. Rainy made a split-second decision. She was here, so why not? Warming to the idea even as she threw a dress over her bathing suit, pushing away thoughts of *him* and focusing solely on her mother. The way things currently felt in the group, she wouldn't be missed, and she'd be back before dinner, their last dinner before their flights home in the morning. Her seat on the plane was next to Braithe. She could talk to her then. Sort things out. She grabbed her bag and headed out the door.

It was no less crowded on the street outside their hotel. People swarmed around each other in a frenzied, colorful tempest. Everything smelled of gasoline and food, and Rainy's dinner rolled in her stomach like it didn't want to be there anymore.

She didn't want to be here anymore. But where was here? Vegas? With these strangers? In her new, partnered-up life that was built on a lie? She sat down on a wall, a short distance away from the crowds, and called an Uber, then she tried Grant again. If he answered, she'd tell him everything, because in the moment she couldn't bear the weight. When it just rang, she thought about calling Stephen's phone to see if he was with Grant, but then he might ask her about Braithe, and Rainy didn't want to have to lie to Grant's best friend. She sent him a text, knowing he'd see it later and respond.

Miss you. We really need to talk.

She hit Send and was about to put her phone away when she saw the dots appear on her screen: Grant was texting her back. The relief was a solid thing, like a chunk of concrete. It was moments like these when she realized how deep she'd fallen down the relationship hole. She waited for his words to appear, wondering why he didn't just call, but as suddenly as they appeared they disappeared. Her phone notified her that Riva had arrived in a Jeep.

"The address you put in, it's not showing up on my map—it's just a dot in the desert." The driver pivoted her body sideways toward Rainy, trying to see her where she sat wedged behind the driver's seat.

"It's the right place," Rainy said. "Do you have an issue driving me that far out?"

"Nope, just wanted to make sure you know you're asking to go somewhere I ain't never been."

Rainy turned toward the window then so she could look out as Riva pulled into traffic. The radio was playing a Johnny Cash song that made her think of Taured. No, it wasn't just the song that made her think of him; it was all the dust, too, coating everything in film. She could feel it on her tongue, on her skin, and then suddenly she was somewhere else.

Friendship was a greasy spoon of a town meant to provide highway comforts to drivers before the desert swallowed them up. There was a post office, a diner called Nirvana that doubled as a bar in the evenings, a pharmacy named after its owner, Red, and a highway motel called Charlie's Inn.

Rainy's jaw ached from grinding her teeth for most of the drive, and now that the Jeep was almost there, she was unsure if she'd be able to get out of the car when it stopped. This was the place where her childhood had shriveled up and died. Her chest was tight as they idled at a stop sign; she wished she'd brought a bottle of water with her. She'd buy one at Red's Pharmacy, if it was still there.

"Nice place," Riva snorted, turning onto Main Street. "Would you like me to leave you at the pharmacy, the dollar store or what looks like a bar over there..."

The bar was new. The building was modern, and it looked funny standing amid all the old buildings that had been there since before Rainy's time.

"Drop me at Red's," Rainy said. The Jeep made a sudden stop and her forehead bumped against the window. She poured out of the back seat and onto the sidewalk, already missing the air-conditioning.

"And how are you going to get back?" Riva looked over her sunglasses at Rainy, who had gotten out of the car and was standing by the driver's-side window. She had one arm propped on the window, and as she waited for Rainy's answer, she wiped her face with a yellow bandanna and then tossed it on the passenger seat.

"I don't know yet," she said. She looked over at the dollar store and wondered if Slav was still around; he owned the only taxi in a fifty-mile radius. She turned toward Riva. "I'll figure it out."

Riva rolled up her window and Rainy watched as the Jeep disappeared in a cloud of dust.

She couldn't get close to the compound; they had it watched around the clock. But Rainy didn't want anything to do with the compound; she didn't want to see the pale cream walls or smell the fry oil that permeated the air. Everything in this shithole town was owned in some way by Taured. He supported them and they supported him. If she wanted to know things, she'd have to find someone willing to talk.

Main Street was deserted, but there were a few cars parked outside the diner. The one-story yellow brick building—the old diner had a new name: the Canary. She wondered if they named it that so they wouldn't have to bother painting the outside.

Rainy spat on the ground outside Red's doors. The back of her neck stung as the sun's rays hit her skin. It was the hottest part of the day, and no one was outside. If she went into the Canary, chances were, it would get back to Taured. Though probably her very presence in Friendship would get back to him, anyway. She touched the ends of her hair, glancing at the newly built bar. He probably owned that, too. She could walk into either building and run into Sammy, or Frank, or any one of Taured's goons. Looking between the two, she decided on the Canary; chances were the same, and she was hungry.

The Canary, she noticed, still had the same giant bubble gum machine that had been there when she was a kid. It looked to be pretty empty, the shells from the candy coating dusting the bottom. The breakfast counter looked the same, too: a trucker in a red flannel slouched over his plate, an old man with a shiny egg for a head reading a novel and drinking coffee. A young couple sat in a booth across from the breakfast bar wearing matching Las Vegas hats: tourists on a road trip. Rainy sat at the breakfast bar a few seats down from the old man. A young server came over, a guy maybe in his twenties but not quite; he still had a smattering of acne across his chin. His name tag said Derek.

Rainy ordered a coffee and a large stack of pancakes from Derek and settled back to study the place. It had undergone a little face-lift: the paint and posters were different, but other than that it looked to be the same old place. She sipped the coffee Derek brought her and looked at the old guy. He wasn't wearing glasses as he read his novel; she was impressed. He was pushing seventy at least. He'd talk to her, she knew it; that's what old-timers did.

"That stuff will kill you," he said, putting his book down and picking up his mug. He was referring to the fake sugar she was pouring into her coffee.

"Gotta die some way." She shrugged. He seemed to like that, and he spun his chair an inch or two toward her.

"I always said cigarettes would kill me and here I am eighty-two years later." He patted his shirt pocket where a pack of Marlboros stuck out. "I'm Marvin."

A memory slammed into her, dragging her beneath the belly of a truck: she could almost feel the heat of the asphalt on her back. She looked away, but Marvin's sharp eyes caught what she was trying to hide. Her brain was galloping loops. *That* Marvin? How could she ever forget that name or that conversation?

"You smoke?"

"Not anymore." She hadn't smoked since her New York days, but the feel of this place was making her crave it.

"Good, why don't you come outside and keep an old man company."

Rainy smiled. "Sure thing."

They stood by a patch of shriveled saltbush as Marvin smoked his cigarette while leaning against the side of the building. Rainy faced the parking lot, keeping her eye on things. The heat was pulling up memories of endlessly long days spent outside. She wanted a cigarette badly.

"You from around here?" Marvin spat in the dirt and then smiled at her, a fleck of spit resting on his bottom lip like a blister.

"Do I look like I'm from around here?"

He eyed her for a beat before saying, "All right, all right," chuckling to himself. He reminded her of a lizard, beady-eyed and darty, his skin scaled with age. "You look like someone I used to know, that's all."

"Oh? Who was that?" Rainy asked.

"I can't put my finger on it."

She smiled. *Liar.*

"Who owns this place?" She looked back at the Canary.

"I used to."

She put effort into her surprised face, raising her brows as high as they would go. Marvin loved it. Encouraged by the height of her eyebrows, he did what old men do: regaled her with a story from the past.

"Owned it for thirty years, sold it ten years ago. Was called the Nirvana before, but the new owner hated the band and wanted to change it. I said, why ruin a good thing, but he wouldn't hear it." Marvin tossed his butt but didn't bother to crush it.

"Well, the food's still good, I see," she said. "Or are you coming for the excellent service?"

He grinned. He still hadn't told her who owned the place now.

"You used to live around here, up at the compound."

"The what?" Rainy made her jaw hang open and hoped she looked as stupid as she felt.

"Old women's prison. Never mind. Must have been your doppelgänger. You're too young to be her."

She raised her eyebrows. She sensed that he wanted to talk, so she shut up and let him.

"Guy came through here in '94 and bought the women's prison, moved a bunch of roughnecks in to work for him, then came the women and children. Pretty soon he had a whole operation going on over there."

"Oh, yeah, like drugs?" She made her eyes big, but she hardly needed to; old Marvin was on a roll.

"Nah, nothing like that. It was all legit. He had an orchard out there that generated some money, but rumor was he was a computer guy—was training all the kids on them computers, figured he could build an army via the web. You know old-timers like me didn't think much of it back then, but now the guy has all of these damn nerds working for him from all over the country, building websites and selling them for a profit. Made millions at one point…" He spat again. "They come in here wearing those little glasses and leather jackets!" Shaking his head, Marvin eyed her clothes. "Weak-minded, enthralled by their emotions," he added. "Perfectly culty."

"Why did he stay here? If he made all that money why not move on?"

Marvin shrugged. "Snakes like the desert." A laugh wrapped in a throaty cough followed. "Why would he leave? He owns this part of the desert."

A good enough answer. Rainy was almost done with him.

Taured had been enthusiastic about technology. Mostly, she thought, it was to manipulate them. Now, in light of Marvin's words, it sort of made sense. He'd been dismissive of the adults spending time in the computer lab; Summer had never seen her mother use a computer while she was at the compound. But the kids were a different story: in addition to the journals he made them send him via email, he went as far as having them take lessons with Gerry Lackey, a former programmer who taught them a computer science class. Taured told them he had met Gerry online, and wasn't that amazing that you could meet people from all over the world and have them become your family.

"How do you know all this?" Rainy was genuinely curious.

He laughed. "Ain't got nothing else to do." He pointed a finger in the air, his head shaking as he spoke. "This place is not even a town proper—a highway rest stop, really."

He wasn't wrong. This was the town she'd known as a kid, and back then, it had seemed a lot larger.

"So he owns this place, then—that guy you're talking about?"

The kid who took her order—she'd already forgotten his name—stuck his head out the door.

"Food's up," he said, not meeting her eyes.

"Yeah, he owns it," Marvin said, starting to walk back inside. "And everything else, too."

"So how'd he get your restaurant?"

"That's a story for another day," he said, looking at her more carefully. Now that they were back inside and the sun wasn't shining in his eyes, he was studying her again, a strange look on his face. *He's seeing my mother*, she realized, and wondered how often the two of them had crossed paths. Her mother was gone so much on the so-called mission trips, but she supposed they'd stopped in town on their way in and out. Mostly, the people in this place were probably hungry for the gossip that came from the compound, gleaning information like the desert scavengers they were.

Rainy took her time walking to her seat, taking in the details of the place. Picking up her knife and fork, she cut into her pancakes. Her mother's death hadn't been mentioned anywhere: not in the papers or, years later, on crime blogs where ordinary people could pick over cases in detail. According to the world, there had never been a murder. Lorraine had died of an overdose. Another day, another drug addict: the police moved on after they interviewed people at the compound, who all confirmed that Lorraine had been using drugs. Furthermore, they told police that she was a deeply disturbed woman who often disappeared for months at a time, leaving her teenage daughter behind for them to take care of. Taured had backed up these stories, adding that Lorraine had been trying to hide her drug dependency and had come to him for help. In his statement to police, he'd said, "By the time she asked for help it was already too late, and she died the next day."

Her grandparents had believed all of it. Given the years-long rift between them and Lorraine, and Rainy's dad's own drug problem, it was an easy thing for them to believe. Gilda and Mark hadn't seen their estranged daughter in years, and they no longer knew anything about her. Rainy had been too traumatized to say more than a few words at a time; though her grandparents were better than Taured—their religious fervor seemed to have mellowed in the years Lorraine was gone, as they had even begun to watch a few TV shows— they were still strangers. And although they'd never said so, she thought they must have regretted how they treated Lorraine, how their behavior drove her from them and into the clutches of someone worse.

"That boy that served you them pancakes, he's the big shot's son." Rainy's fork stilled on the way to her mouth.

The kid was topping off a Coke at the soda fountain, and all she could see was the back of his head. Someone in the kitchen called, "Order up!" and he turned his head to look. She studied his profile, his hair, the pull of his shoulders, searching for Taured. Realizing she was paying too much attention to the kid, she looked down at her soggy pancakes. She could get a knife, wait until after his shift, say she needed help...

Oh my God, Rainy, oh my God. It might not even be Taured's kid. She bit her tongue and flinched: she deserved it. What type of person had thoughts like that?

The sins of the parents will be visited on their children.

"You know him, don't you?"

Rainy stared at Marvin.

Turning back to his coffee, he said, "You're not the first

who's come through here looking for a glimpse of him. Must've had a dozen kids like you, making the pilgrimage."

"His children?"

He looked at her hard. "Nah, the ones like you who want something else."

True that. How many kids had lived at the compound and had been brainwashed into adulthood to do his bidding? When Rainy looked at the pimply kid behind the counter, she realized that some of them could still be there—*Sara* could still be there. Had she ever considered that? No. She had actively tried not to think about that place. But she was here now, and there was no way around the thoughts.

"What do they want from him?"

Marvin turned his mean, old eyes on her, and she could see his rot in the yolky whites. "Same thing you do, I expect."

Rainy took a sip of coffee, pressing her lips together as she eyed the bentness of him; he looked like a branch ready to snap.

"I doubt that, Marvin." He'd lived so long and her mother had lived so briefly. The injustice of the good dying young was especially potent in that moment. Smacking her lips together, she set down her mug. "What's he up to nowadays?" She didn't see any point in lying to Marvin, who'd already made up his mind about who she was.

"He's making money. Still lives up at the prison, but it's just him and his closest now. He runs a couple online gigs, uses the space as a warehouse." Marvin laughed. "His slave is the internet, not all those folks he had working for him for free."

That made sense. He couldn't continue doing what he was doing once social media happened: underage kids working his orchards for free, underage kids learning to build websites and what else? She thought of the photo, the one she'd taken from the front seat of his car, and she dropped her fork. It clattered to her plate. *That's what else.* Reaching back, she pulled her hair across her shoulder and began to unbraid it. Her fingers flicked through the strands, detangling as her brain forced her to remember the photo: Feena wearing only her skin…clearly underage…clearly drugged…

She swallowed, but her throat was so dry it locked. Draining her water glass, she swung her stool outward so she was facing the parking lot.

"You think there are any rooms at Charlie's Inn?" she asked, shaking her hair out. She reached for her bag and hauled it into her lap, making eye contact with the old man. She wanted him to remember her.

"Heh!" He choked out a laugh. "They ain't seen a no-vacancy sign since they opened. You planning on stayin' the night?"

She studied his graying skin, the liver spots that decorated it. Why would he eat here and give his money to the man who had most likely conned him out of his restaurant? Eat his eggs, and drink his coffee? "Figured it would be easier to get a ride out come morning. You gonna tell him I'm here?"

Marvin turned away from her, back to his coffee, and picked up his novel.

"Tell him who was here?"

She tossed a twenty on the counter. "Coffee's on me next time, Marv." She lingered long enough to see him smile before she walked out. Marvin. It was a great cover: harmless old man pretending to be bitter over the loss of his business, waiting to call the compound and warn the gang about who was showing up in Friendship. A spy. In fact, they probably had video of Rainy in the restaurant. Her stomach dropped as she walked through the motel office's doors and handed her card to the guy behind the desk. If Taured owned the town, of course he would want to see who came through. Marvin had already been under Taured's control; she knew that from

when she'd hidden under the truck and overheard his conversation with Sammy. He'd asked for waitresses, and Taured
had told Sammy to send the sisters. *God, what was your big plan
in coming here, Rainy?* she asked herself.

She looked out the motel's doors. She looked like her mother;
that's why she'd thought to take her hair down to try to hide
the resemblance on the camera—to use it as a curtain—but of
course it had been too late. Stupid to put herself on his radar.
She didn't even have a car—she couldn't get away quickly. She
took the room key from the clerk's hand, smiled, walked back
outside into the thick air. The thought of Taured showing up
to her room didn't scare her; it was the thought of not being
prepared for him that did. The room was sparse and ugly, but
cleaner than she had expected. She took off her shoes and sat
on the edge of the bed. She fell back onto the white coverlet
and, holding her phone above her face, she texted the group.

Won't be at dinner tonight. Got stuck doing some tourist
thing. Tell you about it tomorrow.

She hit Send and dropped her phone. Would they even notice if she didn't come back to the room later that night? She
doubted it. They'd accept her text because she was the strange,
independent one, anyway.

She stripped down to her underwear and crawled under the
covers, naked except for her necklace and exhausted from the
day—the weekend—the month. *No one knows where I am*, she
thought as she drifted to sleep...an honest lie.

17

Then

They let her pack her mother's personal things into two plastic milk crates they found in the kitchen. Her clothes and shoes were distributed to the remaining women, which left her with some of her mother's books, a Bible, two old photo albums and a box of trinkets that had no meaning to Summer. She watched as the women carried off the rest, fighting over her mother's nicest shoes, which were too big for Summer. All she took for herself was her mother's necklace, a simple gold chain her dad had given her when they got married.

"It's not much but it's real," her mother used to say. Now it was the only real, physical thing she had left of Lorraine. When she put it on for the first time, the metal had warmed instantly to her skin, but when she reached up to touch it, the gold had been cool beneath her fingertips.

"You're getting a roommate," Ama told her the morning after she'd seen her mother's body in the freezer.

"You mean a cellmate," she said. These days, Ama seemed to love delivering news she knew wouldn't be received well. Ama ignored her and prattled on about how it wasn't good to be alone, that people were created to need each other. Summer barely heard her as she stared at the still-full lunch tray they'd brought to the room. There was a bowl of something that looked like gravy with three biscuits beside it. She picked up the iced tea and drank it slowly so she wouldn't have to talk.

"But first, Sara would like to visit with you and express her sorrow at your mother's passing. She is outside." Sara's parents had complete faith in her loyalty to them and Taured. If she was asking to see Summer, it could only mean that their precious daughter wanted to help. But Summer knew what they didn't: that the girl behind the stoic facade was as angry inside as she herself was. She'd decided to forgive Sara, at least for the moment; she wanted to hear what the girl had to say.

She sat up straighter, nodded.

Ama left and a moment later Sara slipped in, closing the door softly behind her. With her came the smell of laundry detergent, underscored by sweat. Her nose was red, like she'd been crying. Summer studied her friend, glad to see her, despite her earlier anger. Sara was tall and ashamed of it—she rounded her shoulders when she walked and ducked her head to make herself look smaller. When she did look you in the face, she was pretty, or at least Summer thought so.

"I'm sorry." Sara's voice broke. She shook her head and tried again. "I'm sorry. I didn't know." She stayed where she was, head bowed, her guilt so painful to look at as Summer stood up and went to her. They met in the middle, clinging to each other as they cried.

Since the day Sara had invited her to eat with her parents, they'd been friends, co-conspirators and sisters. They didn't give much away publicly about their friendship. Sara called it

keeping things professional. In front of everyone in the compound, they barely acknowledged each other, but alone in
the bathroom or dorms, they'd laugh and do their best im-
pressions of the adults. Sometimes they snuck to the kitchens
after midnight when they knew everyone would be asleep
and stole the baked goods set aside for breakfast. They'd end
their feast in the walk-in refrigerator, drinking milk that had
come from one of the compound's cows. They'd once gone
into the freezer to see how long they could make it before
they got too cold. *Seven minutes*, she remembered.

"I have to tell you something," Sara said, pulling away. She
wouldn't look at Summer as she sat on the edge of Lorraine's
bed and traced the roses on the bedspread with her finger,
her eyes wide. She looked nervous, scared. It was unlike her.

"I heard my dad talking to him."

Tom, as the doctor and the first to move his family into
the compound, was one of the most respected men in the
community other than Taured himself. It wasn't unusual for
them to have private talks. Summer had seen them walking
the parameter of the compound together many times in deep
conversation, the same at dinners.

Summer frowned. Whatever her friend had to say was going
to be awful, she already knew it. She didn't have words, so
she wrapped her arms around her body and sank next to Sara
on the bed.

"They've reported your mom's death to the police and
they're coming to get her body. They had to report it. Taured
is paying someone inside the Friendship police to tell him
stuff, and your grandparents called the cops after you two
never showed up."

Summer reached for Sara's hands, grasping them between
her own. "Taured took me to see her body. He showed me…
she had these marks between her toes that he said were track

marks and that she was on drugs. He's going to tell the police she was an addict and she overdosed. But I know she'd never do that. Drugs killed my dad and she hated them. Taured did it to her and that's why she died."

Sara squeezed her hands hard so that Summer looked up in surprise. "He plans to keep you here, that's what I heard him say to my dad."

"Taured," Summer whispered. It wasn't a question. It wasn't even a surprise, but somehow, saying it out loud made her feel woozy and light-headed. Taured thought everything belonged to him, including her. Sara said nothing for several seconds, watching Summer's face.

"They can't keep me here. If my mom is…gone, they'll send me to her parents, right?"

"They're going to say you ran away a few weeks ago and that's what made your mom overdose on drugs. They're pretending you're not here, Summer. They're going to keep you locked up."

Her heart was her whole body, thudding until she was shaking so much Sara got up and threw a blanket around her shoulders.

"Listen, I've been thinking about it…"

Sara's face, which was naturally serious, looked almost pinched in its earnestness.

"There's more. Your mom had a life insurance policy. She got it after your dad died. You're the beneficiary. Taured wants it." Sara's nostrils were flaring as she looked Summer in the eye, her own eyes brimming with tears.

"What?" Summer hissed. "Just say it."

"They talked about him marrying you." It rushed out of her mouth in a jumble. She hiccuped and covered her mouth with her hand.

Summer shook her head. "What?"

Sara bit her lip. "I don't know. They…my dad…they don't know if they can pull it off, but they're going to try."

She shook her head. "No." Her voice broke. That wasn't right, couldn't be.

And why would her mother even have a life insurance policy? She'd never mentioned anything like that to Summer.

"You're underage, so you'd normally need your mother's permission. But with her gone, they can forge her signature." Sara dipped her chin, looked at her hard, like she really needed Summer to understand.

"He will do it. He will find a way. Do you understand?"
She nodded.

"Sara." Ama stuck her head in the door, almost making the two of them jump. "Time for Summer to rest. You can see her again for a bit tomorrow."

"Just another minute, Mama. I'd like to pray with her, if you don't mind," Sara said. They grasped hands, touching foreheads. Ama nodded and closed the door.

"The police will know something's up. If I'm apparently missing, the police will ask them why they didn't report it."

"He's going to say that your mother told him she reported you missing. They're going to have Frank say he drove her to the police station and waited in the car for her." Frank, whom her mother hated and who hated her back—of course he was willing to lie for Taured.

"Frank is just going to play dumb and say he saw her go inside. You have to leave with the police, Summer, it's the only way."

"How? They won't let me out of their sight now if that's the case."

"They're going to lock you in my parents' room while the police are here."

Summer was quiet as she thought. Sara was right. Without

her mother's protection, they could do anything they wanted to her, especially if everyone thought she'd run away. Would her grandparents believe she'd run away? *Ha! Why wouldn't they?* According to Lorraine, they had always wanted to believe the worst about their own daughter, so why would they question a story about the granddaughter they'd never met? Yet...they were all she had. Duty would make them take care of her; her mama had said something of that nature once. No matter what, she had to get out of here. Taured had killed her mother, and eventually, he would kill her, too. The memory of him standing in the cafeteria, staring at her as they led her away to her mother's funeral, surfaced in her mind. Chilled, she looked with new resolve at her brave friend, who was risking everything to help her.

Ama's parents had the most private room other than Taured himself; it was in the south wing of the compound, near the infirmary and far away from Taured's office and the chapel.

"I'll come let you out when it's time. I promise," Sara said.

Something was brewing now in her belly beside the pain, beside the yearning of grief; it was determination.

They whispered for a few more minutes, making plans. Summer squeezed her friend's hand, not knowing what else to say, feeling the dampness of her palms and being comforted by it. Sara was the only person on the planet she cared about anymore. And if everything went right, she'd never see Sara again.

The door opened and the girls said "Amen" at the same time; Summer had to fight to hide her smile.

"Thank you for your help today," Summer said, speaking formally for Ama's benefit. She squeezed her friend's hand three times: *I...love...you.* Sara squeezed back three times and then Ama and her daughter were gone. It felt terrible, the loss and loneliness. All she could do now was wait.

18

—

Now

Mackenzie was taking the first flight out the next morning to Arizona to see her parents. The rest of them were supposed to land at SeaTac together on the midday flight. Rainy was staring at the ceiling of Charlie's Inn at five a.m., composing her text. She'd send it to their group chat so she could deal with them all at once. She heard the rolling of suitcase wheels outside her room; someone was leaving early. She hadn't been able to sleep, the events of the previous day playing out over and over in her mind till she felt loopy from them, and now she had a headache. At midnight she'd left her room and walked. There was a place she wanted to see, and she needed the darkness to see it, lest she be noticed.

Once Rainy had sent the text, she got out of bed. Grabbing a hair tie off the nightstand, she braided her hair. Everything that had happened with the Tiger Mountain group made her feel sick now. It was too much—being in Friendship and thinking about the things her supposed friends had said. *Like a tornado and a hurricane in one heart,* Rainy thought.

Ursa had let it slip that Braithe had called Grant "boo." Had they been together at some point? Why hadn't Grant told her? In the bathroom she turned on the shower, studying her reflection in the mirror. Grant encouraged her friendship with Braithe, which seemed like a strange thing to do if he'd been with her in that way. And why when people said "it was nothing" did that always mean it was something? That was an unspoken rule.

After her shower, Rainy put on yesterday's clothes and headed to Red's for aspirin and some toiletries. Her headache was starting to make her feel fried. Red had a soda fountain along the back near the pharmacy, and she ordered a coffee and a bagel with cream cheese. She watched the few stragglers ambling about—mostly employees dressed in red vests. A man drank from a water bottle near the automatic doors, his suit sagging off his body like it was more exhausted than he was. She pulled her phone from her bag and stared at the screen. She touched cool fingertips to her eyelids, breathing in. The bagel rolled in her stomach, threatening to slide back up on a wave of cream cheese.

Rainy finished off the rest of her coffee and tossed the cup in the trash. She urgently needed to be done with this place and to get out of there. Her headache hadn't subsided with the caffeine and aspirin as she'd hoped.

She checked her phone again. Only a text from the gallery in New York saying they'd sold her *Jar of Parts* piece to a private collector. The piece had sold for a hundred thousand dollars, an amount that was impressive and worth celebrating, yet the moment fell flat.

When she looked at her phone again, there was a string of texts from the Tiger Mountain group.

Ursa: What? Braithe's not flying home with us, either. She finally got an appointment with that psychic she's obsessed with.

The whole psychic thing hit differently today.

Rainy crossed Main Street, leaving Red's behind her. So Braithe had found a reason to stay, as well. It bothered her, but she couldn't put her finger on why.

Mac: Let us know when you get back and stay SAFE.

Tara still hadn't responded to any part of the thread when Rainy tucked her phone in her back pocket, and neither had Braithe.

She went to the Canary for breakfast, where the same kid was there, setting out sugar caddies on the tables. Derek. Marvin had said he was Taured's kid. Taured probably had a dozen kids by now; when she lived at the compound, there had been rumors that he'd fathered some of the pregnant women's babies—she remembered the bratty, crying kid from her very first day, Enoch Aaron—but at fifteen, looking into that hadn't been a priority.

She decided to sit at a table this time, and Derek came over with a menu as soon as she'd seated herself. He didn't make eye contact when she asked for a coffee. The one from Red's hadn't been enough. Instead, he nodded at his shoes and scurried off. Rainy took out her phone. The group chat had ten new messages. She'd look at them later; right now, she wanted to see if she could find an Uber. It was twenty minutes away. She was the only customer, and while she sat, nursing her coffee, she realized that Taured could walk in the door at any sec-

ond. What would she do? She didn't know, but the mere idea
of seeing him made every hair on her body stand at attention.
Even more disturbing was the possibility that she *wanted* him
to see her. But what was she going to do about it? She sipped
her coffee and stared at the door. When Derek came by again,
she asked him where he went to school.

"I was homeschooled," he said, looking embarrassed about
it.

"You an only child?"

He looked startled by her question.

"No… I have brothers and sisters. I'm…the oldest." He said
it like it was a bad thing.

"You're setting a great example for them by being responsible and working." Rainy smiled, and for the first time he
looked her in the eye. While she had him, she ordered eggs
and toast and asked for her coffee to be topped off. When he
brought the pot back, she asked how long he'd been working there.

He was skittish, trying too hard to be careful and seemingly
in perpetual terror of messing up. "Just the last two months,
since I graduated. My dad owns this place, so—" His voice
dropped off hopelessly.

"He wanted you to learn the business," she interrupted
him, rolling her eyes.

He blushed. "Something like that." Now that she was looking at him—really looking—she could see a resemblance, and
not just to Taured. The wide shoulders, the height, the neck
pushed forward. *Is it in your head?* she asked herself.

"Sometimes dads suck," she said truthfully. He looked like
he wanted to say something, but a voice barked his name from
the kitchen and Derek's head snapped toward it. A trucker
walked in and sat at the breakfast bar, putting his hat on the
counter beside him.

"Gotta go," he said. "Be back with your eggs in a few."

She left her phone next to her coffee mug when she went to the bathroom; there was a Jansport backpack resting in the little alcove where the cash register was, propped against the wall. Before she could think, she grabbed it, carrying it to the bathroom and locking the door. She set it in the sink, unzipping it and peering inside. Notebooks. She took one out and flipped through, finding a series of sketches. The kid was not half bad. His drawings were on the religious side, but she couldn't hold that against him. His wallet was in the front pocket: Gideon Derek Browley, eighteen years old, his address the compound. Remorse washed through her with such violence she began to tremble.

Sitting abruptly on the closed seat of the toilet, she stared at his driver's license. Half the shock was in knowing she'd been right. If her math was correct, he'd have been born when Sara was seventeen, two years after Rainy had left. And how many underage mothers had there been in the twenty years since she'd fled from that place? And, of course, none of the children took Taured's last name, because if he was caught, he'd go to prison for statutory rape. Stuffing the license back into the brown leather wallet, she dug further, uncovering nothing particularly interesting until her fingers closed around an envelope. It was from the art school at Hunter College, City University of New York. He'd been accepted into the graphics program. Poor kid. Taured would never let him leave…unless. Maybe he was planning to take things into his own hands. She put everything back except the notebook and, borrowing one of his charcoal pencils, she wrote him a note while sitting on the toilet lid. When she was done, she slipped the bag back into the alcove and went to eat her eggs.

By the time Rainy was finished with her food, the breakfast bar had filled with a variety of singles and one family of four. Sara's son. She could see Sara in the way he slouched his shoulders. He darted around the dining room, a coffeepot forever in his hand. Around eight, another server came in and Derek came over with her check, looking almost embarrassed to hand it to her. She handed him cash and he started digging around in his apron to make change, but Rainy said, "Keep it."

"Really?" he said. Rainy had left him an eighty-dollar tip.

"Yeah," she said, standing up. "I wanted to leave my town, too." She bent down to grab her phone from the table and saw that she had texts from Grant in addition to the Tiger Mountain group.

Instead of looking surprised, he looked relieved she'd said it. "Did you leave it?" His liquid brown eyes reminded her so much of Sara's, the way they dipped down at their outer corners. His skin was pale like hers, too, and he had three dark moles on his cheek. Sara hated her moles, said she was going to get them burned off when she was an adult.

"Hell, yes," Rainy said, and he smiled. His teeth were crooked, but clean and white. The kid seemed more upbeat as he stuffed the money into his apron and nodded at the floor. She watched him in amusement, remembering her first restaurant job in New York as a hostess and then, later, a server. He could leave here and work at any restaurant; it was good money if you found the right place and got decent shifts. He could make it. When she'd first seen him, knowing he was Taured's kid, she'd wanted him to leave, get the hell out of Dodge, and now that she saw Sara's face when she looked at the boy, her heart ached.

"Your mom," Rainy said, staring into his eyes and thinking of her own. "Always let her know you're okay." She supposed it wasn't such a strange thing for a woman to say to a kid; she could have been a mom herself for all he knew, making sure some other mom's kid didn't run off without her knowing.

Derek seemed frozen in place. He blinked at her and then finally said, "My mom's dead."

Rainy hadn't bitten her nails since she was nineteen and her college psych professor called her out for it in front of the class. It had been a humbling experience in not showing her tells. But as her Uber sped through the desert, she bit them till they bled. In her lap: the rescued Ziploc bag she'd dug up after burying it twenty years prior. She was purposefully not looking at it, afraid of what it might make her feel. Her jeans were brown with the dirt they were carrying; she imagined her face didn't look any better. How had it stayed undisturbed for so long? But Rainy knew how; she'd chosen the spot for that very purpose. The locals called it Charlie Cactus: a thirty-foot saguaro cactus that Rainy agreed was impressive. She'd come here with Sara on their few trips into town for nonperishable food. It grew behind Red's, away from the freeway and a five-minute walk up a hill. None of the adults had cared enough that they'd wanted to go see it each time they were in town, but it became a thing for the girls to walk over to visit Charlie.

She'd buried her baggie deep beneath Charlie Cactus on one of those trips, double-wrapped in plastic bags from Red's. Sara had kept lookout. Sara hadn't asked what was in the bag; she'd just helped Rainy get rid of it. That meant that after she left the compound for good, Sara could have gone back for it and dug it up.

She'd been so lost in thought thinking about Sara and her son that she'd forgotten about the texts on her phone. She read through the updates Grant had sent first. He didn't mention anything about her staying in Vegas, which meant that the husbands were still out of the loop. She looked at the time, calculating the difference between her and Grant. It was three o'clock in the morning for him, so she'd text him when she got settled in the hotel and he had a chance to wake up for the day. There were four texts from Viola, asking what time she was getting back, detailing the snowfall the night before, and then another, sent an hour later, saying, Never mind, they told me you're staying an extra day, party animal. In the group chat, Ursa had taken to updating their status through the check-in process like Rainy might change her mind at any minute and come after them. Braithe and Tara were strangely quiet. She decided to ask Viola if she knew anything more about Braithe staying behind. Viola sent a voice text.

"I texted her whatsup this morning and she told me she'd stayed. She seemed to be fine. She sounded elated actually. She mentioned getting a flight early tomorrow, said she'd be back before you all had time to unpack. That was before she knew about you staying, too, and—"

Viola's voice cut off abruptly and Rainy frowned while she waited. When the text never came, she sent a question mark.

A few seconds later, a shorter voice text appeared. "Sorry... I totally forgot we're late for a doctor's appointment. Tata is pulling the car around, talk soon."

Rainy sent a quick message wishing them good luck and leaned her head back against the seat.

19

Then

They weren't allowed watches, so she had no way of know-ing what time it was. Dawn and Frank came to get her, and just like Sara said, they took her to Ama and Tom's room.

"Why do I have to stay here?"

Dawn pretended not to hear. Sara had told her she'd have to wait at least an hour before Sara could come and free her, but the wait already felt agonizing. She pounded the door with both fists in frustration. Sara would come. She had to. It was Summer's only chance.

Sometime later she was sitting on the floor, head between her knees, when she heard a key in the lock. Jumping to her feet, she waited for the door to open. Five seconds...ten... nothing happened. Going to the door, Summer tested the lock; it was open. She hadn't even heard the door being unlocked.

The hallway was empty, but hanging on the outside of the

doorknob was Sara's favorite scrunchie. Summer slipped it
onto her wrist and ran.

What if she missed them, what if they left without her?
What would happen without her mother here to protect her?
Who would she belong to? The answer to that was so terrifying she ran faster. It was late—maybe midnight; everyone else
was in bed. Would this be the last time she ran through these
halls? If she failed at this, they would never let her see the outside again; she knew that deep in her gut, because she would
never stop trying to leave and she would never do what they
said. They had killed her mother, and they would kill her, too,
for refusing to marry Taured. As she approached the old sign
that still said Chapel with all its letters, she made a sign of the
cross like her mother sometimes used to do. She could hear
voices, faintly, like they were coming from outside instead of
Taured's office. But no—as she neared the door and pressed
her ear to the wood, she could hear them inside. Sara's father,
Taured and three other voices she didn't recognize: two men
and a woman. They were outsiders, the timbre and tone un-
familiar to her. She placed her hand over the doorknob and
blew out the contents of her lungs.

Her forehead was touching the door as she prayed to her
mother's God, pleaded with him to help her. The god behind
the door was a falsehood, a killer, and his people worshipped
him out of fear. She didn't know what life would meet her
past the doors of the compound, but she wasn't afraid of it.

Four people were seated in chairs in front of Taured's desk
in formal clothing. They all looked up in surprise when she
stepped into the room. She was wearing an ankle-length dress
and she felt embarrassed to be standing in front of them barefoot, but her shoes had been taken after her mother had died.
For a few terrible seconds, her vision blurred in and out, and
she thought she was going to faint. She didn't look at Taured,

who she knew was sitting behind his desk, or Sara's father, who stood slightly behind his pastor, ready to carry out instructions at a moment's notice. She stood in front of the three men and one woman. She heard her name spoken from behind her, but she ignored it. The female police officer didn't look happy to be there and since Summer wasn't, either, she directed her words to her.

"My name is Summer Downey. My mother was Lorraine Downey. My father is dead, too, and I want to go live with my grandparents, Mark and Gilda."

"This is the minor that you said ran away?" The female police officer stood. Her hand was on the holster at her waist.

The man sitting next to her, a jowly, bald man, said, "Sit down, O'Connor." O'Connor sat down. "Where have you been, young lady?"

"They locked me away so I couldn't speak to you," she said.

He turned to Taured, his little downturned mouth wriggling unhappily. "Explain this, Taured."

They weren't asking her, she realized. But then he did something that straight-out shocked her. Taured looked Summer in the eyes and said, "Why don't we let the young lady explain herself."

Not what she was expecting.

She turned to the woman—O'Connor. "He killed my mother. It wasn't an accident."

The toad man spoke up. "Young lady, we know it wasn't an accident. Your mother was ill in heart and mind. She was an addict. Do you understand that?"

"There was nothing wrong with her. She was fine. She would never take drugs. She hated what they did to my dad." Summer stared between the three strangers, trying to understand why they were reacting the way they were. The only one who looked disturbed by what she'd just said was O'Connor.

Summer looked at the third person now, a man who'd been quiet for the exchange. Seemingly unbothered by the entire ordeal, he looked at his watch.

"We've tried to protect her from a lot of it," Taured said.

"That's a lie! He locked her in a room and starved her—he tortured her! And not just her. He's done it before! Ask anyone!" She was shaking now—her entire body and her voice. The quiet man looked at Taured.

"These are serious accusations." He spoke softly and with a slight lisp. You had to strain to hear him, which made everyone listen very carefully when he spoke. "Is there truth in this?" he said to Taured.

"Of course not. Dr. Browley can speak to Lorraine's condition in the last couple years, as he was her physician."

"He wasn't," Summer said. They all turned to look at her, but she didn't shrink back.

"Is there someone here who can corroborate your story?" the man with the lisp asked.

Any name she gave them would result in the same thing: they'd lie to protect Taured and their standing in the community—young or old, the rules were the same. Also, any person she named might be punished later just because she mentioned them. In her own mind, she'd made the comparison to the Salem witch trials, which she'd read about on Taured's precious internet. No matter what she said, she'd be punished, or someone else would.

"Sara," she said desperately, despite the crushing guilt she felt. She saw the surprise on Dr. Browley's face, then the anger. Summer knew she had crossed a line, especially after Sara had got her this far. His daughter would now be dragged before these people.

"Get the person of whom she speaks."

He didn't have a lisp, she realized; it was an accent.

Taured nodded at the doctor, who left the room to get his daughter. After Sara had risked everything to help her, she would be forced to take a side and the side she'd choose was obvious to Summer: blood ran thicker than water, as her dad used to say.

"Lorraine was my high school best friend," Taured said. "She came to me for help when her husband died. Summer was only yea high…"

She looked over to see Taured measuring her adolescent self below his open palm. "She was nothing but knees and elbows and now she's our star softball player." He winked in her direction, like they were sharing an inside joke. Cold pinched down her spine. She was so sure she was going to be sick she swayed on her feet, lifting her palm to her mouth. She knew what he was doing and it was too late. While the men were listening to Taured, the woman's gaze rested on Summer's face, watching. She asked for help with her eyes and hoped that her urgency was understood. The more words she said, the deeper she fell into his trap. When Browley returned with Sara, her head was down. Summer recognized her friend's fear in the curve of her shoulders and felt an uncertainty that made her want to run from the room. This was wrong. She was causing problems for people she cared about.

"Sara, I'm Mr. Nava. We're going to ask you a few questions."

Her nod was vigorous, but it wasn't enough, and he asked her to look at him. Sara did so slowly, her eyes darting to Summer and back to Mr. Nava.

"Summer says that her mother's death wasn't an accident. Is that true?"

"Summer thinks it's true," Sara said quickly. She cast another wayward glance at Summer. "Her mom left her here a lot. She wasn't around, you know?"

The men in the room nodded; *a lot of bobbleheads*, Summer

thought bitterly. O'Connor didn't bob her head. She kept looking at Summer while Sara lied.

"So what you're saying is that Summer is a very confused young lady?"

Sara nodded. Summer looked at her feet. The churning inside of her was becoming unbearable, feelings expanding in her chest like a bubble of gas.

Taured watched, his expression completely content with how things were working out for him.

"The truth is, Summer," he said, looking at her, "your mother wanted you to stay here with us. She named me as your legal guardian in her last will and testament." He looked at the officers. "I will, of course, produce Lorraine's will for you. Lorraine didn't want Summer being raised near her parents— she expressed to me that she wanted to protect her daughter from them." He lowered his voice on the last part, letting the weight of insinuation sink in.

"He's a liar!" Her yell made Sara flinch. "My mother would never leave me alone in a room with this pig, never mind leaving me with him for good."

The silence that followed lasted only a few thickly awkward seconds, but Summer could see their faces change.

"That's quite enough, young lady." The jowly man pushed himself forward in his seat and then hoisted himself to standing position. "You need to show some respect for yourself and everyone else in this room."

Was this happening? Her mother was dead, murdered at the hands of this madman, and the police were telling her to watch her manners?

"You're not listening to me," she tried again. "They locked my mother in a room—both of us—and tortured her. They made it look like she overdosed, but they gave her those drugs against her will."

"Oh, my," he said, narrowing his eyes. "You, as well? They locked both of you up and tortured you?"

Summer's mouth hung open. Taured sat behind his desk, a pained smile on his face.

"With all due respect, sir, the girl has just lost her mother."

She couldn't believe he'd defended her. Looking between them in confusion, she finally turned to Sara, her face screwed up, and she started crying before she could get the words out.

"Sara...tell...them...please." The tears were flowing freely now, dripping off her chin. She tried to rub them away, but it was too much. Summer clasped her arms around herself, rocking on her heels. She wanted her mother, but there was no one here who would protect her, no one left in the world. A small cry escaped her throat.

"That's enough." Dr. Browley stepped behind Sara, resting a hand on her shoulder. "Clearly this girl is very upset and I'm not letting my daughter get dragged into this mess."

It all happened so quickly. She locked eyes with Sara over her shoulder, seeing the remorse that echoed her own, and then her friend was gone. Summer was alone with them, but she wasn't hearing anymore.

Her panic was so great that she reached out for something to steady herself and missed, stumbling to the side.

"Whoa, whoa." O'Connor was coming toward her as she swayed. The room was dancing around her in odd jerks.

Summer saw the officer's face, pale and oval like an egg, swim in front of her. But it was Taured's hands she felt on her body, grabbing her by the shoulders and leading her to a chair. She wanted to rip herself away from him, but she was afraid and disoriented. With his hands gripped around her upper arms, he lowered her into the chair closest to his desk, and asked Sara's dad to get her a glass of water.

Then he knelt on one knee in front of her. Summer froze.

There were streaks of gray in his beard and on his temples. She'd never been this close to him—*had she?*—aside from the night he'd knocked on her door, and she had the same thought then as she did now: behind his eyes, behind the amber of his iris, and the large pupils, was something insatiably hungry, and it wasn't human.

She held the words she wanted to say behind her gritted teeth. *Please let me go.*

"I'm… I—" She couldn't finish her sentence.

They were speaking around her, to her sometimes, but she couldn't focus on what they were saying.

"Social services will place her in a foster home until then." Summer looked up to see the female officer speaking to Taured. He was standing next to her chair now, with his hand on her shoulder. She felt the shift in his body, the tightening of his fingers by just a fraction.

"With all due respect, Officer, this is her home. The child's mother has just died. To remove her from everything she knows would add to her trauma. Here are the documents." As if on cue, Taured produced a cream-colored envelope that he handed to the detective. "We have been both forthcoming and compliant in regard to law enforcement and Lorraine's body, but as you can see, I am the legal guardian of her daughter and you have no right nor reason to remove her from her home."

They were speaking again, the men. Summer sought the female officer's eyes and found them drilling into her. She looked to see if the men noticed, but together, they were examining the papers. Gingerly, she met the woman's eyes, a strange sensation rising behind her ribs. She was younger than Summer's mother, maybe in her twenties. She was very blonde and very tan, her hair pulled back severely and knotted at the nape of her neck. She was narrowing her eyes, moving them from Summer to the floor and back again. And then, with a little jerk of her head, O'Connor squeezed her own eyes closed. Summer understood. She stood up rather suddenly and, from the corner of her eye, saw all four men pivot their heads to look at her. Then she let her whole body go limp. It didn't even hurt when she hit the ground.

She heard the sound of their feet, the clamor of voices, and then the female officer sternly say, "Step back, all of you, give her some room. Byron, call an ambulance."

"No need," Taured said. "Tom here is a doctor."

Summer lay limp and still, breathing in tiny gasps.

"I want her taken to a hospital to be checked out," O'Connor said. A second later, Summer heard her speaking, and then the crackling sound of a radio saying an ambulance was on its way.

"I think you're overacting." Taured's voice sounded strained.

"She's a fifteen-year-old girl whose mother has just died. She's collapsed, she could be severely dehydrated or worse. He said she was a runaway, yet here she is. She's telling us she's been abused. She needs to be checked out physically." O'Connor was addressing one of her male colleagues. Summer's heart was pounding so hard she wondered if they could hear it.

"She's grieving, she's exhausted," Taured argued. "We will take very good care of her. Tom here has been her doctor for the last five years. Gentlemen…?"

Taured did not like when women acted like men, as he called it. He was petitioning to the men in the room: he assumed the men had more power.

There were several lingering seconds, and then Nava spoke. "It would be best if she were taken to a hospital and checked out thoroughly. The ambulance is on the way." There was a silence so abrupt and thick Summer had trouble keeping still. And then she heard it: the sound of the siren, so beautiful. It would take her out of this place.

20

Now

After she checked into her room, Rainy FaceTimed with
Grant.

She was jarred when she saw his unshaven face.

"Do you like it?" he asked, stroking a week's worth of fa-
cial hair. She knew that he shaved every day, but she'd had no
idea he could grow a beard that quickly. It made her wonder
what else she didn't know about him.

"It's different," she said. In truth, she hated it. It reminded
her of Taured.

His eyes were laughing as he fingered his chin. "Don't
worry, it'll be gone by the time I get home. The guys here
wanted me to do it because they didn't believe I could grow
a full beard in a week." And then he showed her the view
outside of his hotel and Rainy oohed and aahed. When he sat
back down and they settled into their chat, she lost the will to

describe the trip. She kept him busy, talking about things on his end, but finally he asked the dreaded question: "So how did it go, huh? Did you have fun or what, party girl?"

"As much fun as a party girl would have in…the library."

She was choosing her words carefully. She'd also chosen to sit against a white wall while she FaceTimed him so he wouldn't know she wasn't home. She hoped the news hadn't reached him yet. She didn't feel like explaining. She couldn't even explain to herself what she thought she was still doing here.

His laugh was infectious, and she missed him fiercely. "Eight more days," she said.

"Eight more days," he repeated in the low drawl that meant intimate things only they understood. They hung up and Rainy wrestled with the guilt of her dishonesty. First, she'd insisted that she didn't want to go on the trip, and then she'd extended said trip—which reminded her that she hadn't booked her flight back yet. Now that she was here, somehow the drive to go back to the place where the nightmare had started had felt natural, unavoidable. She'd needed to go, that's all she knew, and she hadn't even made it to the compound—just skirted Friendship's shitty main street. Now she was in a single room at the same hotel she'd shared with the Tiger Mountain girls, curled on top of the covers like a shrimp. What ending was she looking for?

She must have fallen asleep, because some while later, Rainy woke to the sound of her phone. It wasn't a regular ring—it was FaceTime again. It was ten o'clock, and it was dark outside her window.

Tara's name and photo were on her screen. Ignoring the instant anxiety at seeing Tara's name, Rainy reset her face into a pleasant smile and hit Accept.

Tara's lumpy ponytail told her that some type of shit had hit some type of fan.

"Is everything okay?" Rainy asked. Tara had never Face-Timed her.

"It's Braithe." The words were out of Tara's mouth before she could say anything else. She was wearing an oversize Sea-hawks sweatshirt with a bleach stain on the shoulder.

"What about her?"

"She texted me a few hours ago, said she was unhappy with Steve and that…that psychic person told her to—to—leave! She says she's not coming back."

Rainy swung her legs over the side of the bed and walked over to the minifridge. She needed to buy a few seconds and unfold these sentences, which weren't making sense. Reaching in, she grabbed a water; pausing, she thought better of just the water and took out the vodka and OJ, as well.

"Rainy, did you hear me? We have to do something. She hasn't even told Stephen…he's in Japan, for God's sake. He doesn't even know she's not back."

Rainy propped the phone against the coffee machine and made her drink. Tara stared at her from the other side of the screen.

Finally, Rainy said, "Why is that any of our business?"

Tara gaped. Her eyes were watery pink. "Are you kidding me? She's our friend. She's making the biggest mistake of her life and we… I don't know…" Tara waved a hand above her head. "We're partially responsible."

"Why?" Rainy said. "Because we happened to be there?"

"Yes, because we were there! And none of us knew what she was feeling. She's been miserable all this time and we carried on without asking her how she was. We should have known something was off when she wanted to see a psychic!"

Rainy took a sip of her warm screwdriver and sat on the love seat.

"First of all, Tara, you all peddled the psychic thing to me as fun, so why would I think it was Braithe's cry for help?" She unscrewed the cap on her water and chugged it down. The cold water seared her insides. She closed one eye and said, "Maybe you're the one feeling guilty. Because she's your best friend and you didn't know. That doesn't mean I want to join you. I've only known Braithe for a year."

Tara's mouth fell open again, which Rainy thought was dramatic. If Tara wanted to get involved in whatever drama Braithe was swimming around in, so be it. Rainy didn't want any part of it.

"It's because of you, you know." Tara's voice was acidic and slurred. Rainy was pretty sure she'd had her own version of a screwdriver before this call.

For the last two days, Rainy had agonized over what she had done to upset the women, so this accusation stung even more. The fact that Tara would blame her for anything in regard to Braithe was ridiculous.

"What the hell, Tara?" she said slowly. "You guys begged me to go on the trip, then pretty much iced me out after the first day, and now you're trying to blame me for Braithe's decisions?"

Tara sighed, ducking her head. Her ponytail fell forward over her shoulder, and when she looked up, her eyes looked like they did in her marathon photos, the ones Rainy had seen online. Fierce, determined. Tara was ready to square off with her.

"Braithe and Grant used to be a thing. Did you know that?"

Tara's words trickled like ice water into her brain. So it *was* true.

"She dated him before Stephen, and she chose Stephen…

but you know how old love never dies." Her voice trailed off suggestively.

"Grant would have told me." Rainy's voice was firm, but her mind was bulging with questions. *Would* Grant have told her if he'd dated Braithe? It had never been implied; no one ever brought it up. But Stephen was his best friend: there was just no way.

Tara was studying her face. She said, "Stephen knows—he was around when they dated. He sort of felt like he stole the girl and was always grateful to Grant for being so cool about it."

"What does this have to do with me?"

Tara smiled, knowing she'd hit her target; Rainy was visibly upset now. "What do you think all of this has been? The invites, being the favorite new person she shines her light on—she's interested in you. Sure, she may even like you, but it's only because you're with Grant. Grant being the beginning and end of everything she's done since she realized she married the wrong guy."

"This is nuts, Tara. You have no right to tell me this. These aren't your stories to tell."

"You being with him drove her over the edge," she pushed on. "She's not a bad person. She's just a confused person."

"Did she tell you that?"

Tara's mouth tightened.

Suddenly Tara's dislike of her made sense. All the animosity she'd felt had been on account of Braithe's feelings for Grant. She almost felt sorry for Tara; framing the past weekend in light of this current information, things were clicking together very quickly. The looks over the weekend, the tense moments and the tidy bitchiness that never quite warranted a callout—Tara had been torn between disapproving of Braithe's decisions, trying to be loyal to her best friend and feeling angry at the attention she was giving Rainy.

"So why did you agree to invite me on the trip? As I recall, you were the one who pushed me that night, hand-holding and all."

Tara's answer didn't roll off her tongue quite as easily this time. "I didn't know what was going on—I mean, I knew she'd been pining for Grant for a decade, but when he started dating you, she seemed genuinely happy for him, and things with Stephen were going really well. It wasn't until after we invited you on the trip that she told me how she really felt." Tara paused to take a sip of beer and Rainy braced herself for what she was going to say next.

"She made it seem like a game. We were going to get the scoop on you and Grant. See how serious you really were."

"That's really fucked up."

"Yeah."

She didn't say sorry. That was telling.

"Were the others in on this, too... Viola?"

Tara's headshake was emphatic this time. "No, they—we never spoke about that stuff around them. I guess I always felt privileged that she chose me, you know?"

This version of Tara was a lot different than the one Rainy had come to know. She took in the ruffled, worried, strangely vulnerable woman. She felt nothing but anger.

"You could have been a decent person. Instead, you connived to gather information from me for Braithe, who is carrying a ten-year torch for my partner and is now planning on leaving her husband because of what a psychic said—and you want me to help you convince her to come back? Why would she listen to me, anyway?"

"Okay, when you say it like that it sounds ridiculous."

"Oh my God, Tara, because it is." Rainy downed the rest of her warm drink and slammed it on the table next to the phone.

"Braithe is an adult. The decisions she makes for her marriage and life have nothing to do with us. Even if she is in love with Grant, he's mine." Rainy was over it. She wanted to—needed to—get off this call.

"So you're just not going to do anything?" Tara's mouth gaped open unattractively. "What if she, like…commits suicide?"

"What are you asking me to do? She's literally plotting to steal my boyfriend."

"That's a little dramatic, don't you think? Text her, see if she will meet up with you. Maybe you can talk some sense into her. Look, I know you don't want to hear this right now, but she actually does like you. Respects you. I think on some level she realizes she can't compete with you for Grant. I mean, I think she knows she messed up big-time."

"Does she know you're telling me all of this?"

Tara shook her head. "I made the decision, thinking it would help if you spoke to her."

"I am the last one Braithe wants to hear from. You have this all wrong." Rainy released the knot of hair wrapped on the crest of her skull and her hair tumbled down.

Sturdy, steady Braithe with her marbled brown eyes and sophisticated maturity didn't seem the type to connive and scheme, but Rainy supposed that was why she'd been able to get away with it.

"I don't want anything to do with her, or you, or any of you, ever again," Rainy said.

"I should have known," Tara said, her face red. "People like you tout feminism and claim you give a shit about other women, but in the end you only care about yourself. You're

willing to leave her behind because she didn't fit your narrative."

"That's such a load of bullshit, Tara. No one helps the person who stabs them in the back!" But Rainy was staring at
an empty screen: Tara had hung up on her. A vicious anger
was ripping through her, violent and affirming. She paced
the small room until she wanted to scream. *You don't have to
stay here*, she thought. *This is Vegas. You can do pretty much anything you want.* Grabbing her bag, she headed out of the room.

21

—

Now

"Why are you being like this?" The hurt in Grant's eyes was enough to rip the last of her reserve from where she loosely held it. Rainy's hands made knots in her lap. She stared at the computer's keyboard instead of the grainy image of him on the screen. They'd barely managed a connection, and now they were fighting.

"Why didn't you tell me that the two of you were a thing?"

"It was a long time ago, Rainy. She's married to my best friend. And you and I don't talk about the past—we just don't."

That was fair. She never asked questions because she didn't want the same asked of her. But something like this seemed like more of a problem: *I used to sleep with the woman we see every week.*

"Maybe just a heads-up would have been nice. I'm in your world, Grant. Playing with your people, on your territory. I moved my life to be with you. I'd really appreciate understanding the landscape I'm navigating. I feel like a fool because everyone knows you two were a thing except me."

He blinked at her and she could see his frustration, but she didn't care. As far as she was concerned, he'd sent her to the wolves when he encouraged her to go to Vegas.

"Did you know she still has feelings for you?"

The silence was painful, a reminder of how little she belonged in his world. She wanted to ask if he had feelings for Braithe, too, but she was too afraid of his answer. Finally, he spoke, and his voice was low and serious. "She called me."

"What? When?"

He was uncomfortable; she could tell by the way he was shifting around in his seat.

"Can we talk about this when I get home?"

"Your ex-girlfriend, your best friend's wife, calls you in Japan, while you're there with her husband—and you don't think that's important enough to talk about right now?"

She pressed her lips together so hard she thought she might have a headache for it later.

"She sounded pretty drunk. At first, I thought she was calling because something happened to you, but she started talking about her feelings."

"Were you going to tell me?"

"Of course, Rainy. I just didn't think it was the time."

She felt bad, she did. He was on the most important trip of his career to date; it wasn't fair of her to do this now.

"Look, I get how this looks. I'm sorry," he said. "Braithe and I dated our senior year of high school. I went to school out east and she and Stephen went to UCLA together. They ended up having more in common than we did." There was no resentment in his voice, no sadness. "But you need to know that I love you, and only you."

"Okay," she said.

Grant leaned toward the computer until she could no longer see his hotel room, his face filling her screen.

"Rainy, it's you for me."

She nodded.

They ended the call and she felt worse than she had before, Grant's words doing little to soothe her. She was angry and embarrassed, and more than that, she didn't know if she believed Grant, and that was a whole problem in itself.

Rainy didn't go to sleep or even close her eyes; she sat propped in her bed till the early hours of the morning, too afraid of the dreams that would come if she tried.

She must have drifted off around five in the morning; when she woke, it was only an hour later, and her phone was ringing. Viola.

"What? Why are you calling so early?"

"Rude," said Viola. "That's the problem with you New Yorkers."

Rainy laughed, wishing that were the problem; how simple life would be if her personality was a product of where she lived instead of what had been done to her.

"You know why I'm calling?"

"I'm assuming it has something to do with Vegas and Braithe." She sighed, sitting up in bed and frowning.

"You assume correctly. Tara showed up at my house yesterday."

"I wish she hadn't done that. You don't need that type of stress."

"Braithe is my friend," Viola said firmly. "I've known that woman for eight years. This just isn't like her. I'd go talk sense into her if I could, at least try to convince her to come home and talk it out with Stephen."

"Why doesn't Tara go?" Rainy's throat was dry, and she

grabbed a juice from the minifridge, propping the phone against her shoulder. She didn't like where the conversation was going.

"She's prepared to fly back, but Braithe told her not to come. She was pretty firm about it, so sending Tara might make things worse than they already are. Tara isn't exactly a calming presence to be around."

Rainy lifted her chin, wishing the next minute away. "Viola…"

"Please, Rainy."

"I'm not the one to ask. The others know her better." But even as Rainy finished her sentence, she was doubting it.

"God, Rainy, I know, and I'm sorry. But damn, what is Braithe thinking? I am in shock. Like, did I ever even know her? All kinds of things are lining up in my head right now that I never saw before."

"Like what?"

"Okay, remember when Grant covered your living room in flowers on your one-year anniversary?"

How could she forget? Four dozen red roses and that did not include the petals carpeting the floor. She didn't know anyone knew about that night.

"I guess Grant told Stephen his plans, and of course Stephen told Braithe. I distinctly remember her being annoyed. She said it was ridiculous and wasteful. We teased her about being a salty bitch and she laughed it off, saying she was having a bad day, but later I went to the bathroom, and you know how their bedroom is near the guest bath?"

Rainy nodded even though Viola couldn't see her.

"I could hear her sobbing in her room. I never asked her about it because—well, obviously it was awkward that I overheard it in the first place. It's just weird, you know?"

Braithe crying in her room after making a couple comments about flowers didn't really prove anything, but it was nice that Viola was offering her this information.

"When she was texting me," Viola went on slowly, "she was saying how unhappy she's been for a long time and that for the first time in her life, she feels like she can breathe. But she'd never ever even hinted at being unhappy before that, so either I'm the worst friend in the world, or she's the best liar."

"What's Stephen going to do?"

They were both quiet as they contemplated that. Rainy swallowed hard. "Maybe she'll come back when she's ready." It was such a callous thing to say, but even as they spoke, she eyed the Ziploc bag from her past, resting on the hotel's dresser; she hadn't even started processing that.

Viola agreed. "You're right, I'm just overly emotional and in hyper-mother mode. I'm going to step off this cause right now and take a bath."

They hung up and Rainy decided to follow suit and take a shower. The guilt was gnawing at her, but she pushed it away each time. The hot water did little to calm her, and Rainy sat on the bed, wrapped in the hotel robe a few minutes later, staring at her phone.

She tried calling first, but her call was sent to voice mail. She left a short message asking Braithe to call her back, and then she hung up and texted, too.

Braithe, can we talk? It's about you and Grant.

She felt sick even typing those words. Rainy hated confrontation and she wasn't good at having friends. The people she'd hung out with in New York had been just as busy and distracted as she was; their meetups had included late-night dinners and gallery parties with people you knew but didn't really know. She'd liked the simplicity of those shallow relationships: talking about art over seventeen-dollar cocktails, gossiping about a peer's affair over sushi. No one wanted to know what your daddy issues were or where you were raised. They had been *right now* friends, and not one of them had contacted her in the year she'd been gone. The response from Braithe didn't come right away; when it did, Rainy had to read it twice.

Why would you be asking me questions about your husband?

She stared at her phone and read the text again. Was Braithe making a jab at her, at the fact that Rainy and Grant weren't married? It was confusing. Why would she call Grant her husband? She decided to answer using the same tone. When Rainy hit Send it felt good.

Probably because you're still in love with him.

She wanted to understand why Braithe had pretended to be her friend and if it had all been a play for Grant. She also wanted to know why she had been stupid enough to fall for it. Hadn't she learned how to spot disingenuous people by now? She'd certainly had enough therapy to understand what toxic behavior looked like. She was rubbing her forehead when the text came.

You have my attention...

She blinked at the text. "What the fuck," she said under her breath. This felt like a game, one where she was being baited. She left the phone upside down on the counter and went to make herself a drink. This was nuts. This didn't feel right or like Braithe. Halfway to the minibar, she changed her mind and picked up her phone, her thumbs moving furiously across the screen.

I don't just want your attention, she typed. I want an explanation.

She watched the text bubbles appear and disappear; she imagined Braithe typing something angry and then erasing it. In her current state of mind, Braithe clearly didn't believe she owed her own husband an explanation for her behavior; she definitely wasn't going to tell Rainy anything. She could push harder.

Tara told me that the whole reason you came to Vegas was to see that psychic to ask about you and Grant. Is she telling me the truth, Braithe? You're in love with Grant?

It looked like Braithe was composing a novel; the text in progress dots danced on the screen for what felt like ten minutes before her reply lit up Rainy's screen.

What we had was special and he feels the same way. I can prove it.

She didn't want to hear from Braithe again, not until she'd had a chance to talk to Grant face-to-face. That was fair, she thought; they'd both been holding back information. She could at least give him the truth about her own past.

She saw that Braithe had texted her again, and she almost deleted it without reading…almost. Curiosity won. Braithe had sent four photos. Letters laid out on a white bedspread.

When Rainy zoomed in, she saw that they were photos of handwritten letters from Grant, or at least his name was signed to them. She wouldn't read the content. Braithe was trying to bait her. She slammed her phone on the counter and thought about calling Grant; this was nuts, what exactly was she trying to prove?

Those are old letters, she sent back.

Lol. They are. You're too sharp for your own good, Rainy.

She stared hard at the text, her face contorting as she tried to work out what was bugging her. She'd spent the last year getting to know Braithe, and had never once seen this side of her, or any hint of it. Maybe she was drinking, maybe she was having an emotional breakdown; someone—her family— needed to stage an intervention. She thought about sending a screenshot to Viola, but decided against it. Viola needed to soak up these days softly, not be embroiled in drama. After a few minutes of deliberation, she typed out a text to Braithe and hit Send.

Braithe, you need to talk to Stephen. You need help. Please stop texting me.

There. And she could always block her number if she didn't. Ticking behind her eyes was the start of a headache that promised to hit hard.

She put her phone down, stepped away. Rainy tried to bring herself back to the present, to the problem, to the people involved—but the past was an oily, gelatinous thing rotting in the periphery of her mind. She purposefully lived in places that gave her no muscle memory for *that* place: first the city and then the forest. *This is your fault,* she told herself. *You went back there and opened a door for the demons to sneak back in.* But she didn't believe that. Or did she? She was still staring at the phone when she heard the ping of a message received. She didn't even need to open it to see what it said.

This isn't Braithe.

22

Now

Stop playing games. Who is this?

She waited five minutes...ten. The dots had disappeared; Rainy was pacing in front of the window, chewing the inside of her cheek.

"This isn't real," she said to no one. She hit the call button; it rang twice before Braithe's soothing voice told her to leave a message. She tried Grant and Stephen next; neither of them picked up.

She stared at the ceiling. She could find Braithe's family on social media—she had a sister she spoke about—and tell them what? She couldn't out whatever this was to Braithe's family if she hadn't even told her own husband.

"I have to call Tara back," she said aloud. "Oh my God." She hit the call button before she could change her mind and waited. Tara's voice was curt when she answered; Rainy could hear a buzz of noise behind her.

"Hello."

"Hey, it's Rainy. Do you have a minute to talk? It's about Braithe."

"Hold on," Tara said.

She heard muffled voices, and then, seconds later, Tara spoke so loudly Rainy jerked her head back from the receiver.

"What is it, Rainy? I'm out with Mike and I only have a few minutes."

Okay...how exactly was she supposed to sum this up in a few minutes? God, Tara was a pain in the ass.

"Braithe is being weird—and I don't think it's Braithe."

Tara cut in. "You don't have to tell me, okay—she actually had the audacity to threaten me. Like, I am over it. Done."

"Wait—what do you mean, she threatened you?"

She heard Tara say, "Shit, shit, shit—sorry. Hold on—"

Rainy switched her phone from one ear to the other.

"I did something a few years ago," Tara said. "I don't want to get into it, but Braithe sent me screenshots and basically told me that if I got involved in this, she was going to...share them." She sounded scared now. "That would, like, ruin my life. She's such a bitch."

"Okay, but you don't think that's weird, Tara?" Rainy plugged a finger into her own ear to try to hear Tara better, but there was more noise coming from Tara's end of the line.

"It's *all* weird. Mike doesn't want me to hang out with her anymore, not after—ugh. Listen, I have to go."

"Okay, but wait, she was texting me and she—someone— said that it wasn't Braithe. This isn't making any sense... I think someone might have Braithe's phone."

"Rainy, it's Braithe, okay. She's going through something and—"

"But what if it's not her? What if something's really wrong?"

Tara was silent. When she spoke again her voice almost sounded bored. "She plotted for months to take Grant from you. I'm sorry, but you are delusional if you think she's some saint. I hate to break it to you, but you got played, I got played. Whatever victim thing she's doing, whatever game she's playing—I'm not buying it. You know the night of Viola's shower...?" Tara's voice changed. "She was with Grant. That's why she pretended to be sick. She wanted to talk to him about her feelings. So she ambushes him on your doorstep before you get home. And you know what? I freaking covered for her."

Rainy's shock was obvious to Tara, who sighed deeply. "If it makes any difference to you, he rejected her."

It did make a difference, but she didn't want to hear any of this from Tara. Why hadn't Grant told her? She thought back to that night, how he'd been acting. Rainy swallowed, her throat tight and dry. She wanted to do nothing more than crawl into bed and process everything, but right now...right at this very moment, it couldn't be about Grant; Braithe was in trouble. She closed her eyes, exhaling through her nose, and tried again.

"What if she's in trouble? You just don't care?"

"She threatened me after everything I did for her. *She* doesn't care. Sorry, Rainy." Tara hung up. She wasn't sorry. This was going from bad to worse.

"Wow, okay." Rainy set her phone on the floor near her foot and leaned her torso backward until it was resting against the wall. She thought for the hundredth time about calling the police, but didn't know what to say to them. Was Braithe still at the same hotel they stayed at, or had she left and gone somewhere else? Rainy was half-asleep when her phone pinged.

She wanted it to be Grant. But when she lifted the phone to her face, the text was from Braithe.

Tattling to Tara, it said.

Rainy dropped the phone, chills running up her arms. She shook her hands out like something nasty had touched them. That was fast. Tara must have shot some hot-worded text to Braithe's phone right after she'd spoken to Rainy.

You two having trouble? She was stalling, trying to think of what to ask next. Maybe if she knew where Braithe was, she could call someone to check in on her.

I only know Tara through her insipid social media posts. And the screenshots. Did you know that little Braithe has organized folders of her friends' texts?

Who are you?

Now that's a good question.

Prove that you're not Braithe. Send me a voice text.

I don't have to prove anything to you.

You want my attention, so you do actually.

Lol

She waited while the dots appeared again, shaking her foot from side to side as she started at the screen.

The voice memo appeared. It was three seconds long. Rainy hit Play.

"Hello, Rainy."

She stood up, holding her hand over her own mouth; the room seeming to hum around her in a silent panic.

The voice was male. The voice was male. The voice was male.

"Fuck," Rainy said. Then she started typing, her thumbs stiff with fear.

Where is Braithe?

Here with me ☺

Who are you?

Greetings, fellow bondservant! This is Paul!

Paul who? Am I supposed to believe you're some rando who kidnapped my friend?

She was digging her fingernails into her palms, eyes tightly shut. He was addressing her in a way that was...familiar. A coil of a sentence misted through her brain, but when she reached for it, it was gone. Was this happening? This was happening. Her body felt wired. Her phone pinged, the sound violent in her ears. Paul had sent his response:

That's the question, Rainy! Now you're getting somewhere. Who. Am. I.

She tossed her phone on the bed, frustrated.

Paul was a Biblical name, one of the most important figures in the New Testament. What else did she know? *Think. He was Saul before he was Paul...that's right...*

She paced in small circles, her brain really whirring now.

He was a persecutor of the first church until he had a con-
version experience on the road to Damascus, after which he
became Paul. None of this made sense.

Paul who was converted on the road to Damascus, or
Paul the Beatle, or are you your own fucked-up type of
specialty Paul?

Choices, choices…

Okay…so what do you want?

Now that's an interesting question! You're really on a
roll here.

Stop fucking around, you're wasting my time.

☺ ☺ ☺On the contrary, you have all the time in the
world. Braithe does not.

Rainy tried calling, but Paul sent her to voice mail.
"Dammit!"

We're a little under the weather, Rainy. Let's stick with
texting for now.

Where are you?

But Paul didn't answer her question. Instead, the reply read,
I'm mostly up to date on Tara's and Braithe's texts. They never
did figure out why you were so averse to their little predatory
trip. Do you want to tell me? They spent hours talking about it
and I gotta admit—I'm curious ☺ ☺ ☺

Rainy made her way over to her laptop. She lifted the lid and typed in her password.

You tell me something about you and I'll tell you something about me.

When she hit Send, she thought she'd made a mistake. If someone truly had kidnapped Braithe, making him angry was the last thing she wanted to do. But everything about this guy's tone indicated he enjoyed banter. *But only if he has the upper hand*, she thought. That's how bullies worked. If she could keep his mood light, she might be able to get him to tell her something useful.

You like to play games! What a night you girls had playing games, wasn't it?

Were you watching?

No. But I got the firsthand account from Braithe, and boy is that girl a talker when she is drunk. Yowza!

Braithe had gone to a bar the second night alone, hadn't she? So, whoever this guy was, he'd positioned himself to meet her.

Where'd you meet?

That's not important. What's important is what I know.

She pressed her fists to her eyes, the coolness of her hands grounding her. She was hot and cold, scared and angry; every time this guy sent a text, the hairs on her arms stood up. **Which is what?** she sent back.

It was getting dark outside; she could see the indigo of the sky above the strip. For her, time seemed suspended in this nightmare, but below her the city throbbed, unknowing.

I know that Stephen has no idea that his perfect wife is so unhappy. I'm wondering how I should tell him...

Why are you telling me this? I don't care what you tell Stephen or anyone about Braithe. Are you a jilted lover, is that what this is? She rejected you and now you have her phone?

☺ ☺ ☺ Guess again. Think carefully, Rainy.

She tried logging into her Facebook account; it had been so long it took her three tries to guess the password. She'd added Braithe and the rest of the girls long ago when they used the app to share information about their get-togethers. Eventually, they'd switched to text, and she'd stopped going on altogether. She went to Braithe's profile and clicked on her friends; then, typing "Paul" into the search box, she waited for the results.

"Paul, Paul..." She tapped her fingers on the table as the computer filtered the results. There was no one named Paul among her friends. She went through Stephen's friends next, then Tara's, and finally Grant's. There were Pauls—one of them was an ex-professor both Grant and Stephen were friends with; he lived in Minnesota with his wife now. The other was a youngish guy in Stephen's friend list who turned out to be his cousin. When Rainy stalked the shit out of him she found out he was in Boston, going to college. He'd posted a photo of himself the night before at a bar with his friends. She checked out the bar before logging out of Facebook. She decided to say nothing else until Paul texted her again. She was going to need this as evidence…for the police. She searched "Saul," too, but that landed her similar results. Whoever he was, she was certain that neither moniker was his real name.

Someone had Braithe, and police would take her seriously when they saw the texts, heard his voice. "You have to call the police," she said out loud. "Right now."

But she didn't. Had Braithe been missing for twenty-four hours? Police wouldn't do anything until then; she'd listened to enough *Dateline* specials to know that. If she was actively texting people from her phone, could she be considered missing or in danger?

You are the reason she's here. And if I make her dead, that will be your fault, too.

Wow. I guess I can put being gaslit by a psychopath on my résumé.

Also: *Make her dead?* The guy's phrasing drifted from Biblical to preschool.

It was a few minutes before he texted back, and she wondered if what she'd texted had made him angry. There were three types of people as far as Rainy was concerned: the people who knew who they were, the people who didn't and the people who didn't want to. She fell into the last category, marked by an early life that included shame conditioning. Rainy had no idea who she really was. She was just existing, making art about her untapped feelings. And did she want to know what type of monster those years had created—a monster she ignored and kept guarded? Nope. But guys like this: they either relished it or denied it was there.

Don't you want to know what she told me, Rainy? About her and your guy?

Cold dread blew through her chest and gusted out of her mouth in an exhale. *Three years. You've only known Grant for three years.* Had he been lying to her all this time? No. Why would he ask her to move out to Washington if there was someone else? Was it because Braithe was married?

She pressed all ten of her fingers onto her forehead; she would have known if something was wrong between her and Grant. If he was in love with someone else, he would have been…off. There would have been tells…or had there been, and she'd been too distracted to notice? No. Paul was just baiting her.

There is nothing between them.

The dots appeared immediately; he'd been waiting for this, waiting to drop the next bomb.

She was waiting for rebuttal text, but what came through was a voice recording. Rainy clicked on it and was immediately met with the sound of Braithe's voice.

"We went away together. It was before her. My husband was away for work, and so we just drove through the border and went to Canada for the weekend, you know? It was really romantic, and I thought…I thought that that was it, he wanted to be with me, and I'd leave Stephen."

Rainy's breath hitched; the sandwich she'd eaten for lunch felt heavy in her belly. She didn't want to hear more, but she couldn't not hear it; the weight of Braithe's words clutched her throat and squeezed.

Braithe's voice broke off, and for a second, Rainy thought that the recording was over, and then Braithe's voice came back, weaker this time—she was crying. *"But then when we came back, he pretended like it didn't happen. He... I don't know..."* Her voice was so wet with emotion Rainy found herself holding her breath, waiting for what she would say next.

But then another voice spoke, and it was male. *"Made you think you were going to be together and then abandoned you?"*

"Yes," Braithe said.

"Why do you think he did it?"

Rainy could hear the tinkling of glasses and the sound of other voices in the background. Was this the bar where Braithe had gone after they parted ways that night?

When Braithe spoke again, her voice sounded hard, cold. Could the woman who had always been so kind to her, so inclusive, have secretly hated her? It was too much to process. Rainy would have to sit down and unpack every memory she had with the woman. Myriad emotions bloomed in her chest. *She was obviously trying to get close to you for other reasons, those reasons being Grant, like Tara said*, Rainy thought, squeezing her eyes closed.

"Because he's the type of guy who thinks he owes everyone...my husband is his best friend," she said. *"He could never hurt him. His new partner is an artist. She moved her whole life for him. He's never going to up and leave her."*

It was true. Braithe was right.

She saved the voice clip to listen to later. Right now, he wanted a reaction, and she was going to give it to him.

She could be talking about anyone, she sent back.

He sent another audio message, this one shorter than the first. Braithe's voice was slurred.

"I said that to Grant, I told him exactly how I felt."

It wasn't just the use of Grant's name, but rather the familiarity of how Braithe used it that sent a chill through Rainy. Did she have any memories of them behaving oddly together?

She searched her mind, but came up with none. She'd always thought Braithe and Stephen were the perfect couple, and she'd never seen so much as a crack in their relationship. *But you weren't looking.*

But more importantly, how had Paul captured Braithe? All this talk of Braithe and Grant was a distraction. How long had he been watching; what else did he know about their group? The thought was terrifying.

He's been waiting for something like us to play with, Rainy thought. He was creating situations to feed on, and their group had been there at the right time. What would he do if she refused to play his games?

I'm calling the police.

☺ What will you tell them?

She had to think about that for a minute. So far, all she had for evidence were a bunch of texts from Braithe's number. Coy, playful texts were not a cause for alarm. All of Braithe's other friends believed she was blowing off marital steam. He had isolated her from them with texts. It was actually brilliant.

Hate to tell you this, but you're the reason she's here, Summer. And no one is going to believe you. By the time you get them to believe you I'll have cut through her vocal cords.

Rainy went cold.

She stared at her phone for a long time, unmoving. *Summer.* He knew. He had Braithe, but this wasn't about her at all. And he didn't say he would kill her; he'd specifically said *cut through her vocal cords.* He was telling her he had a plan. Whoever he was, he was here for her. No matter what Braithe had or hadn't done, she couldn't let her die at the hands of someone who was after...

Summer.

Taured. Or was it? After all these years, she knew his tone, his style. This was not Taured. But what did he want? As she sat, trying to fight the fog in her brain, it occurred to her. A fragment of an idea began to form in her mind. *Sara*. She opened up a browser on her laptop.

Okay, she texted back. **What do you want?**

23

Then

She'd woken in a hospital room alone, not afraid, but relieved. O'Connor was in the room, sitting in a chair, and a man stood next to her, this one short, bespectacled and bald.

"May I have something to drink, please?" Her voice was a rasp. A nurse brought her water and sat her up in bed. Then O'Connor turned to her. "Summer, this is Dan Malari. He's a social worker with the state and he's been assigned your case."

"What case? I have grandparents, I told you their names. I—"

"It's just procedure to open a case file, Summer. When there are accusations and a removal of a minor from a home, we have to investigate for your well-being." Dan Malari didn't smile at her when he spoke, but Summer felt that he was an okay guy, anyway. There was something calm about him.

"But I don't have to go back there?"

"No, you've been removed from that place and it is currently under investigation."

Summer felt like she could breathe for the first time since... when? Forever. She could breathe so long as they never sent her back to that place. She touched her neck and felt bare skin. "Where's my mother's necklace?"

"I'm sure they're keeping it safe for you. They might have taken it off while making sure you were okay."

If it was gone... Her face bunched up and she dissolved into tears.

"What about my mother? Will they be investigated for what they did to her?"

"What did they do to her?"

"They locked her in a room and killed her."

"How? With what?"

"She didn't take drugs, no matter what anyone says. I know she didn't. They injected her against her will."

He looked embarrassed for her, but he nodded slowly. "We'll let the coroner do their job, okay? My job is to find out where the safest place for you is."

Summer closed her eyes; the safest place for her was with her mother.

"If there was foul play involved in her death, police will move forward with an investigation."

Summer looked at O'Connor and the woman nodded; she didn't feel good about that, but she didn't feel bad, either. Things were still in the air, as her dad used to say.

"What if they can't prove foul play?" she asked carefully.

"Then there is no case," O'Connor said matter-of-factly. Summer nodded, settling back into her pillow.

"Good news is, your grandparents are on their way. They should be here in a few hours," Dan said.

"I'll be able to live with them?"

"Yes."

She didn't know how it started; suddenly, she was gasping, and then the gasps hurt so much that she couldn't get around them, or around her own air, which somehow seemed to be pressing into her. A nurse rushed in and her two visitors stepped back. She could only hear her own gasps, feel her own feelings, but the last thing Summer saw before she sank heavily into unconsciousness was O'Connor mouthing the words: *You're safe now, it's okay. You're safe now, it's okay...*

After her mother died, Summer's body had been physically free of the compound, but her mind had stayed trapped behind its walls. For a while, her grandparents tried to get Summer to work with a specialist who dealt with former cult members, but she'd refused to speak to him, saying it wasn't her who'd been part of the cult but her mother. She'd only been a kid. She'd screamed this at the grief counselor until he'd smiled and said they were finally getting somewhere. When her free counseling ended, her grandparents shifted her from therapist to therapist, trying to find someone to coax her out of her depression. But no one could understand what she was feeling, and she didn't want them to. It was her private hurt.

Her therapist suggested she get a part-time job, and her grandparents latched on to the idea, citing all the opportunities that came with having a job. They also offered to buy her a used car to get to and from work, which was the only reason she agreed. A car meant freedom, and that was a precious commodity. She got a job at a local restaurant, busing tables and then later working as a server. The tips were good and she had nothing to spend her money on, so she saved it. What else was there to do? Summer had gone over the options, things like cheerleading and chess club, and the sport that must not be named—softball. She had no interest in doing things that normal kids did; nothing brought her joy. In the morning, she'd drive to school, and after school she'd drive to work, from work it was home: easy-peasy.

On nights when she didn't work, she sat between Mark and Gilda as they watched their shows: the news (so they could bemoan the wickedness of the younger generations), *The 700 Club* (Pat Robertson was her grandma's crush) and *Dr. Quinn, Medicine Woman* reruns. It was her favorite time and not because she enjoyed the content. No, Summer daydreamed during those hours, hands pressed between her knees, her eyes glazed over. She thought of who she was going to be next, and where she was going next, and most importantly, she thought of all the things she wanted to do to Taured to punish him for killing her mother. She used whatever they were watching on TV to come up with her fantasy: if Pat Robertson was talking about the fires of hell, that's where Summer would send him. If Sully was bitten by a rattlesnake, Summer would have Taured bitten by one, as well, but instead of saving him, as the brave Dr. Quinn would have, she'd watch him die, writhing on the floor in pain. It was nice, better therapy than the therapy, if she were honest.

After the shows, she'd fall into her mother's old bed and sleep deep and heavy, momentarily sated with revenge. And that's how it went.

When Summer graduated high school, she legally changed her name to Lorraine Ives—her mother's maiden name, which she shortened to Rainy—and moved to New York. Her grandparents wrote to her regularly, folding a religious tract into each card or letter they sent. Rainy kept every piece of Christian propaganda in a shoebox in her closet because she thought her mom would find that funny. Shortly after her graduation, Mark and Gilda died, within eight months of each other.

She enrolled in art school after a year of working the New

York restaurant scene, using the money from the sale of her grandparents' house for her first year's tuition. Rainy was not an artist; Taured had cared about educating the young ones with his skewed view of the Bible, art falling very low on his list of accepted activities. But art was the way people gave voice to truly important things. When she'd walked through MoMA for the first time, she'd felt like every cell in her body had come to life. You could say anything you wanted to— anything at all, and hide its meaning between layers of paint, or in the bend of metal, or in the folds of performance art. During her visit, Rainy had overheard two friends discussing an exhibit, which consisted of a piece of linen wrapped around a rope.

"I swear to God I can't wait until this class is over. What the hell does Campsey want us to say about this. I cannot..." The taller of the two unhooked her arm from her friend's and went over to examine the display, getting so close Rainy swore her nose brushed against the rope.

"It says nothing. I hate it." The girl backed up, joining her friend, who was draped over her phone, not even looking.

Rainy couldn't disagree with her more. Both the rope and the linen had been created from the same fabric, yet each was woven into a distinct texture, and then they had been wound around each other. She'd gone back to the room she rented and Googled Professor Campsey on her laptop as she ate pickle chips from a bag. Daniel Campsey taught at NYU. In his photo on the college website, he had a round face with two rosy spots high on his cheeks that made it look like he was wearing blush. He looked like a shaved Santa Claus, and she wanted to take one of his classes. It was a gut feeling, and since she was living on those lately, she licked her fingers clean of pickle crumbs and filled out an online application.

When Rainy found out that she was accepted, there was

no one to tell. She wrote a letter to Taured detailing her life after the loss of her mother. The letter was six pages long; she burned it in the kitchen sink after she reread it, ashamed both of how weak she sounded and that her first instinct had been to write him at all. She didn't want to send Taured a letter detailing her hurt; she wanted to make him hurt back.

There had indeed been an investigation into her mother's death, but Taured's people had protected him, backing up the story that her mother was mentally ill and had overdosed on drugs, either accidentally or on purpose. There was no way to prove that she had been injected against her will. The community was asked why they hadn't contacted anyone for help about Lorraine's drug addition, and Taured had said that they hadn't known; Lorraine had taken great pains to hide it from everyone. Her death had been ruled an accident, and Taured got away with it—all of it. The only thing he didn't get was Rainy herself: the courts had ruled that she would stay with her grandparents. He'd never gotten her back. She knew how enraged that would make him.

She took classes slowly, while working forty hours a week at a sports bar, serving beer and burgers to the late-night crowd. Nothing fit quite like the feel of welding iron. At first, the idea of spitting fire at metal seemed like hot, heavy work. But despite her reservations, she'd loved it, and had taken more classes, choosing metal sculpture for her senior project, a depiction of inner self using an outer medium. She chose to make a full-body sculpture of herself as an old woman, using reclaimed metal. She wanted to show not who she was in her current state, but who she would be. It took her months just to find the pieces of metal she wanted to work with, scouring junkyards and old construction sites. She hoarded scrap metal for months, stacking it against the wall in her bedroom. When it was finally time to start working, she sketched drawings of herself as she thought she'd be in fifty years. Nothing was working, and she couldn't get it right until one day she realized that she needed to go deeper than skin. She stripped her sculpture of its topical flesh and started making a figure out of muscle. She hadn't wanted to make something beautiful, as so many of her classmates had; rather, she wanted to make something so ugly it was a warning. At the end of a grueling ten months of work, Rainy submitted her piece: a five-foot-five statue of her seventy-year-old self, her back rigidly straight, but the muscles on her arms sagging low in hammocks of flesh as she gripped a walking stick that looked like a baseball bat.

Her senior project made it into the school's yearly art show and a reporter was there to do a write-up. He'd interviewed her and asked to take a photo of her standing next to her work; when she'd refused to be in the photo, he'd taken one of her hand touching the hand of the sculpture instead. He called the piece *A Millennial View of Self* and put the photo of Rainy's hand reaching for her sculptures alongside the article.

She never could pinpoint what it was about the piece that captured the art world so suddenly, and she didn't have time to think on it. Suddenly, Rainy's sculpture was on the front page of the art section in the *Times* and interview requests began to pour in. Her first commission after she graduated was for the public library and was put directly in the vast lobby with a plaque with her name on it. *Caught Up in Books* is what she called it: a ten-foot tornado of books hurtling in every direction. It was a whirlwind of fame and acclaim that could never be attached to her real name or her face. She'd never allowed a photo of herself to be taken, in case he were to see it. What would he do after all these years if he saw her photo in some magazine? But still, she lived in fear, walking in the shadows in case he noticed her. How angry it made her on some days that she had to live her life both without her mother and constantly looking over her shoulder. But she wasn't angry enough to not be scared.

24

Now

Rainy stared out the window at the gaudy lights and the silent desert beyond. Beside her, on the seat, sat her phone.

I'm going to kill her. You'd better come if you want to save her, the text had read.

She looked up at the cabdriver. "If you could drop me off a couple blocks away, I'd appreciate it." She looked down at her hands as they shook in her lap, the chipped red nail polish reminding her of her mother.

A brief nod from the driver and the car veered sideways. It was too early for the city to be beautiful; Vegas was a moon child, and under the sun's microscope, she looked like costume jewelry. Hands pressed between her knees, she stared at the Bellum, the crawl of it toward the sky. A vertical tomb.

Go to the Bellum Hotel. Wear dark leggings and a yoga

top, no bra. Tight clothes with no pockets. I don't want
to have to pat you down.

Her dread was feasting on her thoughts, a dark dive into
all the ways this could go wrong. She'd bought the top on
the strip: sleeveless, with a high neck. *I don't want to have to
pat you down.* He liked to toy with women, hurt them, but
what he was doing wasn't sexual, she was convinced of that.
Rainy—Summer—knew the verbal cues of a sexual preda-
tor; the way interaction with them made you feel violated
and probed without ever being touched. She'd always got that
feeling from Taured; that's why her gut told her this wasn't
him. Nothing about Paul gave her pervert vibes; no, he was
creatively angry. She had a theory, and she'd checked the articles about Sara and Feena on her laptop from the hotel: neither of them had been sexually assaulted. He wasn't a rapist,
he was a murderer.

The car reached the curb.

Overthinking is not a practical thing for an impulsive person to do.
Fifteen years of therapy had trained the impulse to ask permission, to wait in a corner like an eager but well-trained dog.
But for fifteen years, her fury had been closing in, and now
there was nowhere to go but into the impulse.

Rainy slid cash through the window slot.

"No change."

The driver held up his hand in thanks and she slipped out,
dragging her duffel with her.

She looked down at her phone, at the last text he'd sent her.

At seven p.m., go to the buffet at the Greenery. There
you'll find a room key. You'll know it when you see it. Go
into the room, drink what I've left you, then lie on the
bed. If anything happens to me, no one will be able to

find Braithe in time to save her life. So before you act, remember that you're not the one in control. One wrong move and she's dead. I am the only one with access to Braithe.

She was breathing through her mouth: in and out, trying to calm herself. Paul, Paul—the name bothered her. Had she known a Paul at the compound? But again...there was no way he was using his real name. She supposed Taured could still be behind all of this, luring her here with one of his guys, but somehow, it didn't feel that way to Rainy. Paul was acting on his own anger, playing his own game. The men who did Taured's bidding weren't witty or explosive: they were reliable soldiers.

She stopped at a Quick Mart two blocks away, gathering what she needed and dropping it on the counter in front of a stoop-shouldered woman whose name tag read Susan and who looked bored. At the last minute, she ran back to the fridge to get water and an energy drink. The bottle with the yellow label caught her eye—the one the bartender had shown her. Something was loosening in her memory, but she couldn't quite grasp it yet. Grabbing the bottle of coffee syrup, she carried it to the register with her drinks. "I'll have a pack of Capris, a lighter and that phone," Rainy said, pointing, and pulling out her cash. Sad-looking Susan turned to grab the cigarettes and phone from the back wall. She looked at the coffee syrup with interest before sliding it into the bag with the box of Band-Aids, the phone and the drinks.

"Want these out?" She held up the cigarettes and lighter and Rainy nodded.

"I don't actually want to buy the coffee syrup. I just have kind of a weird question about it. And do you get a lot of regulars over here from the hotel staff?"

"Oh, yeah." She looked over at Rainy and annoyance lined

her face just as much as the sun had. "They treat this place like it's their lunchroom. It's cheaper to buy stuff over here, you know? So they stop on the way in and on the way out."

Rainy pursed her lips, nodding slowly. "Anyone come in here to buy this coffee syrup on the regular?" Rainy had that feeling again: it was the mist that kept showing up in her head, the mist she couldn't see through. The bartender hadn't been the only guy she'd known who drank that syrup. The compound had been a mecca for weirdos from all over America, and one of those weirdos had that bottle at the compound.

"Yeah, there are a couple guys who love that stuff. Say you can't find that brand anywhere else around here."

"Yeah? The guys ever heard of Amazon?"

Susan found that remark hilarious and her face didn't look so sad anymore. She winked at Rainy before slipping the lighter into the paper bag without ringing it up. Rainy could be generous, too. And since they were playing that game…

"Hey, do you happen to know their names? The guys who buy the syrup."

Susan frowned as she studied the lotto tickets thoughtfully. "They come in here separately. I don't think they know each other."

"Oh," Rainy said.

Susan was looking at her differently now, eyeing her almost regretfully. She was sad Susan again. Rainy was disappointing her.

"I'm not a cop or anything," Rainy added.

"Yeah, like I haven't heard that one before." Susan looked put off, so Rainy slid over the fifty dollars she'd been palming, the bill she'd marked. It was like the movies, but with no promise of the outcome: Susan could spit in her face. To her relief, the money disappeared beneath Susan's palm.

"There's, like, four restaurants in there. Don't know which

one he's at. He never stops talking. Told me he's using the stuff in some of the drinks he makes. The other one doesn't say much, just buys a couple things—the syrup, energy drinks and candy bars—and is on his way. Happy?"

"Not yet." Rainy stepped aside to let a family carrying chips and sodas check out. "What does the other guy—the one who's not the bartender—look like?"

The father of the chip-and-soda family side-eyed her as he swiped his card and his wife said something to him in a language Rainy thought might be Russian. She glanced at Rainy before ushering her children out the doors to wait for their father.

Susan waited for the man to leave before her head snapped toward Rainy. She wasn't in friendly mode anymore.

"You're going to get me in trouble."

"Then answer fast and I'll be on my way."

She shrugged. "He's, like, a few inches taller than you. White like a vampire. Black hair, light eyes. He's just a guy." The look on her face said, *Get the fuck outta here.*

But Rainy couldn't do that just yet. This was an information-gathering mission. If she didn't get enough of it, or get it right, she'd die.

"Anything special about him?"

Susan blew air out of her mouth with a *pffft* sound.

"Yeah," she said. "He drinks that coffee syrup."

Rainy smirked. "What about any tattoos?"

That got a little pause. "No," she said finally. "No tattoos. But his roots were showing like he hadn't dyed his hair in a bit…and they were light."

"Hey, thanks," Rainy said. She ducked out of the store. That would have to be enough.

Her duffel slung across her back, Rainy lit a cigarette and walked along the shrubbery-lined walk that led to the back alley of the Bellum. She hadn't smoked since New York—she'd given it up for Grant—but the rush of acrid smoke filling her lungs had a dangerous *welcome home* quality. Slipping through the gap in the fence that divided the gas station from the hotel, she noticed a couple strands of blond hair clinging to one of the fence prongs. She wasn't the only one who'd noticed the shortcut advantage. She wondered if Paul went to work this way, buying his coffee syrup and slinking off to stalk women. She choked down smoke as she surveyed the back end of the grand Bellum Hotel; like everything in Vegas, it was garish, hideous in the daylight. Without the night and the oozing neons to disguise the ugly, the sun revealed it for everything it was—loading docks, the stench of trash rotting in the heat, and construction. Rainy smoked two cigarettes before she kicked off from the wall, spitting down a grate as she walked over it. That was the part she hated: the trash-mouth aftertaste. Slowing down, she realized that people were coming and going from the docks; she caught a glimpse of a long hallway as a woman slipped outside through a service door and pulled a pack of Marlboroughs from her apron pocket.

"Here…" Rainy offered her a light before she could find one of her own. The woman eyed her suspiciously but took it, anyway, never taking her eyes off Rainy as she rolled the wheel and the flame licked her cigarette to life.

"Thanks, I always forget mine in my bag," she said, frowning. "You looking for a job? Because there's a right way and a wrong way to do things and you can't go sneaking around the back—"

"I'm looking for a person actually."

The woman sucked twice on her cigarette, and then paused to flick something off her lips. She didn't look at Rainy when she said, "Who is it, then?"

"Just a guy." She shrugged. "I need to find him."

She rolled her eyes. "You're going to have to give me more than that. Hundreds of people work here."

Rainy shrugged. "His first name is Paul, I don't know the rest."

"Oh God," she sighed. "We got a lotta Pauls at the Bellum. Is he, like, a server, a manager or what?"

Rainy shook her head. "I'm not sure."

"We have a Paul who's a line cook, and another four of them front of house that I know personally. Oh, and I drink with some of the housekeepers after work and they call the maintenance guy Vucifer—Vegas Lucifer, get it?—but I think his real name's Paul." She dropped her cigarette butt and started walking for the door marked with a big number twelve.

"Wait! Are any of them from the east coast? Or does he, like…drink coffee syrup?"

The woman's hand froze on the door handle. Rainy thought she looked a little nervous when her head swiveled around to look at her. "Yeah," she said quickly. "And he's a mean man."

She was about to lose the woman, and she still had items on her fucked-up shopping list.

"Hey, do you think you could get something from Barry for me?"

She whipped around pretty fast, arms crossed over her chest. Rainy hadn't expected that. Suddenly, her new friend looked hostile.

"Are you fucking with me? Are you?"

"Nope." Money was the universal soother. Rainy pulled two hundred dollars out of her pocket and held it up for her to see. "This is for you. All you have to do is get something for me from Barry. When you bring it to me, I'll give you two hundred more, plus the cost of the product."

"How do I know you're not a cop?"

"How do I know *you're* not a cop?" Rainy shrugged. "I'd

be a real cunt to do that to a woman who was just trying to make a living, right? What does a cop gain from a middleman like you? All I want is what's on this list—just take a look." She extended her receipt from the Quick Mart on which she'd scribbled three words.

"It's a four-hundred-dollar gamble," Rainy said. "This is Vegas."

The woman took the list and the money and disappeared inside wordlessly. *She won't come back*, Rainy thought. *She's going to take the two hundred and split.* The door opened when two male housekeepers stepped out to smoke…or sample Barry's wares. They took one look at her, sitting against the wall, swore profusely and went back inside. Thirty minutes later, when Rainy was convinced she'd been ghosted, the door opened again. Rainy stood up, smiling. The woman wordlessly handed her a tiny envelope.

"You're a lifesaver," Rainy said, handing her the rest of the bills.

The woman nodded curtly and disappeared through the door again.

"You're definitely a New Englander, Paulie." She typed a few notes into her phone and sent a text before making her way back to the front of the Bellum. Ditching her phone in the trash can out front like he'd told her to do, she stood in eyesight of the lobby and waited, counting to two hundred. He'd wanted to see her do it, then he wanted to have time to get away. She searched their faces: the comers and goers, the staff—there were too many bodies, too many options.

Fuck, fuck, fuck, said her heart.

She walked in.

At seven o clock, Rainy went to the buffet. She scanned the bodies at the various hot stations and spun around to look at the salad bar, where a line of gray-haired ladies was calling out to each other about cottage cheese. There were people everywhere, walking in twos, threes and fours. Rainy felt numb with a side of nausea. Grabbing a plate, she got in line, trying not to look at mounds of mayonnaise salad, keeping her eyes peeled for whatever Paul intended for her to see. Staff were positioned around the room in sparkling dinner jackets, looking ready to jump into action or song. It was a lot to keep track of. No wonder this was where he'd sent her; there was too much chaos for her to watch everything that was going on. He could be anywhere, posing as anyone. Rainy's plate was still empty as the line crawled past the lettuce. She grabbed spinach with the tongs, her gaze carefully combing the area. This was stupid—ridiculous. What if he was toying with her? The ache of anxiety riding in her chest crested when there was nothing significant near the trays of onions and cucumber, and she thought of the message again; he'd told her to go through the buffet lines, and that she'd know what she was seeing when she was seeing it. She had no clue what that was supposed to mean, except that he was in charge and she had to do what he said. *For now*, she told herself. That made her feel better, the idea that she was just playing his game until she could play her own.

There was no sign of anything weird at the meat-cutting stations, so she turned left toward the soup, and then there it was: her name on a placard above one of the lidded soup containers: *Rainy Chowder*. Rainy peered closer, thinking that maybe it was a coincidence, but the script on the first word was slightly smaller than the second. It was an envelope, small and white, stuck to the top of the placard. She pulled it off to reveal the *Corn*. The envelope fit comfortably into her palm. Rainy abandoned her plate on a trolley of dirty dishes and walked straight for the door.

She didn't open the envelope until she was safely in a bath-room stall. Her name was written with black marker in near-perfect script. She turned it over and used her nail to open the envelope, sliding out a rectangular room card. Handwritten in the bottom corner in permanent marker was the number 447. She was to go there now. He was probably watching her. She felt suddenly exposed, the stall around her flimsy pro-tection. She signed into her email account from the burner phone, found the draft she'd been working on. What she had on the phone was her version of a police composite: what she thought he looked like, where she thought he worked, where he was from, where he'd instructed her to go. With more time, she could have tracked him down herself, but with Braithe's life hanging in the balance, she had to trust the job to someone else.

And she did. If she trusted him to be able to do anything, it was this: find what he wanted, what he'd believe to be his. Paul had left a trail, albeit a small one, but it might be enough. She added one last line to the end of her email. It was more of a hopeful line, a hunch. If she couldn't pull it off, he'd be looking for the wrong person.

He'll have a broken nose, she typed. She sent the email, then threw the burner phone in the tampon disposal.

Reaching for the box of Band-Aids, she began to work.

The first letter from Taured had come to her apartment in New York. It was on his official church stationery and her first instinct upon opening the envelope was to toss it away from her as far as it would go. But she hadn't; she'd clutched the paper in her closed fist until she felt ready to read it. She read the letter the same way she would read the five others he sent shortly after, with all the lights in the apartment on and her gun sitting on the counter in front of her. Loaded. How had he found her?

His tone was friendly and light, the threats buried under Bible verses and zealous concerns about her well-being. Last he'd seen her, she'd been just a young girl, and now here he was, reading about her on the internet. She was famous! Hopefully, one day, they'd be able to catch up. The last part had given her nightmares for a week. If Rainy had shown that letter to the police, they would have cocked an eyebrow at her and asked what the problem was. You had to know his language, understand the euphemisms he so often used to dig out what he was really saying:

Hello, I'm still watching you.

She'd moved after that, subletting an apartment from a friend so her name wasn't attached to an address. The letters came to the galleries instead. Rainy would get calls saying a letter had arrived for her. It wasn't completely unheard of to receive correspondence through a gallery, thank God. Rainy would take a cab to go pick them up and carry them home unopened.

To prep herself to read them, she'd get very, very drunk. Most of them said the same thing: Taured marveling over her accomplishments, Taured saying he prayed for her, Taured saying he hoped to one day see her again. He ended the letters with: *Till He returns, Taured.*

She'd only started thinking about getting out of New York when she met Grant, flirting with the possibilities of a move to the Caribbean or perhaps Europe. The farther away, the better, and her art provided enough money for her to live well.

Grant had changed the course of her life, luring her to cold, rainy Washington instead. It had all happened so fast. And why? Because he loved her art? She had plenty of people who fawned over her, calling her gifted. But what mattered to Rainy was the way Grant accepted her for who she was in the moment.

Now, she stood in front of the room, her hand held to the door as if she were feeling for a heartbeat. Glancing around to make sure no one was watching, she slid the keycard into the slot, and a second later, the lock opened with a satisfying click. Was he here, somewhere just out of sight, watching her? *You are so fucking stupid*, she thought before pushing the door open and walking inside. Rainy stood, staring around at the empty room and contemplating the man who called himself Paul. He worked here. The room faced the service alley that ran alongside the hotel, a bleak stretch of tar bordered by a parking lot. She doubted these rooms were used by guests unless it was an emergency. To prove it, she walked over to the minibar and cracked open the door to the fridge. It was bare inside and smelled funny.

Next to the bed on the nightstand was a hotel glass filled with a milky-looking liquid. And propped against it was a typed note that said: *Drink me.* Rainy considered the liquid, holding it up to the light, and then smelling it. So was he the Cheshire Cat or the White Rabbit, and what was supposed to happen when she fell into his world? She knew he wouldn't kill her...not right away. He would want to stretch out the experience, really play with his toys. She didn't care, though, not enough to stop herself from tipping the glass to her lips and taking a few gulping sips; the taste was bitter. Psychological warfare had been Taured's specialty and Rainy had learned the rhythm and beat of it. If she didn't come, he was going to kill Braithe. She sat on the bed after she'd swallowed the last bit and waited to feel something.

She was awake. The room opened itself to her sideways, her face pressed against cold concrete. She licked her lips, which felt stiff and dry, and tried to sit up, but her limbs felt weighted. No, they weren't weighted but restricted: she was tied up. She'd been in the hotel room, and now she was in what looked like a very large, industrial-size kitchen. She could see the large metal doors of a fridge to her right, draped in plastic that been half pulled off. On her left were what looked like more fridges, only these had narrow doors. She wriggled her wrists and realized they were bound by handcuffs.

"Paul..." It was more of a wheeze than a shout. Rainy barely got his name out before she started coughing. As she spoke, she saw brown work boots walking toward her from the far end of the room. They stopped abruptly, close to her face. If she stuck out her tongue, she'd taste the toe of his right shoe. Tilting her head up toward the light and the owner of the boots, she got her first look at his face, her eyes water-logged from coughing.

Paul was long-faced, with skin the color and texture of sweaty American cheese. He had a nose for days: a nose you couldn't miss. How disappointed she was in Quick Mart Susan and her weak description. His hair was tucked under a beanie, but she could see the oily black strands of it curling at his neck. His face told a different story: a wiry beard hid the bottom half of his face, a tangle of reddish brown. She'd pin him right under thirty, but she couldn't be sure in this dim light. There was a meanness to his mouth, lips that didn't curve up or down but slashed a straight line under his beard. She couldn't see his eyes until he bent down to haul her into a sitting position. They were blue and very clear, like a Nevada sky staring back at her. How could something so evil have such beautiful eyes? *Who was he?* He was so familiar.

Her neck felt like it was made of cooked pasta. Her head bobbed on her shoulder and she got a good whiff of him. She could smell the fry oil on his skin, the grime of the kitchen.

She was grasping at something…what was it? He was a cook…
or maybe a server—*he could even be the manager*, she thought.
Unblinking, he studied her face as she studied his. The vein
in his temple was throbbing. Rainy could see it, fat and swollen beneath his skin like an earthworm. She kept the barest
hint of a smile on her lips but said nothing.

When he seemed satisfied, he stood up and she was looking at the dark blue knees of his jeans. He backed away rather
than turning around and she understood why: he held a phone
at chest level and was taking photos of Rainy where she sat
handcuffed to the steel leg of the table.

She was angry, she wanted him to stop taking photos, but
she couldn't find the words to say so. She tried to hold up her
hand, to block her face from his camera where a line of drool
hung lazily from her lower lip, but it was chained to the leg
of the table.

"What are you doing?" She slumped forward and the handcuffs bit into her wrists. He was tall—six feet, maybe—and
narrow in the chest. When he was finished taking his photos,
he set his phone down on one of the metal tables. He leaned
back, crossing his legs at the ankles, smiling at her pleasantly
like she was a visitor. He was wearing a plain black T-shirt
and his arms, which were crossed over his chest, were lean
and muscular.

"I'm surprised you came." He said this casually, as if they
were having lunch. "And I'm not exactly sure why you came,
to be honest, especially after this one—" he jabbed a thumb
over his shoulder "—has been trying to steal your man."

Her eyes followed his gesture. There were two stainless-
steel prep tables bolted to the floor in a T shape. Rainy's hands
were handcuffed around the leg at the top left of the T while
another slumped figure—Braithe!—was handcuffed to the
bottom of the T, her back to Rainy.

"It's a restaurant. One of many. It's being renovated, and no one is here. So no one will hear you, I've made sure of that."

He stared at her, a little impatiently, Rainy noticed, waiting for her to give an explanation as to why she had come for Braithe. She wasn't going to. Braithe was clearly more heavily drugged than she was, but she was alive.

"Not in the mood to talk, I see." He started walking toward her with a bottle of water. Rainy watched him unscrew the cap. Paul held the lip to her mouth and she sucked up as much as she could before he pulled it away. His hands were ringless, his clothes mundane; there was nothing that would draw your attention if you passed him on a street.

"What did you give me?" Her voice was hoarse.

"What does it matter?"

Water dripped down her chin, and without the adrenaline pumping wildly at her decisions, she was afraid.

"Oh, I wanted to play," he continued. "As soon as you started texting our little Braithe here with your accusations, I wanted to play with you. I realized you were the reason she was even here. She's a little boring, if I'm telling the truth. I can see why our beloved Grant chose you."

Rainy blinked at him, wondering if Braithe was awake and had heard him say that.

"Well, now I'm here to play, so let her go."

"Oh, come on now. You didn't really think I'd do that? You're not a stupid girl, Rainy. Funny, though, I looked for you on the wonderful wide web and found next to nothing. No personal life, no particular place you grew up...no addresses. That couldn't be because you're lying about your real name, could it?"

Braithe looked up, her eyes glassy and unfocused.

"Maybe," Rainy said. "But what difference does it make to you?"

"I like to bond with my victims."

"Yeah? I knew a man who liked to bond that way, too."

He smiled and she saw the expensive dental work, porcelain veneers; her grandmother had had them. It was the first time a smile had lit up his eyes, and it was creepy. She recognized her mistake: he was trying to throw her off-balance, make her so emotional she couldn't think clearly.

Rainy tried to keep her face neutral. He was smart, and she needed to be smarter.

"Where is he now, little liar Rainy, and what is your real name?"

"Fuck you. You obviously know what my real name is. You texted it to me." Rainy spat at his feet and he smiled without malice. "But you're not using your real name, either. You obviously have a connection to the compound." But he didn't answer her, just continued to smile beatifically. Obviously, he wasn't going to explain anything to her. At least, not until he was ready. He looked past her to Braithe and made kissy noises at her.

"This one has been such an angel. I'm not used to all this spice. You're like a little hot pocket, aren't you?"

"Did your daddy talk to you like that? No...that's not right," Rainy said slowly. "It was your mama, wasn't it? That's why you hate women."

Paul's smile froze. He took three jerky strides to Rainy and she felt the sting of his hand as he slapped her clean across the face. He caught her lip and she felt it split open like ripe fruit. Braithe moaned from somewhere behind her and Rainy heard the rattling of handcuffs on the table leg.

Paul stood over her, his clear blue eyes clouded. Rainy watched him clench and unclench his fists like he was trying to pump his anger out of them. She felt strangely calm, or perhaps it was the drugs—either way, she stared on impassively as Braithe began to cry softly from her end of the table.

He was thin, thinner than most men of his height, but what struck Rainy most were the veneers. An eating disorder would cause the signs of malnutrition on Paul's face, and she'd bet his teeth were rotting from years of bulimia before he shelled out the money for his Ronald Reagan teeth.

"Does it bother you to work with food when you have such an unhealthy relationship with it?" She'd won again; she could see it on his face. *Everyone from the compound has a fucked-up relationship with food.* He was bothered, his sallow skin flushing all the way to his eyeballs. He took another step toward her and stopped abruptly. Rainy could hear her own ragged, angry breath in the pause before he turned. She watched his sure strides toward Braithe and her stomach clenched.

Braithe couldn't keep her head up when Paul crouched down next to her. It bobbed upright for a minute and then settled back on her shoulder. There was a narrow window, high above where Braithe was tied; the light that filtered through made it look like she was wearing a yellow T-shirt. Rainy could only see the back of Braithe's head, but Paul was looking at Rainy as he leaned over the woman. He slapped her, hard, across the face. Braithe barely made a sound, which could mean she was too drugged to realize it had happened or it had happened so often she was used to it. Rainy kept her face impassive; she would not give him control that easily.

"Our little Braithe was sitting at the bar, drinking white wine like a bad cliché, when I showed up. Rocked your world, didn't I, B?"

Rainy made her face as wooden as possible as she listened to him; she wouldn't give him anything to work with if she could help it.

"You know what I thought when I saw her sitting there, Rainy?"

She didn't like the way he said her name, dragging out the *a, Ray-nee.*

"I thought, what a sad little queen bee, sitting on that stool in her cold shoulder blouse, looking like someone just broke her heart." Paul let all his features sag, mimicking what must have been Braithe's posture at the bar. *God,* thought Rainy, *why was Braithe in that bar that night?* Had she called Stephen, or had she just needed to get away?

"And someone had broken her heart, Ray-nee, that someone was your guy, wasn't it? Your Grant." He paused for her reaction, his narrow face turning serious with his tone.

His blue, fishy eyes studied Braithe, and he tilted his head to the side so that it matched the angle of hers. He looked like a puppet relaxed on its strings.

"Said she'd flown here from Washington with some girl-friends for a weekend getaway. So I asked what she wanted to get away from—" He clapped his hands twice, bouncing on one leg with the flair of a performer. *Of course,* Rainy thought: *Vegas, he's a showman.*

"She thought that was so, so funny. Do you know what she told me next, Rainy?"

"I can't wait for you to tell me, Paul," she answered dryly.

"She said she was there to call her ex, the man she was still in love with." Rainy swallowed; she wished she had water to cool the aching in her throat. How long had she been here? Paul stared at her, his eyes mesmerizing.

"She took your little game as a sign, you see? And then the psychic...you girls just had to stop to talk to that cracked nut, didn't you?" He tapped a closed fist to the side of his head, clicking his tongue.

"It's not my business who she's in love with. It's not recip-rocated."

"Well, see there, that's what I thought, as well—this poor, delusional woman who arranged this...special weekend so she could come to Vegas and have a psychic confirm her high school boyfriend was the one." He laughed, slapping his knee like it was the funniest joke he'd ever heard, and then he suddenly became very serious.

"She showed me the text she was planning on sending him, you know..." He placed a hand over his heart, his bottom lip drooping out. "It was good, Rainy, that's all I'll say. Braithe should have been a writer."

"That's all you'll say, huh?" Somehow she really doubted that.

Paul grinned, making the motion of zipping his lips and throwing away the key.

From across the room Braithe moaned. Paul either didn't hear her or didn't care; he was engrossed in telling his story. "We had a toast together to celebrate, but I could tell she was nervous the whole time, waiting for Grant to text her back."

Rainy bit down on her tongue, forcing herself not to use it. She needed to hear him out, wanted to, but she was spitting angry that she was being forced to hear the truth from a sociopath instead of Grant. And how much of the truth was he actually giving her? Braithe wasn't conscious enough to contradict his story.

"He did text her back. Not right away, but his response was equally as thoughtful as hers."

She couldn't hold back for another second. The anger rose like vomit. "Fuck you!" If he didn't have her chained, she'd launch herself at him. "I need water," she said.

Paul shrugged. "Why should I give you water when you're being so very rude?"

"A dehydrated girl is no fun to play with, Paul."

He kicked off the fridge he was leaning against and Rainy gave a silent prayer of thanks when he pulled a bottle of water from the pack on the counter and casually walked over. She kept eye contact with him the whole time he held the bottle to her lips. Cold, mean chips of blue buried beneath a spray of blond lashes. They were unblinking as they watched her, like he didn't want to miss a second of her suffering. She was so, so close, but she couldn't quite place him yet.

She tried to drink slowly to give him less of a thrill, but she sucked down the whole bottle in seconds. He carried the empty bottle over to a garbage bag and tucked it inside, then he took a bottle over to Braithe. Rainy heard the seal on the lid snap before he bent over her with the water. She couldn't tell if Braithe was conscious enough to drink, but after a few seconds he stood up, setting the bottle on the table above her head. Was this really happening? *Yes, because you made it happen.* She didn't want to look at him. She'd been staring into his eyes less than twenty seconds ago and it had been a hollow experience. She suddenly felt exhausted. She leaned her head against the pole behind her and closed her eyes.

When she woke, the window on the wall above Braithe was dark. She had the strong urge to pee, and her mouth was so dry she had to work her tongue free of her teeth. What time was it? He must have put something in her water.

"Braithe...are you awake?" Her voice cracked; she scooted her butt forward in an attempt to get her blood moving and tented her knees. "Braithe...I need you to wake up," she called louder. No answer.

"Hey! Hey! Can anyone hear me? Help! Help!" She rocked against the table, trying to move it, but Rainy knew it was no use; it was bolted down. "Hey!" she yelled again. "Help us!

"Braithe!" she called. "Wake up! We need to get out of here."

"You can't." The words preceded his footsteps like he'd been just around the corner, listening. Rainy went so still she could hear her own raspy breath. A few seconds later, Paul walked into view, carrying a large paper bag that smelled of food.

"This—" he said, after setting the bag on the table that separated her from Braithe "—is in the new wing of the hotel. Construction is only set to resume in a few months, and by then we will be long gone, won't we, B?" He tossed his keys on the counter. "No one can hear you, Rainy—these professional kitchens are well insulated. Chefs like to be able to scream at their kitchen staff without the dining room hearing." As he spoke, he stacked containers on the table, his movements fast and jerky. Rainy could smell him from where she sat. Had he just left a shift?

She glanced at the window and saw that the sky was lightening to an indigo. When she looked over again, he was unlocking Braithe's handcuffs. He pulled her to her feet, where she swayed, unsteady, and then he led her to the food. Rainy watched as he sat her on a stool and placed a fork in her hand. It was the first time she was seeing Braithe's face since the night of the dinner. Her hair was still in the topknot she'd worn that night, but it sagged off the side of her head like a piece of fruit past its prime. A few strands had escaped their pins and hung limply around her face. She didn't have bruises, not that Rainy could see, but Braithe was so gray she matched the concrete floor. Her eyes looked swollen, but that could have been from crying. She didn't look up when Rainy said her name.

"She's so zonked out she doesn't know who you are," Paul said, stroking her head. She was staring down at whatever was in the container, the fork poised above it. "Go on, be a good girl and take a bite." When Braithe didn't move, he spoke again. "Hey! I'm talking to you, you ungrateful shit, eat! God!" Throwing his hands up, he paced behind her chair.

"You said it yourself, she's drugged. Untie me and I'll feed her."

"I don't think so," he said. "We've already been through this, Rainy." He took the fork from Braithe and speared something in the box. Braithe opened her mouth and Paul spooned what looked like pancakes through her lips. She chewed unenthusiastically, her eyes on the table. He handed her the fork and she took over, robotically.

"Braithe wouldn't eat at first, you see. She can be really stubborn, as I'm sure you know. Anyway, we came to a deal—she eats what I bring her, and I don't leave her in the freezer all day."

"You fucking psycho."

"Now, now, Rainy, it's right over there—" he pointed to his right and Rainy followed his gaze to two large steel doors with what looked like vault handles on the front "—waiting for a new bitch to freeze. You're up next!" he said cheerfully. "I brought you bacon and eggs."

He hummed as he unwrapped her food, setting it on the counter. He glanced over every few seconds to make sure Braithe was eating.

"I need to go to the bathroom," Rainy said.

Paul nodded. "Soon as she's done."

Rainy searched Braithe's face, looking for something—a message or a plea for help, anything—but her head remained bowed, her movements mechanical. Rainy sighed, frustrated.

When Braithe dropped her fork to signal that she was done, Paul led her to the bathroom, where she spent no more than five minutes. He had her handcuffed back at her spot with not a peep. She was as docile as a deer.

He came toward Rainy with his keys. As he crouched behind her, she felt the pressure on her shoulders ease and the
handcuffs release, and she was able to move her arms forward.
It took her a minute to get up, the feeling slowly moving back
into her limbs in needlelike pricks. Paul's presence behind her
made her move forward, her steps an awkward shuffle. She
didn't want him behind her, she needed to see what he was up
to. Glancing over her shoulder, she saw that he was smiling.

"Move," he said, shoving the barrel of the gun into the
small of her back.

"Did you see that in a movie?" she asked. The blow felt
sharp, and then wet; he'd struck her on the back of the head.
Rainy fell, sliding across the floor as her vision flashed to
bright white and then black. Was there blood? She felt for it,
and her fingers came away sticky.

"Get up. You have two minutes."

She did as she was told, pulling herself up by the bathroom
door handle and glancing back at him.

He was still smiling.

Rainy peed with her eyes closed. When she was finished,
she washed her hands and then wet a paper towel, dabbing it
on the back of her head as gently as possible. She was going
to have the king of headaches. When she walked out of the
bathroom, Rainy didn't think—she just walked toward him
until she was standing right in front of him. He was taller
than her, but only by a few inches. She took a natural stance,
tucking her head down and clenching her jaw. Then she said
something in barely a whisper. Paul cocked his head and then
leaned toward her to better hear her. "What was that?"

Rainy said it again, but only a fraction louder. The gun
hung limply at his side. His head dipped closer. Rearing her
head back, she repeated the rules to herself: if you went in
mouth gaping, you'd risk biting off your own tongue, and if

you weren't braced for impact, you could damage your neck. She snapped her head toward her target, using her body to propel her, aiming for his nose. She heard the crack before she felt it. Paul's first scream was muffled, the second loud and pained, but he moved quickly. Rainy didn't have time to move before the butt of the gun hit her in the temple. *So this is the way you die*, she thought as she fell.

She wasn't dead. She was cold and in pain. Sitting up, she groaned at the *wrongness* of the feeling in her head. It felt big and heavy, a dull ache dragged across her forehead and into the base of her skull. She'd hit Paul and he'd hit her back, but where was he? She scooted to a sitting position, leaning her head back. She was freezing. Duct tape stretched over her mouth, she supposed, as part of her punishment, since no one could hear her in here, anyway. She felt her internal panic clock ticking faster. The walls pressed in and Rainy dropped her chin to her chest and tried to be somewhere else, but her control was a paper town. The last time she'd been inside a walk-in freezer, she'd seen her mother's lifeless body. Did he know? Had he been there, too? She tried to think, but the pain in her head was as distracting as the cold.

Paul's blood was everywhere—her pants, the floor—and she knew that if she looked in a mirror, she would see it on her face. She could smell it. He was nowhere to be seen, though for all she knew he was out there beyond the freezer doors, doing something to Braithe in retaliation for what Rainy had done to his face. She squirmed against her bonds, but it was no use. *Conserve your energy, Rainy, think.* She could do that; she knew *how*. She'd spent the torturous hours in solitary, thinking. She hadn't checked out and she hadn't pretended to be somewhere else: that had been her time to examine what was happening to her and why. She swayed from side to side, eyes closed, doing her best to keep moving without exerting herself. *He knows how your mother died, he knows how Taured used to punish the women at the compound. He might even know that Sara helped you get away. Fuck*, she thought, and from deep in her subconscious, she began to remember.

Paul had been in Kids' Camp with her—she was sure of it. He had experienced similar atrocities, and he had become… this. She'd read about the murders as she sat in the hotel room: Sara's and Feena's. After Derek had told her that Sara had been murdered, it had occurred to her to Google Feena Wycliffe. There had been only two articles about Feena's death: the first had been after her body was found in her car at a concert venue. She'd been strangled from behind and left in her car. A security guard found her in the early hours of the next morning. Police had asked the public for help, urging them to come forward if they had seen anything. The next article was published on the one-year anniversary of the murder. Still, police had nothing: no DNA, no fingerprints. All Feena's friends had alibis, and since Feena's purse and wallet were still in the car, undisturbed, the police could only conclude the motive was personal, but they had no idea what it was. According to her friends, she hadn't had a boyfriend or love interest.

Surely, if they'd questioned Feena's friends properly, they'd know about her time in the compound…unless, like Rainy herself, she'd never told them. That sounded more likely. She'd been living a new life somewhere else and the chances that her friends hadn't known were strong. After all, Rainy had chosen something similar for herself. It had been harder to read about Sara—her Sara. The details in her death were gruesome. Different. The police had no reason to connect the two…yet. If Paul had succeeded in killing her, Rainy was sure the police would connect all three of them back to the compound. She knew it. That's exactly what Taured didn't want to happen. Whether or not Paul was trying to incriminate Taured, or just lead police in his direction, she didn't know, but she had the feeling he was out to get his former leader's attention one way or another. And that was exactly why she'd gone to him for help. Two vultures with one stone.

Shit. It was so cold…

What if he doesn't come? But she knew him: she'd been thinking about, obsessing about…and psychoanalyzing every facet of his personality for years.

Her eyes snapped open. There it was. The connection she'd been grasping at and failing to make. He'd killed Feena by strangling her, he'd killed Sarah by shooting her. He was giving them the deaths he thought they deserved: Taured's "special girls." Feena had taken too much of Taured's attention, so he'd cut off her air. Sara had given Taured a baby, taking Taured farther away from Paul or whoever he had been back then—so he'd shot her in the stomach and left her to bleed to death in the desert.

Rainy had a sick feeling that her own death would include some type of poison…or drug, like her mother's had. Taured had used food to lure Rainy into his office the night he'd drugged her and taken those photos of her. He'd fed her apricots in the cafeteria the night he'd convinced her to tour Kids' Camp. And who had been there watching very carefully? Someone had been studying Taured and the unique relationship he had with each of his girls, someone obsessed with Taured and winning his approval, being the most important person to him.

Ginger.

25

Now

"**B**raithe, do you hear me? Do not eat or drink what he gives you... Braithe!"

Braithe wasn't hearing her; she was lying on her side on the ground, still handcuffed to the table, but Ginger had left her legs free. He must not see her as much of a flight risk. That was good. If he underestimated Braithe, they could use that.

Rainy had been trying to wake her for a good thirty minutes, ever since Ginger had left, clanking her handcuffs against the table leg and calling out to her. But she was seriously dehydrated and her vocal cords were raw from the screaming she'd done in the freezer. She didn't know how long he'd be gone, but the little fucker had run off without gagging her.

He'd let her out of the freezer, his nose bandaged and his eyes looking slightly doped. Good. Rainy figured he'd gone to urgent care and come right back, even though it hadn't felt like right back. But the four or five hours she'd spent in the cold had seemed like much more. Eventually, she'd fallen asleep, and when she'd woken up, Ginger had been standing over her. Without speaking he'd dragged her out of the freezer and back to her spot against the table leg. As soon as he ripped the duct tape from her face, she'd said, "I'd like to upgrade to a suite."

He'd shoved her down, hard. The back of her head hit the table and she moaned, dropping her chin to her chest, dizzy. He didn't use the handcuffs to secure her to the table this time: Rainy saw him reach for his pocket, where he pulled out pink zip ties. He secured her arms around the table leg with the zip ties before he took off the cuffs and tossed them aside. Pink zip ties. She almost asked if he'd ordered them on Amazon, but she wanted a shot at some water.

Pink, pink, your feet stink! She could hear her dad yelling that across their small apartment living room before charging for her: the tickle monster. Had he been high when he'd done that? Drunk? On a sober kick? Did she care? He was never scary to her; his sideburns were too big to be taken seriously and his laugh was contagious. Pink. She felt encouraged: this was so stupid and yet so real. Her dad had taught her how to break someone's nose with her forehead; he'd demonstrated it many times in their living room. She'd thought it was hilarious, especially when he mimicked grabbing an imaginary someone by their shirt collar and rearing back his head, to "head-bash" them as he'd called it. *"This is how you do it, Summer, are you watching?"* Little had she known how that lesson would serve her now.

"Time out for noisemaking?" she asked. He didn't look at her, not in the mood for jokes after getting his ass beat, she supposed. *Oh, how smug you are, tied-up woman!* she told herself. Either way, she could see the dark bruises beneath his eyes and it pleased her somewhere deep and feral: she'd got him good. *Thanks, Dad.*

Ginger had said no one could hear them because the restaurant was in a wing that was being remodeled, yet he was never winded when he arrived with his armful of groceries. That meant the elevators were probably working, and Ginger—as staff—would have access to the key codes that would allow him up here. He didn't seem at all worried about the sound.

When she looked over at Braithe, she was sitting up. It took a minute for Rainy's mind to catch up to what she was seeing. She tried to say Braithe's name, but it caught in her dry throat.

"Rainy—" Braithe's voice was so shocking in the silence that for a few seconds Rainy's tongue stayed glued to the roof of her mouth as she tried to work it free.

"Rainy…" she said again, more desperately.

"Y—es. I'm here." It had not felt real until now, a fever dream, but with Braithe's cracked voice filling the room, Rainy started to wake up.

"I'm so sorry. I never imagined…" It sounded like it hurt for her to speak. Rainy saw her look longingly toward the water bottle. She made a noise that sounded like she was trying to clear her throat. She knew it was ridiculous, given the situation they were in, but she needed to know.

"He'll come back soon. What happened between you and Grant during the baby shower?"

The kitchen retuned to an awkward silence. Rainy could hear Braithe's labored breaths.

"Nothing," she said finally. "God, absolutely nothing."

"But you tried…"

Her answer came slower this time, labored. "Yes, I tried."

"Why did you pretend to be my friend?" She licked her lips. Everything hurt.

"That was real. I like you."

Rainy tried to laugh but it was just a crackle. Braithe had used her to have more access to Grant: the couples' nights, the dinners, had put her in his life more soundly than it had with just her and Stephen. Now, in light of everything, she was seeing Braithe differently. Not as the elegant, kind friend, but as a conniving, manipulative liar. Maybe she had liked Rainy, but it was only to use her.

"But you liked Grant more."

"Yes, I suppose you could see it like that. At first, I thought I was making the right choice, with Stephen," she said softly. "He was so good to me, and Grant…well, he was never as into me as I was into him, if I'm being honest. When we were together, I was like an afterthought. I suppose that's when the addiction really started."

"The addiction to what, Braithe? To Grant? To wanting what you don't have?"

"That's fair… I get it. But he didn't want me back, Rainy. And I don't know what's going to happen here, but you should know that."

Rainy leaned her head forward and hit it backward against the table leg. It hurt but it felt good, woke her up a little. She wasn't going to thank Braithe for telling her that Grant wouldn't cheat on her. This woman was not her friend.

"He's who you were talking about the night we played that game." It wasn't a question, and Braithe didn't try to answer it. "And you're the one who asked my question, not Tara. What were you going to do if I didn't draw that question? Use it as an opening to ask me, anyway?"

Braithe's silence confirmed that she was correct.

"Did you call Grant that night?"

Even in the dim light, Rainy could see her head bounce in a nod.

"Yeah. I called to tell him again how I felt."

"And what did he say to you?" Did she really want to know? That night, she'd tried to call Grant herself, and he'd sent her calls to voice mail because he had Braithe on the other line, pouring out her feelings. Why hadn't he told her? Why hadn't Viola said something? They'd all just let her be a fool. Anger at all of them burned in her chest, so much it almost made her cry out.

There was a long pause. Rainy wasn't sure if Braithe was crying. She did not care, she did not. The last year of her life had been a complete lie.

"That he didn't feel the same way."

She ground her teeth, wondering if she should believe her. Braithe needed Rainy on her side if they were both going to get out of here. "How do I know you're telling me the truth?"

"Okay, why would I lie about that, Rainy? I may have been harboring feelings for Grant since the beginning of time, but that doesn't mean I wasn't sincere about liking you."

"You didn't give a shit about me, Braithe. You were using me to stay close to Grant."

Braithe's lack of response pinned the tail on the donkey. Rainy turned her face away. She didn't want to look at any part of her, not even her lying, shitface profile.

"Why did you come?"

"What?"

"You heard me." There was an edge to her voice now.

Oh, are we seeing the real Braithe Mattson? Rainy thought.

"Why. Did. You. Come? You made a choice to come here when Paul texted you from my phone. If you hate me so much, explain why you did it."

"He said he was going to kill you."

"So, why not let him?"

"Oh, for God's sake, listen to yourself. I should let someone kill you because you fucked my boyfriend once upon a time in high school and you still have a thing for him?"

"Fuck, Rainy. Okay. What are we going to do?"

She licked her lips. "I think I know this guy. I've been thinking and I have a few plans. None of them are actually very good but—"

"Oh my God," Braithe said.

"I think he was watching me...maybe before now. But he saw us together and he—"

"Used me," Braithe finished.

"I'm sorry."

Braithe whimpered.

"We have to focus." Her backside was numb, and she shifted her position, painfully aware of the cuffs. "I set some things in motion before I got here. But first, I need to tell you about my past."

It was light out when Ginger came back, this time carrying a black duffel bag, the same dingy beanie still on his head. His face was different. What was it? He turned his back to her to set the bag on the table; it made a solid noise when it hit the surface: it was heavy. How long had it been since she'd woken up in here? No more than seventy-two hours. Would that give him enough time to find her? *Hurry, Taured.*

If he comes...

He will come.

Ginger dumped out the rest of the bag on the small table behind her. The noise of the objects hitting the tabletop was loud and metallic. There were a limited number of things that could fit in a bag of that size and be that heavy. Glancing at Braithe nervously, she saw her playing along, her head resting on her shoulder. He would kill Braithe first, she knew it.

He'd played with her the longest, but she hadn't been his real target, anyway.

He smelled…stank. Rainy wrinkled her nose, watching his movements closely. *Beer and unwashed body*, she thought. He'd gotten a drink this time…probably a lot of drinks, judging by the smell of alcohol.

"Paul," she said, keeping her voice low. "Are you okay?"

His shoulders hunched but he didn't turn around.

He'd been manic so far, riding his own chaotic energy. This was a crash. This is what she'd been hoping for.

"Ginger," she said clearly. "I have to pee. She probably does, too."

He froze. She could see his fingers gripping the edge of steel table, gnawing without teeth at the metal until the knuckles turned white. He'd heard her.

Fuck. Maybe that was too far. Licking her lips, she tried again. "Did you think that I didn't know who you were?"

Still, he said nothing, his back to her.

"You were closest to him, weren't you? I saw you the night of my mother's…her funeral, or whatever he called that spectacle. I saw you other times, too…" She let that linger. "I know what he did to you. And I know what you did to Sara."

His torso jerked and then he turned around. He was smiling, one side of his mouth jerked up like a cartoon character.

"Hey, Summer."

Something was different, wrong. Not wrong—right. That was it: he'd shaved. Without the beard, he looked a lot more like a kid. She could still see that kid in her memories, tripping over his words and his feet…being tripped. Looking like he'd explode every time Taured paid attention to him.

He'd been on the receiving end of Skye's right arm, just like her. At the time, she'd only heard the rumors about what had happened to him; it hadn't been out in the open, in front of most of the compound, like with her. Some of the boys had seen it, and then there was Sara, who, when taking her father his dinner tray, had seen Ginger in the infirmary.

"But why?" Summer had asked. Sara hadn't wanted to tell her, but Summer had pressed her, so she had: *Taured caught Ginger touching his thing. Looking at something bad and touching his thing. Taured said it was a terrible sin. So he had Skye hit him so hard his jaw dislocated.*

That had been a few weeks before Skye had launched the baseball at her own face. After that, everything had snow-balled, and Ginger had receded to the back of her mind with everything else that happened at the compound. To be happy was to forget, but something had changed in Rainy. Remembering hadn't felt painful when she went back to Friendship. That had surprised her. She'd expected to feel depleted being there and, instead, felt energized, furious. She'd stayed away for so long to protect Summer, not realizing that it wasn't Summer who'd be going back: it would be Rainy.

She had just disfigured his face further by breaking his nose. Ginger wasn't going to poison her anymore, she realized. She'd changed the course of her punishment.

"Skye got you, too," she said, and his smile dropped. "Do you remember when he broke my nose?"

"*He* didn't break your nose," Ginger said quickly. "*Taured* broke your nose."

"He was too much of a coward to do it himself." Rainy laughed. It was a genuine sound, and Ginger looked startled. "He used kids to do his dirty work."

Ginger was visibly upset now. "He was the coach—the one in control."

"And now what? You're the one in control?"

"Looks like it."

He was still drunk, she realized, swishy on his feet. He took a step toward her and thought better of it. Turning his back to her, he opened the bag. The zipper was loud. Out of the corner of her eye, she saw Braithe move. Ginger saw it, too, and his head snapped sideways. She saw the twisted side of his face where his jaw had never quite healed properly, more visible now. He'd used his beard to hide it, like wearing a mask, but today he wanted her to see. Why?

He's going to kill you, and he wanted you to know who he is first. The thought came in clear and sharp. She watched him take a hammer out of the bag, set it neatly on the table. He glanced at her, and then kept working. Another hammer, and then another, and he was organizing them. Not by size: he took out a small hammer painted entirely gold and set it next to a silver one with a black handle. He was lining them up like a collection. It felt like there was an anchor in her intestines: the drop and pull hurt. *Oh my God, he's going to make you suffer...*

The sweat beaded at her hairline and trickled down the side of her face.

Derek's face had paled when she'd asked him how his mother passed. She'd sworn she could see his heart pounding beneath the polyester of his shirt and had immediately regretted asking. She'd expected him to say cancer; that had been a hopeful thought on Rainy's part, wishing for Sara to have died of something...normal? Cancer seemed safer than what he'd said; she could understand cancer.

"It was a homicide," he'd mumbled. "They've never found her killer."

This is what she'd known in her gut ever since he'd told her Sara had died. But she'd thought right away that it was Taured. He'd killed her mother; why not Derek's?

Until she got back to the hotel in Vegas and had opened the Ziploc bag—the floppy disk, the photos, the driver's licenses, both her mother's and Feena's dad's—and she'd put it all together. Taured was a killer, but his insanity had created other killers. The one standing before her was working his way through the floppy disk, punishing the women Taured had already punished by taking those photos in the first place. *But why?*

"Isn't it enough that I—that Sara—had to live through that place? That he drugged teenage girls and photographed them naked to blackmail them and their parents? That he destroyed our lives? Now you want to hunt us down and kill us?" Spittle flew out of her mouth, clinging to her chin. She'd screamed the last part and now Ginger was red with outrage. But he seemed to collect himself, and in the next minute he was smiling again. God, she wished he hadn't shaved his beard. What he said next made the hairs on the back of her neck stand at attention.

"Don't be stupid. I never had to hunt Sara. She was a lamb. I just took her while she was visiting that cactus you girls used to love. Do you remember how you'd get all horny for that cactus?"

She opened her jaw and screamed at him in anger, her neck extended as far as it would go. That did it. He stalked toward Braithe, the little gold hammer in his hand.

"No! No!" Rainy knew she shouldn't have screamed. "I won't yell again—"

But it was too late: he swung the hammer. She saw Braithe tilt her head up to look at him; she made a noise in the back of her throat, and then the hammer came down. Braithe's head fell once more to the side. The breath whooshed out of Rainy; her lungs pushed but they wouldn't pull. Straining against her cuffs, she yanked forward, but she was held fast.

He's killed her, he's killed her, she thought as she saw the blood drip from Braithe's ear to the floor. *He killed Sara, and now Braithe…*

She took her first breath in; her lungs expanded. She was going to scream again because this time Paul was heading to her, the little gold hammer wet with Braithe's blood.

A crime scene, she thought, watching another drip hit the floor. He was a serial killer. She'd be dead and she'd never know if they caught him. How many murders did it take to class someone as a serial killer? *Three*, she thought. And she would be the third, assuming he hadn't killed anyone else first. Her photos had been third on the disk, behind Feena's and then Sara's.

She'd searched Jon's last name, too, and two pages of articles had popped up, his obituary among them. Jon died of a heart attack years before Ginger killed Feena. They'd been living in Texas at the time. Feena had later moved to Colorado to be near some family, and that's where Ginger had tracked her down.

"You killed Feena, too," she said.

He didn't acknowledge this, but he didn't need to. "She started using her real name after Jon died. You were the hardest to find." He was standing in front of her now. "Who would have thought you'd be D-list famous? I was looking in the slums and our girl was eating caviar in the city. I thought I'd have to travel to see you, but then—I couldn't believe it!—you brought yourself right to me. Can you believe how lucky I am?"

Crouching down, he reached out and chucked her beneath the chin. "It was fun, too, the whole little game to draw you out. I make it my mission to know my girls. And you, Summer—Rainy...whatever you want your name to be—carry a lot of guilt. Despite how Braithe treated you, I knew you'd come after her. A person can be controlled by their weakness." His crooked mouth pulled to the side.

"What's your weakness, Ginge? Taured?"

She remembered the boys taunting him with nicknames worse than his actual name. And another taunt:

"Ginger has a finger…" someone would say. *"Up Taured's ass!"* someone else would chant.

"Ginger has a finger…" she said under her breath, looking at him through her lashes. His face was such a tell; it got red—redder than his hair used to be.

He slapped her, but it didn't hurt as much as it could have. It felt good to poke his sore spot.

She leaned her head against the table leg. She could taste blood. She laughed because she could, closing her eyes and rolling her head from side to side against the metal. When she opened her eyes, he was staring at her, a thoughtful expression in his too-close-together eyes.

"Do you think that he'll be happy you're killing us?" Rainy asked. "You can't possibly think that. When he finds out what you're doing, he'll kill you himself."

Ginger's eyes narrowed. "You don't think he had some kind of plan for all of you? Why do you think he took those photos of you? You think he wants you all out there, living the way you want, godless, ignoring everything he ever taught you?"

"A good and faithful servant," Rainy said dryly. "You're delusional if you think this is the key to finally getting his approval."

He studied her, amusement in his face. "I hope the next five are as fun as you."

"You'll never get within a thousand feet of those women. I sent my trusty floppy disk to the police station, along with all the information I had about Feena and Sara." Rainy had no idea if the police would be able to pull anything off the disk after it had been buried in the desert for twenty years, but at least she'd also had the hard-copy Polaroids of herself and Feena. She'd left it at the buffet with a note for the police, right where Ginger had left her the room key: *Police Chowder*. And under the word *police*, just to make sure: *SOS Give to Police*. Someone would notice. Hundreds of people must go through that buffet every day.

"Ha! What information? You don't know anything. You're smart, but not that smart, Summer." He was sweating profusely, the hamster-and-bologna smell of him close in her nostrils.

"How did you get a copy of that disk?"

His neck jerked back like he was surprised at her question. "A disk? He showed me. He used to sit me on his knee and show me the photos of all those women on his computer. It was easy to remember them."

Rainy turned her head, closed her eyes; she was going to be sick. She couldn't look at him, but then she thought better of it and snapped her eyes open aggressively.

"I don't know what he did to you, but I know he did terrible things that no child deserves. He abused you in every way. This choice you're making, to do this sick shit, is on you."

"Boop." He touched the tip of her nose with his finger and quickly stood up when she tried to bite him. "You care too much." He took a step back to look at her. "You came for the whore of Babylon—" he said, jerking his head toward a limp Braithe "—because you couldn't help your friend Sara, is that right?"

For the first time, she considered that this might not work. He might not—

Suddenly, there was a noise at the door. She heard the whoosh of air that left Ginger's lungs as he heard the noise, too. He walked backward, keeping his eyes on the door. He lifted the hammer, swinging it around expertly. He looked sharp, tactical. Flattening himself behind the door, he waited, gun up near his face and ready.

Then door opened and she saw him. The man from her nightmares.

"Taured!" Rainy cried out. "He's behind the door!"

As the hammer came down, Taured turned sideways, raising his arm to cover his face. He was taller than Ginger, larger. Rainy's neck was turned as far as it would go as they struggled in and out of her line of sight. Their bodies twisted and she saw the look of shock on Ginger's face when he saw Taured. It stalled him. The hammer caught Taured's forearm and Rainy heard him grunt in surprise. His reflexes were fast, and he grabbed for the hammer with his other hand, but Ginger had already lifted it, ready to strike again, and it was coming down like an ax. Rainy waited for the crunch of metal on bone, but again Taured was too fast. Throwing himself backward, he hit the wall and the hammer swung through the empty air. Using the wall as leverage, Taured threw himself at Ginger, grabbing the hammer with one hand and Ginger's throat with the other. They swung in a circle like they were dancing, the hammer still clutched between them as they stumbled out of her vision toward Braithe. Ginger had a gun; where was it now? If he used it to shoot Taured, someone would likely hear the gunshot in the hotel, even though this wing was under construction.

And then what, you dummy? He turns the gun on you and Braithe. She clanked her handcuffs against the table leg in a fruitless attempt to move the bolted-down table.

"Wake up, Braithe!" she shouted. Was it possible she was still alive?

Braithe was stirring, her head bobbing. And then she looked semialert, holding her head at a steady-ish angle.

Open your eyes, open your eyes! Rainy had a purely comical thought: *The boys are fighting!*

Braithe, who had her knees pulled up to her chest, straightened one leg.

As they grappled, they lost their balance, and Ginger took the brunt of the fall, hitting the ground and staying there, pinned by Taured's weight. They'd collapsed just beyond where Braithe sat against her own table leg, struggling.

Rainy couldn't see what happened next. The men's feet were kicking, and she saw flashes of gray boots. Ginger tried to reach for his gun, but Taured was a bigger man with longer arms, and he got there first. She braced herself for a gunshot, her vision swimming as the grunting continued, but the only sound that came was two dull thumps. Braithe was watching, she had a better view than Rainy, and she was trying to keep out of their way, pulling her legs up to her chest. As Taured stood, Braithe's head followed him, tilting all the way back.

Everything felt perfectly still in those moments, and the light from the high window was shining directly on Rainy's face, bright white and blinding. She blinked once…twice…and then Taured rose from the ground, a disoriented victor. Rainy could just see Ginger's boots, unmoving, beyond Braithe.

Taured stumbled back into Rainy's view, glancing at Braithe and stepping into the greater part of the room. There was blood on his hands and shirt, but he didn't seem to notice. He was looking for her. It was her turn to tremble, the weight of her stupid, ridiculous plan crashing down on her. Handcuffed to a table leg on an abandoned floor of a hotel, at the mercy not only of a would-be killer but her worst enemy. She started laughing at the absurdity of it: How had she thought she should deal with a kidnapper herself?

She couldn't contain the laughter that bubbled from her lips. *All because she grew up in a cult and had a lot of great therapy, she'd thought she could outsmart a sociopath.* Her laughter was almost beautiful even to her own ears, illogical yet melodious in this impossible situation.

"Hello, Taured," she said, and as he crouched down in front of her, he was grinning. Blood was running steadily from his nose where Ginger had got him good. She wondered if Ginger were still alive. The light wasn't good, but it looked like there was a lot of blood on that side of the room.

"You're not so different," she said.

He grabbed her chin and turned her head from side to side.

"You're very different."

When he let her go, her skin tingled where his fingers had been.

"That's good. Want to let me out of these handcuffs? My wrists are killing me."

Taured made a face like, *Wow, okay*, and stood up.

"Who's your friend?" He glanced back at Braithe, who was sitting very still.

"Her name is Braithe. Who's yours? Do you remember him?"

Taured looked over to where Ginger lay motionless. "Ginger. Of course I remember him. I got your email. You can imagine how shocked I was, Summer, to see your name pop up from that old email address."

She'd used the email he'd had them send their daily journals to, knowing he would still have access to it, would look at it, even after all these years. He needed those trophies.

"The subject line got me." He pushed off from the wall and took the few steps needed to reach her. Then, like he'd done a moment ago, he lowered himself in front of her, eyes sparkling. She was in kicking distance of his crotch, the arrogant bastard. She could see the pores on his face, the individual hairs that grew down his neck. The freckle on his earlobe that looked like the tiny stud of an earring. She remembered noticing that as a child. She'd thought, when she'd first met him, that the illusion of an earring made him look cooler.

You should kick him now; you might not get another chance later.

"Now, I know you're this fancy sculptor. I've seen the accolades and awards—" he held his hands up, shaking his head "—but you really should try your hand at writing, Summertime."

As he looked at her like—like she was a meal, she remembered why she was here. She curled her toes up in her boots. Paul—Ginger—hadn't said she couldn't wear boots.

Taured was still speaking. "The description you sent. Very good detective work, by the way. I knew it was our Ginger." He glanced up at the ceiling like he was recalling something. "'Taured, I need your help. A man has taken my friend captive and he's asked me to surrender myself to save her. He told me that if I contacted the police his first order of business would be to kill her, but if I came willingly, he'd spare her life for mine. All I can offer is a rough description of him...'"

Rainy exhaled, a sort of laugh that sounded choked. He was imitating her tone like he'd been listening to her speak for the last dozen years. He was creepy...sick. She yanked on her cuffs in anger.

"Look for a broken nose." He sounded purely delighted by this point. "And then you actually managed to break his nose!" He shook his head in proud disbelief. "You were always so determined, so dead set on what you wanted. I know that because I read half of your thoughts. The beautiful innocent thoughts of a young girl in her prime."

Her head ached in the spot it had met Ginger's nose.

"Before he left, he'd been causing problems. You know how disgruntled people get. But thanks to you, that problem is now—" he looked over at the body and then back at Rainy with a gleeful expression "—dead."

He spared her more of his fucked-up thoughts when he went to look over his handiwork. He stood, a foot in the puddle of Ginger's blood, hands on hips, then suddenly he bent down. Legs extended, Rainy bounced on her left side, then right, trying to get blood flowing.

Fuck. Shit. He was dragging the body toward her. Ginger's head was not okay. She closed her eyes when Taured propped him opposite her against the door to the walk-in freezer.

"Hey!" She heard him clap his hands. "He had the sense to turn the freezer on! Do you think it was for you and your friend?"

Rainy opened her eyes, looked at Ginger this time. Taured had pistol-whipped him pretty good. One side of his head was…dented. Along with the broken nose she'd given him, he was almost unrecognizable.

Nice way of saying it. Her mother's voice in her head.

Rainy looked away quickly, the tears in her eyes fat but unfallen. "I don't know what he wanted to do. I just did what he said."

The idea that he was in some way affiliated with Taured and his cult had crossed her mind. At first, she'd wondered if he could be Frank, Sammy or Marshall. All those guys had been Taured's henchmen, but they'd all lacked something she picked up right away in Ginger: he was smart, really smart. That wouldn't have gone down well at the compound. Taured couldn't keep smart men because they always eventually called him out. The women had been different: they stayed because they were in love with him, but it hadn't mattered how smart they were because their feelings for him won out, even if they probably just had Stockholm syndrome. Ginger's black hair had thrown her off, but then she remembered. It was when the lady at the Quick Mart had said that one of the two men who bought the syrup dyed his hair, had light roots under-

neath. The little boy who'd followed Taured around the compound until everyone made fun of him: he'd loved Taured,
too. And Taured had used that love against him. He'd been
training all the kids up to serve him, so possibly he thought
of Ginger as the future Frank/Sammy/Marshall. And somewhere along the line his love for Taured started the rot that
spread through the rest of him.

She felt the vomit piling up behind her throat. Turning her
head to the left, she let it come, and she was sick across the
floor. This kitchen was having an odd baptism. When she
looked back at Taured, he seemed pleased. Of course he was:
he fed on the emotions he caused. It didn't matter how gross
the outcome was. After another torturous minute of watching her, he dragged Ginger's body into the walk-in freezer
and kicked the door closed, dusting his hands.

"He hit her pretty good." Rainy licked her lips, nodding
toward Braithe. "Can you check on her?"

Taured nodded. He walked over to where Braithe sat, taking her in, before lowering himself to his haunches. She was
no longer sitting up, alert; her legs were extended in front of
her and her head was lolling again. He touched her neck and
looked at Rainy. "She's alive," he said. Then, as he stood up,
he said, "You care about her."

"I do."

"You offered yourself up to this to save her."

"I suppose that's what it looks like," she said.

"No greater love than this, a man who gives up his life for
his friend…" He looked down at Braithe for another few seconds, considering either her beauty or her value to Rainy—
she didn't know which—then he walked toward Rainy along
the length of table that separated her from Braithe. When he
was in front of Rainy, with his back to the freezer, he leaned
against it, crossing his ankles.

"You were never transparent about what you cared about, except for your mother. It was all a mystery to me—what parts you were faking and what parts were real."

Rainy thought back to the journaling he'd had them do, the way she'd always try to write things that would please him. And that's what he was doing back then: brainwashing a bunch of kids into believing their life's purpose was to please him. Pillaging their brains for information and then using it against them and their families.

"Ditto," Rainy said. She wished he'd given her some of that water, too, but she was too proud to ask.

"Wonderful," he said, throwing his hands up. "Let's get to know each other again, then—what do you say?"

"I'd say it's about time."

Taured looked pleased with that. He surveyed Ginger's array of food on the counter, his lips pursed.

"I'll get us something better," he said, bypassing the vegetables Ginger had so carefully lined up. "You want a steak, Summer? Who am I kidding, everyone likes a steak, right? Except maybe that guy."

"Fine," Rainy said. "A steak is great." She wanted him to leave for a bit so she could think and gather herself. She knew he wasn't going to just let her out of these cuffs. But that was stage two, and she wasn't there yet.

She watched him wash his hands using the little bottle of detergent Ginger had brought, washing off Ginger's blood with Ginger's soap. She didn't feel bad for him; the bastard intended to harm both her and Braithe.

Taured whistled while he scrubbed. Rainy didn't recognize the tune, but it sounded like something sung at church. When he was done, he pulled off his shirt, making sure to face her as he did it. He was all muscle, tough like a bull. Even his neck had thick cords running through it, veins standing at attention. Dropping the bloody shirt on the floor, he turned away from Rainy; she saw the gun in the waistband of his pants, as she supposed he wanted her to.

She'd seen him shirtless only once, when she'd accidentally walked into the makeshift clinic for a Band-Aid. He'd been sitting on the examination table, kicking his feet like a kid. Rainy had been so alarmed that he was there she almost hadn't noticed that he wasn't wearing anything on top, and then when she did notice, she must have turned a shade of ultrasonic violet, because Taured had laughed.

"They're just tattoos, Summa, Summa, Summatime..." And then he'd shown her each one, without getting off the table: animals exploding from leaves across his shoulder blades, and a snake draped across his chest, the tip of its tail touching his belly button. His arms were clean of tattoos, which, he explained, gave the world what they wanted: a respectable man.

"And I am the *most* respectable man, Summer, wouldn't you agree?"

It was then her job to say, "Yes, Taured."

Even then, she'd wanted to laugh when Taured used the word *respectable* so generously on himself.

Then he was shrugging on another shirt, a tight, white undershirt he pulled from his pocket. He looked like a dick, she noted, not above being petty in this moment. He picked up the duct tape and walked over.

No, no, no—she needed to be able to talk to Braithe. He was gentle at least, spreading two layers over her mouth before backing away to look at his handiwork. She watched him walk over to Braithe and survey her. He kicked her leg.

"She's out cold," he said. "She won't bother us tonight." And then he left.

Rainy kicked at the air. Trying to make noise under the tape was exhausting and then the feeling that she was suffocating would creep in and she'd have to calm herself down. But it was only five—maybe ten—minutes after he left that Braithe began to stir.

"Rain-nee," she slurred.

Rainy clanked her handcuffs against the table leg.

And then what sounded like a sob. "He's dead."

For God's sake, Rainy wanted say. *He wanted to kill us. One down, one to go!*

"This was your plan?" Braithe continued. "Trading one psycho for another? We're never going to get out of here, oh my God…" Her head dropped as she cried into her knees.

Stick with the plan, stick with the plan… Rainy clanked her handcuffs again, trying to get her to focus.

"I know, okay…I *know*."

And then she was quiet for so long Rainy was sure she'd fallen asleep. She jumped when Braithe's voice sounded, her vowels stretched long, like taffy. "I'm sooo sooorry, Renny," she slurred. "My fault…"

It wasn't her fault, though, and it made Rainy angry— the itchy kind of angry that she would scratch at for hours. She wasn't exactly on loving terms with Braithe right now, but nothing either woman had done warranted this madness. *That's good*, she thought, settling back against her pole. *Keep the anger. It's better than fear.*

When Taured came back, the light in the room had changed completely. It had to be early evening. No one would notice him coming or going at this time of day as families and couples shlepped back to their rooms from the pool. The lobby would be swarming with people checking in.

He set two bags of groceries on the counter where Ginger had set his just hours before and began to unpack them. He was enjoying her pain—the duct tape. She sat still and patient like a good girl until he wandered over to her and abruptly ripped the duct tape off her mouth. That made her yell, and she dropped her head like Braithe did so he couldn't see her expression. Her bladder burned to be released. She wanted to cry and sob with relief at the same time.

"I have to use the toilet," she said.

He didn't answer.

"Hey! I need to go now!"

He unpacked his bags, removing several items and setting them on the counter next to his other supplies, before acknowledging her. New day, same games. He was so predictable she wanted to scream it in his face, tell him she knew how to play now, too.

She licked her lips as she watched him stroll casually toward her, dusting his hands off. She was so thirsty she could scream. He knelt behind her on one knee; she could see him out of the corner of her eye as she twisted around. His fingers touched her wrists and she wanted to be sick. Her muscles recoiled away from him, but there was nowhere to go. *The devil is on your skin*, she thought. She was trapped by the handcuffs, forced to endure his skin on hers until she heard the clank of metal that indicated she was free. Rainy moved slowly, bringing her arms around until they rested in her lap, sore and stiff. She let her muscles adjust with her eyes closed. She didn't want to see him.

Taured had Ginger's gun pointed at her. So he'd found it. She could smell it, almost taste the metal in the back of her throat. She lifted herself unsteadily to her feet. If Taured had a reaction, she couldn't see it, because he was still behind her; she could feel his presence pulsing the same way it had when she was a child. He could fill up a room just by standing in the doorway.

Braithe stirred from where she lay, moaning, and Rainy

felt a jolt of hope. But before she could get a good look, Taured was steering her toward the bathroom. Rainy's left hand was free; the handcuffs dangled from her right. She caught a glimpse of Taured in the mirror above the sink before he shoved her inside. She was suddenly alone, with only his feet visible from beneath the door. She slid the lock in place gently, and a little jerk of his head through the space between the stall door told her he'd noticed. His back remained mercifully turned as she pulled down her pants and lowered herself to the bowl. She kept her eyes on the part of him she could see through the crack in the door: the perfectly trimmed hairline—he had his hair cut every few weeks—and the black outline of ink beneath his white T-shirt, snaking up above the neckline.

The tinkling of her urine hitting the water below made her shut her eyes, shame temporarily crawling up her spine. The monster guarding her stall shifted slightly to say he'd heard, too. How many seconds did she have? Her fingers found the edge of the Band-Aid and began to tug, her eyes darting from the gap between the stalls to her work. She'd made the cut high on her inner thigh, not flinching as she sliced a line deep enough to draw some blood. She'd made two more on the other side, but she focused on the first one. The cut was angry, the pad of the Band-Aid yellowed with blood.

Rainy's pee was tinkering off. Taured knocked on the door and she jumped. Her finger was underneath the cloth padding of the Band-Aid, coaxing. The plastic slid free, and she flushed the toilet, tossing the used Band-Aids inside. Rainy pulled up her pants: leggings, as Ginger had told her to wear. It was smart: you couldn't hide weapons or anything else under the constrictive spandex. But he hadn't realized that women's leggings often have a tiny, hidden pocket in the waistband. She slipped the pills from Barry inside, and tugging her shirt over the waist, she rattled the lock to let Taured know she was done. He took his time stepping away from the door, so Rainy took her time washing her hands, pretending to be unmoved that he was behind her, watching her in the mirror.

Enjoy it while you can, freak.

He looked the same, just a little worn, but he wore the same clothes as he had fifteen years ago and parted his hair the same way. He was a monster of habit. That was good. That was really good, in fact; because Rainy was counting on being able to predict him. And she needed him to think he could predict her. There was a hint of a smirk around his eyes as he studied her. One could almost mistake it for fatherly pride, if they didn't know better. He followed her from the bathroom without saying a word.

He walked behind her, the gun pointed at her back. She tried to get a look at Braithe's head to see how bad it was, but he shoved her forward. She'd been slurring the last time she was conscious. Instead of making her sit in her usual place on the floor, he led her to the counter, where the wine and raw steak sat waiting next to the grill.

"A meal," he said, looking at her carefully. "Like old times."

She kept her eyes on the fat of the steak, at the pinkish white running through the meat. The tightening in her chest was painful, her breath threatening to come too fast—or not at all.

One look at it and she was hurtled into the past—into Summer.

She was painting her toenails in front of the squat window that sat high on the wall of their room, the glass pane wedged open by her mother, who'd used a stool to reach it. They weren't technically allowed to paint their nails, but she'd come to her mother's room to feel close to her and had found the little bottle on the nightstand. She painted her last toe—the baby—and leaned back to look. It was bold, and people would notice. She felt a burst of defiance. Let them look! Hadn't that

been what her mother intended when she bought it? She was so deeply
sorry for the things she'd said the last time they'd spoken.

Suddenly, she heard voices and the sound of laughter. Someone
was walking in the hall outside her mother's room. She perched on
her haunches, her ears strained and her heart racing. She was supposed to be in the kitchen tonight, helping with dinner, but she'd left
minutes after arriving, slipping out before anyone noticed. The little
bottle of blue polish sat near her feet, and she deftly swept it under the
bed as the knock sounded. The smell of it still lingered in the air. The
knock sounded again, knuckles rapping on the wood right in front of
her face, and she jumped back, hesitating, and then swung open the
door. She'd forgotten to put her socks back on—she should have, even
though the polish was still wet—and now she stood barefoot in front
of Taured, ten little sins exposed.

"Hey there." He smiled. "Wanna take a walk?"

The sins of the parents will be visited upon their children…

Had he followed her, or did someone tell him she was here? Lately,
she'd been skirting her chores, skipping journaling. She felt…different.

"A walk where?" Had she ever felt this angry, and defiant, and
afraid, all at the same time?

"Does it matter?"

It wouldn't have a month ago, she thought, sliding her feet into her
shoes. A week ago, even.

"I s'pose not. The compound is the compound." She was trying
to make light of the situation, but Taured frowned. She'd said something wrong.

He never called it the compound. To him, this place of bleak blocks
and chain-link fencing was a refuge from the rest of the world, not a
prison. His smile did not reach his eyes as she stepped out and pulled
the door closed.

Mama, she thought. I want my mama.

"Is my mother—?"

"She's fine."

So where are we going? Why do you pay so much attention to Feena? Why does my mother keep bringing back people if she hates it here? *She held all these thoughts behind her teeth, trying to make herself as small as possible as she walked beside him.*

"Where are we going?"

"To the kitchen for a snack. Are you hungry?"

"I am," she said.

But instead of turning left down the main hallway that led to the kitchen, he turned right. That was wrong. Something ugly tickled her spine and she wondered what would happen if she just ran for it.

Taured stopped when they reached his office. She opened her mouth to ask why as he swung the door wide. Her mouth was still open when the smell hit her. Summer took a step closer, taking it all in: fist-size dinner rolls, a plate of melon and grapes, fried chicken and a tower of mashed potatoes. It wasn't a holiday, but this was a holiday meal. Her mouth grew sticky with spit and her head felt light. She hadn't eaten today. Had she eaten yesterday? After all her fasting, she couldn't re-member; food wasn't on her to-do list right now.

"Please, sit," Taured said. "I had this meal prepared so we could spend some time together. I'm afraid that in my overall business I've neglected you girls..."

She sat; the smell of the food felt overpowering.

"First, we drink." He poured iced tea from a pitcher into a wine-glass and handed it to her. But instead of pouring tea for himself, he lifted his glass to a box on his sideboard and, as he poured from a de-canter, dark red wine tumbled into his glass. Summer sipped. She was scared, but soon that started to drain away. There was music playing... the radio. She hadn't heard that type of music in a long time, and she closed her eyes, humming all over with the vibrations.

He made a plate for her. Summer had never seen Taured serve anyone. She was so hungry. She ate too fast, the food delicious; she was sloppy. She kept apologizing for the mess she was making, but

*Taured would just smile and sip his wine. And then she was so full
and so happy she closed her eyes and…*

"Wonderful," she said now, pivoting her body toward him,
as if the sight of the uncooked food had had no effect on her.
"Who will be cooking?"

She knew the answer to that. Taured couldn't cook; he liked
to pretend he could, because God forbid there be something
the almighty Taured couldn't do, but there was always a cook
behind his meals. He needed people to feel like they had to
do things for him.

This is too easy, she thought.

*Don't get cocky right now. You're just another woman cooking his
meals, and that smell you're wrinkling your nose at is your own fear.*
Her mother's voice this time.

She unwrapped the meat from its packaging. The range was
huge, but fortunately she'd used one like this before. She'd
been a server all through college, and for one summer, she'd
dated a line cook.

The broiler was a Viking, and the pilot light was on. She lit
the range and stood with her back to Taured to watch it, but
more to show him that she trusted he was in control.

If you could see my face, you'd know I want to kill you.

She closed her eyes, smoothed down her disgust until it
was an indecipherable lump under her surface and then she
turned. He'd never lit the range at the compound, he had
women to do that for him. One thing about Taured: he appreciated a useful woman. He smiled at her and it was almost
fatherly. It was the same smile she'd seen the first day at the
compound when she was barely thirteen; she'd fallen right into
that smile, into those arms. She thought of Derek, his reedy
unsure son—Sara's son. Male lions sometimes ate their own
cubs, she reminded herself. She stretched then, and, hands on
her waist, she extended her neck back, rolling it from side to

side. Taured watched her, making no move to stop her. Instead, he took a step back to give her space. Even farther behind him, at the end of the table, she thought she saw Braithe move. She withdrew her eyes quickly so he wouldn't notice.

"It has to heat up," she said, taking up warrior one pose in the space behind the range and the wall. "Being tied up like that messed with my back." She took deep breaths without turning around, letting her body stretch out of the last few days, but more importantly, allowing her mind to stretch. *Go slowly.*

"You can pour yourself a drink if you want. I have to tenderize the meat."

She bit the insides of her cheeks, latched the soft tissue between her molars to stay focused.

He regarded her for a moment, then said, "I'll make us both one."

"I don't drink," she lied, reaching for the package of steak. The wrapper was bloody as she unrolled the paper.

"I've seen you drink."

This time her breath did betray her. The wall in front of her was stainless steel, nothing to look at, but she looked. Stared.

"What?" Taured feigned innocence. She shook it off… shook her head and asked for one of Ginger's plastic sporks.

Digging one out from the box, he put it in her outstretched hand. Rainy bent her head over the steaks, stabbing the meat with small, aggressive jabs. What was this dance? What was his plan? *Focus.*

Taured was to her right, blocking her view of Braithe and the door. He looked at their wine option and signaled her with the gun. "You'll have to open it."

He'd been watching her? When? How? But she couldn't let him see that he'd rattled her. She needed him to be relaxed.

"What are you talking about?"

"Isn't it obvious?" He took his time answering, obviously wanting to drag out the moment so he could enjoy her discomfort. "The boxed wine. I need you to open it."

He's toying with you. Don't let him see a thing, Rainy.

Resolute, she took the four steps to where he pointed, wiping her palms on her pants. He was holding the gun loosely at his side, standing slightly to the right of the boxed wine, waiting. She was close to him again, his heat perverting the air like a wild animal.

The box of wine sat next to a stack of plastic punch glasses next to her left hand on the much smaller prep table against the wall. She grabbed two of the glasses, turning them over. The wine still had the orange price sticker attached.

Boxed wine! Because why give Rainy the chance to hit you with a bottle or stab you with a corkscrew? She got to work, keeping her eyes off his face and her back to him, like she was afraid of him. He was gobbling this up; she didn't have to look at him to know that. She was fidgeting with the spout on the box-of-shit-wine, trying to get it to work, trying to—when she felt him behind her. *Fuck.* Had he noticed anything?

"Like this," he said, leaning into her and letting wine slosh into the plastic glass. His free hand brushed hers, the one that was holding the glass, and she dropped it. She jumped back, out of range of his hand and the splash, the prep table behind her penning her in, ramming into her waist. She kept her head down, holding her arm with one hand. The shame was real and it burned in her cheeks and in her gut: a twenty-year-old ember blown to life. Evil existed only to feed itself and here it stood in front of her. She thought she could do this, but her hands were clammy with fear, barely able to flex, let alone fight.

"Try again," he said. "Rookie mistake."

"Rookie mistake, Summertime…"

The rage bubbled. It was almost too hot to keep down. Rainy lifted her head; his eyes were waiting for hers. *Right now, your rival is you, not him.* Little girls grew into women and women grew into hunters. *You are the hunter now, Rainy,* she told herself.

He can't even cook his own steak. She stepped toward the task, renewed. *It's fine,* she thought; he'd seen something real in her reaction. Who she was five minutes ago was not who she was now. *I will recharge, I will resurface, I will rebound.*

He grinned, holding up both hands, one of them still holding the gun, and took another step back to give her space.

"When would you have seen me drink?" She picked up another glass, this time holding it with more confidence as she opened the spout.

"In the articles about you. They never showed your face, but you always had a glass in your hand. I knew it was you."

"Props," she said quickly. "Grape juice for wine. In the art scene, they like you to smoke and drink, or you're not glamorous enough to hang. But you remember my father died of addiction. It's not my thing."

He appeared to consider this for a moment, then he nodded.

"Well, you're having one tonight."

"Okay," she said, hoping she sounded bored. She poured half of what she'd put into the first cup and took a slow sip, blinking at him over the rim. "It's terrible," she said, frowning. "Bitter." She feigned a sip. When he saw that she'd underpoured herself, he swapped glasses with her, handing her the full-to-the-brim cup.

"Drink," he said.

She took two giant sips and stared at him. "Did you put something in here?" she asked, staring into the wine.

He laughed. "You saw me, just now. I was standing in front

of you the whole time. Besides, you just opened the box. It was sealed."

Rainy let her shoulders relax and she took another sip.

"I don't want any more," she said, putting the cup down.

"Have another sip," he said. It wasn't a suggestion. Rainy took another sip to satisfy him, flinching as she swallowed.

"I have to check the range," she said. As she walked away, he took a sip from his glass. She could hear him swallow.

His eyes were all over her back. She felt as defenseless as she had at fifteen. *No...no...this time it's different.* Light-headed, she picked up the raw meat with her bare hand and set it on the grill. There was a hiss, and seconds later, the aroma of charring meat filled her nose. She was hungry. He meant to get her drunk with the boxed wine, and she needed to eat something.

"Ginger put cheese and some salami in the freezer back there," she said, jerking her head to the walk-in. It was comical, her talking about Ginger so casually as he sat propped in the freezer like a Christmas ham. Taured kept his eyes on her as he walked backward to the metal doors of the fridge and yanked them open. He reached inside, keeping his foot in the door to keep it from shutting.

He carried Ginger's dinner party leftovers to the table.

Then, abruptly: "You've always thought I was responsible for your mother's death."

She said nothing; she couldn't. He was responsible, and they both knew it.

"Her death was her own fault."

Still Rainy said nothing. *Careful what you do, Rainy. He thinks he knows you.*

She watched him, transfixed, the heat from the range billowing around her, dampening her skin. She licked her lips, cracking her neck. He was gearing up to launch his slander campaign against her mother.

"Your mother and I were close…"

Sure, why not? Rainy nodded. They had been once.

"We had a sexual relationship—" he paused here for effect "—and she confided in me often, and when things became difficult for her, when her depression became too much to handle, she…well, the drugs started in Portland, and she didn't want you to know that, of course."

"What is your point here, Taured? Haven't you told me these lies before?" It was getting so hot. But Rainy had tried hot yoga a couple times and found it cleansing. She leaned into that feeling now. Taured was sweating, patches of damp forming on his shirt under his arms.

"They're not lies, Summer. She was willing to leave you behind if I gave her the same amount of money she arrived with. Where do you think the money came for the tickets she bought for New Mexico? That wasn't from your grandparents. She tried to steal from me. She went back on our deal." His teeth were getting a nice wine bath, marooning themselves around his gumline.

He drank his wine. He spoke and he drank. He was so transfixed by the sound of his own voice that he'd stopped pressing her to drink hers. Narcissists were unfailingly distracted by themselves. He wasn't even pausing to make sure his lies made sense.

"She tried to steal what from you? Me?" She saw the look in his eyes and it almost made her go blind with rage. "I wasn't yours. I never have been."

"I saved your life, back then and today. You owe me."

Rainy sighed. The thing about her rage was that it was silent. She didn't need to cry, or become hysterical, or accuse him of things he'd done. She'd already done that: held his trial in her own mind. The screaming had been had and done and now she was resolved to end the nightmare for good. Her sigh was a little leak of insanity.

"It doesn't matter what she did or said. My mother isn't on trial here, you are." When she looked back at him, she could tell he was replaying her words more slowly. Thinking on them. She was sure things were getting a little foggy for him in the thoughts department. Looking around, she saw the mess on the floor: the vomit, the blood, the spilled wine.

"What is it, Taured? Have you never thought that you might have to pay for what you've done? Let's talk about what you did to those little girls at the compound...the little boy that was Ginger. Sara...Feena...me..."

Beneath the neatly trimmed beard, his full lips twitched. She liked that crack in his facade. He was not impenetrable, not the god he thought himself to be. It was just the two of them here, his disciples a hundred miles away.

"You don't sound very grateful," he said. "I saved your life."

"Well, you certainly get an A-plus for following my directions well."

He didn't like that.

"I would have recognized him without the broken nose."

Rainy frowned. "Maybe so, but I wanted you to recognize me."

Rainy touched her tongue to her front teeth and shook her head from side to side. Maybe his thinking was getting slow, or maybe he was studying her, but there was something odd about the look on his face.

"You are the same, Summer. The same fire, the same defiance. You haven't changed at all. That's what I admired about you. I could always count on your defiance. My sweet Summertime."

"You never met a trauma you didn't like to poke." She shook her head in disgust.

"Haven't you heard that the light gets in through the cracks?" He said this like there was a joke hiding behind his words, because they both knew he orchestrated those cracks just so he could provide the religious salve for them. It created a cycle of psychological dependency in his followers.

"I know about the photos you took of my mother, of the other mothers…of their fucking daughters! That was your thing, right? You held their children captive by draining their bank accounts so they couldn't leave, and then you took dirty photos of them. You blackmailed them. You are on trial tonight, Taured."

Rainy enjoyed the look on his face. It was the face of a man who didn't believe anything bad could happen to him, that every threat was made by a lesser person and held no ground. She enjoyed it because she intended to wipe the smug expression from his face once and for all.

"A trial without evidence? A childish notion. I promise you, Rainy—" he tried the name out like he was humoring her "—there is none. All of your claims have always been false."

"This isn't a court of law, Taured. This is two people chatting in a kitchen…ah…excuse me…" She turned the steaks with the spork, then licked her lips, wanting her words to hit in the right way. "This is *my* court."

"Your court? Do you mean to judge me?"

"I do." Could he tell that something was wrong? His movement was nonexistent at this point; he was still, only his eyes and mouth moving.

He laughed, just a little laugh—like a chuckle. The past came back to her in a hurry: the heat of the day, the way the bat had felt in her hands on the softball field, slippery and heavy…the fear. Oh God, the fear was so big and she had been so small.

He had big hands, and he'd grown wider in the intervening years; he was no longer a lanky thirtysomething, but a guy in his late fifties. He was half-perched on the stool Ginger had pulled over, the gun on his knee, his finger still curved around the trigger. One of his feet was settled firmly on the floor, the other resting on the stool's rung.

"I stole a floppy disk back then. Out of an envelope in your car... Do you still have that old piece-of-shit BMW?"

Did the expression on his face change? She thought she saw something like fear, and then it was gone.

He cracked his neck, and there it was: Rainy could see it. A cataract of anger dropped over his eyes again. All traces of his earlier amusement were gone. He was getting with the program, seeing his rival for the first time.

"I think you wanted to kill me yourself, didn't you? That's why you're here today. I got away back then and you saw my call for help as a way to help yourself...to me?"

"You've drugged me. How?"

She reached behind her back and began to braid her hair. The steaks were really cooking now, probably past well-done. The meat smelled good, wild. Or maybe she felt wild.

"Anger, as it turns out, is an even greater medium to work with than metal. My anger bends the material as much as the heat does." She flipped the half-braided hair over her shoulder, her fingers moving rhythmically as she finished. "Can you hand me that, please?" She pointed to a rubber band on the table in front of him.

Taured's face was slack. He picked up the rubber band, looked at it, then held it across the table toward her. He wasn't as sloppy as she needed him. The drug was present, but hadn't taken full effect yet. The band was a little thing, pinched between his fingers. She reached across casually and took it from him, holding his eyes. He had hunted her for years. Well, this was hunting, too.

"You took my glass," she said, lightly turning her back to him. "I softened some quaaludes for you in my mouth and spat them in." She stopped, looked over at him with her face scrunched up. "I promise you I'm not the first person to spit in your drink."

She finished tying off her braid and looked at him like a woman who was ready for a drink.

"I met your son, you know, while I was posturing over in Friendship, trying to get you to notice me. Marvin, I assume, let you know I was in town..."

The steaks were smoking now. The air smelled charred.

Taured stood up.

In New York, Rainy had taken a self-defense class once a week called Fighter Flow in a former storefront with blacked-out windows. She did a lot of stuff like that back then: photography classes, a wilderness survival class. Once, she'd taken up archery, only to give it up for fencing. But Fighter Flow was different. She'd heard someone talking about it on the train. Snippets of conversation, a woman whose sister had been mugged in her driveway was taking the class to feel safe.

"I don't know what the instructor did, but it worked, because she's a different person. He made her—" They'd stepped off the train, their conversation lost to her forever.

When Rainy got back to her studio, she'd looked the place up online. The only things on the website were testimonials and a phone number. When she called, a woman answered.

"How did you hear about us?"

"On the train... I was eavesdropping."

The woman laughed a little and then asked for her email. "I'm going to send you a questionnaire. Answer it and shoot it back to me tonight if you can. I can see if you're a good fit and we can go from there."

Rainy had agreed and hung up. She was intrigued; the woman on the phone had given her no information, but she filled out the questionnaire, anyway, and sent it back. She was making herself a sandwich for dinner a week later when she got the call back; she'd forgotten about Fighter Flow. Licking mustard off her finger, she'd carried her plate to the table, balancing the phone against her shoulder.

"We have two available time slots for you—Mondays at seven a.m. or Saturdays eleven p.m. Your choice, but you're going to have to give me an answer right now because there are other people who want to fill these slots."

"Mondays," she said quickly. And she jotted down the address the woman gave her.

It was taught by a retired marine corp veteran who asked her to call him Tito.

She'd dropped her chin and asked, "Tito like the tequila...?"

And he'd lifted his chin and said, "Yup."

At six feet even, Tito looked like the guy you should be running from. His scars had scars and three of his teeth had been knocked out in fights and replaced with gold. "Street fighting made me this beautiful," he told her. "I light up the whole airport when I go through security. I have enough metal in my body to make me the tin man."

His first rule: "My gym caters to people who *need* self-defense, not those who merely want it. For that reason, I make things comfortable and private. You refer someone if they need help. Otherwise...?"

"You don't talk about fight club."

He nodded. "Good answer."

"It's not a matter of how big or strong someone is or whether you're 'tough,' it's a matter of being trained, being prepared. Knowing your enemy. Got it? I can prepare you, but you have to put the mental work in."

"Is it possible for a woman to feel safe in a world where men leverage their physical strength?"

"Saf*er*," Tito told her. "No one's gonna get you if you can help it, eh? You're gonna be the last woman that man ever fucks with because there will be nothing left of him when you're done."

She didn't believe him then.

When he stood up from the stool, he didn't sway, and that's what she'd wanted to see. Instead, he took a step toward her, lifting the gun. She was cornered between him and the grill, his body a barricade.

"I have a drug dealer. What happens in Vegas stays in Vegas, right?" She made a face. "I wasn't really sure what you used on us back in the cult days, so I had to guess."

He lunged to grab her, but she dove right under the table and peddled backward on her palms. On the other side of the table, Rainy was on her feet in three seconds. Adrenaline was a good drug. Anger was a better one.

"I smuggled them in under Band-Aids." A burst of laughter rippled from her throat. "And now here we are." She rubbed the palms of her hands on her thighs.

He hadn't lifted the gun yet but she knew he would. Her back was to the walk-in freezer; it pressed against her shoulder blades. Taured considered the table between them. He perched on the edge, on one side of his buttocks, never lowering the gun. Swinging his legs over, he landed on the other side. Rainy was impressed. She'd never stopped moving away from him, small, shuffled steps.

"You can shoot me, but it won't matter. You're going to jail this time. I sent the police everything you'd thought you'd hidden." The air was heavy, and it burned through her nose and deep into her lungs. She ducked and ran, and she heard the gun go off. So, so loud. And then she felt a white-hot pain in her upper arm, the impact almost throwing her off-balance. The pain in her arm was fire—a burning hot stone.

She turned to look at him; he was chasing her, but he slipped in her vomit. A piercing noise suddenly split the air: the fire alarm. She could still see him, and he was standing up now. Lungs straining, she ran for Braithe, who was still cuffed to the table leg. She yanked at the cuffs, swearing. The key had to still be on Ginger.

Braithe was limp, and Rainy felt for her pulse as Taured got to his feet. She didn't have the keys for the door to the hotel, and without it she was trapped here with him. She could head toward the range and around to the server's area where the bathroom was, lock them in until the fire department came, but depending on how many bullets he had...

Braithe groaned, opening her eyes. She saw the smoke, saw Taured and seemed to pull on the last of her strength. "Get the key," she said, shoving weakly at Rainy.

"Take shallow breaths and stay low," she said in Braithe's ear. She stood up as he lumbered toward her. He was holding his arm, his clothes checkered with her vomit. He was hurt and his eyes looked strange. Coupled with the drugs, it was enough to slow him down. Maybe.

She charged for him, yelling, and he lifted the gun. Rainy dove right. The bullet hit the wall with the windows, four feet above Braithe's head. His aim was way off. She needed him to follow her, to get him away from Braithe. When help came, it would come through those doors, and they'd see Braithe first. She picked up a bottle of water Ginger left on the table and threw it at Taured's head. He didn't lift the gun this time, but he followed her instead. The smoke was bad, her lungs exhausted, struggling with the lack of air. She ran for the source of the smoke, back toward her steaks.

She passed through it, choking. She could hear him behind her, ducking through the kitchen and into the dining room; her hip banged against the corner of something hard and she cried out. Taured lunged for her—he was closer than she thought. There was less smoke here. None of the tables had arrived for the new restaurant, and the dining room stood bare, exposing her to Taured.

She ran, so many parts of her throbbing she couldn't pinpoint the pain. The lobby...the host stand. The door that led to the hotel was bolted.

She turned, expecting to hear more shots.

Taured was in the dining room, but he wasn't holding the gun. He had one of Ginger's hammers in his hand.

"No more bullets?" Rainy asked. "Come on, then," she said.

He came for her, eyes bloodshot, lips slack. She sidestepped him and then turned around to watch as he swayed on his feet. She'd mushed both of the pills and held them on her tongue, not daring to swallow until she spat them into her wine. But even now, she felt dizzy from the smoke and from whatever drugs had made it into her system. She was not, however, as dizzy as Taured. Running past him, back through the server's area, back to the grill, she waited.

He came. He was disoriented enough to stumble as he made his way around the corner. Instinctively, he reached his hand out to steady himself, grabbing the red-hot grill. His scream made her leap backward. Holding his hand in front of his face, he tried to study the wound, but there was too much smoke.

If they weren't going to die from each other they'd die from this.

While he was still preoccupied with his hand, she launched her weight into him, knocking him sideways. He twisted, landing stomach-down on the grill. It didn't take much—

that's what she'd think later. Maybe it was the drug she'd given him or maybe it was the smoke, but he went down and stayed down. Using the wall as leverage behind her, she pushed her boots on his ass and held him there as he screamed. As he tried to lift himself off the grill, he burned his hand, too, and he flailed helplessly. There was a different smell this time— burning flesh.

"Summer! Help me!"

"I'm not your fucking Summer."

His body spasmed. She could hear the sizzling of his flesh between the whooshes of the fire alarm. He was screaming, so high in pitch it matched the rest of the chaos. He was roasting, this was his hell. She didn't want help to come yet—this wasn't finished—but the sound of shouting filled her ears somewhere beyond the door. She closed her eyes. She heard her name being called. By whom? Braithe? It wasn't being called, it was being screamed—everyone was screaming. It was Rainy they were calling—Rainy, not Summer. *Rainy... Rainy...* The name she'd chosen to outsmart her trauma. Taured had stopped moving. He'd just...stopped. When? She was so tired. She dropped to the floor.

The pounding in her head got louder. When had it started? When would it stop? She couldn't hold on anymore. Collapsing against the wall, she heaved what felt like her last breath as the door burst open and the light streamed in.

EPILOGUE

Nine months later

The city sounded good, like the best dream revisited. The humming, honking vehicles made Ham's head whip back and forth, tail tucked as his gangly legs followed at a matching trot with hers. Rupi, on the other hand, seemed to like the incessant car action, and he stared toward the road transfixed, his little lips pursed in interest.

"I can't believe you lived here," Viola said. Rupi was strapped to her chest in one of his baby wraps, and she had both of his little hands in hers as she kept pace with Rainy and Ham. It was her first time in New York. She'd insisted on coming with Rainy, even though Rupi was only nine months old.

"I'm going to go feed him and change him, which should give you just enough time to say all the things you don't want me to hear. Okay?"

Rainy nodded. They parted ways in the lobby, with Viola

going right toward the elevators that would take her to their room. Rainy stepped into the hotel's restaurant with Ham still beside her.

"I'm meeting someone… Braithe Mattson."

The hostess nodded and led Rainy to the terrace where Braithe was already seated, drinking a glass of red wine and staring at Rainy like she'd been expecting her to walk in at precisely that moment. She didn't stand up when Rainy got to the table, but she did greet Ham, who sniffed at her with interest. They'd purposely chosen a pet-friendly patio.

"I'm sorry about Shep," she said. "He was a good boy."

"He was old," Rainy said. Ham whined and Rainy settled him down before taking a seat herself. Shep had died a few months after they got back from Vegas. Cancer. Ham was a good boy, too; he just needed practice.

"Is Viola here with Rupert?"

"Yeah, she'll be down in a minute."

Braithe nodded. She'd changed a bit: she wasn't so polished. Rainy had seen on Instagram that she'd chopped her hair and had given up the beiges and golds for blacks and grays. As far as Rainy was concerned, Braithe could make anything look good—especially this edgier self.

"How has it been?"

The waiter poured her a glass of water, asked what she wanted to drink. Braithe waited until she was gone to answer the question.

"I love it. I wouldn't have before… I know that. But—"

"It lets you get lost enough to think."

"Yeah. And I've never been on my own like this. I'm a real adult at forty-three. Paying my own bills and all." She rolled her eyes to say how silly it was, but Rainy could also see Braithe's true pleasure in these facts, as well. She'd split from Stephen after they got back from Vegas. Rainy hadn't seen her after they parted ways at the airport.

Grant had met her as she walked through, rushing, running, holding her in all the right ways. Braithe had stayed with Tara for a few weeks before moving to New York, where her sister's family lived. Stephen put the house up for sale a month after. He and Grant still spoke occasionally, but after everything that had happened, he moved to Montana and was living with a new woman.

"Nice ring." Braithe nodded at her finger.

"Thanks." It was simple: an emerald cut on a gold band. She'd chosen a plain gold band for her wedding ring and now wore them paired and with pride. Grant said he would have married her even if she'd rejoined the cult. It was a terrible joke, and he'd apologized for days. Either way, they were happy.

"Your hair is pretty badass that length, if you don't mind me saying."

Rainy smiled her most genuine smile. "I most certainly don't mind you saying," she teased. She'd learned that the best way to honor her mother was through her life, not the length of her hair. She'd cut it to her chin in the "baddest" bob and never looked back.

"You sure you don't want to do the interview? It might be good to talk about it."

Braithe shook her head, but it was the look of horror in her eyes that made it clear to Rainy: she would never talk about what happened. "I was caught in it, but that's your story to tell. Besides, there's nothing more that I want than to move on with my life and put all that behind me. I lost so many things through that experience."

Rainy nodded. Her wine arrived. Tomorrow she was doing a TV interview with a morning show on what the media was calling Tauredia. In the wake of Taured's death—which the police had easily seen was self-defense on Rainy's part—what was left of the compound had dissolved, those remaining members detained and Taured's cult the subject of multiple documentaries and podcasts currently in production. Everyone wanted to talk to Rainy, the woman who'd gotten away from it all and taken down the leader. The floppy disk and the photos she'd stolen all those years ago were now part of ongoing investigations into the dark side of the web and Taured's part in it. Taured had sent their photos to other email addresses, and those recipients were now being investigated, too. The only reason she'd agreed and flown to New York to do the interview was to raise awareness about women in positions like the one her mother had been in.

Viola, who still felt bitter about being left out of the Vegas saga, insisted on coming to New York.

"Bitches aren't leaving me out of the action anymore. Baby is coming!"

"I still can't believe we made it out of that alive. And I still can't believe you didn't have a better plan."

Rainy smiled. *Act now, think later* had worked for her, but barely.

"I wasn't really given much time to plan. But I had a couple backups."

"Like the note at the soup station?" Braithe's eyebrows were all the way up, her smile repressed.

"Well, sure." The note at the soup station was a favorite topic on the blogs. Rainy liked to pretend she didn't see the memes of the chowder bowl with the scared face holding a Help, Police! I'm Chowder! sign.

"I also wrote a note on the fifty dollars I slipped to the clerk at that corner store," she offered.

"I guess…" Braithe looked less than impressed, and Rainy snort-laughed into her palm.

"Rainy!"

Susan had confirmed her story to the police and, miracle of miracles, still had the fifty dollars to show them when they questioned her. It was a backup plan, but one in which she'd meant to clear herself of any wrongdoing. Around the margins and in any clear space she'd written:

I am Rainy Ives. I'm being held captive along with Braithe Mattson. Anyone who reads this should contact police about Taured, the man from Friendship, Nevada: second-degree murderer, forced-labor conspiracy, attempted sex trafficking, possession of child porn, racketeering conspiracy, wire-fraud conspiracy. It's because of him we are here. I've got proof.

"But, Rainy, he didn't have anything to do with Ginger, not at that point, in that way. And not until you pulled him into it by emailing him."

"He had everything to do with Ginger."

"Yeah, I get what you're saying. But I hope you get what I'm saying, too."

"I did what I thought was right in the situation."

"You planned on trying to kill him or you thought Ginger would do it for you?" Braithe wasn't being accusatory; Rainy recognized her need for answers.

"I gambled. I knew Taured would come and I knew one of them would die as a result of it. I figured I'd have a chance at the other one. At the time, I didn't know who exactly Ginger was. All I knew was that he'd been at the compound at the same time as me. And if he was doing these atrocities, it was because Taured had nurtured him toward them. Either way, I had one to deal with the other."

"It's like you're giving Ginger a pass."

"He's dead, isn't he?"

At those words, Braithe's face smoothed into what Rainy perceived as relief. She nodded. She took a sip of her water, not meeting Rainy's eyes for several minutes. Then she said, "I'm glad he's dead. I don't care if that makes me a bad person. He was a monster."

"Why?" Rainy asked. "Why was he a monster?"

Braithe was angry now, but not at Rainy. "He fucking kidnapped me, he tied me up and drugged me. I can't sleep. I wasn't sure who I was before, but I'm less so now. I hate him."

Rainy made a noise in the back of her throat. "Well, I'm glad Taured's dead...*he* was a monster." She tried to clear the emotion out of her voice but gave up on it; it was just the two of them at the table today, and she owed Braithe her truth. "He kidnapped my mother and in turn kidnapped me. He tied me up, he drugged me, he took photos of me that he used to blackmail my mother. But I can sleep now...now that he's dead. I don't feel bad about that, either, because he was the first monster. And I ended him."

Summer had been there for all of it. She saw what he did to the minds of those children and what he'd tried to do to her. If you weren't there, you couldn't speak on it.

Rainy decided that there was very little difference between her and Ginger; she'd just chosen to put her anger in a different place. She'd gone to the source and shut off the tap. Braithe would reject the idea of her being like Ginger, but there it was.

Braithe nodded. "Everything else happened like you said it did?"

"Pretty much."

Braithe stared at her, hard, before nodding.

And then she was looking over Rainy's shoulder at Viola, jumping to her feet to greet their friend.

"Let's welcome back Rainy Ives, the woman who took down Tauredia." The host had big teeth. She nodded around at her unseen audience before turning to Rainy, growing serious. "Why did you risk your life instead of walking away from Braithe?"

"It was fight or flight, and I was tired of flying. Braithe was there because of me, because Ginger happened to see her with me that night. I didn't see another option, because Sara saved my life all those years ago. And once someone has extended that courtesy, the wealth of gratitude never goes away."

"Do you regret not going back for Sara? And do you think it would have made a difference if you had?"

"I don't know. I'll live there forever, though, wondering. I was too afraid to think about her back then, but I'm not afraid to think about her anymore."

"Rainy, can you take us back to that day when Sara helped you escape from the compound? We know now that Sara later became the victim of a serial killer who, fifteen years later, kidnapped your friend Braithe and held her captive. My God, the twists in this story!" She turned to the audience. Looking back at Rainy, she said, "Is there something you wish you could say to Sara and your mother all these years later?"

Rainy knew her face was on full display, including the mist in her eyes, which she tried to hide by turning away. But there was nowhere to go on live television. She thought of the note she'd slipped into Derek's backpack. *Your mother saved my life once. She unlocked a door that led to my freedom. Here's yours.* She'd included a wad of cash that she hoped would set him up for at least a little while.

She looked over at him now, where he sat at the back of the

studio. He'd set down his sketchbook to watch. Rainy pulled a strand of hair from the corner of her mouth and looked directly into the camera.

"Your children are going to be okay."

★ ★ ★ ★ ★

ACKNOWLEDGMENTS

This was a very lonesome book to write. I didn't include many people in the process. My largest thanks goes to Brittany Lavery, my editor, whose skill, patience and insight I am deeply grateful for. Sean, who designed another brilliant cover. The team at Graydon House: Pam, Justine, Heather, Randy, and everyone in marketing, sales and publicity. Thanks to Jane, my agent, and everyone at DG&B.

Thanks to Serena Knautz for being my right hand and taking care of things that overwhelm me.

I'm always grateful to my family, who support and stand by me through this dream journey I'm taking: Mom, Scarlet, Ryder, Avett—I do this shit for you. Special thanks to James Reynolds for his brilliant ideas.

To the bloggers and bookstagrammers: you guys are the wheels that make the books go round. Thank you for your passion. And to every librarian who's ever pushed one of my books into a reader's hand—huge gratitude. And to my readers, the ones who know what *Ra ta ta ta* means—#pln4life.

To my guy, thank you for picking up the slack, for the emotional support and for the daily back massages—I love you, Joshua. And finally a thanks to Jolene, who influenced my young life so deeply her name has shown up in two books. You taught me who I wanted to be: a badass.

AN
HONEST
LIE

TARRYN FISHER

Reader's Guide

GRAYDON
HOUSE

1. At its core, this book is about women fighting back against misogyny. While Rainy's experience is more extreme, how does this relate to recent news headlines—and the effects of the patriarchy on society overall?

2. How does Taured compare to and contrast with other real-life cult leaders? Think of Jim Jones, Charles Manson, Keith Raniere and others.

3. Discuss this book's feminist themes. Particularly, how did it make you feel when Rainy decided to rescue Braithe, despite how Braithe treated her? Why do you think she did it? If you were Rainy, would you have gone after Braithe?

4. What did you make of Rainy's decision to adopt her mother's maiden name as her own?

5. What role does art play in this story?

6. Rainy has a lot of insecurities about her relationship with

Grant, and these insecurities make her feel very human and relatable. How do you think her past informs that particular vulnerability?

7. The phrase "the sins of the parents will be visited upon the children" appears frequently in the story. Where do you think this phrase comes from, and do you see this sentiment playing a role in our larger society? How do you think Rainy takes that idea and flips it on its head?

8. Have you read any other books or watched any films or television shows about cults? How does Rainy deal with her trauma compared to other characters you've seen or read about?

9. Are there any parallels between Taured and Rainy's grandparents? Why or why not?

10. What did you make of the ending?

1. What inspired you to write this book?

A need to read it. I was thinking about the many male-driven movies of the '90s like Face/Off and Con Air and I wanted to translate that into a female-driven book.

2. How did Rainy's character evolve? Did the character come first and lead you to the story, or did you build the story around this character?

As I was finishing up The Wrong Family I began to see a woman in the recesses of my mind. She was urgent and she had long dark hair, and since I was still writing The Wrong Family I tried my best to ignore her. So I'd say in this case the character drove the story all the way.

3. What research did you do for this book?

I started with psychological research for the villain of the story. What type of personality disorder was I dealing with? How does my villain manipulate and why? I watched just about every documentary on serial killers and cult leaders that I could find.

4. Why the Vegas setting?

I was writing the final chapters of The Wrong Family *when the pandemic hit and we went into lockdown. And if you've read that book you know it takes place in an old, dark house. My brain needed a vacation from not only pandemic gloom, but the setting of my last novel in general. So, I decided to set the next book in Las Vegas...and what do you know? It rains while they're there. Sorry, not sorry.*

5. You write about strong, complex women who are flawed in a very human way. Can you speak a little about the book's feminist themes?

To me, that is all women: strong, complex, organically flawed. What I like to examine in my books are the ways our complex personalities overlap in society. In my last two books I wrote about how they overlap in a negative way, so this time I went in a different direction. I wanted to showcase a female bond that surpassed circumstance and situation. There is a choice being made in this book to do what is right regardless of how dangerous it is.

6. We see a lot of similar behavior and beliefs from men who lead cults. Was Taured inspired by anyone in particular, either from real life or fiction, or is he more an amalgam of these kinds of men?

Cult leaders of the '70s and '80s never seemed to plan ahead; their impulse-driven personalities were the draw to many of their followers. So, I thought: What would happen if there was a cult leader playing the long game back then? Taured's goal was to raise the children in his cult to be his true loyalists. He was working with progression, not against it, which makes him a different kind of '80s or '90s cult leader.

7. Lorraine, Rainy's mother—while only in the "Past" sections, nonetheless looms large in this story. Talk to us about her character.

Lorraine escaped her controlling religious family only to walk into a different type of controlling religious family. She represents the cycle women become stuck in. She was always willing to take action to change her circumstance, but she was often forced to make decisions out of desperation. No matter her mistakes, she loved her kid. She was a doer, and that's what Rainy absorbed from being around her.

8. For you, what is the most important thing for readers to take away from this story?

Strength.

9. Your characters' names are always so interesting and memorable. How do you come up with them?

I named Rainy after Mt. Rainier in Washington State. My own name means tower or hill in Gaelic and I wanted her to be a mountain of a force. Braithe was a shortening of the last name Braithwaite, which I thought was beautiful. The rest just fell in my head at the right time.